PRAISE FOR *ROCK ISLAND ROCK*

"Price has proven he is more than a one-hit wonder. All the while he is weaving the lyrics of a novelist's song, he draws the reader into a world of rock and roll and supernatural intrigue. Eyre Price is rock fiction's front man."—Rick Robinson, bestselling author of *Alligator Alley*

"*Rock Island Rock* is a gripping thriller, as raw and compelling as the music that underscores its pages."—Melinda Leigh, bestselling author of *Midnight Sacrifice*

"Price handles a keyboard the way Keith Richards handles a black, three pick-up Gibson Les Paul Custom on 'Sympathy For The Devil.'" —Michael Sherer, author of *Night Blind*

"With *Rock Island Rock*, Eyre Price lets us know that he's here to stay. The Crossroads series is destined for big things... Price weaves his story into the heart of America and her music and tells it like it is. Fast-paced, with a dark sense of humor and characters who remind me of many people I have known, make it unputdownable. *Rock Island Rock* will knock you out." —Robert Pobi, international bestselling author of *Bloodman*

"Mesmerizing and original, *Rock Island Rock* perfectly blends lyrical prose, Elmore Leonard-like grit, and a dose of the supernatural in this tale of a music man who's done some bad, bad things. It's a mystery, a story of good versus evil, and a love letter to rock and roll. Eyre Price is one of the best new voices in the genre."—Anthony J. Franze, author of *The Last Justice*

"Price moves the reader at a blazing pace through Daniel Erickson's frenetic world, a world punctuated by violence, desperation, crime, and redemption. Poured over all this is the soul of rock and roll, which gives the story its truly original flavor. Kudos to Price for this literary rock opera."—Carter Wilson, author of *Final Crossing*

ROCK ISLAND ROCK

ROCK ISLAND ROCK

BY EYRE PRICE

Printed in the United States of America.

Published by Thomas & Mercer
P.O. Box 400818
Las Vegas, NV 89140

ISBN-13: 9781612183657
ISBN-10: 1612183654
Library of Congress Control Number: 2012923475

This one is for Kat, Hollie, Cody, Nate, and Bear, who slept at my feet while I wrote, walked with me when the words wouldn't come, and never offered me anything but their unconditional love. And for NOLA and Voodoo, too.

I would go down to the river
Jump into the water
And cross my fingers
Just to see if you loved me.

"Trust"
Dylan Myers-Price

CHAPTER ONE

Queens. The borough often gets lost in the shadows created by the spotlight constantly trained on Manhattan, but across the East River, on the "other" banks of that tidal strait, is rock-and-roll hallowed ground.

Shea Stadium was the landing point for the British Invasion, when the Beatles turned the entire nation into a rabid pack of squealing teenage girls. A young Robert Zimmerman followed Woody Guthrie's folk trail to 150th Street, and Simon first met Garfunkel just across the Fifty-Ninth Street Bridge. Gene Simmons and Paul Stanley were inspired to name their band while driving down Kissena Boulevard, and their band played its first show at a club on Queens Boulevard. Anthrax and Metallica honed their chops there. And the Ramones formed their (not-so) happy family at a rock-and-roll high school not far from Rockaway Beach.

One of the tastier musical landmarks is an out-of-the-way spot in Astoria called Lox 'n' Roll, where East (Tel Aviv) meets West (Beijing) in a kitchen that turns out potato pancake dim sum, brisket egg rolls, or spicy Szechuan noodle kugel. The Legs McNeil–inspired dining room ties it all together with Formica and chrome tables and booths made out of Chrysler and Plymouth bench seats. Along the walls, menorahs and fat-bellied Buddhas sporting Wayfarers share space with autographed eight-by-tens of rock-and-roll royalty and their battle-worn drumheads and shattered guitars.

For early March, the night was more lamb than lion, more promise of spring than last gasp of winter. The melting snow-turned-slush made the night air heavy with moisture, and the new moon, full and high in the midnight sky, was shrouded in mist like Stevie Nicks wrapped in a witchy shawl of fog.

Daniel Erickson stood in the baby spot of moonlight and looked as deeply into Vicki Bean's eyes as she would allow. "Stop. Think about this. Be absolutely sure. Because if you take this step, you can't ever go back. Nothing will be the same. Not ever."

Before he'd ever made the arrangements at Lox 'n' Roll, Daniel had made a full disclosure to Vicki. He'd shared everything she needed to know to make her decision, including that bit about how he'd foolishly borrowed a million dollars from a Russian mobster who'd sent two hit men after him when their deal went sour. He'd made a particular point of carefully explaining how one of those hit men had left a trail of blood in his wake, and the FBI had erroneously—though understandably—blamed Daniel for those heinous crimes.

Whether he karmically deserved his fate or not, Daniel had made it painfully clear to Vicki that he was, above everything else, a man on the run. The only life he could offer her was one on the lam.

If that wasn't exactly the fairy-tale proposal most little girls grow up dreaming about, Vicki Bean had never been most little girls. Early on, she'd learned rock and roll was the only make-believe that was real, and so she'd grown up playing guitar, not princess. She'd heard everything Daniel told her and convinced herself she understood the sacrifices she had to make to be with him. There wasn't a sane woman in the world who would've even considered the prospect, but as far as she was concerned that was just one more reason to look him in the eyes and tell him, "Yes."

"You're sure?" Daniel was enough of a businessman not to question a yes until it became a no, but her answer was too important for him to settle for the one he wanted. "Absolutely, positively sure?"

"I'm sure," Vicki told him. "Absolutely, positively."

And even if that wasn't completely true, she knew for a fact that she just couldn't go back. She never went back.

Daniel kissed her like she'd just sold him the winning Mega Millions ticket. "Then here we go."

Against his better judgment, he searched her eyes one last time for any traces of doubt. Whether he didn't actually see them or simply ignored them hopefully, he nevertheless pushed open the door and held it for her. "This is where we get our new start."

* * *

Daniel checked his watch to make sure they were on time. Twelve o'clock on the dot.

Above the entrance to Lox 'n' Roll was a bright red *bagwa*, a Chinese talisman believed to ward off dark chi. Daniel passed beneath it, wondering just what sort of evil the totem was there to protect against. As he pulled the door open and held it for Vicki, it occurred to him for half a second that maybe *he* was the one it was guarding against.

Just inside the entrance, a young woman at the hostess station was cursing in Chinese as she tried to restore order to a disorganized stack of laminated menus. She was squeezed into a short-sleeved red silk dress with a mandarin collar. The frock was pretty enough, but so restrictive that her every movement seemed painfully difficult, and apparently that included mustering up a smile. "We close."

Daniel looked past her and out to the dining room floor. There wasn't a single patron there to suggest she was lying, but something in the two syllables she'd uttered made him find it difficult to believe her.

The instructions he'd received had been simple enough. He'd been careful, following them to the letter. Of course he'd received them from the friend of some guy whose ex-brother-in-law had once asked Moog to recommend some muscle who could collect on past-due debts. It was an admittedly tenuous connection, and Daniel was painfully aware that there was a distinct possibility something had been lost in translation.

Still, they had come too far to simply turn around now. Daniel leaned into the hostess, far closer than she would have preferred, and whispered confidentially, "I'm looking for a man called Lee Ho Fook."

The name got her attention, but her grim face tightened further into a full-fledged scowl. "No one here by that name," she snapped in fractured English she'd learned from cartoons. "No have cow. Eat shorts."

"I was told to get a big bowl of corned beef chow mein," he added confidently, with a knowing wink to confirm the code.

That only deepened her simmering resentment. "Very spicy dish. You no like."

"I think I'd like very much." Daniel looked straight at her. "Very much."

With a heavy sigh, the young woman went to the door, turned the lock, and then changed the hanging Open sign to show its flip side to the outside world: "You Don't Have to Go Home, but You Can't Eat Here." She returned to the stack of menus she'd been straightening, took two from the top, and turned to Daniel and Vicki. "Walk this way."

The hostess led them through a maze of empty tables to a booth at the very back of the restaurant, where she put the menus down, one beside the other. "You sit here, Doc." She pointed at the left side of the booth, and they both slid onto the bench, first Vicki and then Daniel.

Without another word of instruction (or taking a drink order), the woman turned and stormed off toward the kitchen, disappearing through the double doors that separated it from the dining room.

"Are you sure about this?" Vicki asked. She looked around the room and tried to place the Steven Seagal movie in which she'd seen the setup.

Daniel's nerves had ambushed his appetite, but he looked up from the menu he'd been browsing out of sheer curiosity. He slipped his left arm around her and gently rubbed her shoulders. "Everything's going to be all right." He looked straight into her eyes the way people do when they're really trying to sell a lie.

"Sure it will," she lied right back.

He deepened his gaze into her sea-green eyes, partly to convince her he was confident he could back up his guarantee, and partly to determine if she was buying his act. Daniel was so distracted by his inability to get a read on what he saw there that he never noticed the well-dressed man until he'd already slid into the booth across from them.

"'Ello, duckies." The man wore a bespoke suit, navy ten-month wool with the faintest of pinstripes to it. Beneath the suit coat, a slate-gray silk shirt was open to reveal an abundant covering of dark, curly chest hair. His features seemed concealed behind a mustache-beard combo, as full as a covering of face fur but impeccably trimmed and kempt. His hair was perfect, combed back, styled tight, and held there with product. It was clear he was going for well-groomed gentleman, but the overall effect made him look like Larry Talbot from a Lon Chaney Jr. flick.

Daniel was startled by the man's sudden appearance. "We're looking for—"

"Coo, but you're an excitable boy," the stranger called out. "I bleedin' know who you're lookin' for." He gestured to himself. "And you've found him, 'aven't you?" The English accent was thicker than London fog, but seemed a fitting accessory to his ensemble. "An' I knows what you come lookin' for too, I do."

"I'm sorry," Vicki interrupted. "And you are?"

The man smiled as if he had a secret he enjoyed too much to share. "You can call me Jim."

Daniel looked nervously about the empty room. "Well then, Jim?"

"Got yourself a bit of Barney Rubble, 'aven't you?" the man observed coyly.

"What's that now?"

"Trouble," the Brit translated. "You got trouble. A bloody lot of it, too."

Daniel sensed the growing unease next to him and slid a comforting hand down to Vicki's thigh to reassure her. "I'm just looking to buy a pair of IDs."

Jim held up his hands with alarm. "Mind your tongue," he cautioned, checking over each shoulder to see if anyone could be listening in on their conversation. Aside from two waiters who'd apparently wandered into the room to set the tables for the next day's service, there weren't any eavesdroppers.

"I know what you want." Jim gave the room another quick check. "Twenty grand. Apiece."

It was the price Daniel had been told to expect. He reached into the breast pocket of his jacket, pulled out an envelope containing the cash, and surreptitiously slid it across the table. "Done."

The man put a hairy hand on the envelope and claimed it for his own. He slid the package to his lap and counted the contents to himself. When he was satisfied the money was all there, he placed it in the breast pocket of his own jacket. "Done."

"And now?" Daniel asked.

"What do you mean?" Since claiming the cash, Jim seemed to have grown ignorant or innocent.

"Our IDs," Daniel whispered, careful to keep his voice down. "The passports. The papers."

"Yeah…" Jim drew out the syllable, hesitating a bit before finally flashing a toothy smile. "You're new to this, then?"

He didn't wait for his assessment to be confirmed by Daniel's look of confusion. "Here's the thing. Looking for forged papers is a bit of a sticky wicket. It requires a bit of a leap of faith, now, don't it? I mean, what with it bein' a crime an' all."

Daniel wasn't sure where Jim was leading him now, but he had a growing feeling in his belly that he didn't want to follow.

"Which means you can only get 'em from criminals"—Jim stopped to humbly lay a hairy hand upon his furry chest— "which, if I'm to be honest with you, is exactly what I am." He looked around the room. "What we all are."

That last part bothered Daniel. "We?"

Jim gestured in the air as if calling the waiters over to order, and the only two other men in the room trotted over obediently.

Both men were short and birdlike in build, but what they lacked in muscular bulk they more than made up for with the pistols they pulled from their waiter's smocks. Without a word, one slid next to his boss and the other forced himself next to Daniel and Vicki, crowding them both further into the booth.

Jim smiled at their arrival and continued with the Big Reveal portion of his plan. "And the thing about criminals is that they're just not to be trusted, are they?"

"You would've thought I would've picked up on that by now," Daniel observed dryly.

Jim ran a hand over his perfect hair. "You see, mate. We know who you are. Why you're here. And where you got this money." He tapped his pocket where he'd stashed the cash-stuffed envelope. "And we know you've got more."

Daniel felt fear. And anger. "I don't have any more."

"Not on you." The calmness in Jim's voice made it clear that this development was not unexpected. "But we know you can get it." Jim looked straight at Vicki. "With the right motivation."

Daniel felt less fear. More anger. "And just what exactly would that be?"

Jim raised a hairy finger to his lips, smugly pretending to think on it for a minute. "'Ow about I keep your bint company while you and my boys go fetch the cash an' bring it back 'ere?"

The irony lodged in the request like a bone in the throat wasn't lost on Daniel. "I should tell you what happened the last time someone sent me off to collect some cash with what they thought was a badass chaperone."

Jim nodded, acknowledging what everyone in the underworld already knew. "I think you'll find these two are just a little bit *more* badass."

"Well, then." Daniel looked over at the kung fu goon sitting next to him and then at the other across the table. "You haven't left me much of a choice," he conceded.

"None at all, mate." Jim nodded toward each of his men. "If there's any funny business from you, Ah Quen and Chen Ching 'ere can kill you more ways than you could count with a bleedin' abacus." He grinned triumphantly. "An' that'd leave your bit of stuff there alone with me."

Jim looked Vicki up and down like a pawnbroker checking out a Hondo guitar fitted with a Gibson headstock and offered as the real deal. "The bird's a bit too long in the tooth to fetch the top coin—"

"I'm too what in the who—" Vicki started to explode before Daniel restrained her.

The hairy-handed gent just chuckled. "But she's got more than her share of spirit, don't she? I'm sure I could find a buyer for her." He made some mental calculations in his deviant head. "Something fetish, you know."

"No need for that." Daniel didn't feel any fear at all now. "I just need to make a phone call, and I can have the money brought here." Now there was nothing but anger.

Jim flashed a victory smile. "You got twenty minutes, an' then my lads here start kicking your arse." He licked his lips ever so slightly. "And I start tappin' hers."

Daniel reached for his cell phone, but the henchman beside him grabbed his hand faster than a cobra strike.

"I'm just going for my phone." Daniel tried to pull his hand free, but couldn't.

Jim gestured once, and the kung fu goon released Daniel's wrist.

With his cell phone in hand, Daniel pushed speed dial and listened. It only rang once, suggesting someone was expecting the call. "I need the money. All of it. Twenty minutes, or they say they're going to kill us." He paused to listen to something. "I know you told me so, but this really isn't the time, is it?" He waited for the answer he wanted. And got it. "Good. I'll tell him." Daniel ended the call.

"Good news?" Jim gloated.

"For you," Daniel responded glumly, before turning to Vicki and asking her as cheerfully as their dire straits would allow, "Do you remember when I told you there would be days filled with danger?"

She was not amused. "I don't remember you saying they'd be *filled*."

CHAPTER TWO

Daniel Erickson was many things. A flawed soul, for sure. A victim of circumstances, maybe. He was not, however, an innocent man.

The Russian mobster *had* set a pair of hit men on his ass, but Daniel had shot one of them in the head. Daniel had killed those motorcycle club members the Russian had hired as extra muscle, too. And he'd played no small part in throwing that Russian mobster off a penthouse balcony. Daniel wasn't exactly sure where the body count stood—high enough that it was just a number—but his hands were washed too deeply in blood to ever claim innocence.

In his mind, Daniel justified the lives he'd taken as the unfortunate but unavoidable consequence of saving his son's life—and his own. In his heart, he realized he carried an unpaid tab for the blood he'd spilled. Somewhere deep in his soul, he hid the secret that how he'd come to the killing in the first place was a matter of dark mystery.

But whatever else Daniel Erickson might have been, he was not innocent.

He turned back to the self-satisfied man across the table, who was already mentally spending the money he'd yet to collect. "I'm betting you're sitting there thinking I'm one of those guys you don't have to take seriously."

"Honestly?" Jim leaned forward like a big cat about to pounce on a little mouse. "From the first moment I saw you"—he paused to stroke his perfect hair for effect—"I *knew* you were mine."

"Well, there are men you can push around," Daniel admitted, even as he looked deep into his newest foe's eyes. "But I'm not one of them."

"Is that right?" Jim bluffed, although truthfully he'd been unnerved by something unexpectedly dark he'd seen flash in Daniel's eyes. Still, he was unwilling to make a million-dollar admission by failing to rise to the unspoken dare. "Well then, just what kind of man are you?"

Daniel felt the familiar cold fury returning to his blood as his eyes turned tombstone dead. "I'm a push-back man."

A tense silence descended.

Daniel leaned back in the booth as if his declaration had won the day and reached to put his cell phone back. The gesture of returning something to the breast pocket of his coat seemed so natural and nonthreatening that no one in the group took any particular note of it until Daniel had already exchanged the phone for the butterfly knife he kept there, too.

Before the henchman squeezed next to him could grab him again, Daniel flipped the knife open and stabbed Ah Quen's hand, pinning it to the table with the blade. The man let loose a rabbit's howl, an eerie shriek that rose in its agonized pitch as, an instant later, Daniel snatched a set of chopsticks from the table's place setting and drove them through the man's left eye.

Across the table, Jim and Chen Ching sat stunned in shock for a second before the splatter of blood from their unfortunate cohort startled them to their senses. By the time they realized the proverbial shit had hit the metaphorical fan, it was already too late.

Daniel shot up to his feet, tipping the table toward them and driving it forward until both men were knocked backward, their bench overturned beneath them.

Daniel grabbed Vicki's hand and pulled her past Ah Quen, who was desperately trying to free his hand from the flipped bench.

They managed to take a step or two together before some sixth sense warned Daniel it was time to hit the deck. Without hesitation, he pulled her to the ground and rolled them to their right just as the shots struck the floor where they'd been. They rolled twice again, and Daniel looked up to see Jim and Chen Ching taking aim at them.

That's when the car came through the front window.

The Chrysler 300 SRT8 was as black as the night it came busting out of, a rolling tsunami of shattered glass, splintered framing, and Detroit steel. It skidded across the dining room, tossing aside tables and chairs before coming to a stop, wall-mounted Buddhas and decorative celebrity guitars crashing to the ground in a swirl of debris around it.

Almost immediately the sedan drew gunfire from Jim and Chen Ching, who'd managed to pull themselves from the overturned booth and flip the table on its side to use as cover. Each man emptied a clip into the intruding auto, but the shots buried themselves in the idling Chrysler without finding a victim.

It was a critical error.

As the pair stopped to frantically reload, Moog Turner emerged from the driver's side of his now scratched and dented 300. Like a very pissed-off Zeus, he raised his chromed hand-cannon and fired six of the seven .50 lightning bolts in the Desert Eagle's clip into the table Jim and Chen Ching were hiding behind. An engine block will stop a .9mm round, but two inches of laminated pressboard draped in a red linen tablecloth might as well be a wet tissue to a .50 round from a Desert Eagle.

Moog didn't bother to wait for bodies to hit the floor. He knew from experience that there were things a man could survive and things he couldn't. What he'd just unleashed was the latter.

The big man got back in his car and spun the wheels until her nose was pointed toward the sedan-size entrance wound he'd opened in the side of the building.

Daniel got to his feet and pulled Vicki to hers. Together they lurched toward their waiting evac, but only managed to take a step or two before Daniel was tackled, sending them both back to the floor.

Not until Daniel was pinned to the floor did he realize that Ah Quen had managed to free his pierced hand and was now intent on returning the blade—straight into Daniel's heart.

Daniel turned to the side just as the man thrust the knife, the blade burying itself in the flesh of his left arm. He howled in pain, but all he really felt was the cold fury transforming him again into the angel of death he'd been on that night in Vegas.

In the midst of the melee, the hostess returned from the kitchen, looking no happier than she had when she'd first seated them. She screamed *"Diu nei!"*—the Cantonese equivalent of "Fuck you!"—as she raised a Norinco QSZ-92 pistol and took aim at Daniel.

Before she could get off the shot, Vicki tackled her like Ray Lewis coming up the middle. The hit Vicki laid down knocked them both to the ground and jarred the pistol loose from the hostess's hand. The weapon slid across the floor as the women struggled to their feet, both gasping for air.

The hostess staggered a step or two and then forced herself to assume kung fu's Universal Post position, readying herself to strike. "*Jinhu-Liu duan*," she said proudly, announcing her rank as a martial artist. "Golden Tiger." She seemed confident her opponent would be rendered helpless by such intimidating credentials. For further effect, she went into a brief demonstration of her mastery of martial arts forms.

Vicki hit her in the head with a guitar.

It was a 1979 Les Paul autographed by onetime Queens resident Joe Walsh. Vicki had picked it out of the rubble left in the 300's wake and swung it at the hostess's head like she was aiming for the bleachers in Citi Field.

"You think you're tough?" Vicki called down to the woman sprawled across the floor, blood trickling from her nose and ears. "I played up front in an all-women's punk band for fifteen years," she declared, just as proud of *her* credentials. The hostess made no response. Vicki threw the broken ax down on the unconscious woman and spat contemptuously. "Stupid bitch."

What Vicki knew should have horrified her only filled her with epinephrine and exhilaration, like the first time she'd jumped from the stage and into the crowd. She stood for a moment, savoring the long-lost rush.

Across the room, Daniel was still pinned on his back, a knife in his arm and a highly agitated martial arts fighter straddling his chest, ready to deliver a finishing move.

Fortunately for Daniel, Ah Quen had exercised preternatural self-discipline and abided by the most fundamental principles of first aid: never pull a foreign object from a puncture wound.

With the flat of his hand, Daniel desperately swatted at the protruding chopsticks and drove them as far into Ah Quen's head as he could. It was far enough that the man clutched at his eye for an instant and then simply fell off Daniel, slumping to the right, where he convulsed on the floor once or twice and then lay still.

This time it was Vicki who helped Daniel to his feet. They ran together to the waiting car and pulled open the rear passenger door. Vicki was the first to slide in. Daniel was about to follow her when he suddenly stopped, turned, and headed back across the debris-strewn floor, making his way to the overturned table at the back of the restaurant.

"We ain't got time for no takeout," Moog yelled over the throaty hum of the idling engine. "We gotta go."

Daniel knew his friend was right, but ignored him anyway.

The table now had six large holes in it. Daniel flipped it over and discovered that each of them matched a corresponding (but much bigger) hole in the men who'd been hiding behind it.

Daniel bent down and reached into Jim's blood-soaked suit coat. Forty grand was more than he was willing to leave as a tip. As he pulled the envelope free, Jim's hand grabbed his wrist. The unexpected sign of life made him jump.

"They'll find you." Jim's words, meant as a threat, were little more than last gasps. "There are too many looking for you. One of 'em will find you—"

"Maybe," Daniel was willing to concede. "But they'll all find out exactly what you did."

Jim shuddered, but it wasn't clear whether it was his pain or Daniel's words.

"You can't push around a push-back man." Daniel rose to his feet, took a step toward the waiting car, and then turned back one last time.

Jim's empty pistol was still useless in his hand. The clip it needed was just out of reach on the floor beside him. Daniel bent down, picked them both up, and united them.

He stood over Jim. "Oh, and about what you said to the lady—" Daniel chambered a round.

The man was slipping beyond words, but his flickering eyes looked up as if to ask, "Yeah. What about it?"

Daniel responded with a single shot.

He trotted back to the car, and before the door was closed behind him, Moog's size-fourteen Ferragamos had stomped down on the Chrysler's accelerator.

The sedan shot out of the restaurant like a rocket off the launchpad at Cape Canaveral, and the big man never slowed. There were sirens in the distance, but Moog was already speeding down the Grand Central Parkway by the time the first black-and-whites from the 114th Precinct had rolled up on the scene.

Daniel looked over at Vicki, afraid that what she'd just witnessed had scared her out of his life—but more afraid that there was good reason for it. "This probably won't be the last time."

She looked at his arm. After fifteen years in a punk band, it wasn't the first stab wound she'd seen. "You'll live."

"You think so?"

She smiled and nodded, not yet certain but more convinced than ever. "We all will."

CHAPTER THREE

Some men are born to kill, but Daniel Erickson wasn't one of those.

He'd endured all of the adolescent clichés that come from growing up in a small town while having more talent in the arts than on the playing fields or hardwoods. He disappointed everyone but surprised no one when he skipped college to run off to LA and take a shot at the music business.

He was well on his way to proving all of his naysayers right when he managed to snag a writer's credit on "Driving You Out of My Mind," a song he'd had nothing to do with writing, but which nevertheless earned him some serious change over the course of the ten years it was the theme for Ford's line of pickups. Although he was much more the musical scavenger than rock-and-roll predator, that one hit was all he needed to make a life in the Biz.

Success (earned or simply obtained) opens the door to more success. All Daniel had to do was walk through it. He rustled more writing credits and got involved with some midlevel acts. In the end, there was more black ink than red, more credit than creditors: the very definition of success.

He met and married Connie, an aspiring model/actress who quickly became discreet about her days as a "dancer" but brash in her tastes for expensive clothes and jewelry. They got a house in Malibu he could never quite afford and settled down to raise their son, Zack. It was the American Dream.

For a while.

Eventually, perhaps inevitably, the dream segued into darker territories until the nightmare at its core was finally revealed. Music's transition to the digital age made it harder and harder for a scavenger to find a bone. Connie had lived up to the kept-wife cliché with an affair with a muscle-bound D-list actor half her age. And Daniel had reacted with a complete financial, physical, and mental collapse, capping it all off with a fantastically failed suicide attempt.

In the end, the only lifeline thrown to Daniel had come from his son, Zack, by now a man himself. Zack had taken the last bit of money Daniel had squirreled away and used it as bait to lure his father through a tour of American roots music, from the Mississippi Delta's blues all the way to Seattle's grunge scene, hoping that his father might rediscover the spark in his soul.

The boy had never considered that completing this journey might require his father to tender his soul to a figure known as Atibon who walked out of the shadows of the crossroads one moonless Mississippi night. It was nevertheless a touching gesture. It might even have worked, if the money hadn't been owed to a psychotic Russian mobster. But the debt was there when the money wasn't, and Zack's life was the intended penalty on the default. So the well-intentioned lifeline turned out to be a whole lot of bricks.

What else could he do? What would any father do? Daniel Erickson did what he had to do. He became a killer. Not because it was the path he'd been born to walk, but because it was the only way to save his son. And himself.

He became a killer. And everyone (well, everyone except his best friend/bodyguard, Moog) who came for him, or threatened his son, or him—they all died. Hard.

The necessity of the acts, however, did not make them any easier. A man can't take another's life without losing a little piece of his own. Daniel had been warned that drawing blood carried a heavy price, but he had no way of knowing just how steep.

The least of it was that he couldn't sleep. Not for normal stretches, anyway. And never without finding that his troubled dreams would trick him at this turn or that into returning to that Vegas hotel suite where he'd spilled all that blood.

The condition strained his emotions at times and left him virtually narcoleptic at others. The not-so-gradual erosion of the ephemeral wall that separates the dream realm from waking reality opened an unwelcomed portal for nightmarish visitors that he knew in his more lucid moments couldn't possibly be anything more than the strained creations of his overburdened subconscious.

Or at least, that's what he struggled to remind himself when they came.

"Do you really think you can hide?" The words sounded like sharpened steel being dragged slowly and deliberately across a concrete floor. "There's no place you can go where you'll ever be safe."

Even with more than one-third of it missing, Daniel instantly recognized the face staring back at him with what remained of its right eye. He'd been born Jesus Arturo Castillo del Savacar, but he'd spent most of his short life known as Rabidoso because the sick puppy took such pleasure from his business of killing. The little psychotic had been the very worst in the long line of bad men who'd hunted down Daniel and his son. When Rabidoso finally put a gun to Zack's head in Vegas, Daniel had put a slug in the psychotic's skull, splattering that twisted mess of brains across the hotel balcony.

Daniel wasn't one to speculate on heaven or hell or whatever other posthumous fate might have befallen him, but since that fateful night, Rabidoso had become Daniel's most persistent hypnagogic visitor.

"You'll never be safe. Not from him." The specter's face contorted into what would have been a sneer, if there had been enough cheek and chin remaining to achieve the grin. "He knows all about you."

Daniel felt a momentary temptation to panic, but hatred tamped down his fear, exactly as it had done on that night in Vegas. "He?"

"He's coming for you." Rabidoso's silhouette paced predatorily through a backdrop of smoky shadow, his body moving in herky-jerky spasms as if his image were projected from a film with every third frame removed. "And no one can save you this time."

It's just another dream, Daniel repeated silently.

Unable to will himself awake, he stood his ground, staring back defiantly at the fragmented remains of the killer's skull as he struggled to make out what was concealed in the swirling, smoky blackness just beyond the still-stalking corpse. "You used to say nothing could save me from you." Daniel couldn't be certain, but he thought he could just make out the figure of a man hiding back in the murky edge of that impenetrable darkness. "And now look at you."

Rabidoso's ectoplasmic form was a representation of the near-headless corpse Daniel had left on the hotel balcony, and now its flapping jaw drooped open in outrage, revealing a row of gold-capped, blood-caked teeth. What was left of his eye glared at Daniel as his ectoplasmic body first trembled with shudders of anger and then began to vibrate with a building, finally uncontrollable rage. A second before the corpse combusted into an explosive ball of flames fueled by its unquenched hatred, there was a high-pitched, wailing shriek. It was a howl of pain, blended cries for new blood.

Daniel couldn't tell whether the pained wail had come from Rabidoso or from whatever was skulking in the shadows behind him.

The sound was loud and shrill enough to wake Daniel, pulling him from his nightmare like a lifesaving hand plucking a drowning man from a dark and treacherous riptide.

He sat up on the sea grass couch on which he'd fallen asleep. The familiar surroundings of the screened-in porch and the rolling blue sea off on the horizon were comforting, even if his dream had left him unsettled.

He shook off the last images of the dream as if he were shaking water from his ears after a long swim. It cleared his head, but he could still hear the scream.

Shrill and high.

Moving straight toward him.

CHAPTER FOUR

Whushhh. Whushhh. Whushhh.

The sound of the tide against the shore. Reason says this was the first sound Earth could call its own; its infant gasp as it filled its lungs with air enough to wail. It follows that this will be its last sound too; a deathbed confession whispered and then lost in a final exhalation, as whatever cataclysmic force has been patiently waiting since the dawn of creation finally wipes it from existence.

In between, there is the continuous rhythm of water and earth colliding again and again, coming together but never combining, like lovers who can only agree that the sex is good.

Whushhh. Whushhh. Whushhh.

Like a mother's heartbeat in utero, the primal rhythm of the surf had lulled the big man into complacency and then into sleep. Beneath the celestial heat lamp of the tropical sun, he slept on his back, absolutely motionless, like a big, black, snoring rock. He was so perfectly comfortable and so lost in that near-narcotic moment that he never heard the creeping footsteps.

They fell one by one, little more than a whisper of feet across the sand. In a virtually silent serpentine, they drew closer and closer to the sleeping man without ever giving him reason to sense their approach. He slept on in his halcyon daze, oblivious until they were finally just a breath away.

Moog Turner was a killer, not by accident or incident or even psychological imbalance, but by choice and by trade. He'd been trained and tutored in the specialized art as some youths are apprenticed to become vintners or high-wire walkers.

As an angry young man running down Kansas City's Independence Avenue like a bull through Pamplona, Turner had been fated to meet the same end as that bull. But then one fateful night, Moog found himself face-to-face with the legendary Arthur Beagler—on the better end of the stainless steel Mark I Desert Eagle .50 held between them.

No one had ever gotten the drop on Beagler before. In recognition of that achievement and as repayment for the uncharacteristic mercy Moog had shown him in thumbing down the hammer and holstering the pistol, the master took the wilding under his wing. It was the professional assassin's equivalent of studying physics under Stephen Hawking.

In the years that followed, Moog was trained and tutored in 1,001 ways to kill a man. Some were so subtle that their lethal results seemed like nothing more than fate's intercession as a simple accident. Others were so brutal that the murder became a grotesquely eloquent message that needed no translation and could not be ignored.

Throughout his tutelage, however, one lesson had been stressed as supreme. While Moog had been thoroughly schooled in innumerable variations on whacking a guy, what his sensei had stressed as the single most important lesson a hit man could learn was how to avoid becoming a whack*ee*.

There'd been a time when anyone foolish enough to stalk Moog would have simply wound up as a corpse in a brutally efficient expression of Darwinism in action. Back in the day, Moog's senses had been as sharp as the razor he kept in his sock, and even during those brief moments when he allowed himself to sleep, he was still poised and ready to strike. There'd been a time when those things were true, but that page of the calendar had long since been torn off, crumpled up, and thrown away.

But money can change a man. A stash of $5 million can make a man softer than an investment banker's whisky dick. Months of lying low on a Caribbean island with stolen Russian-mob money had added pounds to Moog's six-foot-seven-inch frame, transforming a body that had once seemed sculpted from obsidian by a Kushite artisan into something that looked as if it had melted under a tropical sun.

There had *been* a day, but on this warm Caribbean afternoon, with the ocean's lullaby lapping in the background and a sweet trade wind blowing in from the sea, Moog Turner was soft, drowning in a dream so thick and deep that he never had any sense of what was approaching until it was right on him. And by then it was too late.

A hundred yards away, the only thing Daniel Erickson heard was the scream. It was a shrill, piercing shriek, a pained falsetto far higher in pitch than anyone would've believed a man with Moog's booming bass voice could have hit, no matter how distressed, no matter how far into the pits of terror he'd fallen.

A second later it was followed quickly by another squeal, every bit as contorted by fear into something tortured and bestial. Then there was an agonized wail. Then nothing but silence. Silence and the surf.

Always the surf.

CHAPTER FIVE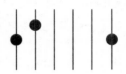

If island life had softened Moog Turner, the same life had hardened Daniel Erickson into a physical form he'd never known before. Whether penance for sins committed or a campaign of self-improvement, daily runs on the beach in the morning and again at evening had given him a sinewy leanness, and a disciplined regimen of push-ups, pull-ups, and sit-ups had provided muscle he'd never carried before.

He easily jumped up to catch the crossbeam of the covered porch and began a series of pull-ups as he tried to calculate how long it would take a man of Moog's size and deteriorated conditioning to run a hundred yards across the afternoon sand.

He dropped back to his feet and waited, knowing it wouldn't be *that* long. A minute later (give or take), the door to the screened porch burst open and then slapped shut behind the big man, who was too winded to do anything but drop his hands to his knees and pant wildly. "Oh, Jesus! Oh, Jesus!" he cried between desperate gasps for air.

"Problem?" Daniel asked with a knowing grin and a barely suppressed laugh.

"Those damn lizards are my goddamn problem." The big man tried to straighten up but quickly thought better of it.

"St. Thomas does have a significant iguana population."

"Well, how about you kiss my ass, Crocodile Hunter? I know there's a damn lizard population, because one of those scaly things just ran right up on me." Just the thought of his reptilian neighbors scampering over his flesh made the big man shudder with revulsion.

"I hate those damn things," Moog said between gasps for breath. "And I'm done hiding out on this island. Man can't even take a day on the beach without some damn Komodo dragon crawling up on him. What kinda shit is that?"

"It was just an iguana," Daniel corrected. "And he probably thought you were a rock."

"Well, I *hit* the thing with a rock," Moog announced proudly. "How you like that, Ranger Rick? Cause you bet your nature-lovin' ass it ain't gonna be crawling up on nobody else no more."

"You know, throughout South and Central America they call them *gallina de palo*."

"That right?"

Daniel tried not to smile. "Chicken of the tree."

"Chicken," the big man grumped. "I ain't had a decent piece of chicken since my sorry ass left Kansas City." He sighed with something between melancholy and resignation. "What I wouldn't give for a bellyful of Stroud's right now." His voice sounded like a giant stomach growling.

"We could go out to Cajun Cap'n Pete's," Daniel offered in what he mistakenly thought might be a consolation.

The big man shrugged off the suggestion. "It ain't Stroud's." He peered out through the screening that enclosed the porch, scanning the horizon for reptiles that might be amassing to seek vengeance for their fallen scaly comrade. There was nothing to see but sand dunes rolling out to pure blue water. Anyone could see it was a view of paradise, but Moog stated what he knew in his heart. "This ain't home."

Vicki Bean stormed out onto the screened-in porch with her green eyes blazing in combative zeal and her hands wrapped around the sawed-off bat she kept at her bedside. "What the hell was that screaming?"

"It was him." Daniel snickered and pointed to Moog, who was silent with embarrassment. "More iguanas."

She cocked an eyebrow in Daniel's direction, her silent way of asking him, *How can you find anything funny in any of this?*

Daniel didn't understand. "What?" He hadn't understood any of her *looks* in weeks. Maybe months.

She was also aware of the divide widening between them. Her arched eyebrow drooped into the vaguely forlorn look she now wore as regular beach attire, along with a bikini top and cutoff jean shorts.

Most people who came to St. Thomas left rested and relaxed after only a week or two, but the uninterrupted months Vicki Bean had spent on the island had left her feeling lost, with new, fine frown lines etched into her face, and dark circles beneath her eyes that even her native tan couldn't conceal.

"What?" Daniel repeated, his tone suggesting she was failing to see the humor in the situation. "What did you think?"

"Oh, I don't know." She used her words like the bat she held at the ready, resting on her tanned shoulder. "Vengeful drug cartel assassins. Pissed-off Russians. Maybe meth-baked bikers come to party." What she intended as a scoff came out with more venom than even she realized she'd built up. "Or maybe just the FBI come to take us away to a federal prison. There are *so* many potential visitors on our guest list."

She turned and started back into the house. He followed after her, unsure what he'd say once he caught her. "Vicki."

She stopped in the hallway, just past the kitchen, and turned to face him. Her teeth were gritted, but even he could tell that it wasn't as much in anger as to keep from crying. "What?"

"It's all OK," he assured her. "We're living in paradise."

"Yeah," she snapped. "A paradise you can't leave is just another prison." If her words sounded caustic, she felt nothing but sad inside. She let the bat drop to her side and turned to go back farther into the house, not so much angry as defeated.

"Vicki."

"*What?*" She turned to him and looked back, her green eyes wide with pent-up anger. "What, Daniel?" She sounded as if she were daring him to show her some pacifying parlor trick she hadn't seen a dozen times before.

Words are hardest to find when they're needed the most. He had nothing. There was no way to assure her their life together would get better—or even just closer to normal. In a year or two, when the heat had died down a little more, maybe then they'd be free to travel, to live their lives—maybe not *their* lives, but lives she could tolerate more easily. Maybe.

"I'm sorry." It was all he could say, but that at least was the truth.

He wished it mattered to her more.

CHAPTER SIX

Preparedness.

That's the extra step on the competition. It's the tipping weight on the scale between failure and success. For those who put themselves out on fate's pass line, it's all too often the difference between life and death.

They made their plan, reworked it, then refined it further, until all remaining uncertainties had been defined and each contingency had been thoroughly considered. They worked it until they'd channeled every possibility in the great sea of chance into finite streams of possible outcomes, any one of which they could accept.

Preparedness was the key. They had done the work. There was nothing left to do now but to wait for the US marshals to hit the door.

That happened about twenty minutes later than scheduled, with a heavy pounding at the door and an entrance that didn't wait for a response. Supervisory Deputy Ken Barters burst into the room like a flash grenade of alpha male pheromones.

"You picked a helluva day for a briefing, Feller." Sarcasm dripped from his words like the icy beads running down his navy jacket with US MARSHAL emblazoned across the back in bold gold letters. "This damn sleet's got the Beltway covered in more ice than the Cap's rink at the Phone Booth, and the Skins are on from Frisco in about forty minutes." He threw his jacket over the back of the chair at the head of the conference table, but he might as well have pissed on it.

"Y-yes, w-w-well…" Special Agent Gerald Feller stammered. He'd worked out every detail of his fugitive-apprehension plan, but he'd long proven unable to prepare himself for interagency rivalries.

"This is Deputy Catherine Wimmers," Barters announced, without looking back over his shoulder at the woman trailing directly behind. "Don't be fooled," he cautioned. "She can drop the hammer as hard as any man I've ever tracked with."

As she nodded a silent acknowledgment, Wimmers's blonde bondage ponytail lent her the ferocious feminine aura of a Russ Meyer heroine. She dropped her well-muscled body into the seat next to Barters with a defiant possession suggesting she might just piss on her chair, too. Just because.

"I'm Special Agent Gerald Feller." His introduction sounded like an apology, as he nervously ran his swollen fingers through the carousel of red hair that ringed his onion-shaped head. Neither of the marshals responded as if this was information of any importance to their operation.

When Feller recognized there wouldn't be a hearty round of good-to-have-ya-on-the-team, he disappointedly gestured toward the young man sitting faithfully by an assemblage of laptops and projectors like a cyber-age RCA dog. "And this is Special Agent Karl Schweeter. He's been working with me on the logistics."

The young man in the freshly pressed Dockers shot to his feet and gave Barters an enthusiastic hand that even the gruff marshal couldn't refuse to shake. "I've been all over your case files. I have to say it's some impressive stuff in there. It's great to have you on the team."

Special Agent Feller smiled approvingly, as if he'd played some role in orchestrating the enthusiastic reception, but inside he was seething at the sort of sycophantic attention no one ever showed toward him.

Barters gave the junior agent a handshake and a "Yeah. You too." It was the sort of unimpressed, by-the-book reaction that Feller thought his prodigy deserved.

"Now that we've got all the howdy-dos out of the way—" Barters checked and then tapped the face of his MTM Pro Ops watch for emphasis. "Kickoff is now thirty-four minutes. Show us what you got."

"Well," Feller hedged, nervously looking up at the clock on the wall. He tugged at the waistband of his slacks, which was already straining like a New Orleans levee to contain the storm surge of his potbelly. "We're just waiting for—"

The door opened again, and everybody turned as a barrel-chested man in his fifties stepped into the room. "This better be good, Feller. Skins are the afternoon game."

"Ross Bovard," Barters exclaimed as he shot out of his chair. "Now we know things are serious." He thrust out his hand and they engaged in a clasp of hands more fitting for a gladiatorial arena than a governmental conference room. "I haven't seen you since—"

"Buffalo," Bovard finished for him. "Those six al-Qaeda assholes." They both laughed heartily at the memories they'd conjured and released their hands without either one claiming victory or conceding defeat.

Barters introduced his deputy, and she took her turn at the Gorilla-Grip-Test-Your-Strength game they had going.

Special Agent Feller stood silently, envying the displays of camaraderie that never included him. His was never the hand people were looking to shake. What was it? he wondered. They were the same damn jokes, but his were always the ones that people resisted.

"Sir. Sir."

The next thing Feller knew, someone was tugging at his elbow. He turned, momentarily disoriented, like a sleepwalker awakened midwalk. Schweeter, his eager, earnest eyes staring straight up at Feller, was urging him on. "The briefing," he whispered, as if the three at the opposite end of the table couldn't hear them.

"I've got a seventy-two-inch plasma screen in my den," Special Agent in Charge Bovard announced; it was both a mannish boast and a simple statement of fact. "I'd rather not have to watch the game here on my iPhone. So let's get on with it." Barters and Wimmers chuckled along. Even Schweeter joined in.

The exact same jokes, Feller silently complained one last time.

"Sir."

"Oh, right," Feller mumbled apologetically before nodding at Schweeter to start the slide show they'd prepared.

The photo of a man appeared on the screen at the far end of the conference room. He wasn't at all sinister looking, as the faces on wanted posters or in newswire suspect photos almost always are. The photo was distinguished only by the subject's sad smile and the distant look in his eyes. "This is Daniel Erickson."

"Looks like my brother-in-law." Bovard chortled. Barters and Wimmers chuckled along.

That wasn't even a joke. Feller kept the bitter observation to himself.

"Sir," Schweeter whispered again.

"Oh, right," Feller covered as he continued. "Daniel Erickson. Age forty-seven. Six feet. One hundred seventy-five pounds. No military training. For twenty-five years he was a music promoter. Seemingly legitimate," he added, "as far as legitimacy in the music industry goes."

Feller pulled at the collar of the sparkling white T-shirt peeking out from the open collar of his blue button-down. "Then he went through a divorce. Lost everything. Had a nervous breakdown. Was committed briefly. Took a trip to rehab. Somehow he emerged from that personal cyclone as a business partner of this man, Filat Preezrakevich."

Schweeter pressed a key on the laptop, and a different face appeared on the screen. This one wasn't smiling at all, but grimacing as if it were physically painful for him to contain his violent rage for even the fraction of a second it had taken to snap the photo. "Preezrakevich was *russkaya mafiya*. The worst of the worst. His body count was so high—even by Russian standards—that the other *bratki* concluded he was too dangerous and conspired to kill him. He fled to the United States and somehow wound up partnered with Erickson." Schweeter clicked through a series of grainy black-and-white stills from security tapes showing the two men together at a casino roulette table.

"Through Preezrakevich," Feller continued, "Erickson partnered up with two men." Another click, another face. This one had a scar running from his left temple across a pair of thin, cruelly sneering lips and then over to the right side of his neck. Even in the photograph it was alarmingly clear the man was dangerous and absolutely batshit crazy. "The first was Jesus Arturo Castillo del Savacar. An assassin with the Cartel del Golfo. His associates with the cartel tagged him Rabidoso because he was such a sick puppy."

Schweeter clicked again.

"The second was this man." The image on the screen changed again, and this time the face was hard and set, like it had been chiseled from stone. "Vernon 'Moog' Turner. Muscle for hire out of Kansas City. Onetime protégé of Arthur Beagler."

"Beagler?" Bovard interrupted. "You're sure of that?"

"Yes, sir," Feller confirmed. "They worked together for some time. There was a split between them. We're not sure over what. Turner went to work for Preezrakevich about five years ago."

Feller noticed that Bovard made an obvious mental note, but didn't share it with anyone in the group. "Go on."

Feller did what he was told. "In February of this year, these three men—Erickson, del Savacar, and Turner—went on a cross-country crime spree." The slides advanced to the photo of a middle-aged woman, naked from the waist up, lying obviously lifeless in a pool of dark blood. "It included the murder of Maria Garcia, Erickson's cleaning lady." No one in the room flinched.

The next slide showed a black garbage bag opened to reveal an assortment of human limbs and body parts. None of it seemed to affect Special Agent Feller at all. "And Randall Baldwick, Erickson's ex-wife's boyfriend," he commented matter-of-factly.

Another click, and a videotape of a CNN broadcast came to life, showing a sea of people churning and bubbling with acts of violence. "Incitement of a riot in New Orleans."

Feller took a deep breath to brace himself as the following photo showed a dozen police cruisers that looked like they'd made a cameo appearance at a monster truck show. "In evading authorities in Chicago, Erickson made an escape in a stolen tractor-trailer, running through a police barricade in the process."

"I'll bet they love you up in Chi-town," Barters quipped. "Just like Steve Bartman and Rod Blagojevich." Wimmers chuckled dutifully. Bovard looked disgustedly off into the distance, like a Little League dad whose awkward son has just lost the championship game with an errant throw into the stands.

Feller wanted to say something in Bovard's defense, but his quiver of comebacks was empty. "Later, the three of them shot it out with five members of the Corpse Corps biker gang in downtown Chicago," he continued pointedly as a slide showed a corpse blocking a southbound lane of Michigan Avenue.

"They started another riot in Cleveland at the Rock and Roll Hall of Fame. Twenty people were hurt in the chaos of the evacuation." Click, and the photo showed ambulances in front of the iconic structure.

Click. More slides and more corpses. "They shot four men on the streets of Philadelphia."

Click. Still more photos of bodies. "Then, four more members of the Corpse Corps on a highway in Oregon."

"Holy shit," Barters couldn't help but call out. "You couldn't follow a trail like this?"

"We followed them to Vegas," Feller started defensively. "In the penthouse of the Hotel du Monde, there was a shootout between these players. Five members of the Corpse Corps were killed. Del Savacar was shot in the head. Preezrakevich, the man whom the Russian mafia couldn't kill, was thrown over the penthouse balcony." The slide showed a hi-def image of how the tiny man had made a plus-size mess all over the hotel driveway.

"Erickson escaped. Along with Turner. There was no money found in the hotel suite, so we believe they took a large sum of money, likely seven figures, from Preezrakevich." There were more stills taken from security footage showing the pair leaving the hotel, with one man carrying a large duffel, climbing into a battered Monte Carlo, and driving off onto the Strip.

"Did you trace the car?" Barters's condescending tone was parental, like he was asking a muddy-handed child if he'd washed up for dinner.

"It was reported stolen in Jersey," Feller answered. "But we haven't recovered it yet."

"Of course you haven't." Barters folded his bulging arms across his muscular chest. "Now what?"

"In March there was an incident in Queens. Three dead." There were photos to document each of them. "We believe Erickson and Turner were attempting to purchase identities to flee the country."

"And did they?" Barters wondered aloud.

"Two weeks ago we got a report that Erickson was in St. Thomas." The next slide showed Daniel, tanned and lean. "We've verified his presence there, along with Turner and an unidentified female." There was a picture of Daniel and a woman at a distance, walking along the beach.

"We've got them trapped on an island. There's no way off but through us—and that means no way out at all." Feller had spent some time practicing the confident delivery.

Barters scoffed. "'Through you' looks like a goddamn swinging door from where I sit." He leaned back in his chair. "But now that the marshals are here—"

"It's still a Bureau operation," Bovard interjected.

"Well, good God, Ross, let's hope we get marshals' results." Barters smiled triumphantly and turned to his partner. "Pack your swimsuit, Deputy Wimmers, we're headed to the Caribbean."

She lit up as if she'd just won a game-show vacation.

"I assume you've got an apprehension plan in place?" Bovard asked Feller, making it sound like a dare.

"Of course," he responded, sounding far less confident than he'd practiced.

Bovard leaned in to the table, "Then let's go over it and see what needs to be fixed." He chuckled. "And what just needs to be thrown out." Wimmers chuckled, too.

"Right. Let's walk through this." Feller resented them both. He looked quickly away and stole a glance through the window at the stormy afternoon, surrendering any hope of getting home before the roads became impassable or the Skins went into the second half.

"We've tracked Erickson here. St. Thomas."

CHAPTER SEVEN

Over a million tourists visit St. Thomas every year.

Sunny skies. Trade winds. Crystal-blue waters lapping at bone-white beaches.

For the vast majority of those who come to the island seeking rest and relaxation, their Caribbean vacation is as close to paradise as any of them are likely to ever get.

St. Thomas is unquestionably a beautiful location, with some of the finest resorts in the Caribbean, but paradise is a front that a lot of people work very hard to maintain without ever enjoying it themselves. It's an illusion sold to those who don't want to give any thought to the fact that the sheets in their seaside bungalow need to be washed, that someone is sweating in the resorts' kitchens to turn out those meals, or that those tropical drinks don't pour themselves into those hollowed-out coconuts.

Beyond the resorts and the private retreats that line the coast or sprawl across the lush, green mountains, an entirely different community struggles to make ends meet on the meager wages paid to service workers. For those hardworking people, the day-to-day reality of St. Thomas is very different from the glossy pictures splashed across the cruise brochures and magazine spreads.

Aaron Ojaso had been born in Savan, the dark heart of that "other" St. Thomas. The area had once been the center of the island's slave market, and nothing had been done over the passage of time to exorcise those hateful spirits. In modern times it's become the center of a different—if not wholly unrelated—bondage, where poverty confines its inhabitants. Dilapidated apartment buildings line narrow streets, and those who can't or won't take advantage of the meager economic opportunities available to them haunt the alleys and abandoned storefronts, looking for a way, any way, to make it through another "perfect" day.

Osajo had met Cozie "A-Volt" Earls when they were just boys, dancing in the Lucky Dollar Buss A Move competition at Randolph Elder Park in Morant Bay. One of them had said something disrespectful to the other—the exact comment was long forgotten now—and before any sense could be made of the situation, a fistfight had broken out. They fought one another to a bloody draw, and when they were finally separated, badly battered and exhausted, each recognized the other as his counterpart. they'd been inseparable ever since.

The two of them shared a small apartment above a T-shirt shop at the nastier end of the main tourist district of Havensight, where docking cruise ships have turned the island community into a shopping mall of souvenirs and trinkets. It was a cramped place, with a stained couch in the living room and a pair of twin beds in an alcove separated by a wall of hanging seashells.

This was the headquarters of what both young men hoped would be a burgeoning criminal empire à la Tony Montana. They had tried to set up their own gang, recruiting younger kids from the surrounding neighborhoods, but soon found themselves stuck in the middle, with Bloods to the left of them and Crips to the right.

Lucky to escape with their lives, the pair resigned themselves to climbing the rungs of the ladder to criminal success by selling grass and coke to errant college kids who weren't afraid to step outside their comfort zones and wander down Back Street after dark. They made some cash at it, and occasionally found a coed who would take a bag of this or that in exchange for another stain on the couch or an hour behind the shell curtain.

More recently A-Volt had found some notoriety as a rapper, even recording a couple of tracks at a homemade studio on the other side of the island to spread among the neighborhood kids and sell to tourists. He'd even managed to attract some attention from a couple of folks who'd achieved some success in the music business.

It was that connection that prompted the call. "Of course I remember." Osajo pointed at the phone excitedly to let A-Volt know it was the call they'd been expecting. "How I forget you, rock star?" He smiled broadly at what he heard on the other end of the conversation.

"No, no, no," he assured the caller. "Whatever you want on Rock City, we get for you."

He listened to what was being asked of him. And started to pace. There weren't more than a dozen steps he could take in any direction in the cramped apartment, but he took them and then turned until he hit another impediment. "No, no. I can do that." His eyes showed doubt, but his voice rang with newly discovered opportunity. "But it gonna cost you."

The big question. How could he not have prepared himself? "How much?" he mouthed to A-Volt.

"For what?" his friend whispered back.

Osajo drew the index finger of his free hand across his throat. A-Volt's eyes widened.

Osajo ran his hand over his dreads, trying to settle on a figure. "Twenty," he finally blurted out when he realized he had to say something. His face contorted in pain at the prospect of losing this lead with such a foolishly greedy demand. And then lit up with triumph. "Half now, half when it done." He waited. And then jumped into the air, joyfully celebrating the realization of all his dreams.

A-Volt wanted to know what was going on. His friend put out a hand to make him wait silently for another moment.

"Down the beach," Osajo repeated, listening carefully to the directions he was being given. "Right. No, I know the place." He nodded encouragingly to his partner. "When we get our money?" The caller interrupted him, but Osajo was emboldened. "No, no, I know who you are, but everybody pay cash, even someone like you." Arrangements were made. "All right. Tonight, then. It's taken care of. He'll be dead before the morning sun come up."

Osajo closed the phone and looked at his partner in crime. "Twenty grand!" A-Volt didn't look as excited as he'd expected him to. "What?"

His friend tried to conceal his trepidation. "I just never killed no one."

Osajo thought on it, trying to think of a way to make his friend feel better about the task they were facing. "Think on it like this," he offered. "Man musta done something bad, or they wouldn't be paying us crazy money to kill him."

CHAPTER EIGHT

Daniel had wanted to follow Vicki as she stormed down their hall, but he knew better than to think there was something to be gained that way. Or at least, he didn't trot after her. He stood and watched her disappear into the room they shared. The door slammed.

A dark cloud of discordance hung over the little house at the end of the beach for the remainder of that sunny afternoon.

Daniel sat alone on his screened-in porch, staring out at the sea, wrestling with an internal desire to simply sink into its depths. Life, he knew, was cyclical, and in the troubled corners of his mind, where he was careful not to wander for too long, panic was building that the disasters of his life were beginning to repeat themselves.

Over the course of his dark days, he'd survived a crazed Russian mafioso, a psychotic cartel hit man, and a murderous motorcycle club. He'd been cut, stabbed, shot at, beaten, and stomped. But it was love that had brought him closest to death's "Open All Night" doors.

He could have lived with his ex-wife's infidelities, if only she would have lived with him. But she wouldn't, and that had left him unwilling to live with himself.

He sensed the same foreshadowing tremors with Vicki now. The walking away, the pained silence—he recognized it all as the uneasy calm before the storm. With those troubling clouds gathering off their personal horizon, he could feel the same familiar panic building in his chest.

He struggled with the realization that he was losing Vicki, that he'd become disposable to her. That he'd become disposable. Again.

The thoughts made him nervous and weird, like they always did. But he also knew that, like the strong currents of the Caribbean out on the horizon, the more he struggled against them, the more quickly he would simply sink into their depths.

CHAPTER NINE

On the other side of the house, Vicki had retreated to the far corner of the ranch, where Daniel had converted two bedrooms into a makeshift recording studio with the idea that she'd have the opportunity to put together a collection of original songs. The idea had been exciting for a while, and then, like everything else on the island, it had gradually lost its appeal until it bored her and then finally just annoyed her. Even she wasn't sure why.

Once or twice she'd gone to town and met a fellow musician or two who was eager for the opportunity to record for free, even at a homemade studio. Those partnerships had been exciting enough to occupy her for a day or two, but as with everything else on the island, she'd been unable to sustain her enthusiasm for the projects for very long.

In the fog of her time there, the idea of her own work faded as well. It wasn't as if someone hiding for her life could launch an album release. It was all a pointless exercise. Like everything else her life had become.

She thought back to those times—and there were more than a few—when the A&R guys had come to her with offers, opportunities to make a life in music. She'd turned them all down. Something about artistic integrity or personal independence. She couldn't remember the reasons she'd given any longer. Now she'd wondered why she'd given them at all. Had the idea of success scared her so much that she embraced failure instead?

And was that what had happened with Daniel? Had she run off with him because of something she felt, something they shared? Or was it simply that becoming the traveling companion of such a broken man was more attractive than hanging around Jersey with the possibility of the last great heartache always perched on the next barstool?

She picked up her Epiphone acoustic and strummed the strings, not playing anything at all. Minor chords mainly. Sad sounds on a guitar.

CHAPTER TEN

There was a dog, short-haired, lean, and scrappy, in the passenger seat of the battered Jeep that rolled down the crushed-shell driveway. The pup barked loudly, as if it were heralding their arrival, then energetically leaped to the ground as soon as the brakes squeaked to a stop.

The dog sprinted off toward the surf to run through the waves and give chase to the flocks of gulls and shorebirds gathered at the foreshore. It padded over and examined the bloodied reptilian mess Moog had left on the beach, then broke straight for the porch at a sprint to rejoin the Jeep's driver.

The man behind the wheel stepped out onto the sand, his bare feet too callused to be bothered by the hot sand or the shell shards. Without any outward sense of irony, he wore a large Hawaiian shirt covered in orchids and hibiscus, so long it practically covered his bright-blue board shorts.

He reached into the back of the Jeep and pulled out a road-beaten guitar case and a wreath of artificial pine, then turned toward the house.

Moog had joined Daniel on the porch, and the two of them watched the man approaching with a shared intensity.

"Something about this guy I really don't like," Moog said, almost to himself. "Like I know him from somewhere." He fought to place the face but couldn't. "And I didn't like him very much back then either."

"Yeah." Daniel's arms were crossed against his chest. "Yeah. I'm not worried about *you* not liking him."

Vicki came out onto the porch without acknowledging Daniel or Moog and called out, "Mark!" She waved enthusiastically, and the man returned the gesture with the hand that held the wreath. She trotted out to greet him with a hug, and he returned it.

Moog turned and flashed an I-*really*-don't-like-him look, and Daniel returned it.

"I got you something," the newcomer said to Vicki. He handed the wreath to her.

She looked at it curiously before making the connection. "Oh my God, is it Christmas?"

"Two weeks," he answered with a smile.

News of the impending holiday and the wreath in her hand seemed to transport her to some other time or place. She stood stone silent for a moment, clearly disturbed to be caught between the two locations.

"You OK?"

"I'm fine," she lied and gave him a second hug. "I'd just totally forgotten. Thanks, Mark."

Mark Wannaman was a mysterious figure by any standards, and seemingly by design. His long hair, somewhere between windswept and hipster-matted, was streaked with gray, but it was impossible to pin his age down more closely than anywhere between the late twenties and early fifties. He wore a long beard that didn't quite do enough to conceal the deep scars that marked his face. When his eyes weren't hidden behind the darkest black

Retro Rocker shades, they seemed to drift off to the far distance, as if he was scoping out the path to something bigger, or trying to catch a glimpse of whatever it was he was running from.

St. Thomas was lousy with guys just like him.

The painful irony—which was not lost on Daniel—was that he was the one responsible for bringing Mark Wannaman into their lives. Six weeks earlier, he'd run into the bearded stranger while picking up a new guitar as a "see, it's not so bad being stranded in Paradise" present for Vicki. The two of them had gotten to talking about guitars. And then music. Then Daniel had let it slip that he had a makeshift recording studio in his home and that every once in a while he would let some of the local kids come and record a track or two for whatever get-me-off-this-rock project they might be compiling. Before he knew what had happened, Wannaman had invited himself to record a few tracks there.

Moog had been furious when he learned of the arrangement. The local kids were bad enough, but a strange middle-aged white guy appearing out of the blue was a greater risk than Moog thought his little family on the run should take. Eventually Daniel was able to convince the big man that the music-making cover might provide curious neighbors with an explanation for why the three of them were at the house, but Moog's guard was never down when Mark was around.

And then Vicki met Mark. A casual introduction of the new visitor to the house had turned into a conversation, and from there a request for her to lend a new guitar part for this song or backing vocals for that one. In no time at all, Wannaman's solo project seemed to have become a duo, and it became painfully clear to Daniel that whatever the nature of the relationship they'd formed, it was something they alone shared.

"I didn't think you were due to come over today," Daniel called from the porch as Mark and Vicki made their way back to the house.

"Yeah, well," Mark started in his distinctive gravel-road growl, as if he'd just smoked an entire pack of unfiltered Camels in one big puff and then washed it down with a boot of Rebel Yell. It wasn't a voice that was ever going to win one of those prime-time singing game shows, but it had an appealing earthy tone and an undeniable confidence. "I woke up this afternoon overcome with inspiration, and I wanted to get it all down while it's still there."

Spontaneity made Moog nervous. And suspicious. "So you just dropped by, huh?"

"You can't wait too long with inspiration. You never know how long it'll last." His attempt at an ingratiating grin did nothing to disarm Moog's distrust. "Life is all about time, and we're all running out of it, right?"

"It's not a problem," Vicki assured everyone. "We don't have any plans."

"Well, actually we were all about to go get a bite to eat," Daniel said.

"You two go ahead," Vicki volunteered. "I'm not hungry. I'd rather stay back anyway."

"Cool," Mark chimed in. "You're sure you don't mind?"

"Not at all," she said with a smile.

"Well, all right." Daniel tried to recover. "I guess we'll just eat in tonight."

"It's fine. You two go on without me." Vicki's tone was unwavering and her eyes dared Daniel to make a bigger issue of it. "Mark and I will stay here and just work on whatever has inspired him."

"Nah, we're not hungry either," Daniel said.

"You just said you'd made plans," Vicki said. "If you made plans, then go eat. Why would you stay here?"

There was no way to answer her question without detonating one of the IEDs she'd set in the conversation. "Well, all right, then." Daniel tried to swerve the conversation. "We'll just step on over to Pete's, and you guys—"

"Man…" Moog stopped his friend, pointing out that Mark and Vicki had already begun to drift off toward the porch and the studio at the far end of the house.

"I just don't trust that guy," the big man observed as they watched the pair disappear into the house.

Daniel found his voice failing him as he struggled for a deep breath that the familiar pressure across his chest would not let him take. There was only one thing to do. "Let's go get a drink."

CHAPTER ELEVEN

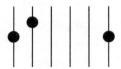

The "studio" Daniel had made for Vicki was nothing more than two small bedrooms. One of them he'd lined with Auralex studio foam, and in the other he'd set her up with Pro Tools 10 on a iMac and a Focusrite mixer. It wasn't the Record Plant, but it worked.

Without any studio rental fees, it worked just fine for Mark Wannaman, too.

"Daniel seemed a little tense," he observed without ever taking his attention from the Taylor acoustic in his lap. "Even for him."

"What?" Vicki had gone out of her way to drive Daniel off, but now that he was gone, she found he'd taken her thoughts with him.

"Your man," he repeated. "Seemed tense."

"He's fine." She ran her thumb down the open strings of her Epiphone and hoped she was right. It took another moment or two before his exact words hit her. "And he's not 'my man.'"

"Cool." He eagerly put the guitar back in its stand. "'Cause I been sensing—"

"No." She hadn't intended to open that particular door. "That's not what I meant, either. I was saying it's not like he *owns* me or

anything." She gave some thought to how that soun
I own him."

He seemed unfazed by her distinctions. "That's co

He was really starting to piss her off. "I mean, we're ̣ ̣ner."

"Right."

He was pissing her off *a lot*. "We're totally a couple." she'd never said those words aloud. Now that she had, they struck her ear as strange and somehow inaccurate.

"OK."

"Why are you being like this?" she snapped when she couldn't take his prodding and poking any longer.

"Being like what?"

"With all the questions."

"I didn't ask you anything," he pled innocently.

The truth was an ineffectual defense. "Daniel and I are a couple," she declared. Not for him, but for herself. She tested it out and drove it around the block a time or two. It seemed to have some miles on it. "We may not be getting married." *Had she actually said that?* "You know, tomorrow." *Married?* "Or ever." *Married?* She fell silent.

He picked his guitar back up. "I didn't mean to start anything."

"It's fine." And it was. There wasn't any need to think beyond the day she was living. She'd lived her whole life that way, and there was no reason to change now.

He stood up and adjusted the vocal microphone's height.

Welcomed silence.

And then, "It's just that—"

What is it with guys? "It's just what?"

"I just can't see you two together." That wasn't exactly it. "I mean, obviously I see you two together. He just doesn't seem like your type."

She didn't find that any better. "My *type*?"

"You know what I mean."

And she did. "He's not." The admission surprised her more than it did him. "But I guess that's why I'm with him."

"And why's that?" He strummed something soft and low.

She had no ready answer, but offered him the best she had. "I was born with a broken Chooser."

The blank look on his face made it clear he was waiting for a fuller explanation. "A broken what, now?"

"Chooser." Daniel had understood what she'd meant from the moment she'd let him in on her secret. "It's what I call whatever it is that guides you to choose, you know, who you're going to be with." She felt self-conscious about having shared this thought with Mark. "And who you're not."

"Got it."

"And, well, mine's broken. I choose guys who are exactly 'my type.' Hard-living guys with tattoos and guitars."

He looked at the sleeves of ink covering his arms and self-consciously twisted his silver bracelet of woven guitar strings. "Guys like me?"

She hadn't thought of it that way, but…"Yes," she said, shrugging. She slung the guitar's strap over her head and let it fall taut against her bare, suntanned shoulders. "And guys like that are fun."

He grinned. "True, that."

"But only for a while." She played a quick chord progression. "And then they leave. Even if they stay with you…" Her voice trailed off for a moment. "Even if they stay in the same apartment or house or whatever, one way or another, they leave you. They're not *there* anymore. Not how it counts." The memories she'd conjured were sadder than she remembered them being.

Her words seemed to have the same effect on him.

"But Daniel was the one who came back," she reminded herself. "And he looked like he'd fought his way through hell to do it."

"What do you mean?" Her comment piqued his interest. "Fought his way through what?"

She realized she'd already said too much. "It's complicated."

"Everything's complicated."

She acknowledged that point with a silent nod but couldn't be goaded into spilling more. "But *he* came back. He came back and he's stayed, and I guess I feel like I can't walk out on *that* guy."

"Even though you want to, because you're a tattooed, guitar-playing gypsy yourself?" He waited for her answer, not the words, but the way her body reacted.

"No. Not anymore." She folded her arms across her chest. "Not all the time..." She strummed a little more. "I just don't know what happens if you walk away from the one who came back for you." She played a soft, melancholy tune. "I guess I'm just not ready to roll that particular pair of dice just yet."

"So I'm guessing we're not going to be getting it on." A Cheshire-cat smile blossomed through his unkempt beard. "Just joking."

She smiled. "Right..."

"Because, you know, if you wanted to..." he started, not sure if she'd meant something more.

"No."

"Right." His smile faded, but didn't die. He loudly strummed a series of chords. "Well, since we're not going to fuck, why don't we do something *really* intimate, like make music?"

She smiled right back. "Let's."

CHAPTER TWELVE

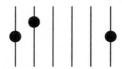

Daniel hadn't had a drink in more than two years. Sobriety had come courtesy of a court-ordered stay in rehab. Maintenance had been a matter of sheer survival. Leaving Vicki back at the studio with Mark Wannaman, however, had rekindled his thirst.

They got a table at Cajun Cap'n Pete's, a restaurant/bar for tourists that overplayed the nautical themes to an extreme just on the shy side of a cease-and-desist order from the suits at Margaritaville, Inc.

Daniel had a rum and Coke. Then he had another. After the third, he found that old habits brought back old thoughts.

His ex-wife, Connie, hadn't crossed his mind in months. Not in any significant way. But the flushed sensation in his ears and the swirling vortex of dark thoughts the drink had released brought the memory of her right back as if she were seated discontentedly next to him.

"The thing about being cuckolded—" Daniel offered, with a drunkard's self-delusion and without noticing Moog brace himself for a conversation he didn't want to have. "Being a cuckold is like having malaria. Even if you survive, every little fevered cough you have over the course of your life just makes you panic that the agony is returning again." He finished drink number three and raised it over his head as a signal to their overworked waitress.

"I don't think you have anything to worry about," Moog said. It wasn't that he necessarily believed that to be the case, but he knew it was what a friend should say. And, selfishly, he just didn't want to spend the evening talking about it.

It didn't work.

"The problem with relationships," Daniel continued, "is that once they start to go south and you realize they need resuscitation, it's too late. You just get all nervous and weird trying to fix it, but all you're doing is giving mouth-to-mouth to a dead man."

The waitress brought another round of drinks, and Daniel started right in on his.

"The problem isn't that they're sleeping with someone else." He stopped to reconsider what he'd said. "Well, that's a big-ass problem, too. But what's worse is being dismissed like that. You know?"

"Not really," Moog confessed. "I got ninety-nine problems, same as everyone else, but being easily dismissed ain't never been one of them."

"It's like neither one of them thinks you're significant enough to be a factor in their risk calculations. It's them saying, 'Oh, don't worry about him. What can someone like that do to us?' Well, I'll tell you what I can do!" He set his glass down to make a point, but in his rapidly deteriorating state it hit the table harder than he'd intended and spilled a bit over the side.

An attractive woman in a floral-print wrap dress walked across the restaurant floor, and Moog's attention was momentarily diverted as she passed by the table and then disappeared out into the bar area.

"Do you ever miss it?" Daniel asked.

"What?" Moog hoped his wandering attention had gone unnoticed. "This back-and-forth worryin' about a full-time woman? Hell, no." He took a drink. "Tried once, but my line of work don't make no room for love."

"No." Daniel leaned back in his chair, shaking off the suggestion he was still talking about something trivial. "The killing. Do you ever miss the killing?"

The question fell heavily on the big man. Spoken aloud, it almost seemed to him like a betrayal of a sacred secret, a dark bond they shared, but about which they never spoke. After all, their friendship wasn't based on killing, but on *not* killing.

Less than a year ago, killing had been Moog's living. Daniel had been just another assignment, and the big man had done his level best to bust a cap in his ass. But sometimes fate—or something even more mysterious—intervenes, and Moog found himself unexpectedly at the mercy of his intended target. It wasn't a willingness to spill blood that had earned Moog's admiration; it was Daniel's compassion that had won Moog's loyalty

Did he miss the killing? Moog was quick and unequivocal with his answer, hoping to end the discussion before it could begin. "Not a single goddamn day."

"What does it say about me that I do?"

"That answer ain't up to me."

Daniel leaned forward in his seat, his words soft and full of guilt as if he was in a confessional. "I could lie and tell you my mind's on Vicki right now, but that's not it. I'm sitting here thinking about that night in Vegas. The one night in my whole life when I couldn't be dismissed, when I wasn't insignificant."

Moog had seen too much blood spilled not to be troubled by his friend's perspective. "It ain't the gun that makes you significant. Can't be. 'Cause this world is too filled with assholes carrying pieces, and they're *all* insignificant."

"Maybe *feared* is as close to *significant* as I'm ever going to get," Daniel conceded. "And if that's how it is, then I liked being feared. I mean, I *liked* it. I've missed it. And now I'm not thinking about Vicki so much as I want the opportunity to feel that way again."

"You be careful," the big man warned, leaning in so he could lend necessary emphasis to his words without raising his booming voice and risking being overheard. "That kinda blood lust is the same drug your boy Rabidoso got to huffing on, and you seen where that ended him up at. It's the only place where that life can end you up at." He leaned back in his chair again, distancing himself. "That's why I'm glad to be done with it all. People only afraid of monsters, and I don't want to be no monster ever again. It's nothing you should want to be neither."

Daniel dismissed the warning. "A man wants what a man wants."

"A real man controls his wants." Moog put a big finger to the table to emphasize his point. "He ain't controlled *by* them."

"Well, while you been struggling to let it go, I've been fighting to hang on to it. That feeling, that energy, is like a life preserver to me. I feel like if I let go of it, I'll just go back to being what I was— I'll just slip back into those thick, black waters and drown in my own lack of consequence."

"Spillin' blood ain't sippin' whisky, man," the big man warned. "You're either drunk on it or you ain't. It either own you or it don't. But you're lying to yourself if you think there's anything in between."

Daniel didn't respond, but he was clearly unconvinced.

"When I first started…" The big man stopped, searching for a way to make his point without making a confession. There wasn't one. "First man I killed wasn't no man at all. He was just a boy, fifteen or sixteen. I wasn't any older myself, just a wild thing running on streets that were filled with all sorts of wild things. And for a while I thought taking that life made me a man, earned me respect. But you know what it really did?"

"What's that?"

"It sealed my fate." Moog took a drink so the rest of what he had to say wouldn't stick in his throat. "Couple years later I met a man, a professional hitter. Best there's ever been. I guess he saw something in me, 'cause he kinda took me under his wing, taught me how to kill a man proper. Schooled me in how to handle it like a business. Taught me everything.

"But the most important lesson he ever taught me was that they make bullets in pairs. And the first time you use one, its partner, its soul mate, starts down a long, twisting path of inescapable fate and unbelievable coincidences that'll someday bring it right back at you. Killing a man is just a long suicide."

Daniel looked off into the night sky above the patio. "*Life* is just a long suicide."

"No." Moog didn't have anything in his life he could hold up as Exhibit A. Not yet. But it was the fervent prayer that kept him buoyed above the lapping waters of his own darkness. "No, it ain't. And Vicki and that guy ain't nothing. And even if they are, it's not worth taking what we got here and ripping it up by the roots."

"What exactly is it that we got here?"

Moog looked his friend dead in the eye. "Today. We got right now. And that might not mean that much to you if you come to take it for granted, but I know it's a fragile fucking thing. And to my mind, it's the only thing worth fighting for."

Daniel had heard something similar from his mysterious friend Mr. Atibon, and he smiled at the thought of the old man. "So I've been told." He raised his glass. "Today."

Moog joined the toast. "Today."

Daniel finished his drink. "Let's go home and see what we see."

CHAPTER THIRTEEN

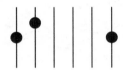

The sea air and the ride home with his head hanging out the passenger-side window had revived Daniel back to dangerous territory for a drinker, that treacherous precipice where one false step delivers a disappointing descent into a splitting headache, insomnia, and sobriety.

Moog drove all the way back to their place without saying a word. Daniel didn't object to the silence. He knew the big man had said everything he'd had to say, and he was aware that there was little interest in what Daniel might have to add to it.

"Thanks," Daniel said sheepishly as Moog turned over the keys to the Suburban. His head was still swimming in rum, but he recognized all the unwelcome telltale signs that sobriety would soon be making an unwelcome return, bringing a crushing headache with it.

"No problem," Moog answered. The big man took a step or two toward the guesthouse where he stayed, then suddenly turned. "You done all right, you know."

Daniel wasn't sure he'd heard him right. "How's that?"

"A man's significance can't be carried in a holster."

"Right." Daniel kept his doubts to himself.

"It's in his heart." Moog touched a spot on his chest. "And whether the world recognizes it or not, that don't say shit 'bout whether he has it. You saved my life, man. Saved your son's life. You saved a lot of lives you don't even know, folks who woulda had their asses capped if Rabidoso and Mr. P and them others were still alive and runnin' their ways." The big man stopped, wishing he were better with words and feelings and that sort of stuff. "I'd say that makes you pretty damn significant."

"Thanks." Daniel accepted the compliment without pointing out that he'd done all of those things with a gun in his hand.

"I appreciate you, man." Moog offered his hand, and when Daniel took it, he pulled him into an awkward man-hug as proof that he did. "I appreciate you."

"Thanks. You, too." Daniel smiled at his friend, truly grateful for the gesture and fully aware of how difficult it had been for him.

"You gonna be all right?" the big man asked.

"I'm fine."

Whether it was true or not, Moog was grateful all the same. "All right then. Well, good night, then."

"Yeah. Good night."

CHAPTER FOURTEEN

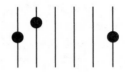

By the time Daniel hit the shotgun hall leading to the pair of rooms he'd converted to a recording studio, all he wanted was to fall into bed with Vicki. Tomorrow would bring whatever the day would bring, but in the dark of the night the only thing he wanted was just to sleep in her arms.

A guitar was playing softly at the end of the hall and he moved toward it like a desert-baked Bedouin chasing an oasis, navigating the corridor with very little trouble, considering his condition. He stumbled once, but it was a loose board that had tripped him up more than once when he was sober.

He reached the room and threw open the door. "I'm sorry, angel."

"Don't sweat it, baby," Mark Wannaman offered with a sly smile.

It was a jarring juxtaposition of expectation and actuality. "What the hell are you doing here?"

The sudden one-two powershift from a lover looking for a gentle reconciliation to a wild-eyed man capable of anything to protect his domestic interests took Mark by surprise, "Whoa, you look like you might not even gimme three steps."

"What can I tell you?" Daniel tried to steady himself against the doorway. "I'm a man who cares."

"Can't say I blame you." He kept playing the same soft chord pattern over and over again. "Vicki went to bed hours ago."

Daniel didn't like the way *that* sounded, and the mayhem in his eyes conveyed the degree of his displeasure more forcefully than any words ever could have.

"Nothing happened, man," Mark offered, understanding what the steely look meant. "But being with someone who's dinking around on you is like swimming with a brick. You shouldn't do it."

"I don't think she's *dinking* around on me," Daniel snapped angrily.

"Then you shouldn't go around acting like she is, man. That's like swimming with two bricks. You got all the shit of someone doing you wrong, *and* you lose someone who was faithful to you. You don't recover from that shit."

"Thanks for the advice," Daniel scoffed.

"Hey, man, I'm not busting your nut for the smiles. I've been through that war." The guitar part he was playing segued into a bluesy rhythm with a Bo Diddley beat. "You ever hear 'Not for You' by Taco Shot?"

Daniel shrugged at the suggestion. Taco Shot had skyrocketed to the top about ten years earlier with a track called "Walking Dead Man," but their ride up the charts had come to an abrupt end when their lead singer wrapped his Porsche around a tree. "I don't know. Maybe."

Mark kept playing his tune. "It was kinda a Lynyrd Skynyrd southern rocker thing." Then he broke into a bluesy rock riff, shut his eyes, and began to sing.

She's a beast in the sheets and I'm not lying
Now you decide if that's worth you dying
Cause you ain't never gonna see her bed
You got a chance to run or you'll end up dead
Ain't no threat that's what I'm gonna do
That's my woman there and she's not for you
That's my woman there and she's not for you

When he opened his eyes again, it was clear that he'd been transported somewhere else in place and time. He looked up expectantly, eagerly reading Daniel's eyes for a sign of recognition.

"I don't think so." Another shake of Daniel's head. "Love Skynyrd, though. Skynyrd, Allman Brothers, Marshall Tucker. They all understood the marriage of rock and the blues."

Mark flashed him a *whatever* look that did little to cover up his obvious disappointment. "Well, it's a pretty cool song." He turned back to his guitar like a bitter little kid whose crayon masterpiece didn't make it to the refrigerator door. "It charted," he muttered under his breath. "On college radio." He played a little more of the riff. "I was just saying that I been through it all."

"I have too."

"Then you know what I'm talking about. Down deep in her heart, every woman is a wild thing, man. You can't wrap her in chains without both of you turning into something that neither of you can live with. You know?"

Daniel did, but he was still too drunk—or too battle-scarred—to let on.

But then he didn't have to. "Yeah. You know," Mark commented confidently. He kept playing his absentminded chords. "Besides, Vicki's solid, man." He looked up. "And I wouldn't screw over someone like you. You got those crazy killer eyes."

There was something about the casualness of the comment that troubled Daniel, as if it somehow betrayed the identity he needed to conceal. "How would you—"

"I don't wear these shades 'cause my future's so bright." Mark smiled to himself. "They're there to conceal *my* crime."

"What crime?" Daniel felt a knot of uneasiness tighten in the pit of his stomach.

"I've done the worst thing a man can do."

There was something in the way the confession had been tossed off that made Daniel ask, "Are you telling me you killed someone?"

"There's far worse than that, man." Wannaman turned his attention back to the six-string in his lap and played a soft tune Daniel found familiar in a plagiaristic sort of way. "But you still don't know who I am, do you?" The question was thrown down like a dare, but seemed to tease, suggesting that Daniel had a personal interest in solving the riddle.

"What are you talking about?"

Mark stopped playing and leaned forward, allowing a little more of the luminescence from the control panel to fall on his face. "Ever since I rolled in here, you been looking at me when you thought I didn't know, trying to place this fucked-up face of mine."

Daniel tried to sputter a denial, but what Mark had said was true.

"And sometimes when we're out here, listening to a track, I can tell your mind's drifting and you're not listening to the mix anymore, you're not weighing whether the bottom needs to come up just a little, you're trying to place where you heard that song before."

That was also true, but Daniel felt uncomfortable being exposed. "You sound like a lot of those guys," he started to ad-lib. "They've all got that contrasting dynamic, the soft verse and the hard chorus. But sounding just like one another is what rock has become today."

"It's what it always was." Mark caught the objection in Daniel's raised eyebrows and beat him to the punch. "I'm just saying, rock hasn't changed nearly as much as some people want to think. It's always the same thing. A bunch of guys, outsiders, with guitars. A bass and a drum."

"I don't know." Daniel wasn't willing to concede the point. "Rock has come a long way from its birthplace in the Delta."

"You know, I hate to admit it, but I don't know a lot about the blues." There was a note of earnest regret in his voice. "I grew up in a little town in Illinois. There wasn't a whole lotta blues going down, so I just never had the exposure."

"You don't know the names maybe, the people and places and history. But you can't pick up a guitar without knowing about the blues. That's just what it is." Daniel braced himself against the doorjamb, beginning to feel that if he didn't have additional support he might simply fall over.

"Starts with people with no voice living hard lives without hope," Daniel continued, trying to find a comfortable spot against the door. "Doesn't matter whether it's the Delta in the thirties or the housing projects of London in the seventies. If it's Capitol Hill in Seattle or Sedgwick Avenue in the Bronx. There's just something in the human soul that's got to rise above it, even if things are so shitty it seems like there's nothing to celebrate. They need to make music for today because they can't be sure there's a tomorrow. Just playing today music, you know."

"Today music?" Mark thought it over. "Yeah. That's what punk was like when I first heard it. Grunge, too."

"Yeah, well. Grunge is just the blues dressed up in flannel and with louder guitars. That whole scene was just kids who didn't have an economic future, didn't think there was any place for them. And they found guitars, but they weren't planning any launch into that stratosphere. It was just about playing the show that day. Same thing. Real songs. Today music."

There was a bottle at Mark's feet. He picked it up and unscrewed the top and took a long draw. "Fashion killed grunge. Once every douchebag across the US started wrapping themselves in flannel and cardigan sweaters, grunge was dead."

Daniel didn't disagree. "More than anything else, I always thought that all of that had more to do with that movie *Singles*."

"Never saw it," Daniel confessed.

"I just remember thinking that if they'd filmed it in Minneapolis, the Replacements would have blown up bigger than Pearl Jam and Nirvana put together. And I've always thought they would've deserved it more too."

"Nothing against those other bands, but I always thought if Andy Wood hadn't died, Mother Love Bone would've been *that* band, that era-defining band." Mark took another pull at his bottle and then offered it to Daniel

"Tragic," Daniel agreed, and took the offered drink.

"Kurt was a real loss," Mark offered. "John Lennon, too."

"When you consider what Jimi Hendrix did in five years, I've always wondered what he would've done with another fifty years. Or Robert Johnson. If he'd lived as long as Son House, it would've changed everything."

"Jack Vigliatura and Bill White of For Squirrels," Mark offered. "The best alternative band that never got a chance to be."

"Gram Parsons," Daniel added. "Ronnie Van Zant. Steve Gaines." They both said "Stevie Ray Vaughn" at the same time.

"Too much death." Daniel took another drink. "It's such a small percentage of people who make it in rock, but the number of them who've died tragically just seems disproportional." He closed his eyes, took another drink, and returned the bottle.

"Marco Pharaoh," Mark offered tentatively, as if he was waiting for Daniel's ruling.

"Of Taco Shot?" Daniel shrugged. "Don't get me wrong—I think it's a shame what happened to the guy. But I always thought the band was overproduced. I just don't see him keeping the kind of company we're talking about."

"What about the kind of company you're keeping?" Mark played a riff Daniel recognized as a bit of "That Kinda Girl," a by-the-book four-minute pop-rock single that had briefly charted for Taco Shot when they were on their ascent. He closed his eyes again and broke into a verse.

Crazy things she says and does
Answers "Why?" with "Just because"
She can't be taught and she can't be tamed
And if you fall in love, well, she can't be blamed

Again, it seemed as if the music had whisked Mark far away from the small home studio. He stopped playing abruptly. "What would you say if I told you I wasn't who you think I am?"

"I'd probably say I'm not who you think I am."

Mark slid off his dark glasses so he could look straight into Daniel's eyes. "I know who you are, Daniel." He spoke the words calmly and with absolute conviction. "That's why I came here."

"I don't know what you're talking about," Daniel lied. Badly. He tried to hedge, "I'm—"

"You're Daniel Erickson, I know." Mark chased the words with a long drink of whisky. "Our mutual friend sent me here."

"I think you better have another drink."

"I'll be glad to, but it won't change the fact that you're Daniel Erickson. Or that I'm Marco Pharaoh." He took that drink. "And we've got an old friend in common."

"Marco Pharaoh? Of Taco Shot?" Daniel asked incredulously. "Getthefuckouttahere! He died five years ago in a car crash."

"No. He didn't. I'm right here." Mark launched into a few bars of Taco Shot's "Sense No More."

Sun keeps rising in the west and the tide, it won't turn
No spark sets to flame and your old photos they won't burn
Sky's not blue and sea's not green, it's all just shades of gray
The whole world went to hell when you went away

It sounded close enough to what Daniel remembered of the song, but it was hardly incontrovertible proof. "It's like four chords. Anyone can play that song."

"Maybe they can play it, but I'm the one who wrote it." Mark stopped strumming to emphasize the seriousness of what he was saying. "I'm telling you. I was in a car crash, but I didn't die. That wasn't me." He took a drink like he needed one. "That was my friend. The one I let die."

"Not that I believe you—because I don't think I do—but you're telling me that you walked away from one of the hottest bands out there? To what? Play dead? Why?"

The answer was simple. And one that Daniel understood. "To keep my wife and kid alive." There was a bit more. "Keep me alive too."

"You played dead to stay alive?"

"The irony doesn't negate the truth," Mark offered. "But you're right, Taco Shot was overproduced. It was over-everything. It wasn't ever what I'd heard in my head, and the money never changed that. After a while, it wasn't what I wanted to do anymore, you know?"

Daniel took the bottle Mark offered.

"They wanted to put out a new album, but not *my* new album. They were going to put out a greatest hits album. Greatest hits? We had three albums out there! Including a live one! How do you get any greatest hits out of that?"

"I'm sure the moneymen appreciated that stance." Daniel knew from painful experience what an artist's stand on principles and creative integrity could do to a bottom line.

"No one appreciated it. Not the moneymen. Not the other guys in the band. Not even my wife. Everybody just wanted to keep the cash stream flowing. Everybody just wanted me to keep the wheels turning. But I had a little girl, you know. I could lie to everyone else, but I couldn't lie to her. And suddenly that meant I had to quit lying to myself."

Daniel understood only too well.

"So I was ready to take my ball and leave the playground, but one day someone messes with my Porsche and it winds up wrapped around a tree. Only thing is, I wasn't driving. I was all messed up from the crash"—he made a circular motion around his face and the beard that tried to conceal it—"but it wasn't me they killed."

"Not you?"

He fidgeted, fingering his braided bracelet. "I was so scared, man. I didn't know what had happened. I didn't know who'd done it." Whether he was offering excuses or explanations, it was clear he hadn't bought any of them himself. "But I knew the only advantage I had was that whoever had tried to kill me thought they'd gotten the job done. I knew that if I let it be known that they'd failed, they'd only try again. Killing me would be a matter of time. And maybe next time they'd get my wife. Or my little girl, too. So I..." He took a long pull from his bottle. "I set the wreck on fire—with my friend still in it—and I walked away."

"Your friend?"

"He was already dead." It was clear that he'd spent years convincing himself of that fact, but that he still had some work to do on it.

"And the cops?"

"They jumped to conclusions about the body in the burned wreck and ID'd it as me. But the people closest to me must've known it wasn't me."

"What makes you think that?"

"This." Wannaman fingered his bracelet. "I wrote 'Sweet Spot' for my wife, Adeline, one night." He launched into a few bars.

A thousand angels could dance on by
I swear I wouldn't care
All I want is what I got
I got life in a sweet spot
We live life in a sweet spot

He glanced down at the steel around his wrist. "When I woke up in the morning, my guitar was stripped of its strings and she'd braided them into this bracelet. She said it was so that I'd never lose the love that inspired that song." He spun the bands around a time or two. "And, good times, bad times, I never have."

"Maybe they just overlooked it," Daniel offered.

Mark nodded as if he was considering the possibility. "There's that. But then just to be safe, someone stole the body—the body they thought was me—and burned what was left."

"Like Gram Parsons?"

"But without the friendship."

Daniel was engaged in the story. "So who—"

"I spent the next years trying to find out who'd done it." He sighed deeply. "And that's what all of this has been about." He gestured broadly at the small studio.

The liquor was making it hard for Daniel to concentrate. "All what was about?"

"This." He pointed toward the drive where his weeks of work had been burned to a disc. "*Rock Island Rock*. The album I've been recording here."

"I don't understand."

"I knew I couldn't go to the cops. With what? It doesn't take a lot of money to make the wheels of justice grind, and there was a lot of money at play. I couldn't go public without knowing what had happened."

Daniel could see how that might be a concern.

"And then it came to me." Mark's eyes brightened with excitement. "Music was the answer. So I took everything I learned in my investigation and I put it into my album here. When I release *Rock Island Rock*, millions of folks are going to get it and listen to it and understand the story behind it. It's like my take on *Tommy* or *The Wall*, only it's a true-life crime story. When my fans have it, when they get it, then I can come out in the press. Then I can go to the cops. And *then* the bastards behind all of this won't be able to do anything, because there will be a million eyes watching them."

Now Daniel was impressed. "A million eyes, huh?"

"And that's when our mutual friend stepped in again," Mark continued.

Daniel felt it necessary to maintain the charade. "Our friend?"

"I call him Papa," Mark said warmly. "You may call him something else."

74

Daniel wanted to profess his ignorance, but he knew it wouldn't be convincing. The truth of the matter was that a year earlier, when Daniel had been searching for the money to save his son, he'd met an old man who'd introduced himself as Mr. Atibon. Since that introduction, Daniel's life had changed in mysterious ways. "How do you know—"

Mark was eager to explain. "I was just a kid starting out. Rock-and-roll cliché. Bad home, bad hair, bad attitude. My band was going nowhere. My whole life was going nowhere. One moonless night in the middle of winter, I'm speeding through my hometown, drunk off my ass. I'm like twenty-five, and I already got two DUIs behind me. All of a sudden, right there where Twenty-Ninth Avenue crosses Twelfth Street, a guy just steps out of the dark, like he's just strolling out of the Chippiannock Cemetery. Just walks right out in front of me.

"I slam on my brakes," he continued. "Old Camaro built outta Bondo. It starts spinning on the black ice and I'm just hanging on like it's some carnival ride from hell, because if I hit this dude with a load on after the two DUIs I already got, I know it's Joliet for me."

"What happened?"

"Car comes to a stop right there against the curb like I'd just parallel parked it there, you know? I get out to check on the guy, because if he's not dead, I'm gonna kill him." He smiled to himself, remembering the encounter.

"Next thing I know, I'm driving him over to Lee's for some pecan pancakes. Along the way he's telling me this story, singing this song for me. The story. The song. It all worked out as 'Walking Dead Man.' The song that made us. Eight months later I'm playing the Roxy, hanging out at the Chateau Marmont, and snacking on crispy calamari with puttanesca. Man, I still don't know what the hell puttanesca is, but overnight we're rock stars."

75

"And the old man?"

"Kept popping up here and there. He's the one that told me it'd be cool of me if I gave my friend a chance to drive the Porsche. Then about six months ago, I tell him that I have the album worked out. He tells me I have to come to St. Thomas to record it. So I do."

Daniel understood.

"And then once I'm here, I'm thinking I'm going to be checking out ISW Studios or something, but he pops up again and tells me that I have to come to you."

"He told you to find me?" Daniel's thoughts were admittedly muddied by drink, but he couldn't conceive of any reason why Mr. Atibon would want their lives to cross. "Did he tell you why?"

"No. But nothing is a coincidence with Papa."

Daniel began to grow tired, more tired than he'd ever been before in his whole life. "No. Nothing's ever a coincidence with the old man."

CHAPTER FIFTEEN

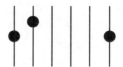

Thump. Thump. Thump.

It took Daniel a moment or two to determine whether the insistent pounding was coming from the screen door or the inside of his head. He looked up from where he was lying on the floor of the screened-in porch, saw the figure silhouetted against the sun just risen off the eastern shore, and realized it was both.

Thump. Thump. Thump.

"All right. All right." It had been a long time since Daniel had awoken with his head caught in the tightening jaws of a hangover, but the sensation was still a familiar one, and it immediately retrieved throbbing memories of a lifetime worth of rock bottoms he'd sunk to since his life had jumped the tracks. Without a clear recollection of how he'd ended up on the porch, he struggled to his feet like a punchy fighter who's been hit too many times to know when he should just stay down. "I'm coming. I'm coming."

Thump. Thump. Thump.

"I said I'm coming!" With Moog's expert input, Daniel had created a strict protocol for responding to the odd knock at the door, but those procedures had been lost in a sea of drink along with everything else in the past twenty-four hours. He stumbled toward the door and then held on to it for badly needed support. "What the hell—"

While all the policeman in the Caribbean look like cruise directors, with their Bermuda shorts and their socks pulled up to their knees, that doesn't make it any less alarming when they show up at the door.

"Daniel Erickson?" The officer's accent suggested he might be from another island, but his tone was stern and official just the same.

"No," Daniel lied. "You're mistaken. There's no Daniel Erickson here." It was pointless. Even if his fuzzy head could've come up with a convincing lie, his thick tongue wouldn't have been able to tell it. "I'm not—"

Despite the knee socks, the officer looked like a very imposing cruise director. He was obviously bored by the theatrics. "Open the door, Mr. Erickson."

"I already told you—"

"And I told you to open the door, Mr. Erickson."

Surging adrenaline sent a shock racing up and down his spine and turned his thoughts to running. They only lasted for a second or two, no longer than it would have taken the able-bodied officer at the door to chase him down and tackle him in the sand.

Then Daniel's thoughts left him altogether. "I said I'm not—"

"You said you're not, but we both know that you are." He pulled at the screen door and found it latched. "Do I need to force my way in?" He considered the ridiculousness of the situation. "Good god, it's a screen door, mon!"

Daniel had anticipated a day when the law might catch up with him, and he'd prepared himself for it. With a quick look over his shoulder back at the sea-grass couch, he eyed the hiding spot where a .45 Colt was tucked under the orchid-festooned cushions. Maybe he could make it before the officer reached for his sidearm, and maybe he couldn't. But right now, the officer was only interested in *him*. If Daniel put up a fight, he could pull the whole house of cards down on Vicki and Moog, too.

Maybe his run had come to an end, and so what? He could still protect the people who mattered.

"All right." He flipped the latch on the screen door and opened it wide enough for the officer to enter.

"Well, don't just stand there," the officer said, gesturing with a sweeping motion of his arm. "You don't look any better on this side of the door than you did on that."

"Excuse me?"

"Get going. I got more to do today than just taking care of you." Without another word he turned and walked back to the navy GMC Envoy with a vinyl sticker reading POLICE VIRGIN ISLANDS WORKING WITH YOU 24/7 across the door.

Daniel followed him unsteadily a step or two and then realized that he'd just gotten up after a night of drinking. "Can you hang on a minute?"

The officer turned. "Well, go piss on that tree, because you're not pissing in me car."

Daniel made it over to the palm. He looked out over the ocean, rhythmically rolling to the shore, and felt the sea breeze, cool against the liquor-tinged sweat that bathed his body. The simple freedom of pissing outside. He wondered what it would be like to live out the remainder of his life without any freedom at all.

Remainder of his life? He was going to a federal prison, and he'd killed a Russian mafia don, a Mexican cartel assassin, and a half-dozen motorcycle club members. The remainder of his life was going to top out at about two weeks. No, a lockup didn't offer any kind of future.

He shook off the last of his piss and looked up again at the sea. He couldn't outrun the policeman, not to freedom anyway, but he could probably beat him to the water. The water was the answer. He could jump into her open, waiting arms and just keep falling into her embrace until there was nothing. Nothing at all.

"Why don't you put that thing away and get in the vehicle, Mr. Erickson." Daniel looked back over his shoulder at the bobby-socked policeman, whose hand was resting on the pistol holstered on his hip. "Too damn early to shoot your ass."

It had been a long while since Daniel had done anything he was told, and he didn't like it any better than he'd remembered.

"Where are you taking me?" Daniel demanded from the backseat.

The policeman looked up from the twisty road that snaked along the coast and flashed a big, bright smile. "Exactly where you're supposed to be going."

"It wasn't an existential question," Daniel insisted. "Are you taking me into Charlotte Amalie? Or are the Feds waiting to whisk me away?"

"Feds?" the policeman asked, seemingly surprised by the suggestion. "You talk like you are a bad man. Are you a bad man, Mr. Erickson?"

Daniel sat back on the rear bench seat, turned away from the cage, and looked out at the scenery speeding past too quickly for his liking. "I used to be."

"And perhaps you can be again." The policeman burst out with a deep, body-shaking laugh.

Daniel had resolved not to say another word until he could lawyer up, but he began to worry when the policeman turned off the main road and began to follow one of the dirt-covered arteries that pass for roads in the tropics as it wound its way up into the hills like a cane snake. "Where are we going?"

"I told you." The dirt rut they were following crossed over another, and the policeman stepped on the brake. "I'm taking you exactly where you're supposed to be."

The Envoy kicked up a cloud of dust as it slid to an abrupt stop. "This is as far as you go." The policeman got out from behind the wheel and pulled open the rear door. "Get out."

Daniel looked around. There was nothing but jungle overgrowth as far as he could see. "This isn't Charlotte Amalie."

"Charlotte Amalie not where you're supposed to be, mon." His words were confident, but not very reassuring. "Come on. Time's runnin' away."

Daniel slid out, and the sound of the SUV's door slamming shut behind him echoed in the tropical canopy like a gallows trapdoor falling open beneath his feet. It was all so obvious now: he wasn't in the custody of USVIPD, CAPD, FBI, or any other alphabet anagram. It was much, much worse.

Island policemen may look like friendly cruise crew, but they're like cops all over the world. So there's a percentage of them (no need to argue how significant that percentage may be) who have decided that "to protect and serve" isn't so much a higher duty as an opportunity for personal gain.

It all made sense now. Despite its *Pirates of the Caribbean* set dressings, St. Thomas is really small-town America. Someone must have gotten curious about the odd house down on the cove. Maybe one of the kids whom Vicki had taken an interest in and invited to come record. Maybe Wannaman with his bullshit dead-rock-star cover story. *Someone*, however, had done some due diligence to ferret out their true identities, found out about the money, and now wanted what was left.

Daniel wasn't being arrested, he was being executed.

The perfect-day photo ops were for tourists, but no one could live on the island for any period of time without hearing whispers of the shadowy figures controlling the drugs and smuggling, the gambling and prostitution. More often than not, the stories of those who found themselves in the darkness of those shadows were punctuated with acts of violence. The End!

"I'm not going to tell you anything," Daniel declared, intending to demonstrate he wouldn't be complicit in his own robbery and execution.

The policeman grinned. "I'm not going to ask you anything."

"Whatever you got planned, it won't be the first time I've gone through this dance." Daniel held up his left hand, emphasizing the missing pinkie finger that the Russian mobster had taken as a trophy. "The bastard that did this died very badly."

The policeman had seen worse. He looked straight at Daniel. "No one dies easy."

Daniel stood in the middle of the intersection. All by himself. Keys dangled temptingly from the Envoy's ignition. He thought of Vicki, lying in their bed, ashes of anger still smoldering, but maybe waiting for him to come with an apology and make up. All he wanted was to be in her arms.

Suddenly, Daniel realized the regrettable but irrefutable truth: if he was going to survive—if *Vicki* was going to survive—this cop had to die. Now.

Daniel started to walk, slowly but deliberately, toward the cop. The officer sensed the approach, and his hand went to his sidearm. "Don't." He looked around the jungle surrounding them like curtains, clearly watching for signs of confederates he was expecting to step out of the tree line.

"I'm not going to die on my knees," Daniel declared. With every word he approached, not stealthily, but like a big cat just shaking off the tranquilizer and intent on paying his respects to the guy with the dart gun who just shot him in the ass.

"I'm warning you." These are three of the most pointless words a man can speak. By the time the cop's wasted warning was echoing with bird chatter and jungle noises, Daniel's hand had already grabbed for the pistol the policeman was just clearing from its holster.

The two men struggled to control the weapon, staggering back and forth in a violent embrace, like awkward celebs in a dancing contest. Their energies focused on the gun, moving back and forth between them as each man pulled and twisted, trying to gain possession.

Boom!

A shot went off. Immediately, all of the sounds of their struggle were lost to a high, piercing ringing and Daniel felt a sharp pain in his ears—not a wound but a deafening concussion from the blast near his ear.

Except for the distant ringing, it was perfectly silent. Nothing made a sound. Not the birds or the jungle. Not even the policeman as Daniel snapped a knee up into his khaki-clad crotch and then swept his feet from beneath him, sending the man falling onto the flat of his back.

The policeman made a desperate gasp as his still smoking service weapon was wrenched from his hand, but Daniel never actually heard it. The painful ringing completely drowned out the cop's terrified pleas as he squirmed on his back and held up his hands as if he had some magical powers that would deflect the bullet Daniel was about to put into his chest.

Daniel looked down the line of the pistol and into the cop's eyes. It was a sight he hadn't seen in a while, but familiar and, if he was honest with himself, not entirely unwelcome. He wanted to say something to his victim, to explain that he was going to be pulling the trigger in another heartbeat or two because the cop had brought a threat to Daniel's door, to the place where the people he cared about were sleeping even now. He wanted to make perfectly clear that if the cop had just left him alone, they could both be off in the arms of loved ones right now. But now the policeman had to die, because if he didn't, it would just be a matter of time before someone else showed up back at Daniel's door. He wanted to make sure the cop understood it was a mistake to push a push-back man.

So much to be said, but there was work to be done. Besides, with one pull of a trigger it'd be like Daniel had just said it to himself.

The man kept screaming, making pleas that Daniel couldn't hear—and wouldn't have heeded if he had. Daniel raised the pistol, pulled back the hammer, and began to search for the exact spot where he would rip open the man's torso. His hand began to tighten around the weapon as he started to slowly squeeze the trigger.

"Don't!" The word came from behind him, but it was as clear and as strong as if it'd come from inside Daniel's own head. Startled, he turned instinctively toward it, pointing the pistol out in front as he did.

"Don't do that neither, *mi key*." The old man standing at the center of the crossroads laughed deeply, as if the sight of Daniel pointing a pistol at his chest was the funniest thing he'd seen in ages. "Weren't I right 'bout you," said the man beneath the porkpie hat, laughing all the harder. "You a natural-born killa. Or a natural-born-again killa, might be."

Daniel knew the man well, but still didn't understand. "Atibon?"

CHAPTER SIXTEEN

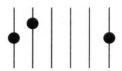

The Fates may be fickle, but good fortune follows hard work.

Aaron Osajo had hoped the blood he'd spilled would grease the wheels of illicit opportunity for him and A-Volt, but neither of the young men could have dreamed it would happen so fast.

"Can you believe this?" Osajo asked, leaning back in the leather seat and trying to imprint the experience on his memory as if he was saving game progress on his Xbox 360. "We livin' like kings."

His friend didn't respond, and Osajo couldn't help but be a little disappointed in A-Volt's reaction to their good fortune. Instead of joining him in celebrating their ascent, his partner had turned silent and sullen.

It wasn't as if it had been easy for Osajo. He'd never taken a man's life before, either. He hadn't realized how much of himself he'd have to surrender to get the bloody deed done. But in the end, he'd done what he'd had to do. Like a man.

The black Mercedes S550 turned off Smith Bay Road into the private drive and waited for the black castiron gates to open before following the paved path that serpentined its way up the hill. The car came to a stop at the bottom of a long stair made of quarried blocks of sculpted coral leading up to the main house.

Immediately, the driver jumped out from behind the wheel and trotted around to open the door for them. The two young men slid out of the car and stood in awe, looking up the stairs at the mansion on the hill.

"Hoia-Baciu House," the driver announced in a voice that made Osajo think of what he called "the gadget dude" from the James Bond movies.

Despite the tropical heat, a manservant dressed in full fig like a butler from *Downton Abbey* stood at the very top, waiting for them to make the ascension. "Good afternoon, gentlemen," he greeted them when they finally made it to the top. His voice was clipped, with an English public school accent. "My name is Cromwell. The master has asked that I show you directly to his office." Without another word he turned and led the two friends across a stone landing to the house's oversize front door.

It was a perfectly quiet afternoon in front of the house, but once the manservant opened the door, that silence was shattered by the ear-crunching din of a raucous party. On the other side of the ebony door, the house was crowded with people who seemed to be having the time of their lives.

People filled the great entranceway, laughing and joking, drinking and dancing. Some smoked reefers rolled up like fat Cohibas, snorted lines of coke from crystal bowls filled to overflowing with powder, or snatched handfuls of pills from candy dishes scattered about.

Electronica music blasted a relentless audio assault as many of the revelers danced to the throbbing beat. Others had paired up in twos and threes and groups of more, in this room or that, all of them entangled in a moaning, writhing knot of bodies.

Osajo looked like a kid who'd come downstairs on Christmas morning and found his parents had gotten him Disneyland. "Can you believe this shit?" he asked his partner excitedly. "We are so fucking rock and roll."

A-Volt said nothing, didn't even seem to take notice of the debauchery surrounding them. If anything, he seemed oddly disturbed by what was going on, and that made Osajo wonder if they were even seeing the same thing.

"This way, gentlemen," Cromwell directed them, and though he didn't raise the volume of his voice, he could still be heard over the party's triple-digit decibels. He led the pair through the crowd, and as he moved the mass of humanity parted before him like the Red Sea making way for Moses. He led them through a labyrinth of hallways, past dozens of rooms that all seemed to be occupied with frenzied partiers, until at last they stood before a set of large double doors, one of which had been painted with black lacquer and the other with red.

Cromwell knocked twice with his gloved fist and then opened the black door, ushering the men inside. The two men followed the invitation and stepped into the room, but were surprised when the door was immediately shut behind them without another word from their guide.

As soon as the door closed shut, the room went completely silent, as if the door were somehow capable of blocking all of the ambient noise from the party being held in the house. Or as if the party had just suddenly been extinguished.

Curtains were drawn across the windows, and the interior of the room was dimly lit and bathed in shadows so that it was difficult to see anything with great detail. Thinking they were alone, Osajo excitedly asked his friend, "Can you believe this shit?"

"Believe it. This shit is real." The startled pair jumped in alarm at the deep voice.

"Please allow me to introduce myself." The man who had been hidden in the shadows stepped out into the dim glow of what little of the fading light could force its way past the heavy silk drapes. The light revealed a man who was tall and almost femininely thin. He was dressed in a gray William Fioravanti bespoke suit with a Dolce & Gabbana shirt the color of dried bone, which he had buttoned to his throat. It was clear the man had seen his share of birthday cakes and mirror balls dropped at midnight, but he still projected a youthful energy of potential physicality.

In his arms he held a good-size iguana, which he stroked along its back with long, exaggerated gestures, as if he found something pleasurable in the motion of the tactile sensation of the reptile's scales. "I am Haden Koschei." He smiled at his own introduction, as if he'd told them a joke he knew they'd never get and thought it was all the funnier because of it.

"I'm not sure who my friend is," Koschei continued, looking down at the reptile snuggled in his arms like a baby. "I found him on the beach this morning. Someone had hit him with a rock and left him for dead, but I think he's responding to my touch. I'm thinking of calling him Whiro." He looked down at the creature in his arms and smiled. "Or maybe Zu."

Osajo wasn't sure what to make of the man, but he felt it was important to make a strong first impression. "I'm Osajo," he announced with as much confidence as he could muster as he nervously toyed with the silver trophy around his wrist. He gestured to his friend. "This be A-Volt."

"Yes," Koschei sneered. "I'm well aware of the two of you." Koschei settled himself into a Pininfarina Ares Line Xten chair behind a large Parnian desk that dominated the room. He positioned the iguana in his lap and then turned his attention back to his human guests. "Gentlemen, please have a seat."

"Thanks," Osajo said ingratiatingly. They each took one of the leather club chairs their host had indicated.

"I'm told by a mutual friend that you two young men have recently begun a certain business enterprise."

Osajo smiled proudly. "We killed a guy, yeah."

"Indeed." It was clear Mr. Koschei was unimpressed by and unaccustomed to such unprofessional displays. It was equally clear, though, that he had a definite role for them to play in his plans. "I prefer to think of it as a service rendered," he corrected. "It so happens that I find myself in need of such services."

"We're your men," Osajo volunteered. A-Volt sat silently, wishing they could leave and just go back to their place above the T-shirt shop.

"There's an individual on the island whom I am told may pose a serious threat to me and my interests in the near future." Koschei grinned, but the contortion of his mouth was more like an animal baring its teeth. "I would very much like to beat him to the punch, so to speak."

"We can take care of that for you," Osajo promised. "Just tell us—"

"I'm told he's living here under an alias. Or two." Koschei reached into a folder on his desk and pulled out the photo of a man with a sad smile and a distant look in his eyes. He slid it across the desk for his two new assassins to have a look.

Osajo reached forward for the file, took a look at the photo, and was silently taken aback by the realization that he knew the intended victim.

"His given name is Daniel Erickson," Koschei added.

For Osajo the personal connection was unsettling, but for A-Volt the connection made the deed unthinkable. "Man, we know that dude," he whispered to his partner. "He's the one lets me record my stuff. He's been good to us. We can't—"

"Is there a problem?" Koschei asked, his voice low and throaty like the growl of a lion with blood on its tongue and a gazelle still twitching on the savannah floor.

"No," Osajo assured him. "No problem at all."

A-Volt had been silent since the night before, but the prospect of more killing—and this time of one of the few people who'd ever done anything for him—was something that he stuck at. "Yeah, man. See, we know this dude. He been a'ight to us—"

"Friend of yours, is he?" Koschei sneered and then nodded as if he understood completely. "I'm failing to see the problem in killing him."

"We can't just go kill someone we know," A-Volt explained, despite Osajo's best efforts to silence him.

"You're mistaken," Koschei corrected. "Not only *can* you, but it's actually much easier to kill someone you know." His strokes along the lizard's spiny back became stronger and more intense. "What you can't do is *not* kill this man." His eyes sparked with intensifying anger, and his preternaturally cool demeanor began to slip away. "This is not a request. It's not a 'Will you please?' It's an instruction. An order."

The madder Koschei got, the more agitated the reptile in his arms became, thrashing its tail back and forth, twisting its head in sudden spasms. Osajo knew it was an important meeting, that impressing a potential client of this stature was important, but he didn't understand.

"Why do you think I sent for you?" Koschei wondered aloud. "Why do you think I'm wasting my time with you two morons right now?" Molten rage began to erupt through the fissures of his controlled facade.

As Koschei became increasingly enraged, the dewlap under the iguana's neck presented, and the lizard began to bob its head and hiss. The animal's body became unnaturally rigid and then began to twitch in fits from tail to snout.

"Could the two of you be so foolish to think I'd lower myself to *ask* something of you?" Only their silence answered. "I sent for you because you're mine to send for."

Whatever discomfort had been afflicting the iguana had now clearly intensified to pain. It hissed loudly as it struggled to escape its captor's grip. Koschei, for his part, didn't seem to notice the flailing lizard's efforts to free itself.

"Did you think you could walk into a man's life last night and take it for your own, without there being greater ripples in the pool?" Koschei's voice rose in anger as the iguana he was ignoring began to frantically hiss an octave higher.

Osajo and A-Volt sat paralyzed in their seats, unable to respond, like small children receiving a parent's wrath. The room began to fill with a sickly sweet scent, simultaneously enticing and noxious, as the air began to cloud with a faint mist of smoke.

"Someone is going to die tonight," Koschei declared. "I'm offering you the chance to make the decision *who*." He looked pointedly at Osajo and then at A-Volt, both of whom had been shocked to silence by the realization that the lizard in their host's arms was the source of the smell and the smoke.

"But make no mistake," Koschei warned them. "If Erickson isn't dead by the time the sun rises tomorrow—" He paused to allow them to consider the possibilities. In that silent moment, the iguana let out a final hiss as its blue-green scales slowly curled and turned brown. "The two of you will be."

"Yes, sir," Osajo answered dutifully.

Obedience wasn't enough for Koschei any longer. "And I assure you that whatever fate you may plan for Mr. Erickson, it will pale in comparison to the orgy of gore you'll find yourselves immersed in if you disappoint me."

Koschei got to his feet, apparently only just then realizing what his rage had done to his adopted pet. He looked down on it with disgust and tossed the roasted lizard to Osajo. "Here."

Instinctively, Osajo tried to catch the object thrown at him, but the lizard's white-hot flesh burned his palms as soon as they touched the scalding corpse. It dropped to the ground at his feet.

"Dinner's on me," Koschei sneered. "I'm told they taste like chicken."

Both men just stared in disbelief at the charred lizard and then back up at the man who had done it.

"And guess what?" Koschei prompted. "So do the two of you."

CHAPTER SEVENTEEN

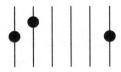

The Mississippi Delta is a primordial landscape, a place of legend and mystery. At its heart there is a place where two highways intersect at perfectly symmetrical angles.

Anyone could drive past the outwardly unremarkable landmark without noticing it at all (and plenty of folks do it every day), but anyone who has walked the highway and stood upon that spot will swear on his grave that the simple crossroad in the dark heart of the Delta is a place filled with unimaginable magic.

What they will disagree about (and often quite fiercely) is whether the enchantment to be found there is a force of good or evil.

A year earlier, Daniel Erickson had stood on that very spot one moonless night. At the time, he was convinced his death was imminent, and Vegas certainly had all the smart money bet that way. But then, out of the darkness, stepped a man who introduced himself only as Mr. Atibon.

That simple introduction changed Daniel's life profoundly and forever.

There was no explanation for how Mr. Atibon knew all the things he knew or did the impossible things he did. He simply knew them. And did them.

Daniel had never exactly been a "man of action," but when he rolled into Vegas and kicked out the jams, he'd never given any real consideration to the role the mysterious Mr. Atibon might have played in those events or the dramatic personal transformation that had allowed him to save his son. Even when ominous harbingers warned Daniel that he'd run up a blood debt and there was a heavy price to pay off that balance, he was only too willing to dismiss it all out of hand.

That wasn't to say he'd forgotten his encounters with the mysterious Mr. Atibon. To the contrary, the mysterious man was never far from his thoughts, and every day Daniel felt that influence in his life in a dozen subtle and unexpected ways. It was just that, despite the old guy's permanent residency in his memories, Daniel just never considered that he and Atibon would come face-to-face ever again.

And now here they were.

Atibon helped the policeman up from the ground where Daniel had knocked him and returned his sidearm to him. The officer pointed angrily and shouted something, but the tinnitus in his ears was all Daniel could hear. Almost all.

While Daniel couldn't hear anything but a constant *whoosh*ing tone echoing in his head, he could somehow clearly make out the old man telling the policeman, "Calm down, Winston. Didn't I stop him from shooting you?"

Daniel couldn't hear the words he used to respond, but the policeman's wild gesticulations were evidence enough that he'd taken very little consolation in Atibon's reassurances.

"You should be glad your tired old carcass ain't down that ravine," the old man scolded. "And be happier still I didn't charge you for that favor." Whatever threat was contained in that seemed to be enough to silence the officer.

Mr. Atibon led the policeman back to his Envoy and held the driver's door open for him. "You're almost paid up, Winston," Daniel overheard. "Now I have just one more errand for you to do, and then we'll be jake."

The policeman seemed to have concerns about the terms of their arrangement.

"I suppose you could leave me hanging," the old man agreed. "But then, you tell me, what choice would that give me with our debt left unsettled between us?"

Daniel didn't understand the one-sided exchange, but it was clear from the interplay between the two men that Atibon had gotten his way. The policeman put his Envoy in gear and angrily pulled away, showering dirt and dust into the air. It was quite a display, but it was obvious that he was just running off on Atibon's errand.

The old man laughed and turned his attention to Daniel. "Now there's a sight." There was a note of paternal pride in his words.

Daniel stood in the middle of the road, covering one ear and then the other, but all the tests produced the same result. "I can't hear."

"Of course you can't hear, boy. Goddamn gun went off about an inch from your ear. You're damn lucky it didn't blow the damn eardrum out altogether." The old man took a look just to be sure. "Nope, you ain't bleedin'. You'll be fine."

"What?"

"Said, 'You'll be fine.'" The old man made a slight concession with a shrug of his shoulders. "In time."

Daniel was still covering and uncovering his ears in some field audiology testing. And still coming to the same conclusion. "Then how come I can hear you right now?"

"What else you need to hear?" That was the end of it as far as Mr. Atibon was concerned. "Now come on, we got a little bit of ground to cover." He started to walk off toward the branch of the crossroad that led off to the right.

Daniel followed a step or two behind. "Where are we going?"

He kept a brisk pace for what seemed like such an old man. "See if you can't keep up now. We got things to do, and there ain't much time."

"What things?"

Atibon scoffed. "You an' your questions." But he didn't answer any of them.

After a half mile of trotting over dirt roads winding through the mountainous jungles, Daniel's questions had to be squeezed in between huffs and puffs. "If we had to go somewhere, why didn't we just meet there?"

The answer seemed obvious to the old man, at least. "Crossroads, son."

"Crossroads?"

"There are rules, boy," Atibon informed him. "The universe don't just spin all helter-skelter like. There are things you can do and things you can't. Even for me."

"What does that mean, 'even for you'?"

Atibon chuckled, quickening his pace. "You'd think with all your runnin' up and down that damn beach chasin' I-don't-know-what that you'd be quicker on your feet than you are."

In half an hour they'd worked their way down from the surrounding hills and out to the beach. They stood in front of a striking home, a postmodern assemblage of boxes and glass set on an oceanfront property. Atibon walked straight to the front door and then paused. "This is it."

Daniel joined the old man on the front porch and noticed that the door was slightly ajar. "Now what?"

"Well, we came all this way." The old man rocked back and forth on his heels, trying to steal a look into the house. "I'd say you step on in."

"Shouldn't we knock?" Daniel tried to peek in too, but couldn't see anything through the slim space.

"Trust me, ain't no one to hear you," the old man said like he knew for sure. "Now get to steppin.'"

Daniel pushed the door all the way open and took the step he'd been told to take. The entryway fed into a large great room. Daniel got the distinct impression that at one time it might have been well furnished, but all of the furniture and furnishings had been turned upside-down or smashed, as if a tropical storm had stopped for a very personal visit with the house's owner. He surveyed the destruction and then turned back to Atibon, who was still standing on the stoop. "Now what?"

"Well, I'd invite me in, if I was you," he huffed impatiently.

"What?"

"Rules, son, rules." The old man shook his head as if that was something he shouldn't have had to explain. "Everyone gots 'em. And everyone gots to follow 'em."

Less and less in life made sense to Daniel, but he'd learned just to let things happen when the two of them were together. "Well, then, won't you please come in?"

"Don't mind if I do." Atibon stepped into the house as if it was his own.

"What happened here?" Daniel asked as he wandered deeper into the house and discovered that the same tidal wave of destruction had washed through there as well.

"Nothin' of any importance." The old man sighed. "It's all just stuff." He walked past it all as if it wasn't even there. "Here's what I brought you to see." The old man pushed his way past a sliding screen door that had been torn off of its track and stepped out.

The backyard of the property was simple and secluded. A small lawn had been sodded and maintained, but at its far edge it gave way to the natural terrain, the sandy beach and the surf beyond. The focal point of the area was a pool that had been set there presumably for people who didn't enjoy an ocean swim or were too lazy to walk the extra two hundred yards.

The pool was forty feet wide and maybe twice again as long. Some island craftsman had spent a good deal of time, skill, and effort tiling the floor with the mosaic of two dolphins breaking through a wave together. All around the pool a number of inviting chairs and sofas and chaise lounges offered comfortable seating options.

It would have been a perfectly lovely place to spend the afternoon, if there hadn't been a corpse floating on the surface of the water.

Daniel looked over the edge of the decking and into the saline-treated waters that were now the color of boxed white zinfandel. The man was naked, floating facedown like the *Nevermind* kid, but presumably without the hopeful grin.

Death is the worst kind of thief. It takes whatever soul it chooses, and then out of sheer spite or mean-spiritedness strips the humanity from the shell it leaves behind so that it's impossible to believe life ever dwelt within something so horrible.

Daniel jumped at the unexpected sight of the floating corpse. The mane of hair he had worn vainly, convinced it made him look forever young despite the encroaching gray, was matted with blackened blood. The back of his head looked like a bowl of *carne guisada*. Whatever other injuries might be concealed beneath the surface, that blow alone would have been more than enough to have written in the double bar to the song of his life. Mr. Atibon didn't jump. Clearly he wasn't surprised by the discovery, and he sat down on one of the chaise longues as if the discovery just made him tired.

Daniel looked at the body again. He couldn't see its face, but he recognized the intricate tattoos that wound their way around both arms in sleeves of dragons, guitars, and naked chicks. "That's—" He paused, as if saying the name out loud could somehow change the outcome of the situation.

"Mark Wannaman," the old man supplied, knowing that nothing would change his fate now. "That *was* him."

Daniel took a step back from the edge, afraid the revelation might push him into the water like a frat boy prankster. "What? I was with him just last—"

Atibon already knew. "You were the last one to see him alive." He regarded the floating corpse. "Well, the second to last."

Every dark thought Daniel had harbored toward the man just a few hours earlier suddenly swooped down on him to attack him with talons of guilt and regret. And then he was struck with an absolutely terrifying thought: "You don't think that I—"

"What? Murdered him?" Atibon cast a suspicious eye in his direction. "Did you?"

Daniel was horrified by the suggestion. "No, of course not." But his answer was less than absolute.

"Of course, I know you didn't, damned fool." At another time, Atibon would have mocked him further, but he felt too tired for that sort of thing under the circumstances. He took off his pork-pie hat, ran his long fingers through what remained of his hair, and replaced the lid. "But I want you to find out who did do it. Not just who put him in that pool like that," he clarified. "The hands don't matter a damn. I need you to find the twisted heart who decided it wanted him put there."

The request seemed more disturbing to Daniel than the accusation. "What?"

"I know you can't hear nothin' else right now, but you can hear me clear as a bell."

That was true, but it didn't change anything for Daniel. "I can't investigate a murder." He thought it out further. "I especially can't investigate a murder in which I'd be the natural first suspect."

"What did I tell you 'bout ever sayin' 'I can't'?" the old man snapped sternly. "You been tellin' everyone who will listen not to underestimate you, not to—what was it—dismiss you? But you're the first person to run yourself down. Every goddamn chance you get."

Daniel didn't have a response.

"Ever since we met, you been doin' a whole lotta things that you *can't* do, and you been doin' 'em all jes' fine."

Daniel silently nodded his admission.

"Well, now it's time to pay the debt you run up with all that. And you're gonna do it by finding out who made that happen to that poor boy."

Daniel took another step back from the edge. "What debt?"

The old man looked hard at him. "Wasn't that you come to the crossroads last year, all beat to hell and drag-assed?"

It wasn't necessarily how Daniel would have characterized it. "Well, I—"

"And what did you come there looking for?" The old man set the question like a worm on a hook.

"A CD," Daniel answered, remembering the musical clues he was following at the time.

"Aw, to hell with those goddamn CDs," the old man growled. "You went there looking for a way to save your son, right?"

"Right," Daniel answered reluctantly.

"And save yourself?"

"I suppose."

"And how's your son today?" The old man didn't wait for an answer. "He's a fine figure of a man. And you're standin' right there in front of me with all your goddamn questions, so you must be jes' fine yourself." Point made. "I held up my end of the bargain. Now it's your turn to pay the price."

"I never made any bargain with you," Daniel insisted.

Atibon cocked an eye at him. "I tell you what. You take a look in your heart. You take a look in your soul. You be honest with yourself. And then you be honest with me. If'n you can tell me you never made no bargain with me, I'll let you walk outta here right now and you'll never see me again." He paused and cocked a finger. "But you'll lose the benefit o' the bargain you say you never made."

Daniel looked pained for a moment, but just a moment. Then he simply sat down in the chair next to Atibon like he was suddenly every bit as tired as the old man. "It's just all of this—everything—it's all so unbelievable."

"Believable." The old man scoffed at the suggestion. "Don't even know what that means, 'cause all sorta people believe all sorta things. If someone believes it, does that make it *believable*? 'Cause if everything folks believe in is *believable*, then damn near everythin' is *believable*. And you best better bet your ass that I'm *believable* too."

Daniel wanted more. "No. What I meant is—" He took a deep breath, as if the simple question was more exertion than he could manage. "How?"

"How?" Was that all? "I don't care *how* you find out who had this done. I got someone made a bargain with me to find it out, and I need you to go out there and get that done."

"No." Daniel sat back in his chair and hung his head. "*How* is it that you do all this?"

"Oh." The old man leaned forward. "You like so many folks, always lookin' for explanations. And, you know what? There ain't a damn soul in this world that don't surprise them own selves every day with the things that they think or say or do. Now, if you don't understand all your own thoughts and deeds, then how do you think you'll ever understand something as limitless as all this?" He waved his hand across the horizon, and just for a second his eyes twinkled with wonderment.

"And 'spose for a minute you did." The old man smiled, considering the prospects. "And you never will. But if you understood it all, what the hell would it change? If you found yourself bobbin' in the water six miles out there"—the old man pointed out past the breakers toward the deep sea—"even if you understood you were in the water, it wouldn't make you dry. And it wouldn't make it easier to swim. It'd probably only make your time out there filled with fear and dread, 'stead of thinking to yourself how lucky you were to be surrounded by the majesty of the ocean."

Daniel didn't look up. He didn't say anything.

"Oh, all right," Atibon conceded. "I'm gonna tell you this. Not because I think I owe you any damn thing, but because you're gonna need to know it yourself in the fullness of time."

"Know what?"

The old man was silent, as if he'd already reconsidered the soundness of the revelation he'd promised. Then he took a deep breath and started anyway. "There's a spirit in this world, a kinda energy. The energy that keeps this life going. It's the spirit of what it is to be alive, to be human. It's what keeps all of you goin' day after day, enduring all the heartbreak and hardships, savoring every kiss and every child's laugh. It's what keeps y'all living when each one of you knows in your heart that sooner or later you're all going to end up like him." The old man pointed at the lifeless body drifting across the pool surface.

"And you?" Daniel wanted to know.

"Me?"

"Who?" That wasn't quite it. "*What* are you?"

"That's harder to explain." The question seemed to spark a moment of melancholy, as if the old man had reason to regret the answer. "In the end, I ain't no more certain about what I am than you are about yourself. But I been at it a whole while longer, and I gleaned that I'm sorta a guardian of that spirit."

"It needs guarding?"

"Of course it do," sputtered Atibon, seeming to take exception to the very suggestion that his role in the cosmos might be superfluous. "We live in a universe of balance, boy. Same as I'm here to protect that life spirit, there's a force out there wants to extinguish it."

"Extinguish it?" Daniel's head ached, and it wasn't just the hangover or the remnants of the concussive damage to his ear. "You mean wipe out humanity?"

"He don't wanna destroy humanity like in wiping out all the peoples. It's more like he wants to destroy all the humanity *in* all the peoples. You know what I mean?"

Daniel wasn't sure he understood anything anymore. "He?"

"Or she," the old man conceded easily. "It ain't always just the same face. It's not like I necessarily know its name or nothin'. We ain't Facebook friends."

"But you two just duke it out for the soul of man?"

"You make it sound like some damn ballroom blitz. There are rules. Rules I didn't make and don't always understand, but rules I got to follow jes' the same. Same with him. And those rules don't let neither of us get involved, leastwise not directly. So that leave us both needin' to do our work through the acts of others."

Need was something Daniel understood—on any level. "And my role in this celestial chess match of yours?"

"Well, it ain't all peace, love, and understanding, son." He gestured out at the pool again. "Every once in a while I need myself a street-fighting man."

Daniel thought on the implications for a minute. "Yeah, that doesn't sound like a position I'd be interested in filling."

"Doesn't it?" The old man cocked his head as if he could actually see the lie lingering in the air between them. "You still can't tell the truth when it'll serve you better than the lie." There was a note of paternal disappointment in his words.

"I don't know what you're talking about," Daniel lied. Again.

"No? You look at your friend Moog."

"What about him?" Daniel was nothing if not defensive of his friends.

"He don't want no part of the fight. Not no more. He gotten soften and fat and he's glad 'bout it. But look at you. You're harder than you ever been. Moog can't sleep 'cause he's haunted by what he's done. You can't sleep 'cause you can't stop thinking 'bout what you done. You think about it day and night."

Daniel got to his feet. "I'm done with this."

"Even if you could be done with it"—Atibon laughed an exaggerated laugh to display his contempt—"how far you think you'd get without the gift I gave you?"

"You think you gave me a gift?"

"A goddamn gift." Atibon spat. "You went into that hotel room and killed everybody up in there. Your boy walked outta there. Your friend walked outta there. And you walked outta there. You're goddamn right I gave you a gift. And I'm callin' that marker in right now."

"Well, guess what? I'm welshing on the debt. How you like that?"

The old man swiped a dismissive paw in the air at him. "You talkin' crazy now. You can't welsh on me. We struck a bargain. And you're gonna live up to your end."

"The only thing I'm living is my life."

"Then live it," the old man shot back. "But how far you think you getting on your own? You were the last man to see that dead man alive." He pointed at Mark's corpse. "And in case you ain't noticed, you ain't makin' a lot of friends with the local constabulary. You think Officer Southier gonna be all professional and polite the next time you two meet?"

Daniel was silent, taken aback by the anger in the old man's voice. And the realizations his words conjured in Daniel's head.

"And whoever did this, what you think they gonna make of you being here right now?" the old man continued.

"*And* you got the only recording of Marco Pharaoh's last album back at your house. What you think that's worth? What you think folks will do to get their hands on that?" It was just browbeating now. "*And* did I mention that your friend Special Agent Gerald Feller just landed on the island? Whatcha gonna do 'bout that without me?"

Daniel was able to choke out a defiant, "I'll manage." But even as he said it he could feel the dread welling in the pit of his stomach at Atibon's words.

"Manage? Son, you hotter than Mississippi asphalt on the Fourth of July. You think those Russian fellows forgot about that money you took?"

"It was Preezrakevich's. And he's dead."

"Money always belongs to someone. You think they gonna be all right, knowin' you got it? Or how 'bout those bikers? You think they don't want to get their oil-caked hands on the man that killed their brothers?"

There wasn't much Daniel could do but look sullen.

"And they ain't the worst of it, son. None of 'em. Not by a god-damn mile and a half." The old man paused for effect. "You think *he* don't know about you?"

The suggestion frightened Daniel more than anything. "Who?"

"I told you, son, he's got more names than I do. But you know him just the same. Everyone knows him one time or another."

Daniel looked blankly at the old man.

"The one you seen hiding in the shadows. The one that Rabidoso feller been bringin' 'round to see you. He's the one I been fightin' with for long as I can remember. He been comin' 'round 'cause he knows what you can do—"

"What can I do?" It was more than just a simple question.

But Atibon had a simple answer. "You can matter."

"How's that?"

"You can turn on the light. Maybe just once and maybe just for a minute. But you can prove him wrong, prove him to be the damn liar he is. You can bring the son of a bitch to his knees, and it scares him."

"Me?" None of it sounded right to Daniel.

There was more. "And he ain't never gonna rest till he get ya." He looked hard into Daniel's eyes. "And I know that somewhere in that sea of doubt you call your mind, you know that for certain."

It wasn't anything Daniel wanted to admit, but that didn't mean he didn't somehow *sense* it was true. "All right. All right. What exactly do you want?"

"I want you to realize that I gave you a gift."

"And what exactly was that?"

"*Boom! Boom! Boom! Boom!* I gave you the power to shoot 'em all down. And that you *need* that gift if you gonna survive, if the people you love is gonna survive. You need that gift more than I need you. So you wanna leave, then get to steppin'. But you best better believe you ain't runnin' into anything but a grave." He took a deep breath. "And you'll be takin' your friend Moog right with you." He took his time finishing. "The woman, too."

"What did you just say about underestimating me?"

"It's not about you," Atibon insisted. "You gotta remember I ain't in this alone. And you ain't neither. If you don't take this charge up, if you stay here on the island—" He paused, as if taking a breath was hard to do. "You'll all be as dead as that boy there before the sun rises again." There was more. "All three of you."

Daniel looked back at the waterlogged remains of the man he'd spent the last evening with and then to the old man, whose eyes were like tombstones set in his head. "Then I don't have much of a choice."

"Same choice as everyone else: Live your life. Or lose it."

"What exactly do you want me to do?"

"You find out who done this." Atibon looked down at the dead man with a paternal sadness and then up with a righteous anger. "That all."

"That all?" Daniel's voice was filled with disbelief.

"For now," Atibon answered, as if it was the only part of a secret he was willing to share.

"Not now," Daniel insisted. "What is it you're asking me to do? Are you asking me to kill whoever's responsible for Mark's death?"

The old man just laughed. "You always rushin' ahead of yourself, son. I ain't worried about the hired hands that dealt the blows. I want you to find the blackheart that had it done. You just concentrate on finding who was behind this. Trust me, when you found that sonbitch, you'll know just exactly what to do next."

"And just how am I supposed to do that?" Daniel threw his hands up to the indifferent sky. "I'm a damn fugitive. How the hell am I supposed to investigate a murder that I'd probably be the prime suspect for?"

The old man smiled. "You just follow the music, and you'll be fine."

Daniel thought on it for a minute. "All right. I'll do it."

"That's *mi key*," the old man said proudly, clapping Daniel on the back as if he was a boy who'd just learned to ride a bike.

Daniel ignored the sentiment. He only had one thing on his mind. "I'll do it, but I want your promise on something."

"There ain't no bargaining, son." Atibon leaned back, surprised by Daniel's gumption. "We already struck our deal."

"No." Daniel shook his head softly. "I don't know what you *really* want from me, but I know for certain you wouldn't be here if you didn't need me to do this. So I'm willing to walk away from this and take my chances on me and my friends seeing tomorrow, because I'm betting they're not all that different from the odds on living through this little assignment of yours."

"It does have its risks," the old man confessed.

"So if I'm going to do this, then you're gonna promise me that you'll protect Vicki and Moog. You guarantee they stay safe, or I don't do this."

"You sure you want to keep bargaining with me? You still owe me for your son's safety."

"I'm sure." Daniel was adamant. "For the exact same reason."

Atibon looked at him the same way he had when they'd first met, like he was trying to calculate just how much he could take the rube for. "I can do what you're askin', but I won't do it for free."

Daniel was beyond caring. "Just so it gets done."

The old man cackled. "You just getting in deeper and deeper."

"What does depth matter to a drowning man?" Daniel looked across at the floating body of Mark Wannaman, gliding across the glassy surface of the pool, spinning on the currents created by the pool filter.

"Well, look who just stood up." He pretended to be offended, but secretly Atibon glowed with pride. "It's a deal. But it'll cost you dearly."

"It always does." Daniel stood up and gave the corpse one last look. "Just put it on my account."

The old man nodded that he would. "Just one more thing."

Daniel turned to the old man but didn't say a word.

"This ain't no long-term situation," Atibon explained. "This needs to be done before the new year."

"Why's that?"

"Because if you don't get the job done and pull out of it what you need to, then you won't live much past then."

Daniel thought on the deadline, but his internal calendar had been converted to island time, and notions of days or months or even years were an unnecessary complication. "That gives me—"

"That's two weeks, son."

Daniel tried to verify the dates in his head but again came up blank. "All right."

"End of the year," Atibon repeated.

"I got it."

"Best be sure you do." The old man laughed aloud.

Without a word, Daniel turned and walked back into the house.

"You runnin' up quite a tab, *mi key*," the old man called after him. "Make sure you don't get no late fees on this then." He laughed as if that was the funniest thing he'd heard in a long, long time.

Wannaman's keys were still on the kitchen counter. Daniel picked them up and walked out to the driveway where the Jeep was parked. Daniel didn't think Mark would mind. It was a long walk back to his place, and it wasn't like the dead man was going to need it anymore.

A ringing *whoosh* from inside his head was still almost all that Daniel could hear, but the old man's laughter was clear as a bell.

CHAPTER EIGHTEEN

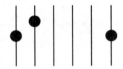

The Gulfstream V carrying a US Marshals Fugitive Recovery and FBI joint task force touched down at Cyril E. King Airport and then taxied to the hangar at the south end of the field to a private hangar where government craft could unload without public scrutiny.

US Marshal Ken Barters was the first of the six-man team to deplane. It wasn't that there was any strategic advantage to being the first man off, or that it followed some mandated intra-agency protocol. He'd rushed off the plane merely because he knew the gesture would seriously piss off the task force's leader, Special Agent Gerald Feller. And he was right.

Barters stretched his arms wide until he felt his back crack and then twisted from side to side to loosen up the middle-aged muscles that stiffened if he sat for too long. The Caribbean sun felt good on his bones.

"I was going to brief the team," Feller called down from the jet's open door.

Barters didn't bother to turn around. "Then brief 'em."

Special Agent Feller knew his mission couldn't tolerate this dissension. "Perhaps you'd like to join us, Marshal Barters?"

"What I'd like," Barters shouted up as he surveyed the hangar, "is all of our equipment off this plane and ready to go within the hour." He looked past Feller and shouted, "Wimmers, get out here."

Twenty seconds later, the athletically built blonde was pushing past Feller and descending the jet stairs.

"Let's get everything ready to roll on our end," Barters barked. She was ready to oblige. "Yes, sir."

"And Wimmers," he added, as she stood awaiting further instructions, "let's make sure we do it *our* way." He made a point of casting a look up at the flummoxed Feller, standing flatfooted at the top of the ladder.

Trying his best to resuscitate his authority, Feller descended the ladder. "All right, let's go," he hollered back up at the jet.

Special Agent Carl Schweeter popped out of the jetway and made his descent. He was followed by Special Agents Todd Connors and Eli Norris, whom the task force had picked up at the San Juan district office. None of them seemed to know who to follow or where to go.

"Feller," Barters snapped. "Get over here."

It was more disrespect than Feller was willing to put up with. "It's Special Agent Gerald Feller," he snapped as he stomped over to where his antagonist stood talking with a man he didn't recognize. The man was tall and fit, dressed in the Bermuda shorts and bobby socks of the local police force—although his uniform was dirty and rumpled, as if he'd been in some sort of fracas earlier.

"Well, I'm going to start calling you 'special ed' Gerald Feller," Barters quipped. "I thought you said you had the locals advised and on board."

"I did," Feller said, his voice somewhat less than absolutely confident. "I do."

"Well, this is Captain Winston Southier of the US Virgin Islands Police Department, and if I can paraphrase, he says you're full of shit." He turned back to his red-faced counterpart. "And who am I to disagree?"

"What?" Feller was clearly confused. "I don't understand."

"That's becoming alarmingly clear," Barters taunted. "Because the good captain here evidently has some problems with the soiree you have planned for this evening."

"What problems?" Feller asked.

"There are some who have concerns about the nature of your presence here in our jurisdiction," Southier announced flatly, almost as if the line had been written for him or fed to him by some third party.

"The nature of our presence?" Feller couldn't quite grasp what was happening. Or why. "I'm afraid that's classified, Captain. And none of your business."

"I beg to disagree," the policeman insisted, not willing to give an inch. "We are unincorporated territory—"

"Of the United States," Feller concluded for him.

"Exactly. We have every right to request that you make clear the nature of your operation in our jurisdiction."

"You can request all that you want, but I'm not answering anything," Feller insisted.

"If that is how you wish to handle the situation," Southier said, getting ready to play his trump card.

"That's how I *am* handing the situation."

"Then I'll call the governor immediately," Captain Southier advised them. "And he'll call your deputy director. And then those gentlemen can continue this conversation for us." Trump card played. "If that's how you wish to handle this situation."

"Goddammit, Feller," Barters interjected. "This operation has a time frame. It needs to stay on schedule. If you can't do this on time, then we just aren't going to do it."

"We'll do it on time," Feller declared.

The marshal shook his head disapprovingly. "This is how you boys get jammed up the way you do."

"What's that supposed to mean?"

"You know exactly what that means, Special Agent Waco."

Feller despaired, thought briefly about how to respond, and then decided it was best to seek a solution. "What exactly do you want, Captain Souther?" he asked clumsily.

"Southier," he corrected, clearly offended by the mispronunciation.

"Way to go, Feller," Barters chimed in.

"What I want is the respect that is due my department," Southier continued. "What I want is to be informed of what your agents will be doing within my jurisdiction."

"I thought you said you took care of this," Barters chirped at Feller.

"I did," Feller fumbled. "I filed all of the necessary paperwork." He ran through a checklist in his head. "I'm certain that Special Agent Schweeter—"

Barters groaned, "Oh, this is perfect."

Feller turned back to the local, desperate to expedite a resolution. "We're here to apprehend a pair of fugitives."

"I see," Southier said. "Then my department will participate."

"Oh, hell no," Barters insisted.

"No. That's not how it works." Feller felt the familiar tightness across his chest intensify. "I'm serious about this. You can't begin to understand the dangerous nature of these men."

"All the more reason for my department to participate."

"No." It was Feller's last stand.

Southier was unmoved. "Then I'll call the governor and begin that process."

In an instant, Feller saw his professional life flashing before his eyes. A governor calling the deputy director. The deputy director calling Bovard. Bovard calling him and telling him to work the situation out. A letter to that effect being put in his folder. Bovard sitting in his office, cursing Feller for the political exposure. Feller being transferred to the El Paso office.

"Welcome aboard, Captain." He extended a hand.

"This is a mistake, Feller."

"What's a mistake?"

"It's all a mistake," Barters called back over his shoulder as he walked away. "I hope you don't get us all killed."

CHAPTER NINETEEN

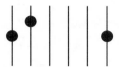

Moog Turner sat on the screened-in porch with a Mossberg 500 tactical shotgun across his lap. He had spent the day waiting for bad news, and the twelve-gauge was the best way he knew to prepare for its inevitable arrival.

It was late in the evening when he noticed headlights on the twin lanes of pitted pavement that ran past their secluded beach house. When the lights slowed and swung down the crushed-shell drive, the big man rose to his feet and worked the pump.

The brakes of the Jeep squeaked as it came to a stop. Moog recognized the shrill sound and casually let the barrel of the shotgun drop toward the ground.

Footsteps crunched to the porch and then banged up the steps. The screen door squeaked as it came open.

"Where you been?" Moog held the shotgun in a way that suggested the answer should be a helluva one.

It wasn't that Daniel didn't take the unspoken threat seriously, but he was too tired to be convincing. "I was driving."

"I mean, what the hell?" Moog was reserved, but clearly in an emotional state far west of simple anger.

"I had a lot to think about," Daniel offered as an exhibit for the defense.

"And why you driving Wannaman's Jeep?" Moog paused a moment to consider that clue, and then all the pieces came together. The obvious conclusion to which they led hit him like a blast from his Mossberg. "Oh shit, you didn't go and kill the guy!"

"I didn't touch the guy."

"Because I ain't digging no grave." Moog shook his head emphatically. "I guarantee you that. Them's the rules. You pop 'em, you plant 'em."

"I didn't kill him," Daniel insisted, loudly enough to get the big man's attention.

"Then what you doing with his wheels?" Moog looked out toward the drive where the battered Jeep sat parked.

"He's not going to need them," Daniel said, as if he was too tired to say anything more. He dropped down to the couch. "He's dead."

The introduction of a corpse into the story line confused Moog. "Wait a minute, I thought you said you didn't—"

"I didn't." Daniel groaned.

"But if the dude is dead—"

"I didn't—"

"I ain't taking him out in no boat neither," the big man assured him.

When he couldn't find the strength to fight for Moog's waning attention any longer, Daniel snapped, "Will you just listen?"

"Listen?" Moog's eyes flashed. "Motherfucker, I been listening to you for damn near on a year now. I've been listening to you when a long time ago I would've shut up any other asshole, taken his money and his woman, and gotten myself gone."

Daniel sat back and exhaled, slowly and exaggeratedly, as if his troubles were something he could simply blow away. "Maybe that's not such a bad idea."

"What the hell you talking about? It's a *very* bad idea."

"I think maybe it's time that—" Daniel stopped midsentence, not wanting to say anything before he could figure out exactly what he was going to do. "I haven't eaten all day. You hungry?"

"I'm always hungry," Moog answered honestly. He propped the shotgun against the wall and followed Daniel down the hall to the small kitchen. "But you think maybe it's time for what?"

"*Maque choux?*"

"You think it's time for mock shoe?"

Daniel looked into the container he'd pulled from the fridge. "No, I was just wondering if this was *maque choux.*"

Moog looked the concoction over. "Guess so. Just heat it and eat it. It don't need a name."

Daniel agreed and plopped whatever the mix was into a frying pan and set it on the burner. He turned the knob, but nothing. "Shit."

"Pilot light?" Moog was familiar with the problems of the old and finicky stove.

Daniel nodded and looked through the junk drawer for matches.

"Forget the stove, man." Moog had questions he wanted answered. "You said you thought it was time. Time for what?"

Daniel found a match and got down on his knees. "Maybe it's time to, you know—"

"Time to *what*?"

Daniel got back to his feet, not wanting to have the discussion from the floor. "Things are unraveling here."

119

Moog stepped back as if his shotgun had gone off. Straight to his chest. "I knew it." He shook his head, trying to think for a moment. "It's bad, ain't it? Real bad."

Daniel didn't respond.

"It's the cops, ain't it? 'Cause prison would be worse than just about anything else, man. It's the cops, ain't it?"

"No."

Moog felt a momentary release of relief. "Whew! 'Cause Vicki said a po-lice car—"

"It's the Feds."

"Oh, fuck me!" The big man took a deep, panicked breath and both his hands went to the top of his head, as if it might come off completely if he didn't hold it down.

"It's worse than that."

"Worse? How can it be worse than the Feds?"

And that's when the dog started barking outside.

Vicki's scream split the night a second later.

CHAPTER TWENTY

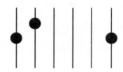

They parked down the road, pulling the dented Honda Civic far off to the side so no one would notice it, and shared a joint to calm their nerves. When Osajo was ready and A-Volt realized there was no way he could talk his friend out of it, they got out of the dented Honda Civic and set off toward the house.

They moved silently through the darkness with a shared purpose, knowing exactly what their objective was and what they each needed to do once they got there.

The house was dark, and they took that as a good sign that they had the advantage of surprise. The front door was locked, but the window to the left was open wide, with nothing other than a screen to keep out the mosquitoes and no-see-ums. The pair wasn't so easily deterred. Osajo put a blade to the wire mesh while A-Volt kept watch.

"Shit, man," A-Volt screamed in a whisper. "I just saw something."

"What? Where?" Osajo searched the area of darkness where his friend was pointing. "I don't see anything."

"I tell you I saw something move out there," A-Volt insisted. "In the darkness, man."

Osajo dismissed it. "It's nothing." He went back to work on the window.

A-Volt couldn't look away. "If it was nothing, then nothing was darker than the shadows and shaped like a man."

Osajo wasn't having any of it. "Come on."

They slipped into the room, which was empty, and moved down the hall on the sides of their feet, rolling from their heels to their toes, so that each footstep would fall silently. It wasn't like the night before had been. This time they knew right where they were going. They had been here before.

"This ain't right," A-Volt argued one last time. "These people been good to us, man. Let us record here—"

"You recorded here," Osajo reminded him in a hoarse whisper. "I sat and watched."

"But still, man."

"And what about the crazy dude, man? You think he was joking 'bout that shit? He microwaved a forest chicken with his hands, man." A-Volt didn't need a reminder. "What do you think he's going to do to us if we screw this up?"

A-Volt didn't have an answer. Or at least, not one he wanted to whisper in the dark.

"It's us or them, man." Osajo would've said it just to get his friend to cooperate, but he knew it was true, too. "And tonight it's going to be them."

Osajo pushed open the door to their right. It creaked a little— every hinge on the island was cranky with rust from the sea air— but the figure in the bed didn't stir at the slight sound.

They crept into the room. What little light was cast by the sliver of moon fell through the uncovered window and shone on the bed. She was alone. A sheet was pulled up to her waist, but that was all that covered her.

"Oh, man." Osajo sighed at the sight of her. "She's so hot just lying there." He turned to A-Volt and smiled.

They had their orders, their objectives, their assignment. They knew what they'd been sent to do, but Osajo couldn't see the harm in a slight deviation from plan. He certainly couldn't see the sense in wasting such a fine opportunity presenting itself so willingly.

He pointed to himself, indicating his intentions to be the first at her, and began to work the buttons on his shorts. A-Volt reached out for his arm, trying to discourage him, but Osajo just shook him off. As he did, the weight of the pistol in his pocket pulled his board shorts to the floor.

Osajo moved to the edge of the bed and leaned in toward her, an outstretched palm ready to clamp down on the scream she'd surely make as soon as he shocked her from her sleep.

And then—for no apparent reason—a dog started barking right outside the window. It was startling and distracting enough that Osajo turned for a moment to look out the window to see where it was and what had upset it.

Before he could pinpoint the source of the disturbance, there was another, more troubling sound. An earsplitting scream. A woman's scream.

When Osajo turned back, the woman had sat upright and was swinging a baseball bat at his head. There was a dull ringing as tubular aluminum made contact with cranium. It would've gone for extra bases.

Osajo crumpled to the floor beside the bed.

Vicki jumped to her feet, stark naked and unconcerned about modesty. Standing on the mattress, she raised the bat high over her head.

A-Volt was caught. He didn't know whether to run or to help his friend or to call out for mercy to this woman who'd been kind to him, but now was terrified and fighting to save her life. He didn't know what to do. So he did nothing.

The bat came down on the top of A-Volt's head and he dropped to the floor as if someone had simply unplugged him.

* * *

Daniel was quicker down the hall than Moog, and he was the first to burst into the room. Vicki stood on the bed, clothed only in moonlight. She held her bat above her head, but she was heaving with exertion and terror and adrenaline. There were two unknown men in the room, and the one without pants was just getting back on his feet. He was fumbling with his fallen board shorts, searching for something.

The sight of it all only convinced Daniel that the old man had been right about him all along. It would've been a lie to claim that he was shocked out of his senses by the situation. To the contrary, he felt the whole world slow down until it seemed as if he were the only one moving. His racing mind provided him with a fully formed thought. He knew exactly what he was going to do and how.

The pantsless guy with his shorts in his hands pulled something from them. Daniel saw the glint of moonlight against the chromed barrel of the pistol and sprinted across the room to tackle the man.

In an instant Daniel was on top of the man, and whatever fire Atibon had lit in him roared to life as an inferno of rage. He threw punch after punch, not wildly like a drunken frat boy, but intending every one of them to chip away at the man.

Osajo tried to cover himself, but there was no way to shield himself from the attack. The man tried to wriggle away, whimpering and crying, but Daniel knew there was nowhere to escape. Nowhere to go but hell.

There was shouting, and Daniel felt hands on him, tugging and trying to pull him away. But he was numb to it all. He was lost in a world of blood and anger, violence and vengeance; a world all his own. He threw punches until there was nothing solid left to hit and no reason left to hit it.

He jumped up from the mess he'd made. He grabbed the chromed pistol and turned toward the other intruder. It was dark. His head was swirling. He saw the other man, took aim at him. And fired.

The shot struck his target and drove him back against the far wall. He slid down its length, leaving behind a Jackson Pollock in blood red across the wall all the way down to the floor.

"What the hell, man?" Moog's eyes were wide and white, but Daniel couldn't tell why.

Daniel took another step back, but there was no stepping out of this. The carnage he'd created surrounded him and there was no way to put the pieces back. Not anymore.

He looked up at Vicki. Her eyes were wide with fear, but he recognized instantly that he was the cause. And its source.

There were no words he could offer, so he silently handed her a robe that had fallen to the floor.

"What is wrong with you?" Moog demanded.

"I don't know, Moog!" Daniel snapped back. "I suppose when I came into my bedroom and found the woman I love—" In the near year they'd spent together, it was the first time he'd ever publicly made that declaration, and the abominable timing of it stopped even Daniel in his tracks. He turned back to Vicki, but she either hadn't heard or had chosen not to acknowledge his words. Either way, he understood.

Moog didn't. "Man, they were just kids."

"What do you mean?"

"They were just kids," Moog informed him. "Those kids that Vicki had recording here last month."

None of it made sense. "What the hell are they doing here?"

"I don't know," Moog answered as he looked from body to body. "And now we never will."

"Don't be so sure." Daniel knelt beside Osajo's body and picked up his limp wrist. It was adorned with a silver bracelet of braided guitar strings. Daniel pulled it free, looked it over, and then slid it onto his own wrist.

"What's that?" Moog asked.

"It's Mark's," Daniel told him, as if that piece of evidence cleared up all of their questions.

Moog thought maybe he understood. "You think these two were the ones who—"

"The ones who what?" Vicki wanted to know. "What does this have to do with Mark?"

That wasn't going to be an easy conversation to have. "I will tell you in a minute. I swear, but right now—"

His answer wasn't good enough. "Are you saying—"

"I'm saying we're going to have to do this, but we can't do this now." He turned to look at Moog, seeking some expert advice.

"Well, there's no way to clean this mess up, and no way to keep living in it." He shook his head with dismay. "I don't know what we do now."

Atibon's words came back to Daniel, and suddenly he understood what had happened. "We get out. Now."

"Get out?" Vicki, still covered with nothing but blood, stood on the bed looking slightly dazed, as if the suggested action plan had hit her as hard as the bat. "Get out *where*?"

"Out," Daniel repeated. "Anywhere is better than here right now."

Outside in the distance, the same dog began to bark again. When they all turned reflexively toward the window, they saw something even more horrifying than the blood-splattered bedroom.

"Jesus Christ," Moog called out. "There are lights coming down the road. Lots of them. Fast. In a line."

Daniel knew. Atibon had warned him. "The Feds."

"It's pretty late for a carnival parade," Moog quipped sarcastically.

"Get her out of here." Daniel pulled Vicki from the bed, wrapped her in the robe she'd yet to put on herself, and ushered her to Moog's protective arms.

"Where?" Moog shot back. "How? Carry her on my back?"

"These two didn't walk here," Daniel snapped. He searched the pockets of the discarded board shorts and came up with a set of keys. "They must have a car parked down the road." He tossed the keys to Moog. "Get to it. I'll meet you there. But if I don't—" Daniel rushed to their closet, kicked out the drywall in the back, and reached through the hole he'd made to pull out the duffel bag that contained the rest of the money he'd stolen from the Russians.

He handed the bag to Moog. "Here. Let's not forget this."

"What are you going to be doing while I'm doing all this?" Moog asked, taking hold of the bag in one hand and Vicki's hand in the other.

Mr. Atibon's words were ringing in his head. *Just follow the music.* "There's something I have to get." Daniel left them and ran to the door. He turned in the hallway just long enough to make out the silhouettes of Vicki and Moog disappearing into the night.

Daniel headed back to the studio, went straight to the iMac, and pressed the eject button. The drawer slowly slid open. "Come on. Come on." There was a disc in the tray. Daniel hoped it was the only copy of the last work of Marco Pharaoh, but he didn't have time to make sure. He snatched it up and ran to the front door to follow Moog and Vicki out into the night.

Daniel took a step out of the door and immediately froze at the sight of a man standing in the front yard with a gun in his hand. He was heavyset, wearing a jacket marked FBI, but he seemed just as startled to see Daniel.

Instinctively, Daniel turned to duck inside the house, but a second later there was a flash in the darkness and a shot ripped past him. Daniel jumped out of the house, landed in the sandy front yard, and sprang to his feet.

The fat guy with the gun readied himself to take the shot that not even he could miss.

And that's when all hell broke loose.

CHAPTER TWENTY-ONE

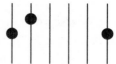

The radio crackled to life. "Outpost Two for Task Force Leader."

Special Agent Feller keyed the mic. "This is Team Leader. Go."

A burst of static. "We've got two figures on the ground approaching the subject property."

"Can you get an ID on them?"

"Negative. Two males. I've got eyes on them but no ID."

Special Agent Gerald Feller ran his swollen fingers over the hairless crown of his head and cursed his situation. He'd been chasing Daniel Erickson for almost a year, and every time he was within striking distance, every time he was just about to get his man, some unforeseeable scenario would arise.

There was the hotel maintenance man who stubbornly wouldn't turn over the elevator keys. The waitress in Queens who swore she didn't recognize the photo he'd shown her, though he knew that she did. Now he had some local cop intent on making a name for himself sticking his thumb in the eyes of a federal operation.

"Call this off, Feller." The voice on the walkie-talkie was gruff and angry and belonged to US Marshal Ken Barters. "We're two hours off our scheduled strike. Now we got unknowns on the ground."

It wasn't a perfect scenario. Feller would've been the first to admit that. But there was no real reason to call off the operation, and no reason of any sort for him to walk into Special Agent in Charge Ross Bovard's office and inform him that the entire operation—with its sizable budget—had been for naught.

He keyed his mic. "Negative. This operation is a go!"

Feller was in the SUV leading the parade, a black Suburban with Special Agent Schweeter at the wheel. In the back sat Special Agents Todd Connors and Eli Norris, ready to explode from the vehicle and storm the subject residence as they'd rehearsed.

US Marshals Barters and Wimmers followed close behind in a Suburban of their own. "Feller," Barters barked. "It's not right."

Behind them, Captain Southier brought up the rear in the USVIPD Envoy.

"Here! Here!" Feller shouted, and Schweeter swung the Suburban into the drive. "Let's go! Let's go!" A second later the two men were running toward the front of the house.

Special Agent Connors, carrying a H&K MP5, and Special Agent Norris, with an M4, scrambled across the sand to cover the east side of the house.

Marshal Barters, with his AR-15, and Wimmers, with her twelve-gauge shotgun, headed for the back of the house.

The marshals were the first into the house, tearing through the porch's screen door and then moving into the interior of the house. "US marshals!"

The very first room they entered was the kitchen, and in an instant both of them knew that something was very wrong. One sniff and they each looked at the other, knowing they needed to get out of there immediately.

"Shit," Barters screamed as he tried to push his deputy out of the door ahead of him.

A second later there was a single gunshot. It left the barrel of Special Agent Feller's Glock 22, traveled straight through the acoustical tile Daniel had hung in Vicki's studio, passed through the control room and into the kitchen, where it struck the refrigerator and caused a spark. It was like a lethal Rube Goldberg contraption.

There were two blasts, really.

The first was a smaller bang, a *puff* almost, caused when the gas that had accumulated from the stove's malfunctioning pilot light initially ignited with the bullet's spark. Then, for what seemed like a sustainable instant, there was no sound or motion at all, nothing but time for the realization to hit Marshals Barters and Wimmers that the flame couldn't help but find its source.

There was a flash. As a fraction of time, it was imperceptible to everyone except Barters and Wimmers, who stood right in the midst of it. To the two of them, the moment seemed endless. There was more than enough time to wonder whether it would be better to survive the blast or to simply surrender to it. There was time to think of family and friends who would either mourn them or nurse them. There was time enough to reconsider what they were doing there anyway, to wonder why they hadn't done something else with their lives, something less likely to end with a fiery blast.

Then the whole world was nothing but flame, blinding light, and blistering heat. The air was thick with shards of glass and splintered wood and household appliances rendered to shrapnel.

And then—just as suddenly as it had been suspended—time was restored, and a shower of debris rained down from the night sky. Remnants of building and fixtures and people came down like a cloudburst in a tropical storm of death and destruction.

* * *

In the chaos and the light of the fire, Feller got back to his feet and stood dumbfounded by what was happening in front him. It couldn't have happened. It simply couldn't have. The heat of the fire and the agonized screams of his team members, though, were undeniable.

Shock washed over him, pulled him down to its numbing depths, down so far that he felt like he was drowning in it. He stood there and simply watched it all burn.

Out of the corner of his eye, he saw movement. A vehicle, he thought. Small and compact, running without any lights. He knew. Somehow he knew.

"It's him! It's Erickson!" he shouted in his mind. But standing on the sand, he just watched it go by, following it for the instant it took to disappear into the night.

CHAPTER TWENTY-TWO

St. Thomas has a population of just over 150,000 souls. When one of them departs under less than natural circumstances, the physical remains are usually removed to the morgue in the basement of the Roy L. Schneider Medical Center in the capital of Charlotte Amalie.

In the six years that he'd maintained order during the overnight shift at the morgue, John Waxler had never seen such chaos. Four new bodies. Two of them US marshals.

The USVIPD had been there. The FBI, too. There'd been bureaucrats from Washington and men from the governor's office. There'd been demands that the bodies remain there for autopsy and insistence that all four be transported to Quantico for the same procedure.

The Feds had won the arguments, of course. they'd marched off to make logistical arrangements. The locals had simply stormed off. And John Waxler had been left alone, charged with readying the bodies for their final flight to Quantico.

"Busy night?" Haden Koschei asked as he stepped out of the shadows.

John jumped, every bit as frightened as he was startled. "Um," he stammered for an instant, trying to collect himself in the presence of the tall, thin man. "There's people all over here tonight," he said nervously. "Been in and out. I don't think this is the night for—"

"Every night is my night," Koschei corrected.

"Yes, but—" Waxler looked nervously about the morgue. It was unclear whether he was more frightened that someone would come in and interrupt them or that someone wouldn't.

"I want to see them," Koschei requested, as calmly as a tourist in the shops down by the harbor might ask to take a look at this trinket or that doodad.

Waxler stammered, "I really don't think—"

Koschei smiled. "That's right, you don't think. You do. Exactly what I tell you to do."

The thin man's gaze caught the four gurneys at the far edge of the room and he strolled over, his Berluti boots clicking against the tiles as he went. "Are these the ones?"

Each of the gurneys bore a black body bag, a container for the parts they'd been able to remove from the debris.

"Um, those are—" Waxler's nervousness grew. "Those are the bodies that they brought in tonight."

"Yes, quite a business," Koshei said as he helped himself to a look at the documents Waxler had prepared and tucked beneath each cadaver. "The island is all ablaze with it." He chuckled to himself. "Kenneth Barters," he read from the first form.

He stepped to the second. "Wimmers, Catherine." He turned to look over his shoulder at the morgue attendant. "Catherine, huh? Any chance you'll be spending some quality time with her before she has to go? Or is this bit beyond repair?"

"I don't know what you're talking about."

"Oh, please, John," Koschei sneered as he moved on to the third gurney. "You can't think this is the first time I've been here." He looked around at the wall of chromed drawers. "This is practically home. I know all about what you do here when you're alone." He corrected himself with a wicked smile. "When you *think* you're alone."

John Waxler looked suddenly as if he belonged in one of his own drawers. "Please—"

"Oh, don't worry. Your little secret is safe with me." He looked over the third set of papers. "For now."

Koschei looked down at the bag. "And this is Vernon Turner?"

"Y-y-y-yes."

Koschei seemed skeptical about the identification, but moved on to the fourth gurney.

"Ah, Daniel Erickson." He zipped open the bag with all the enthusiasm of a child at Christmas finally getting to his big gift. The remains inside were charred black, as if an islander in the holiday spirit had become frustrated with the Caribbean's lack of snow and set about making a charcoal man. "This is Daniel Erickson?"

"Yes," Waxler responded, but there was no certainty in the word.

"And how do you know that?"

"They told me."

"They? They who?" Koschei quizzed him with the promise that there would be Japanese game show punishments for him if he got the answer wrong.

"One of the FBI agents." Waxler scrambled through his rat's nest of a brain for more information to feed to the monster. "Bovard, he said his name was. Special agent in charge. Flew in here special to handle things. Made the identification."

"Made the identification? How?"

"He just came in here and said that's who it was."

Koschei nodded, satisfied that the quaking man was too frightened to lie. He reached into the bag and grabbed the blackened remains of what had once been a head. It made a popping sound as he pulled it loose, and oozed something thick and yellow as he held it up to look into what had once been eyes.

"Well, you can tell Special Agent in Charge Bovard that this is NOT the head of Daniel Erickson!" He threw the handful of remains across the room. "Damnit!"

He pushed the gurney away in disgust. It rolled a foot or two and then simply came to a stop. "Where the hell is Daniel Erickson?"

"Who?" Waxler wondered.

"Exactly," Koschei agreed. "Who is someone like *that* to pose such a threat to someone like *me*?"

"I don't see how anyone could—"

"It doesn't seem fair, does it?" Koschei was quick to agree. "Someone of my nature, who has devoted his very essence to helping people understand the very nature of life."

"The nature of life?" The possible insight was too promising not to explore.

"The nature of life," Koschei repeated for emphasis. He gestured to the chrome-door morgue drawers as if every one of them contained an example. "*This* is the nature of life."

Waxler didn't make any comment, but his disappointment was palpable.

"Look at you," Koschei chided. "Just like all the others, you're so eager to believe the lies because you're afraid of the truth. Surely you must understand that nothingness is your fate."

Waxler nodded as if he did.

"I wouldn't blame you if you didn't." His voice sounded cold and aloof. "You are, all of you, plagued by cruel deceivers who would have you believe that there is something more to this life than what is contained in your own skin." He sighed as if he were boring himself. "But that cruel lie only breeds disappointment and pain. I assure you, everything beyond your own skin is an illusion, a bitter illusion. A pit of hopelessness. And leading people to carry that false hope is the worst kind of cruelty: the kind of pain that doesn't bring anyone any pleasure."

He smiled the kindliest smile he could. "So I've taken it on as my mission to combat the deceivers. To share with even the lowliest of you the irrefutable truth that this life of yours is all too brief, and the only purpose it could possibly contain is simply experiencing as much pleasure as you can feel in that short time. That's all. The fuck you get. The high you get. Hell, even the pain you give, because we all know it feels great to hurt someone."

Waxler smiled. He did know that.

"Because I speak the truth. There are some cruel, deceitful, hateful ones who would silence me for their own purposes, simply because they want to torment people with their false hope. And so my enemies have sent someone to do me harm."

"This Erickson?"

Koschei nodded. "Of course, not everyone can harm one like me. It takes a special man to pose a threat to me. A man who is not really a man. A man without a soul. A walking dead man."

"And this Erickson is one of those?"

"Yes." Koschei sighed. "Whether he knows it or not, Daniel Erickson is such a man." For a minute the thin man drifted off into his own thoughts, and Waxler did not disturb him from them.

When at last Koschei returned his attention to Waxler, it was with an order. "I want to know where this Daniel Erickson is. People find you insignificant. Because of that, they talk in front of you like you're not even there. Listen to what they say to one another and then let me know. I am counting on you to find out where he is. And I assure you, my disappointment will make you wish you were in one of those drawers."

CHAPTER TWENTY-THREE

There are no highways to run down, no buses to catch, and no trains to hop. For most people there are only two ways off an island. By air or by sea.

For fugitives who looked as if they'd just walked through a firefight (because they had), there was really no way to inconspicuously slip through the airport and grab a flight. That left only one way to go.

Realizing their time on St. Thomas had come to an end with the blast that had consumed their house, Moog drove straight to the marina without any discussion or direction. They left the car behind and, with Daniel carrying the cash-filled duffel, they headed toward the docks, none of them knowing exactly where they were going or what they were looking for.

Given the late hour, the marina was largely deserted. The nautical tourists had all settled into their cabins for the night, and it was too early for the fishing excursions to start their predawn departures.

The only ones with any reason to be walking the docks in the middle of the night were smugglers. It was exactly the crowd Daniel and Moog and Vicki were looking to blend in with.

Their casual inquiries at the manned boats they passed were mostly met with silence or obscene suggestions that they look somewhere else. They were just about to give up and consider other options when a voice called out to them through the darkness.

"Hey now, you there."

The three turned, but saw no one. Until he called out again, "You there. You him?"

They turned again, and a short man, five feet if he was standing on a phone book, stepped out of the shadows. An Alan Hale Jr. skipper's hat sat atop his head, a ratty T-shirt and a pair of child-size khakis completing an authentic nautical wardrobe.

"What the hell are you?" Moog asked.

"They call me Petit Pete. And I'm your way off this island, if you're him."

"I'm *a* him," Moog offered.

"Not good enough," the miniature mariner said. "The old man said there'd be someone looking for a way off of the island. If you're him, then I'm your way off this rock, and you're my way outta his debt."

Neither Moog nor Vicki understood, but Daniel did. "I'm him."

"You sure?"

Daniel was. "I am, *mi key*." Without any supporting evidence, he was certain the skipper was there at Atibon's direction.

"You're him," the little man confirmed with a much bigger man's laugh. "Well, then get yourselves on board."

The thirty-foot Owens cabin cruiser bobbing on the waters licking at the dock didn't inspire any more confidence than the man who commanded her. "Are ye climbin' aboard or not?" His breath was a nauseating combination of rum and vomit.

"I ain't getting on that thing," Moog announced emphatically. "Much less getting on that thing with *him*."

"Much less on that thing. With him. Across the Bermuda Triangle," Vicki was quick to point out. It was the first thing she'd said since the three of them had left their home in flames. After she'd said it, she stood silently, hugging herself and staring at the black water.

"What? The Bermuda what? That doesn't look like it could get out of the harbor," Moog argued. "And he don't look like he could captain a boat in his own bathtub."

Internally, Daniel agreed with both of them. The vessel was badly stained along her waterline, and her captain looked like he was, too. It was not a vessel he wanted to board any more than it was a journey he wanted to take, but other considerations had to be factored into the equation.

There were sirens all over the island and helicopters in the air. If the Coast Guard hadn't already shut down the waterways, they would soon, and once that happened, there would be nowhere to run to.

"I don't see you have much choice." Petit Pete grinned.

"He's right." And although he couldn't share his conviction with his traveling companions, Daniel was certain that Atibon was looking out for them.

"What?" Moog was clearly shocked.

"We're on an island," Daniel explained. "We need to get off."

"Off," Moog clarified, "don't mean drowned."

The sirens in the distance somehow seemed louder and more insistent. "Well, we sure as hell aren't driving outta here. I don't think we want to stand in line at the airport right now. We don't exactly have time to book passage on a cruise."

"I get you where you need to be," Petit Pete promised, patting his round belly as if he'd consumed a Bible and it was there to be sworn upon. "I guarantee yer safety, *mi key*. And I'm nothin' if not good to me bargain."

Daniel understood the endorsement, and any embers of doubt he still harbored were immediately extinguished. "If he says he'll get us there, he'll get us there."

"And if I said you was pretty, that don't make you Beyoncé." Moog raised his eyebrows for emphasis, as if he'd just played the trump card.

"We don't have time for this," Daniel insisted. "If Atibon chose this guy, then he'll get us there." He threw the duffel bag of cash on board and then jumped on deck. He turned and held out his hand for Vicki, who took it and followed.

"Atibon?" Moog asked, struck by the strange but somehow familiar name. "Who the hell is Atibon?" he grumbled as he climbed aboard.

CHAPTER TWENTY-FOUR

Special Agent Gerald Feller knocked tentatively and then opened the door. "You wanted to see me, sir?"

Special Agent in Charge Ross Bovard looked up from the three computer monitors on his desk. "As a matter of fact, Feller, of all the seven billion souls on this entire planet, *you* are the very last one I want to see right now. I would rather share the hourly rate for the Friendly Motor Inn's Jacuzzi suite with a syphilitic Arzal ditchdigger from the filthiest back alley in Mumbai than talk to you right now."

Feller stood silently in the doorway, not knowing how to respond to that or what to do next.

"But we have business to attend to, Special Agent—*for now*—Feller. Come in and shut the door, since I have no intention of being seen with you."

Feller did as he was told.

"Feller, do you have any idea of the nastiness of the steaming hot pile of shit you have crapped all over my desk?" Apparently, Feller didn't. "I have two US marshals who were burned to death in an operation planned and led by—the FBI."

"Yes, sir."

Bovard raised a finger to stop him there. "Aaaaaand. There's a recording of the communications from that evening in which the last transmission from one of the now-deceased US marshals is a request to abort the mission." Feller wanted to say something, but the finger came up again. "A request you denied. A request you denied before shooting into the subject residence—completely unaware of the location of your team members—and causing the explosion that killed the two US marshals. The same explosion that left two of our own agents in serious condition and on a likely track to permanent disability."

"I understand, sir." How could he not? "But I don't feel the mission was a complete failure."

"Oh, no, it was," Bovard retorted. "This is one of those incidents the Bureau will make training films about. Future cadets at Quantico will be trained on how not to be a Feller."

"With all due respect, sir," Feller pressed on, "we were able to retrieve evidence from the scene. Specifically, a vehicle that we were able to trace back to—"

"Have you not heard a thing I've said to you?" Bovard demanded, incredulous that one of his agents could be so oblivious to the disaster that had transpired under his command. "I've got the deputy director and the director treating me like the passed-out coed at a community college frat party. I've got the Department of Justice and the inspector general's office preparing to launch independent investigations. And forget the budget presentation to the Appropriations Committee—we'll be lucky if there isn't a congressional investigation, too."

"Yes, sir." Feller knew his only shot at redemption was to finally get his man. "But I've filed a report with you outlining the evidence we recovered. I believe I know where Erickson is headed—"

"Who fucking CARES!" Bovard exploded. "Headed? Erickson isn't headed anywhere. Don't you watch the news? Erickson is dead."

"No, sir." If Feller was sure of one thing in that very uncertain time, it was that Daniel Erickson most definitely was not dead. "I saw him."

"I don't care what you *think* you saw. Daniel Erickson is dead. He is dead if for no other reason than that the Bureau *needs* him to be dead. The entire nation is grieving the deaths of two federal agents. I am not about to tell the entire country that we lost two officers in this circle jerk of an operation and the subjects just slipped through our fingers. I'm just not going to do that."

"But, sir—"

The finger again. "Let me stress this to you, Feller. Daniel Erickson is dead. Any other assertion by you would not only be insubordinate, it might very well be dangerous." One of the phones on Bovard's desk rang. He winced. "Now get out of here. I have to take this."

Feller got up from his chair, shoulders slumped in defeat, but still convinced he had a case to make. He opened his mouth to speak.

Bovard pointed toward the door. "Now!"

There was nothing left to do but follow orders. He silently slumped toward the door and then closed it behind him.

* * *

Bovard waited until he was certain he was alone before putting the receiver to his ear.

"Yes, sir?"

He waited for the screaming on the other end of the line to stop before he made any reply. "Frankly, sir, this has all the splashback potential of a fat guy taking a chili shit. It's just going to get all over everything else unless we take care of it."

There was more yelling.

"I've issued a statement that the two subjects died in the incident. That should keep Joe and Janie Polltaker satisfied. The problem is that they weren't killed. We know that they escaped the scene." More yelling. Bovard was eager to make it clear that it was all Feller's fault, but he knew the excuse would only draw more fire his way.

"Yes, sir. I agree." Bovard turned in his chair and looked out at the light snow falling over DC. "I have a cleaner in mind, sir. Private. Very good. Has a unique relationship to our situation. I think he'll be perfect in resolving the matter."

More yelling. And strict instructions.

"I'm aware of the approaching budget hearings. I understand the implications and consequences if our subjects were to surface now." He held up the report that Feller had filed with him. "We have extensive intelligence on the subjects. We have a clear indication of where they're heading."

Bovard sat and watched the snow fall, no longer listening to the prattling voice. "I assure you, both subjects will be terminated before that becomes a possibility."

"Yes, sir. Merry Christmas to you, too."

CHAPTER TWENTY-FIVE

They made the run from St. Thomas to San Juan without any problems, though the Mona Passage was rough and Vicki spent a good portion of that leg of the journey either vomiting or wishing she could.

Moog, too.

In San Juan, they got fresh clothes and showered at the Club Nautico de San Juan. Then they ate their first meal in a full day while Petit Pete fueled up the *Marie*.

From there, Cap'n Eddie set a course around the Dominican Republic's eastern coast and on to Turks and Caicos. Then on to Long Island. Another fuel stop. By the time they reached Nassau, they had gotten used to ocean travel—and Cap'n Eddie.

From Nassau it was a straight shot to Fort Lauderdale. On the docks of the Lauderdale Marina, Cap'n Eddie promised them it'd just be another two days to Savannah.

That sounded fine to Daniel, but his traveling companions mutinied and informed him that there was absolutely nothing he could do to get them on a boat. Any boat. Especially the *Marie*. Ever again.

They got rooms at the Lago Mar and slept for the better part of a day.

Clean sheets and hot showers have amazing restorative powers for the human soul. When they met the next morning for breakfast on the Seagrape Terrace, the nightmarish events that had driven them from St. Thomas had faded enough to be emotionally compartmentalized. At least, they were compartmentalized enough to be the subject of a hushed conversation over plates of pancakes, bacon, and hash browns.

"Why?" Moog wondered, still chewing through a mouthful. "I mean, why the hell did they blow up the house?"

Daniel shook his head, though he thought he knew the answer. "You know how the gas stove was. The pilot light went out right before—" He stopped, looking over at Vicki, knowing she was better, but still not good, with everything that had happened. "Probably just a spark that set off the gas." He realized there was nothing he could say, and so he filled his mouth with pancake instead.

Vicki, who had been paying more attention to the complimentary newspaper that'd been dropped by her door than to either of them, suddenly exclaimed, "Oh my God!" Rapidly scanning the page, she repeated herself as she raised shocked eyes to meet theirs. "Oh my God!"

"What?" Daniel asked.

She folded the paper in quarters and pushed the article that had her looking like she'd just won the Irish Lottery across the linen tablecloth. He picked it up and began to read. "'US Marshals Killed in Late Night St. Thomas Raid'?" His tone expressed concern over what exactly she'd found so smile-worthy in that headline.

"Read the article," she instructed with a *go-on, go-on* brush of the hand.

He did. He read every word to himself until he came to the passage that pronounced, "Special Agent in Charge Ross Bovard stated that also dead in the blaze were Daniel Marion Erickson and Vernon Turner."

Moog was truly shocked. "Marion?"

"It's a family name."

Vicki snatched back the paper and used it to hit Daniel in the head. And then Moog. "Will you two stop it?"

"Seriously? Marion? Did your parents hate you?" He had a big smile, too.

"First off, Marion was John Wayne's first name."

"Who?"

"And yes, my parents hated me."

"Don't you two realize what this means?" She held the paper up as Exhibit A.

"That they got the story wrong," Daniel ventured.

"No," Vicki assured him. "It means that the FBI won't be looking for you anymore."

Daniel cast a quick look around the room. Old habit. "FBI's not the worst of what's looking for me," he reminded her.

"Well, they won't be looking for you, either," she reasoned. "No one is going to be looking for you anymore, because everyone thinks you're dead."

"Hey," Moog said, his thick eyebrows rising when it finally hit him. "She's right."

"We can start over," Vicki said, slipping her hand on top of Daniel's. "This is what we've been praying for all along."

Daniel gave her a "Yeah," but his eyes didn't dance like hers.

It troubled her. "What's wrong?"

"Nothing's wrong."

"You know what?" Moog looked across the table at the tense situation, which was rapidly brewing into something he didn't want to be a part of. "I think I'm gonna head back up to my room for a bit."

"Everything's fine," Daniel assured him.

"You know, whatever. I'm just gonna—" Before Moog could finish, he was gone.

Daniel went back to his breakfast. He only got through a forkful or two, though, before her laser-guided glare got the best of him. "What?"

"Oh, I don't know." She was hotter than the coffee. "For a fucking year you've been whispering in my ear, 'If only...' and now that we get the chance, now that this wonderful tragedy has taken place, you're sitting there eating pancakes."

"They're good pancakes."

He had to spring from his seat to catch her by the wrist. Gently, he pulled her back to her chair and then leaned in to wipe the tear that had betrayed her and would not be contained. "I was only joking."

"Don't," she said flatly. "Don't take a year of my life, promise me more, and then tell me you're joking."

"I'm not joking about any of that," he swore, with her hand in his and his eyes staring straight into hers. "I want all of that, the today and the tomorrow. All of it, but—"

There was always a "but." Every fairy tale starts with "Once upon a time" and ends with a "but."

Vicki braced herself, her posture daring him to throw down whatever it was that he had. "Go ahead. 'But' what? Just say it."

"But there's something I have to do first."

"What?" she demanded.

With everything that they'd been through, he hadn't told her about what had happened to her friend. Now that it was time to tell her, he didn't know how to begin. "The morning—" he started, finding he wasn't eager to remember it, either. He tried again. "Our last morning on the island—"

She looked at him expectantly.

"When the police took me away…they took me to Mark's house."

"Mark's house?" It was the last thing she'd expected him to bring up. "Why?"

He didn't want to tell her the whole story, but what he could share was more than enough. "They wanted to know what I knew about—"

"About Mark?" The piece-by-piece reveal only confused her. "What about Mark?"

There was nothing to do but tell her. "Mark's dead."

That she understood. "Oh my God." She considered the possibilities. "Did you?"

"Did I do what?" He saw the accusation in the way she looked at him. "No, of course not." It bothered him that it would have crossed her mind.

She shook her head and poked at her pancakes with her fork, but there were no tears. There was nothing close to the total breakdown Daniel had been expecting.

He was ashamed to admit it, but there was satisfaction to be found in the absence.

Still, the few pieces of information he'd given her didn't quite add up. "What does this have to do with us now?"

"I made a promise that I'd find out who killed him."

"A promise? To who?"

"Myself, I guess."

"Then you can let yourself out of it. There's nothing we can do for Mark now. And we can start over now that everyone thinks you're dead."

"Not everyone," Daniel corrected, thinking on his feet. "Whoever sent those two after us, that person knows that the killers didn't come back that night. Whatever the FBI thinks, whatever the rest of the world thinks, the person who sent the killers knows that I'm still alive. If we're going to close everything once and for all, we need to find that person."

"And how do you plan on doing that?"

He pulled out the CD he'd been taking great care of since he'd escaped the fireball that consumed their house and placed the silver disc on the table.

She looked down and knew right away what it meant. "Oh shit. Really?"

CHAPTER TWENTY-SIX

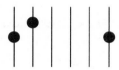

None of what Daniel and Vicki had to say made any sense to the big guy. "Marco Pharaoh? I thought you said the guy's name was Wannaman?"

"It was," Daniel conceded. "Marco Pharaoh was a stage name. Like David Bowie, Alice Cooper, Iggy Pop, or Freddie Mercury."

"I never heard of any of those guys."

"You've never heard of David Bowie?"

"This isn't Modern Music 101, kids," Vicki said, trying to herd them back on point.

"Marco Pharaoh died in a car crash five years ago," Daniel began. "Or so I—and everyone else in the world—had been led to believe."

"Marco Pharaoh?" the big man repeated, like there was something caught between the teeth of his memory and repeating the name might pick it out. "Marco Pharaoh?"

"He told me it was really his friend that died in the crash and that he went on the run." He held up the CD of the album Mark had been recording. "This is *Rock Island Rock*. What Mark was working on at our place was a collection of songs that summarize what he'd discovered after investigating his own death. It was like a musical version of Sherlock Holmes in the parlor confronting all the suspects."

"A CD? Really?" Moog was understandably wary. "Again?"

"That's what I said," Vicki chimed in.

"Again," Daniel said solidly.

"Well, what do the songs say about who did it?" Moog wanted to know.

"It's not like that," Daniel admitted. "They're just songs. The lyrics paint images but it's not like they come right out and say, 'This is the guy who tried to off me.'"

"All right," Vicki started. "What's the first step?"

"I think the first thing we have to see is whether there's anything to his story. Maybe he was another Jim Morrison, but maybe he was just a deluded fan. I say we go to Rock Island—"

"Rock Island?" Moog asked with a note of alarm. "Man, we can't go back to St. Thomas."

"No, no," Daniel assured him. "The island of St. Thomas is Rock City. Rock Island is the city in Illinois where Mark Wannaman was from. And where he died."

"Wait a minute," Moog insisted. "Rock Island, Illinois? This guy, this rock-and-roll dude that wrapped his Carrera around a goddamn pine tree?"

Daniel nodded. "That's what I've been saying."

"Hell, no. I ain't going all the way up to Illinois to poke my nose around that shit."

"What do you mean?"

"I mean, we've had a full year of—trouble. Hell, I've had a lifetime of trouble. And now that we finally get a leg up, millions of dollars, no one looking for us no more…now you want to shit on that and go play detective on some wild goose chase all the way up to Illinois?"

Vicki had agreed to join Daniel—and unbeknownst to her, he'd agreed to take her along in order to keep her safe—but what Moog was saying made a lot of sense to her, too. "No—"

"I understand if you want out," Daniel told his friend.

"Good," Moog said flatly. "I don't want any part of this."

It wasn't what Daniel had been hoping to hear, but…"All right."

"You two are crazy to go put yourselves into something that could blow up real damn quick."

"What are you talking about?" Daniel wondered.

Moog realized he'd come on a little too strong. "Come on," he coaxed. "We can find a place to start over now. Just leave this shit behind us."

"I said I understood," Daniel repeated. "If you don't want to be a part of this, I totally understand."

"And you're going to go?" Moog didn't understand. "Without me?"

"I have to."

"And how far you think you're gonna get without me?"

Daniel wasn't sure of the exact nature of the question, but he couldn't help but feel slighted by it anyway. "As far as I need to."

Both men looked like they were getting ready to walk back to their corners. Vicki was quick to come between them. "We're just going to take a quick run up north. Nobody's looking for us anymore. It'll be no big deal. We'll have a look around and then we can meet up again."

"It's always a big deal with him," Moog said.

"What's that supposed to mean?" Daniel sounded defensive, but inside he knew he had no ground to stand on there.

"And then what?" Moog wanted to know. "You turn over rocks and find a snake. Then what? Or doesn't that matter, like everything else around you?"

Daniel knew he couldn't share that part. Not yet. "What does it matter? I thought you were leaving."

The big man crossed his arms. "You don't know what you're getting into."

"And you do?"

"I know there are some things that are better left alone." Moog stared at his friend.

"And there are some things that you can't let go of." Daniel stared right back. "No matter how hard you try."

"Oh my God," Vicki groaned. "I am so sick of both of you and your bullshit macho mantras. There's so much misguided testosterone here I think I'm growing a set of balls myself."

Moog's arms uncrossed. "All right, I'll go."

"I thought you didn't want to."

"I still don't. But you pay me to watch over you."

Daniel didn't want it to be like that. "You can have the money."

"I finish the job," Moog told him, though cash was the last thing on his mind. "You know that about me."

"All right, we take a quick look," Vicki said, more brightly than she felt. "This time next week, we'll be on a beach on the Mediterranean."

Moog had one concern. "They don't have lizards there, do they?"

"They have lizards everywhere."

CHAPTER TWENTY-SEVEN

Washington, DC, is dotted with shrines, monuments, and venerable old institutions. While each holds its unique place in the nation's history, there is arguably none more revered and beloved than Ben's Chili Bowl. Since the days when Ike was living across town and Chuck Berry first introduced the world to "Johnny B. Goode" and the unique guitar style that would become the cornerstone of rock and roll, Ben's has been serving up world-famous chili half-smokes for presidents and pundits, rockers and Republicans, around the clock.

While most of the District was home and fast asleep, Special Agent Karl Schweeter sat at a table in the very back of the dining room with a late-night half-smoke, an order of chili cheese fries, and a Barq's. He focused his attention on his food and made a point of not looking up when Special Agent Gerald Feller stepped in out of the night and approached his table.

"What's this about?" Feller demanded.

Schweeter looked up from his midnight snack. "Take a chair."

"What's with the late-night greasy-spoon Deep Throat routine, Karl?"

"It's the only way I can be certain we're not being followed," he explained, with a quick look around the room, "and still have a reasonable alibi if we are seen together."

Feller was confused. "Followed?"

"You haven't noticed them?" There was a note of incredulity in Schweeter's voice, suggesting that anyone who had ever so much as seen a Bourne movie should have picked up the tail. "They're ours." His eyes darted around the room again. "It's not a constant detail. I think they're just keeping tabs."

"You think the Bureau's watching us?" Feller's voice contained its own notes of disbelief.

"I'm sure of it," Schweeter affirmed, his mouth blissfully full. "Aren't you going to eat? I'll wait while you order."

Feller shook off the suggestion. "I'm not hungry."

"You sure?" Schweeter cajoled. "It's really fabulous."

"I get it," Feller snapped impatiently. "They're good chili dogs. What I don't get is why you asked me to meet you here at one in the morning." That wasn't all of it. "And why you think the Bureau is surveilling us."

Schweeter wiped his chili-stained mouth with a napkin and nervously looked the place over, checking to see if anyone at the other tables was paying particular attention. When he was confident no one was, he continued in a tone so hushed Feller could barely hear him. "St. Thomas." He took a drink of his root beer and had another look around the room. "And Erickson."

"There's nothing to talk about," Feller pointed out. "The Bureau's gone on record as stating Erickson and Turner are dead."

Schweeter stretched out his hand to caution Feller about raising his voice. "They had to." There was something about the way the junior agent made the pronouncement that took Feller by surprise. If anything, Schweeter had always been too solicitous, too much of an ass-kisser even for him. Now his tone was almost patronizing, like he was pointing out life's little realities to those challenged few who simply hadn't been smart enough to grasp them on their own. "The Bureau can't admit there were agents lost *and* that their fugitives remain on the run. It just doesn't play well with a post-9/11 public. It plays even worse with the Congressional Budget Committee."

"I'll tell you what won't play well." Feller wasn't sure where it was hidden, but he sensed an accusation of incompetence in what Schweeter had just said, and he couldn't help reacting defensively. "When Erickson continues his crime spree and the Bureau has to explain why there's a dead man walking around. *That* won't play well."

"It'll never come to that," Schweeter said calmly but confidently. "I'm sure they're already at work on an operation to turn their fiction into fact."

"What are you suggesting?"

"I'm not suggesting anything. I'm stating plainly that they know what we know. That means they have to be looking for Erickson. The minute they find him"—he paused for effect—"we lose our one and only opportunity to pull ourselves out of what happened in St. Thomas."

Feller hadn't considered the situation quite like that before.

"And," Schweeter continued, gesturing with a chili fry to underscore the importance of his point, "we become the only two people in the whole wide world who can expose their deception." He took the fry in a single bite. "The way I look at it, that's not a position either one of us will survive. Unless—"

"Unless what?"

"Unless we find Erickson before they do."

"How are we going to do that? Bovard will never give us the resources. You said yourself—"

Schweeter smiled knowingly. "Then we'll have to get what we need somewhere else." Another sip of root beer. "Like Russia."

Feller was confused again. "Russia?"

"Erickson killed Preezrakevich, right?" The young man didn't wait for a response. "Took some money, right? Russian mob money. Well, I'm guessing our Eastern friends must want their cash back."

"And I'm sure they're looking—for him, same as we are." Feller stopped to consider the long-range implication of the official announcement that Erickson had been killed. "Or they *were*, before the FBI told the world he was dead." It was all coming together for him.

"Exactly," Schweeter confirmed, glad the student was following along. "But we have leads from St. Thomas, information that points where Erickson is headed. Intel that's as good as anything anyone has right now."

"All right." Feller understood that part.

"And as it happens, I still have a contact in the Bravta from a video-pirating case I worked last year. If we give our lead on Erickson to my guy, the mob will send their own team to hunt him down. All we have to do is bird-dog the Russians, and they'll lead us right to him. Then, before they do anything to him, we nab Erickson ourselves." He said it like it was simple.

It was all making sense now, and Feller was eager to spell out the next steps. "*And* redeem ourselves with the Bureau by arresting—"

"Whoa," Schweeter cautioned. "The whole point of everything is that the Bureau can't let on that it lied about Erickson. So if we don't kill him ourselves, they will." There was an upside, however. "But that will put us back on a career track at the Hoover and buy us both a much-needed insurance policy on our careers. And our lives."

It was all making a lot of sense to Special Agent Gerald Feller. He was shady on what exactly would happen to their prey when the hunt was done, but he saw the campaign as an opportunity to maybe, once and for all, gain the respect that had been denied him for so long. "I'm in."

CHAPTER TWENTY-EIGHT

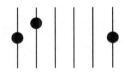

For all of the blood it has spilled in the name of revolution, Russia has never been able to rid itself of its royalty.

Romanovs or Marxists. Stalinists or Khrushchev Communists. Whatever the particular political doctrine, Moscow's grand palaces and opulent great houses have always been occupied by those who held the power.

Those magnificent structures still stand. The same standards apply. But today their tenants are venture capitalists and members of the *russkaya mafiya*—a distinction that is not always clear in Russia's byzantine take on capitalism.

The Pushkinskya Mansion had been built at the dawn of the nineteenth century, but Ivan Nurivov had no interest in the house's history. He climbed the ornately carved marble staircase without appreciation and walked down the hall with a sense of purpose, but without concern for the Giustiniani porcelain tiles beneath his feet. Works from Borovikovsky and Losenko and Kandinsky lined the walls, but he never stopped to pay attention to any of them.

The Cro-Magnon in the leather jacket by the hand-carved mahogany door held out his hand to stop him. "He said he didn't want to be disturbed."

Ivan tried to wave him off. "He's going to want to hear this."

The troglodyte wasn't convinced. "He said he didn't want—"

"If I'm wrong," Ivan interrupted, his impatience barely contained, "then it's going to be me he feeds to his pigs." He arched an eyebrow. "But if I'm right, and you send me away…" He didn't need to finish for the guard's head to be filled with a thousand nightmarish images of death and dismemberment by swine.

"You tell him I tried to stop you," the oaf instructed as he stepped aside, foolishly believing that those words might carry some sway if their boss was displeased.

The bedroom was an enormous cavern of opulence. A mural of angels in adoration or Greek gods frolicking (it was impossible to tell which) spread over the expanse of the ceiling. Embroidered woolwork curtains covered the windows that lined the east and west walls. At the far end of the room was a F. Meltzer & Co. bed, handcrafted and ornately carved from Siberian oak, ten feet long and just as wide.

On the edge of the bed, a naked man with the build and body hair of a small bear straddled a young woman while another rubbed his furry shoulders and giggled. "What is it?" the man growled without looking up from his exertions.

Ivan took a deep breath, knowing that he'd been absolutely right about his excruciating fate if his interruption was deemed unworthy and unwelcomed. "I'm sorry, Mishka." The endearing nickname referenced the Russian cartoon bear, but Igor Grush-enkov was every bit as vicious as the bears of Kamchatka.

"Can't you see I'm occupied?" He gestured at the two young women sharing his bed. The one beneath him tilted her head back to get a look at the intruder.

"I thought you'd want to hear immediately. I've received a message today."

"What of it?" Mishka's attention returned to the women as he kissed one and then the other.

"It was from an agent of the FBI."

Mishka sat upright. "Why would an agent of the FBI be calling you?" The question was laced with enough suspicion to qualify as an allegation.

"He said he had information regarding *Gospodin* Preezrakevich."

"Preezrakevich is dead," Grushenkov snapped with a dismissive wave of his hand. "What more does anyone need to know of a man than that?"

"He said he knows how to find the man who killed him."

Mishka's interest was piqued. "And the money?"

Ivan shrugged, unable to answer with certainty. "If it's still with him. Yes."

It was a tempting proposition. But perhaps too tempting. He needed time to consider its facets. "The vodka," Grushenkov called out, indicating a bottle of Stoli Gold on the antique bar cabinet. "Bring it here."

Ivan did as he was told, handing the bottle to his boss, who took a long drink from it.

Mishka nodded at the woman beneath him and told Ivan, "Hold her hands down." The woman looked up and purred as Ivan took hold of her wrists and pinned them to the sheets.

"And why is our American friend reaching out to us?" Mishka asked casually, as he reached out with his free hand and roughly seized the woman's face with it. Her eyes suddenly widened with alarm.

Ivan tightened his grip as the woman began to fight to free herself, but his voice was calm and his attention focused on business. "The man they say is responsible, the FBI has announced they've already killed this man. If it becomes public they lied about this, it would be bad for them."

"So they are sloppy and they want us to clean up their messes." Grushenkov let loose an exaggerated laugh.

"Pej," he called over his shoulder to the other woman, who'd been feeling ignored. "Hold open her eyes."

The woman smiled sinisterly as her manicured fingers peeled open her friend's eyelids.

"Five million dollars. American," Mishka said aloud, as if he needed to hear the figure in order to consider it. "And the head of the man who killed Preezrakevich would bring honor."

As he silently considered what he stood to gain, he carefully poured the vodka over the young woman's exposed eyes. She cried out beneath Grushenkov's hand when it splashed across her face, but he only increased his grip.

He looked up at Ivan, smiling and eager to answer the question he knew his lieutenant was too smart to ask. "The vodka in the eyes gets them drunker than the drinking and there's never mess with the vomit." He grinned. "Besides, I like it." And everyone in the room knew that was explanation enough.

Mishka let go of the woman's face and gave it a not quite playful slap. "Not so bad, huh? You're feeling better now?" She nodded and tried to hide the whimper beneath her forced smile.

Mishka looked back to Ivan. He'd made his decision. "Go. Find the man. And the money." His eyes narrowed. "But be careful. They offer much, but ask nothing. That is how my papa taught me to trap the bears."

Ivan nodded.

"Good." The beast of a man climbed off the one beneath him and turned his attention to the other. "Now help me with the second whore."

CHAPTER TWENTY-NINE

All the press kits described Marco Pharaoh and his band, Taco Shot, as products of Minneapolis's vibrant music scene, but before any of them had even heard of First Avenue and Seventh Street Entry, they'd been kids running the streets of Rock Island, Illinois.

Rock Island sits on the banks of the Mississippi, looking across the water at Davenport, Iowa. It's the heartland of the heartland. Where teens cruise the Rock Island Parkway in their dualies, just as likely to be blaring Garth Brooks as the Rolling Stones. Where everyone in town goes to Friday's Rock Island High School football game.

"Now what?" Vicki asked.

"I've been listening to the CD," Daniel said, with more enthusiasm than someone who'd just driven from Florida should have.

"We *allll* been listening to that damn CD."

Daniel flashed a disapproving look over his shoulder at Moog's backseat complaint. "That first song, 'Long, Long Way,' is just about his life on the island. 'For No One,' I think, is about the friend he said died in his place. And 'Rock Island Rock' is clearly about—"

"This bum-fuck little town," Moog supplied.

"But even a little town like Rock Island can be a big place," Vicki observed. "Now that we're here, where the hell do we go?"

"His father," Daniel said confidently.

"How'd you come up with that?" Vicki asked.

Daniel had the answer ready. "Listen to this track. 'Be That Hard.'" He pressed the button on the CD deck of the used car they'd bought in Florida, and the song started.

The first verse was backed by an acoustic guitar, almost delicately fingerpicked. Mark's voice, though still as rough as a half mile of back road, seemed emotionally strained to the point of breaking.

Hey now, would it be that hard, one time in your life
Put the motherfucking bottle down, straighten up and get-a
one thing right
Hey now, would it be that hard, one time 'fore I leave
Take me by the hand, look me in the eye, say you're proud of me?

The chorus was an explosion of acoustic and electric guitars mixed together into an angry protest. The vocal was angrier too, but there was something about the defiant declaration that made it sound more like a bluff than a boast.

I put those things behind me
When I walked out your door
I don't need your shit to remind me
I'm not looking for your love anymore.

"I get it," Moog said. "He's talking about his father."

"That's what I get out of it," Daniel agreed.

"His father?" Vicki objected. "He could be talking about any-one. And he probably is. Who sings about wanting their father's love?"

Daniel was incredulous. "Did you listen to music in the nine-ties? Everyone sang about wanting their father to love them. Fil-ter. Staind. Everclear. Pearl Jam. Everyone."

"I gotta go with Daniel on this." Moog was eager to contrib-ute. "I don't know any of those songs there, but there are men that love their fathers, hate their fathers, men that don't ever know their fathers. Hell, I've known more than a couple a men that *killed* their damn fathers. But I ain't never met no man didn't want his father to love him."

"That's right," Daniel concurred.

"Well, go wherever you want to go. I just think you all sound like little boys right now." Vicki turned in her seat to look out of the window as the miles rolled past. "There are worse things in the world than Daddy not loving you *enough*."

She didn't say any more than that. Moog didn't catch the com-ment, and Daniel knew better than to press her any further on it. They drove on in silence, but Daniel couldn't help thinking that this was how people most often revealed themselves, not with the things they said, but with what they purposely left unspoken.

It wasn't too hard to find the childhood home of the town's most famous son. They pulled off the winding two-lane leading out of town and drove down the dirt drive, following it another quarter mile to a large modern house.

"Not what you'd expect for a pig farmer," Moog observed.

"Exactly what you'd expect, for a pig farmer whose kid was a rock star," Daniel commented as he pulled up in front of the house and killed the engine. There was nothing moving out in the yard except some pigs in a far pen.

He turned in his seat. "You guys stay here. I'll go up and ask him a few questions. Find out what I need to know—"

"And then what?" Moog asked, obviously anxious to put it all behind them.

"Depends on what he tells me."

Moog shook his head in frustration, obviously disappointed by the plan.

"So you're just going to walk up to his door, ring the bell, and ask the man if his son is really dead?" The plan seemed preposterous to Vicki, too.

It seemed like a perfectly reasonable plan to Daniel. "Yup." Or at least, that was all he had.

"Well, good luck with that." She folded her arms and leaned against the backseat, daring him to go ahead and prove her misgivings right.

He was undeterred. "I'll be right back."

It wasn't until he'd climbed outside that the full smell of the pigs hit him. He winced at the stench, which had an almost physical presence in the damp morning air.

He walked up to the porch and rang the bell. From somewhere inside the McMansion, he could hear the melodic sounds of electronic door chimes ringing. He waited, but no one came to the door.

Daniel turned and looked back reassuringly toward the car, smiling as if to say, "Just going to ask the folks a quick question." But there were no folks to ask. He rang the bell again. Still no one. He knocked and then knocked again—harder—so whoever was inside would know he was serious, impatient, and not going away just because he was being ignored.

He looked past his own vehicle toward the Ford F-350 parked in the drive. There was no morning ice on the windshield and bits of slush were dropping to the ground from where they'd accumulated on the rocker panels. The truck had been out on the road this morning and whoever had been behind the wheel was likely somewhere around.

Maybe not in the house, but out on the grounds beyond it? Daniel stepped off of the porch and started around behind the house. He offered a modest wave as a sign that he was all right and was just going to have a little look-see around the place. Vicki didn't even bother to look up and Moog just left him hanging there, his hand still raised and looking for a little reciprocal wave.

Daniel walked around behind the house. "Hello?" The only answer was his own voice coming back to him weakly as a barely audible echo. "Hello?"

He turned a corner around the house and discovered he was not alone. The largest dog he'd ever seen in his life was staring at him, its haunches taut, a low growl slipping through its bared teeth.

Daniel raised his hands slowly. "Hey there, big feller." The dog, some mad scientist mix of Saint Bernard and German shepherd, didn't seem to like the new moniker. The growl deepened, and the eyes fixed on Daniel narrowed.

"Take it easy," Daniel cooed. "I'm not going to hurt you. And you're not going to hurt me." He wondered. "Got that, *mi key*?"

The term of endearment that Atibon used often was like the ultimate control word for the dog. It relaxed visibly but approached warily.

Something etched in his DNA made Daniel want to sprint for the car, but he stood his ground and stuck out a fist for the dog to smell. The dog took a whiff and then another, as if he needed confirmation. His tail wagged, and a friendship was formed.

"Where's your owner, boy?"

The dog barked twice and then trotted over toward the pens where the pigs were kept. Daniel followed, trying to tiptoe his way around the filth and mud. He did his best to keep his feet clean and dry, but there was no path he could pick that didn't put his foot square in the shit. He was so distracted by the sounds and the stench that he never heard the rubber Red Wings slosh up behind him. All he heard was the hammer of a pistol being pulled back. *That* he heard clear as a bell.

"Who the hell are you?" the voice asked.

Daniel knew better than to turn back toward the questioner, but he raised his hands slowly to make it clear he wasn't any threat. "I'm looking for Mark Wannaman's father."

"I didn't ask you what you were here after, asked you who you was."

Now it was time to turn around. Slowly, but steadily. The gun came into view first. A .44 revolver. Smith & Wesson. No-nonsense, and as American as deep-fried Coke at the state fair.

Behind the weapon was a lump of a man in a bright orange hunter's cap, an orange camouflage coat, and a pair of filthy Carhartt work pants. His unshaven face was thick and puffy, swollen with softness, and his eyes were small and hard and dark. It seemed to Daniel as if one of the boars had gotten out of the pens and dressed for the day. "Mr. Wannaman?"

His right eye squinted over the pistol barrel he had aimed at the center of Daniel's chest. "S'pose I am. Who'd that make you?"

"It'd make me a friend of your son's."

"Well, that'd make you a damn liar." He pointed his pistol with renewed purpose. "Get your ass down on the ground."

Daniel looked down at the filth at his feet. "What?"

"The ground. You're gonna drop one way or another. The *how* of it don't matter much to me."

Daniel looked at the pistol twenty feet from his chest and then down at the filth. "I just wanted to ask you a question."

"I'm not askin' you."

Daniel looked back over his shoulder, hoping he might find Moog there checking up on him, but he was all alone on this one. "Look, it—"

"All I'm looking at is you, through my sights here. I'm gonna be looking at a goddamn corpse in a minute if you don't get down on the ground."

A face full of pig shit wasn't the way he wanted to start the day, but it beat a chest full of lead. Slowly, Daniel lowered a knee down into the muck. It was every bit as cold and unpleasant as he'd expected. It smelled even worse than it felt. He lowered his other knee.

"All the way down."

Daniel put a hand down in the filth. And then another. The mess was cold against his belly. He felt a boot press him down into the mud and a hand reach into his back pocket.

"So, mister? What is it brings you asking questions about my boy?"

It was hard to talk with his face so close to the shit. "I'm going to find out who killed him."

"He killed himself. Drove into a damn tree like the fool that he was."

"We both know he didn't." Daniel's voice was unwavering. "He died six days ago. In St. Thomas. Someone beat him to death and tossed him in his pool."

The awkward moment it took for the gears of the pig man's brain to spin furiously trying to conceal the truth and then make up a lie answered everything. "He died?"

"Six days ago," Daniel repeated. "I only came here to make certain that everything he told me was true." He started to get up. "Now that I know that it was."

A boot pressed him back down. "I didn't say nothing of the sort."

Daniel spit out a mouthful of what he hoped was just mud. "We both know you just did."

"I told you. He drove himself into a tree five years ago." His voice was loud and desperate as he scrambled to make sense of everything. "You're one of them reporters, ain't you?"

"No. I'm the man who's going to find who killed your son." He managed to get up to his knees, but before he could move from there the boot kicked him back down.

Daniel had had enough. He worked hard to keep his voice calm but unyielding. "But right now I've had enough of your shit here, so I'm telling you that I'm the man who's just going to get to his feet and go. And if you've got a problem with that—"

This time, before the boot could come down, Daniel rolled to his left. The boot struck next to him in the mud, where he'd been lying just moments before. He grabbed the man's ankle and pulled as hard as he could. The fat man fell hard on the flat of his back and the impact knocked his pistol loose. It discharged as it struck the ground, the shot striking a post.

Still on his back, Daniel raised his leg in the air and brought the heel down on the pig man's nose. A fountain of blood opened up.

The dog barked and bounded back and forth, but it was clearly suffering a conflict over just whose ally he should be. Unable to make up its mind between the two men, it just barked and ran around and around the skirmish.

Daniel kicked the man again, and an instant later Daniel was on his feet with the pistol in his hands. "Didn't they ever tell you the most important lesson of handling a gun?"

The pig man dabbed at his nose. "What's that?" he asked, his voice now nasal and pained.

"Don't ever point a gun at a man unless you're going to shoot him." Daniel illustrated the point by taking aim at the center of the pig man's chest.

The pistol's accidental discharge had alerted Moog to the trouble, and he came running around the corner of the house just in time to see Daniel setting his sights on the fat man's chest. "Whoa! Whoa! Whoa!" he called out, his hands raised. "What the hell are you doing, man?"

"I've got this," Daniel assured him without taking his eyes off his target.

"Got what?" Moog asked, his eyes wide with shock. "You said we was gonna come out here, ask the man a couple questions, and go. We ain't got the time for shit like this. And I sure as hell ain't servin' in Stateville because you got it in your twisted head to get all shooty with some crazy redneck pig farmer."

"You gotta help me," the fat man pleaded.

"Shut up, cracker," Moog snapped angrily. "I ain't gotta do nothing you say. And right now I'm trying to keep you from being breakfast for those hogs, so just keep your trash hole shut." He turned his attention back to Daniel.

"I've got this," Daniel insisted again.

"Then take it," Moog snapped, having clearly reached his limit. "'Cause I'm sure as shit not going to step out there. You can clean up that mess your damn self." Moog started off a step or two before turning. "And you best better believe you gonna be riding in the trunk, 'cause I ain't sitting next to you." He stormed off around the corner he'd come from.

"Oh, Jesus!" The man reached for his bleeding nose, but Daniel stepped on the wound and the man screamed.

Moog came back around the corner of the house, but Daniel waved him off.

Moog looked at Daniel, and then at the man bleeding at his feet, and then at the still smoking pistol in his hand. "What the fuck?" he said, then walked back to the car.

Daniel turned his attention back to the man squirming beneath his foot. "Now let's get this straight. I already want to shoot you, so it's in your best interest not to give me a reason to go through with it." He felt confident the pig man understood. "Good. Now why weren't you surprised when I told you your son died this week? Because you thought he was still alive?"

The man tried to get out some defiant protest, but all that came out was a squeal as Daniel applied more pressure on his chest.

"Of course, you knew." Daniel looked at the McMansion and the pig farm. "You got paid for keeping the secret, didn't you?"

The man didn't answer, but he didn't need to.

"The question is, who paid you?"

"I got money from the estate," the man whimpered.

Daniel thought about the lyrics of "Be That Hard" and what it must've taken to write it. "Mark wouldn't have left you any money."

"I didn't inherit it. The estate pays me."

"For what?"

"On account I was his father," the man insisted through gritted teeth.

"You don't have time to lie to me."

"I don't know anything else." He was too desperate to lie. "I get a check twice a year. That's all I know. Money from the record company."

"Pay you for what?"

"I don't know," the man cried. Daniel stepped harder on his chest. "I get paid to stay stupid. I didn't ask questions back then, and I don't ask questions now."

"You made a deal to pretend your son was dead?" Daniel's voice was filled with contempt.

"I ain't the only one." The man offered it up as if company in the offense was a sufficient defense. "Socks done it too," he insisted.

"Who?"

"Billy Wright. Everybody calls him Socks. He drinks down at the Fiesta. His son was Mark's buddy. He was a—roadie for their band. They was like brothers, the two of them."

"He was the one in the car," Daniel surmised aloud.

"Socks knows more than I do," the farmer insisted. "On account—"

Daniel had enough of the pieces to fill this part in. "Because he was the one who actually lost a son." Daniel shook his head dismissively. "You're quite a pair." He let the hand holding the pistol relax so that the weapon was no longer aimed at the man beneath his foot.

"You don't know how it was," the man asserted, a little bolder now that the pistol was no longer pointed at his chest. "You don't know nuthin."

"I know your son loved you. I don't know why. He didn't, either. But he loved you till the end. You should've done better by him—Mark deserved a better father." Daniel turned and walked away.

"Hey," the pig man called after him, awkwardly climbing back to his feet. "Ain't you gonna give me back my gun?"

Daniel didn't bother to turn around. "No. I need it."

"You're a goddamn thief!" the man called after him.

He'd been called worse. He kept walking.

Behind him, Daniel heard the old man cursing out the dog. "Goddamn mutt. I don't keep you 'round here to play fetch with the damn trespassers." There was some commotion and then suddenly the dog let out a pained howl that subsided into a long, drawn-out whimper.

Daniel stopped.

The pig man seemed genuinely surprised to see Daniel walking back toward him. "What do you want now?"

Daniel looked over at the dog, which was limping around the yard, clearly favoring its left rear leg. "Did you just kick that dog?"

"None of your goddamn business if I did," the pig man announced defiantly. "I'll be goddamned if any man is going to come to my property and tell me how I treat my damn dog." He was genuinely exercised by the possibility. "Why, if I wanna—"

Daniel fired once. The pig man dropped to the ground and wailed in pain.

Daniel knelt down beside him. His voice was surprisingly calm. "You're shot in the foot. It's not going to kill you unless you don't get some help soon and you end up lying there in that cold mud for too long and lapse into shock, up to your double chins in pig shit. That'd be a shitty way to die. Do you understand?"

A groan was the man's only response, but it was enough of an acknowledgment for Daniel.

"Now here's how this is going to work," Daniel told him, his voice hard. "I'm not going to finish you off right now. You're going to crawl your fat ass up to your house and get yourself some help. When the ambulance arrives, you're going to tell everyone you had an accident. It could've happened to anyone, understand?"

The man groaned and nodded. "Because if anyone asks me about our little conversation here, I'm going to come back and put one in your head. Understand?"

The man grunted.

Now Daniel grew really serious. "And if you ever hurt that dog—or any dog—ever again. I'm going to come back here and put a slug in your head." Daniel recognized the hole in that. "And, trust me, I'll know. All right?"

The pig man whimpered and then groaned some more.

"OK. I'm going to take off then." Daniel got back to his feet and looked down at the wound. "You really ought to get that looked at."

Daniel turned and walked away. The dog followed him all the way back to the car.

CHAPTER THIRTY

Arthur Beagler kept a close watch in his rearview as he followed US 50 West from his home in St. Michaels, Maryland, into the District of Columbia, then took the Beltway around the city, exiting in Arlington. He drove to the Crystal City Underground and backed his BMW 750i into a spot in the garage near the stairs. A handful of peanuts tossed casually on the ground beside the sedan would look like simple snack spillage to any suburban shopper, but crushed shells when he returned would warn him that someone had approached his vehicle.

He took the stairs off to his right and descended past the shops, all the way down to the Metro station. From Crystal City it was the yellow train all the way to the end of the line at Mt. Vernon Square, with Arthur surreptitiously making mental notes on every passenger who shared his car. At the prompting of the announcement, he left his seat and stepped onto the platform, but then turned back to the same car and rode it back a stop to the Gallery Place station. When he got off the train and ascended the escalator to the Verizon Center, he was absolutely certain that he hadn't been followed.

That only meant whoever had sent the ticket and accompanying instructions hadn't bothered to try to place a tail. It didn't mean that it still wasn't a trap.

Arthur ordered a beer, not to drink but as a prop, his gaze seeming to sink casually into the pale golden liquid, but his eyes constantly scanned the passing faces for a glimpse of something that would tip him off. He looked hard, but nobody rushing past his position took any notice of him as he tried his best to blend in with the crowd—no easy feat for a six-foot-five-inch black man at a hockey game.

When he heard the opening bars of the National Anthem, Arthur realized that whoever had summoned him there had carefully planned the reveal of this trap. There was nothing to do but turn and walk away or step right into it. He threw the beer away and walked into the arena.

Section 121. Row D. Seat 3. Arthur took the seat awkwardly, his arthritic joints unable to smoothly make the necessary contortions. Then a line of men filed in from either side, and the trap was sprung.

Arthur didn't recognize either of the two men who took the seats to his left without ever looking toward him. Their identities didn't matter. Black suits. White shirts. Dark ties. They were generic in every way. Just two Feds who'd been plugged into those seats to keep him from moving left. Seat warmers.

There was, however, nothing generic about the man moving toward Arthur from his right. His face, full with bloat and colored with a drinker's blush, was all too familiar.

Arthur leaned back in the uncomfortable plastic seat and shook his head with a degree of self-reproach. "I should have known."

Special Agent in Charge Russ Bovard grinned triumphantly, as if just sitting down next to Arthur was his endgame. "You would have come anyway."

"Like hell I would've." The big man said it with conviction.

Bovard shrugged off the assertion. "Then we would've just come to you. And that would've been worse."

"Worse for who?"

"Worse for me," Bovard admitted. "I don't have any desire to go to Maryland." He fidgeted in his seat, but couldn't get comfortable, either. "And worse for you, because then we couldn't have a friendly conversation like we're having now." He pointed enthusiastically toward the game being played out on the rink. "And look at this, we're practically on the ice."

"Cold makes my knees ache," Arthur grumbled. He rubbed them as if the admission had made them suddenly hurt more. "You couldn't have done this to me at a basketball game, for God's sake?"

Bovard casually turned his hands toward the ceiling. "The Wizards were out of town."

"I coulda waited."

Bovard's eyes were fixed on the game. "This can't."

On the ice there was a collision and Marcus Johansson fell forward, sliding a distance on the front of his sweater. At the point of impact there was some pushing between some Capitals and part of Toronto's second line, but the referee intervened before gloves were thrown. Above them the speakers announced, "Tripping. Toronto. Two minutes. Number four, Cody Franson." Most of the crowd booed enthusiastically, but it wasn't clear whether they were displeased with the infraction or the ref's interference in a might-have-been-melee.

"Ooh! That's a tough call." Bovard grimaced. "The ice here is as soft as a Democrat's dick."

"Yeah, well, I'm not interested in Democrats or dicks or this fucking silly-ass game or anything else you got for me tonight." Arthur started physical preparations for what he knew would be an arduous and painful extraction from his seat.

"Sit down, Arthur."

The big man looked down incredulously at the liver-spotted hand hanging on to the sleeve of his suit coat and then into the bloodshot eyes staring right back at him. "Don't you ever put a hand to me again." He pulled his arm away defiantly. "And it's *Mister Beagler* to you."

Maybe it was the plainclothes security he'd brought with him, or maybe he simply wasn't aware of the nature of the man he was addressing, but Bovard was unimpressed. "Spare me the Poitier routine, *Arthur*. I've got a mess on my hands, and I'm in no mood."

"You got a mess," Arthur repeated with a snort. "Well, go clean it up your own self. I ain't no janitor."

Bovard leaned menacingly close so his words couldn't be overheard over the crowd's roar. "You're exactly who I say you are. That can go on being the Arthur Beagler who's currently enjoying retirement from—what is it you tell everyone out in St. Michaels, pharmaceutical sales, is it? Or you can just as easily be Arthur Beagler, whose neighbors never suspected he was a Muslim extremist with terrorist ties. Or the head of a white slavery ring. Or any other thing I want to make you. Understand? Declaring who you are is what I do." He stared hard into Arthur's hard brown eyes.

"Why me?"

"We have a situation that has escalated beyond conventional care," Bovard began.

"Two subjects have eluded our grasp. Certain public representations have been made concerning their status. We need—"

Arthur understood exactly what they were after. "You need someone to make your lie the truth."

"I'd like to see it as needing someone to make our truth a reality." A glass-half-full grin spread over Bovard's jowly face.

"You know I'm retired. I ain't taken a job in more than five years. You ain't got someone younger and brighter-eyed than me in your stables?"

"The stables are full," Bovard admitted. "But I thought you'd have a personal incentive to complete this assignment."

Arthur asked the question before he could think better of it. "What gave you that idea?"

"One of the targets is your boy Turner."

Arthur restrained himself from registering a reaction. "Why you think that'd give me incentive to do anything?"

"We were led to believe there was some bad blood—"

"Families fight." That was an end to it for Arthur.

Bovard, however, had a Plan B. "If that subject should come into custody elsewhere, it could put your own status in jeopardy."

Arthur just laughed at the suggestion. "You think my Moog would sell me out?"

"He's become an embarrassment," Bovard responded. "Even if he didn't give you up, the situation would make people—people with even greater resources than me—so nervous that there'd be more conversations like this, conversations in which you'd be the subject, not a participant."

"Are you threatening me?" It seemed an odd question to ask with a light note of amusement. "I'm sixty-four years old. My fucking knees ache so I can barely walk and my back's bent worse than a hound dog's hind leg. I can't fucking sleep half the time and when I do I keep waking up to take a piss, which I can't do half the time, either. I'm retired, got no hobbies, and ain't laid with a woman in more than two years."

This time it was Arthur's turn to make sure there were no misunderstandings. "I ain't scared of death. Death is an old friend I haven't seen in a long, long time. So if you brought me all the way down here just to let me know he's back in town, all I can tell you is send him round. Anytime. I'd enjoy one last go round with that sumbitch before we walk off into the night with our arms over one another's shoulders."

"You misunderstand me, Arthur. I'm not threatening any-one." Bovard smiled as if he was conceding defeat, but it was just on to Part C of his plan. "I'm merely pointing out what men like you and I know too well: this is an unpredictable world. One day you're—oh, I don't know—an adjunct professor of sociology down at Johns Hopkins, and the next thing you know, a robbery has gone wrong. Or your history of depression has left you sui-cidal. Maybe your novelist husband, the recovering addict, finally snaps and sets the house on fire with you in it. Who knows?"

If Arthur Beagler had ever known fear, his eyes were sud-denly wide with it now. "You leave my girl out of this."

"I didn't bring her into this, Arthur. I came to you with a problem I need resolved, and you started reminiscing about your old friend Death. I was merely reminding you that you two may go way back, but he's still on my payroll." Endgame.

Arthur Beagler hadn't seen his daughter since she was seven. Or at least, he hadn't let her see him. He was at her graduation from the Brearley School. And Columbia. And Hopkins. He was the cop outside the church where she was married. And the orderly who stopped and stared at the nursery window when she'd had a daughter of her own.

"I ain't doing it for free," Arthur insisted. "I ain't no man's slave."

Bovard had already anticipated as much. "The usual rate. Waiting to be wired."

Arthur wasn't motivated to ask for more. "When?"

Bovard cringed. "You have a week."

Arthur laughed to himself. "Congressional budgetary meetings."

Bovard looked at him as if someone had stolen his poker hand.

"I'm old and black. I'm not ignorant. You want these boys—my boy—dead before you have to go asking for money, 'cause they don't give money to fools with egg on their face."

"Everything you need is there." Bovard dropped a zip drive into Arthur's huge hand. "That's all of the intel we've got."

"Everything I need except what it takes to get it done," Arthur corrected.

"That's your part."

Arthur nodded, somewhere between understanding and capitulation.

"Now that we've reached an understanding, you'll have to excuse me." Bovard started to get to his feet. "Feel free to stay for the rest of the game."

This time it was Arthur who reached out to stop an untimely exit. "Bovard."

"What?"

"You made a mistake bringing up my baby." His grip tightened as his words intensified. "In a business like ours, men should stick to business."

Bovard tried in vain to free his wrist without causing a scene. "Why's that?"

"Because when you take out the clarity and civility that money brings to matters, when you make it personal, you discover that some of us are monsters."

"Grow up, Arthur." Bovard grinned knowingly. "We're all monsters."

"Maybe." Arthur knew better. "But some of us are scarier than others."

CHAPTER THIRTY-ONE

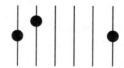

Garlands were strung from bottle to bottle along the back bar, and an assortment of warped cardboard reindeer hung from the ceiling, making the place seem like somewhere an alcoholic Santa might have stopped on the way back from his around-the-world excursion to wind down with a drink or two.

A bright slice of winter afternoon barged into the darkened barroom when the door opened, and the old-timers at the bar turned in unison to regard it with a mix of horror and contempt.

Their look did not soften when a freshly showered (and reshowered) Daniel stepped in through the light. He'd suggested coming alone, and neither Vicki nor Moog were interested in accompanying him any longer.

He took a place at the bar, and the half-dozen regulars rearranged themselves in subtle ways to accommodate the presence of a stranger in their midst.

"What can I get you?" the man behind the bar asked, but there was nothing welcoming in the question.

"I'm looking to talk to Socks," Daniel told him.

"Lookee here," the bartender started, already laughing at the joke he was about to tell. "This here's a bar, ain't no JCPenney."

Some of the regulars laughed and twittered, but no one looked up to make eye contact.

"You want a drink or not?"

Daniel took out a Grant and put it on the bar. "I just want a Coke." The bartender poured the drink from the soda hose and then looked at the bill, more annoyed than hopeful. "I can't break this."

Daniel took a sip from the flat soda. "Tell me where I can find Socks, and you won't have to."

The bartender looked long and hard at the regulars lining the bar and then longer and harder at the fifty-dollar bill. With a quick toss of his head, he indicated the skinny man at the far end of the bar.

Daniel left the bill and walked down the length of a bar that was way too small for stealth. Everyone watched Daniel as he passed. The old man watched him as he approached.

"Socks?"

"You already know I am," the man admitted as he finished off his beer. "Ain't no need to put it as a question."

"I'd like to talk to you if I could."

The old man looked down wistfully at the suds gathered around the bottom of his otherwise empty glass. "My throat's a bit dry for talking."

Daniel put another bill on the bar and gestured to the bartender, who poured and brought a fresh beer.

The bartender looked suspiciously at the bill and then to Daniel, who nodded and indicated the length of the bar. "Everybody."

There were brief mumblings of thanks, but no outpourings of gratitude.

"I want a shot of Wild Turkey," Socks called after the bartender. "Double." He looked down at the portrait of a president he didn't recognize. "Just bring the bottle."

He looked straight ahead at the bar back, never turning to Daniel. "Now what do you think I know that's worth this much liquor."

"It's about Mark Wannaman."

The old man's mood and posture changed. "What about him?"

"Mark Wannaman and your son."

"I said what about him?"

"I met a man recently who said he was Mark Wannaman."

"Don't surprise me none."

"Even though he's been dead—"

"He ain't been nothin' but gone," the old man objected. "You know that, or you wouldn't be here throwin' your money around like this."

"They say your son was a passenger in the car, but he ran off."

"My son never ran off nowhere. That's not how he was. What goddamn reason would he have to do it?"

"So you knew Mark was alive and you didn't say anything about it?"

"Two days after the accident, an envelope turned up at the house. Ten grand in it."

"And you didn't think to say something to someone?"

"You can't pay the mortgage with a dead boy." He didn't need to turn to know the look on Daniel's face. "And you can judge me all you want, but that's the truth of the matter. I got a sick wife and a bad ticker. I grieved my boy same as any father would have." He took a sip of his Wild Turkey. "And I will till they bury me right next to him." Another sip. "Or at least, where he oughta be."

Daniel had a renewed sense of compassion for the man, but how could he not ask, "What do you mean?"

"Well, they stole the body."

"Who?"

"Never did find out. Word was, it was the boys from the band. Some sort of oath they all took. That if one of them died, the others would take the body out into the desert and set him ablaze. I never believed it though." He took another thoughtful sip. "I always thought they'd done it just so I could never prove it was my boy that died."

Daniel thought it over. "Wait a minute. If someone did that to disguise the fact that it was your son who died in the accident, then why keep paying you?"

"I always figured it was Mark, you know. Compensating me for how my son died and all. And for keeping his secret."

Daniel had a hunch. "When's the last time you received money?"

"Beginning of the week. Why?"

"Because whoever's been paying you needs to keep the secret now more than ever."

"Why's that?"

"Because Mark Wannaman really is dead."

"For real?"

"For real. About a week ago."

"Then who—"

"That's what I was about to ask you."

He thought on it hard. "I can't imagine. The only one of the boys I hear from anymore is Alan Lucca. Their bass player. Got a Christmas card from him just the other week."

"You wouldn't happen to have an address from that card, would you?"

"Sure I do."

CHAPTER THIRTY-TWO

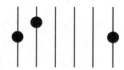

Eight hours earlier, the last of Los Angeles's most fabulous club kids had staggered off for impersonal hookups with similarly sex-starved strangers or sought comfort in a pre-passout breakfast at Nick's Café or the Waffle. Now, with the sun high in the coastal sky, the industrial-chic interior of Tradimento was completely deserted.

Almost.

At the very back of the club, where velvet ropes separated the enormously wealthy and the extremely notorious from the youthful, glitter-covered hoi polloi, Haden Koschei sat on a Victorian couch upholstered in violet velvet, raised on a platform so that the seat—the best in the house—looked out over everything.

He heard the front doors open, then slam shut. He closed his eyes, knowing that Cromwell would be patting them all down. More thoroughly than any of them would find inoffensive. Including the woman.

A satisfied smile snaked across his lips as he took a sip from his absinthe Sazerac. He carefully smoothed the lines of his black

Dolce & Gabbana suit and then brushed a piece of lint from his black Giorgio Armani cashmere T-shirt. He was ready for them.

Footsteps echoed across the vestibule, and the group stepped out into the cavernous space. There were six of them, exactly as he'd expected.

Four of them were merely muscle. Four goons, dressed up in ill-fitting suits to look a part they couldn't play. Koschei had seen them before, but hadn't paid them any attention. He didn't now, either.

The four were guarding Carlos "El Tigre" Silvano, who was the head of the Mexicali cartel and would be until someone in his cadre proved as capable of treachery as he'd demonstrated himself to be.

He'd earned his nickname for his penchant not only for utilizing enemies and rivals (and the occasional civilian) as Meow Mix for his collection of big cats, but also for pacing nervously like his prized liger in its cage. Back and forth, back and forth.

In this setting, however, it was important for him to maintain his posture by standing still—a simple task made all the harder by the natural nervousness he felt being so far north of the border, where his presence would have been of equal interest to federal law enforcement officials and rival drug cartels.

The woman beside him was his wife, Angelina. She'd been born a mere *Chicalona*, but her innate regal nature, startling sensuality, and willingness to do whatever was necessary had combined to lift her from her humble beginnings to a position of considerable power that was not entirely dependent upon her husband.

She had become known throughout the entire Mexicali region as a high priestess in the darker circles of Santa Muerte, feared and respected for her fierce cunning and a taste for blood that exceeded even her husband's. Her devotees had come to regard her as a gateway for Mictecacihuatl, Aztec goddess of death. As such, she'd not only cemented her husband's hold on the cartel, but made herself a persona of considerable power.

"I'm here." El Tigre held out his hands as if he'd been expecting something more and was disappointed. "Just like you asked."

Koschei smiled, amused by a display that he knew was meant to mask his guest's nerves. "Asked," he repeated with an expression of distaste, as if he'd just eaten something off of a men's-room floor. "It suggests that you could have refused, or that your presence here is a gift to me for which I should be thankful." His eyes narrowed. "You were summoned. That's why you're here."

Silvano was not a man accustomed to being put in his place, and he bristled at his host's high-handedness. "You will have to excuse my mood. Travel is difficult when there are so many who would have my head."

"Rest assured"—Koschei smiled coldly—"you have nothing to fear from your enemies. Your head is mine."

"With all due respect"—El Tigre matched the toothy grin, but there was no warmth behind his either—"I'd like to keep it on my neck just the same."

"Well, we can't always get what we want." Koschei offered an outstretched hand and indicated a spot on the couch to his left. "Go ahead, have a seat."

Carlos looked for a moment as if he were considering other options. There weren't any. Reluctantly he took a place on the couch beside Koschei, who patted the cushion to his right and invited, "After you, my dear."

Angelina looked to her husband and then did as his eyes silently instructed, taking the seat that was offered. Anyone would have thought her the obedient wife—if they'd missed the look she shot her host as she crossed before him.

Koschei smiled and patted her knee twice. "So lovely, my dear."

"We have business?" El Tigre interrupted.

"We do." Koschei crossed his legs and turned to his left. "Several pressing matters." He extended his left arm along the top of the couch. "Why don't we start with the new additions to your enterprise?"

"I have developed relationships in the Islamic community," Silvana explained. "They're desperate for cash, and they have the chemicals we need. Straight from the source. Fifty-five-gallon drums," he boasted as he enthusiastically demonstrated with his arms how big around the barrels were. "I have two super labs in operation and two more coming online in the next month. With that I can produce a thousand pounds of meth every week."

"That's quite a bit," Koschei responded, in a way that conveyed he was unimpressed.

"My question to you," Silvana prompted pointedly, offended by Koschei's indifference, "is, can you distribute this much product?"

"Spreading pleasure is what I do." Koschei's arm slid from its position on the couch and patted El Tigre reassuringly. "Whatever you can produce, I can turn into cash."

Silvano smiled. "Good."

"But there's something else I want," Koschei said, as if everything else was a distraction from his true purpose.

"And what's that?"

"There's a man," Koschei explained. "I want you to bring him to me."

"A man?" The matter seemed ridiculous. "Then go get him. I'm not a courier service." He turned to his men and grinned. "Or a dating service." El Tigre and his men all laughed.

Koschei let them. He nodded patiently. "You see, I'm constrained in my actions by a certain set of rules. A protocol, if you will, that prevents me from intervening directly in certain matters. I'm obliged to allow things to work out on their own."

"Well, then?"

"Well, there's no sin in aligning factors to work out in my favor, now is there?"

"I wouldn't know anything about sin."

Koschei looked to his right and smiled at the woman who'd been left out of their conversation. "Oh, I would." She smiled back.

Silvano didn't appreciate the gesture—or the detour their business had taken. "I'm not interested in whatever you have to do with this man of yours. That's not part of our deal."

"*Our* deal? There is no 'our.' The deal is mine. I tell you what it is and what it's not. I own it. Just like I own you. I'm not asking you to find this man. I'm telling you."

El Tigre's eyes bulged with rage. He started to rise. "Nobody tells me—"

Koschei reached out with his left hand and caught the man's shoulder, preventing him from rising further. "*I* tell you. Now I'm telling you to sit down."

The man tried to resist, but he could only comply. His four bodyguards rushed forward, but none got more than a step forward before Koschei turned to face them all, saying, "Not one more step." His words were chilling, but it was the murderous look in his eyes that paralyzed them where they stood.

He returned his attention to Silvano, who screamed in agony as he tried to squirm out of Koschei's grip on his shoulder. "This is what is going to happen. Do you understand?"

Silvano groaned and then, when he realized an answer was expected of him, forced himself to answer. "Uh-huh."

"You and your men are going to find this man for me. You're going to find him and bring him here."

Silvano nodded frantically, beads of sweat running down his brow.

"And to make sure that you bring him to me…" He reached next to him and put his hand on Angelina's knee. Then her thigh. Rather than the excruciating pain El Tigre was experiencing, Koschei's touch seemed to raise a sensual ecstasy in her. She curled up next to him and put her arm over his shoulder. "I'm going to keep something of yours."

Koschei threw his left arm forward, and El Tigre flew forward like a doll, landing at the feet of his stunned bodyguards.

"Bring me Daniel Erickson." He looked over at Angelina, who was beginning to pull herself closer to him. "If I were you, I'd hurry."

CHAPTER THIRTY-THREE

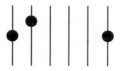

A long, winding drive led to a suburban faux chateau, the architectural bastard love child of an eighteenth-century English manor home and a French provincial cottage—on steroids. The drive ended in a circle in front of the house, and Daniel parked the car by the stone steps that led up to oaken double doors with black iron studs and supports.

"I'm not sure if we should knock or set up a siege," Daniel said as he lifted the iron ring. Neither Vicki nor Moog acknowledged his attempt at history humor, and so he simply let the ring fall back against the door.

"Seriously, neither one of you is talking to me?"

Silence.

"Because I shot the guy in the foot?"

Nothing.

Daniel didn't push it.

They waited silently in the cold. Neither Moog nor Vicki had anything more to say about the time they worried they were wasting or the risk they were running, but neither had to, either. They stood on the front porch, arms crossed, silently judging Daniel.

They were both just about to tell him that they'd come to a dead end and it was time to give up the trail when one of the heavy doors opened and a thin, balding man cautiously stuck his head out. "Hello?"

"Mr. Lucca?" Daniel inquired. "Alan Lucca?"

It was clear from the alarm that flashed in his eyes that he was the man they'd come to see, and from the delay in his response it was equally clear he was hesitant to admit it.

A little girl, maybe six or seven, came running up to inspect the strangers, wrapping herself around her father's leg for reassurance. "Who are you?" she demanded with the refreshing frankness of a child.

It was obvious her father didn't want her to be part of the conversation, but Daniel answered before he could do anything to stop a dialogue from building. "I'm a friend of your father's."

She looked at him skeptically.

"Actually, I'm a friend of a friend of your father's."

"Alice, why don't you go play with your sisters," her father suggested, without making any impression on her at all.

Something about the three strangers tickled her sense of curiosity. "What friend?" She threw down the question as a freckle-nosed dare.

Daniel smiled. "Mark Wannaman."

The man at the door grew pale. "All right, Alice," he said, taking the little girl by her shoulders, gently but firmly. "I need you to go play with your sisters. Stay there. I'll be right there. All right?"

He turned back to the unwanted strangers who were still at his door. "I don't know what this is—about."

Daniel was quick to tell him. "Mark Wannaman was murdered."

"You don't know that," he shot back defensively, as if the simple statement concealed an accusation.

"I do."

"Listen, everybody has their crazy rock-and-roll conspiracy theories. Morrison's hanging out in Paris. Elvis is eating burgers on the beach. Kurt was—"

Daniel wasn't deterred. "I saw him, Alan."

"What does that mean? There were pictures of the wreckage everywhere."

"I'm not talking about the car crash, Alan. I'm not talking about five years ago. I saw Mark last week."

"No. You're crazy." He seemed genuinely surprised.

"I talked to him just last week. A day later I saw his body floating in a pool. He'd been beaten to death."

"Who—" It was a natural question to ask.

"The people who did it are dead." Their death fell from Daniel's tongue like the simple statement of fact that it was. The coldness didn't buy him any points with Vicki. Or Moog.

"Then what are you doing here?"

"Because they were just contractors—they weren't the ones that *wanted* him beaten to death. I'm going to find out who was responsible."

"You can't think—"

"The only thing I know for sure," Daniel told him, "is that it's cold as a mother out here, and I'd really like to come in and talk this over where I'm not freezing my ass off."

He thought about it. "Yeah, I don't think so." He gestured over his shoulder with his thumb. "I've got my girls inside—"

"Alan. I told you I'm going to find who's responsible. Whether you leave me out on your stoop here or not, you and I are going to talk this over. The only questions are when, and where, and what kind of mood I'm in when we do."

"Come in." Once he'd closed the door behind them, he hedged. "I'm afraid I didn't get your names."

"I'm Eric Danielson," Daniel said. He motioned to Vicki. "This is—"

"Nicky Raines." She could think up a crappy fake name herself.

"Taylor," was all that Moog could come up with.

"You have a first name?"

"Mister."

"And you're police officers?"

"Not exactly."

It suddenly occurred to Alan that he might have just made a very serious mistake. "But I thought you said—"

"I said I was looking for whoever was responsible for killing Mark. I never said who sent me looking."

Alan cast a self-conscious eye around the surprisingly sparsely furnished mansion. "Not the home of a rock star, I know. But I've got three girls by the woman who's suing me for divorce now. Four more by two others who already have."

"It's not easy," Daniel said with some authority.

"And listen, I'm just the bass player. Mark would come in to the studio and say, 'I just wrote this or that, can you lay down a bass line to it?' And then guess who's got the writing credit. Not me. I mean, what's 'Bag Full of Monsters' without that bass line?"

"That's gotta piss you off." Daniel dangled the comment like bait.

Alan bit, but didn't take the hook. "What? No. I mean, sure, you know, it hurts. It pisses you off a little. But not enough to kill anyone. If you're going to play the bass, you're used to it."

"And you're used to it?"

"I'm just the bass player, man, and no one gives a shit about the bass player." He thought about it. "Unless he's Flea." He leaned forward on the couch. "You ever hear of anyone spray-painting graffiti 'Jack Bruce Is God'? You got Michael Anthony, for my money the best bass player in America. 'Oh yeah, we'll just replace him with this teenage kid. What's the difference?' John Entwhistle, the best *ever*"—he was adamant about it—"dies, and they're like 'We're still the 'Oo. Let's go play a thousand fucking shows.' You are not the Who. You are two guys from the Who. Not the same thing without the Ox laying that bass line down."

He leaned back, trying to calm himself, but it didn't do any good. "You know what a rock song is without the bass line?" No one had a chance to even take a stab at it. "It's that coffeehouse shit they play these days. Or worse yet, the fucking bass loop they slap on everything now. 'Create an original bass line? Why bother, we'll just slap some computer-generated noise on the thing and no one will know.' Boom. Boom. Boom."

It was a long time since Daniel had seen someone get so worked up over something that wasn't actually trying to kill him. "That's what they did with that Taco Shot greatest hits piece of shit. Called me up and said, 'We're getting the band together again.' Like hell they are. They call me in for two days. It's just a publicity stunt. They take the lines I'd worked out and delete them. Drop in a goddamn loop. And now everyone is going to think I play like a goddamn computer."

He shook his head, "If I didn't have bills to pay—"

Something he'd said triggered a thought for Daniel. "The greatest hits package."

"What about it?"

"You get paid on it, right?"

"I get pennies, man. Nothing compared to—"

"Who?"

"Just about everyone." It was clear that discussing the economics made him uncomfortable.

Daniel was intent on keeping him there. "And if Mark had come back—"

"You mean from the grave?"

"That wasn't him in that grave, and you know it."

"We all had our suspicions," Alan admitted. "But half of everyone under thirty did. I never knew anything. For certain."

"Who did?"

"Herb, maybe. He knew Mark better than any of us." He paused, debating whether he should say something or let it be. "He knew Adeline better too."

"Adeline?"

"Mark's wife. Widow, I guess. Or whatever. I guess she's his widow now."

"Just how well did Herb know Mark's wife?"

"He knew her long and hard enough that if I were you, I'd leave me alone and go take my questions to him."

"And just how would I do that?"

CHAPTER THIRTY-FOUR

The perpetual cloud cover that shrouds Kansas City from November to late March had dropped a dusting of snow that afternoon, but LaTanya Harris didn't notice the faint tracks in the fading light of dusk as she pulled into her garage.

Her hands were filled with bags from Price Chopper, and as she juggled them from one hand to another while she fiddled with the key, she failed to take note of the scrapes on the gold-plated doorknob.

Because she was struggling to put the groceries on the counter without dropping any of them, she never noticed that the lamp in the living room—the one with the automatic timer—had been switched off.

There were signs. Telltale signs. But LaTanya Harris had missed them all.

"Malaika!" she called out, but she wasn't concerned when only silence responded. It wasn't quite dark yet, and with holiday break on for the Blue Valley School District, there was no real reason to insist that her daughter stay home.

LaTanya thought about her own senior year in high school, up in her room listening to Boyz II Men in her bedroom. With her boyfriend. She smiled wistfully at the recollection and then shuddered at the thought that her little girl might be up to the same things they'd gotten up to. Or worse.

She slipped out of her coat and draped it over a stool at the breakfast bar. She was just about to turn her attention to fixing dinner when she heard the voice behind her.

"Hello, LaTanya."

She didn't turn at first. There was no need to. She hadn't heard the deep timbre of those bass tones in more than fifteen years, but she recognized it immediately. "What do you want?"

"You know what I want." His voice was calm and casual, but every word sounded like a threat.

She turned to face him, but wasn't prepared. In the time since she'd last seen him, he'd gotten older than she could've possibly imagined, but Arthur Beagler was no less imposing for the passage of time. She tried to project an aura of strength, to strike a defiant posture, but all she managed to project was how terrified she was.

"Well, he ain't here," she said bravely, though her voice wavered a bit. Her first thoughts weren't for his safety or her own. Her maternal instincts were focused on her daughter, and her heart raced from the fear that maybe he already knew that.

"No," he admitted. "I know he's not. But I also know you know where he is." He considered the possibilities. "Or you know how to get in touch with him."

"The only thing I know is that you took my Vernon away from me," she spat out. The thought of it made her angry, and that anger restored a bit of her spirit. "*You* took him away from *me*." She pointed to her heart. "So it seem to me you oughta be the one knows where he's at. Not *me*."

"That what you let yourself believe?" He smiled at her as if she were a little girl who'd just dropped an ice cream cone.

"He was going to go straight," she protested vehemently.

"Going to go straight." He sneered at the sentiment. "The only thing Moog is going to go straight to is hell." He smiled at the certainty. "Same as me."

"He was going to get himself a job."

"A job," he scoffed. "I gave him a career."

"Killing people isn't a career," she screamed, though she wanted to cry.

"Oh, no?" He looked around the modest but well-appointed house. "But we both know you don't afford this place on your own."

She was offended by the suggestion. "I'll have you know I'm a goddamned licensed dental hygienist."

"And we both know you didn't pay for school on your own. Didn't pay for that Lexus on your own. Didn't pay for any of this on your own." His voice began to show signs that his patience was running out. "Killing paid for all of this."

"No—"

"We both know that it did. Deep down, you know why he came with me, why he wanted me to make him a killer."

"He never wanted—"

"He *did*," Beagler insisted. "He did because it was the only way he could give all of this to you. To your baby."

The words hit hard enough to dislodge the tears she'd been holding back. "No."

"That was his strength. And his fatal flaw. You know it's true. Just as sure as you know where my boy is or how to get in touch with him."

"He's not your boy." She was angry now, but it only made her cry more.

"He'll always be my boy." Beagler's eyes flared. "He's my boy till I say he ain't." He moved toward her like a big, old lion, well aware of what he was capable of doing, but disappointed she was going to make him go to all that trouble.

She knew she had to stand her ground, but his approach made her take a step back and then she couldn't help but take another, and then another, until she was against the counter with nowhere to go. She needed to hurry him, get him out of the house before her daughter came home. She couldn't let the two of them meet.

"I'm not leaving here until I know how to find him." He kept coming, slow and deliberate, until his hands were against the counter on either side of her and his face was close enough to hers that he could have swallowed her. "We both know what that means."

She closed her eyes and braced herself for the pain, but what happened next was worse.

The front door clicked and swung open. A blast of the cold December evening shot into the room along with a bright, "Mom! I'm home!"

It was enough of a distraction that Beagler turned his head toward the door for just an instant.

"Malaika!" LaTanya called out as she reached for the largest of the frying pans that had been soaking in the sink. The skillet came up in a forehand smash that caught Beagler along the left side of his head. The pan rang dully as aluminum struck something far harder, but the impact was enough to cause the big man to stagger for a step or two. But no more than that. He shook off the blow and pulled the pistol holstered under his arm.

The girl rushed into the room, then screamed.

"Malaika, run!"

The girl was too shocked to follow her mother's warning. She ran instead to her mother's side and turned in her arms to face the man who was now holding a gun on them both. "No, baby," LaTanya told her girl in a whispered warning. They stayed in each other's arms, looking up at the man standing over them.

Beagler shook his head clear and focused on maintaining a level of self-control that he hardly ever exercised. "You listen to your mama." He took a moment to catch his breath. Casually he touched his ear, pulled his hand away, and realized there was blood on the fingertip.

"The only other soul ever made me bleed and is walking this earth tonight was your father," he told the girl. "I made one exception for him. I'm making one for your mama right now. But don't you push your luck like he did his."

"Father?" It seemed like a foreign word to the girl.

"She don't have nothing to do with this," LaTanya assured Arthur.

He shrugged off her plea as he'd shaken off the frying pan. "Neither do you. But we both know how this is going to end if I don't get what I came for." There was no compassion in his eyes, but they made it clear that he spoke the truth. "You know, in my own way, I think on her like she was my very own baby grangirl right here. But I don't have time for that now. You gonna tell me what I need to know. We both know that's a fact. I'm just asking you not to make it so I have to spill blood of my own."

LaTanya pulled her daughter close and began to cry. "I'm sorry, baby. I'm so sorry."

CHAPTER THIRTY-FIVE

"Minnesota?" Moog called from the backseat. "Because Illinois in late December isn't cold enough for you?"

"You'll like it. Wait and see."

"What's there to like?" Vicki asked, as if she already knew the answer was nothing.

"I thought you of all people would be excited about a trip to Minnesota."

"I don't understand most of what you do and think." Her tone made clear which of them she blamed for that. "But why would you think I'd have any interest in Minnesota?"

He had an answer ready. "Because Minnesota is the brain of American music."

"The brain?" She was more than a little dubious.

He was up to the challenge. "Think of the Mississippi River as the country's main artery. And music as the blood. The Delta and New Orleans may be the heart and soul of American music, but Minnesota is the brain."

"I'm still not getting it."

Daniel was happy to finally have some conversation to pass the miles. "In the sixties no single individual did more to shape rock and roll than Dylan. Period. End of story."

She rolled her eyes. "Well, as long as you don't overstate your argument."

"He's the piece that ties everything together, from Woody Guthrie and Pete Seeger to Gaslight Anthem, from Charlie Patton and Leadbelly to the Parlor Mob. Dylan's the cornerstone. You absolutely cannot put on a track of rock and roll recorded in the last forty years and not hear something that can be traced back to Bob Dylan. Minnesota, born and bred."

"All right, I'll give you that, Mr. Peabody." She was feeling generous. "And the next?"

"Prince."

"You've gotta be kidding me."

"I kid you not. You go back to the late seventies and music had become as segregated as it had been in the fifties. Springsteen had Clarence Clemmons. Billy Preston went on tour with the Stones. But for the most part rock and roll didn't feature a lot of African-Americans."

"Black people," Moog objected. "You ain't no European-American."

"All right, black people. But there weren't a lot of folks in rock and roll who weren't white men."

"Oh, don't get me started," Vicki interjected. "There are a lot of rockers who aren't male. Stevie Nicks. Joan Jett. Patti Smith. Debbie Harry. Ann and Nancy Wilson. There've always been women who could rock as hard as any man."

"No doubt." Daniel was happy to concede a point he would have gladly made on his own. "I'm not saying they don't kick ass—"

"'Cause they do."

"I'm just saying there aren't as many of them. And the same with black men, until Prince comes along playing everything: Rock. Pop. Funk. Soul. R&B. Prince reunited rock with soul and blues and funk in a way that Jimi Hendrix didn't live long enough to have the opportunity to do. He opened the white world to artists of color in a way that no one else did. Hip-hop may have kicked in the door, but it was only because Prince had already opened it wide."

"And if I give you that one too," Vicki said, "what's your third?"

"The Replacements."

"The Replacements? How you figure that?"

"Punk came from England, right? I'm not going to take anything away from the Ramones or the Dolls or the Dead Boys, but punk is always going to start and end with the Clash. But the Replacements took punk and made it something distinctly American. Before Mark Arm ever proclaimed Mudhoney 'Pure grunge! Pure noise! Pure shit!' the Replacements took all of punk's frenetic energy, added a little melody, and sowed the seeds of what everyone now calls alternative." Daniel held out his hand. "Arguably the three biggest turning points in American music, and all of them from Minnesota."

Moog was unimpressed. "None of that makes this Arctic shit any warmer," he lamented, watching the frozen miles speeding past. "I thought Kansas City got cold, but goddamn, this is like living on an Eskimo Pie."

"Well, this has all been fascinating." Daniel was relieved to hear just the smallest bit of playfulness creep back into Vicki's voice. "But I need to stop."

There was a truck stop off the next exit, and Daniel pulled in, the tires crunching across the frozen pavement.

Vicki ran for the door as soon as the car stopped moving. Daniel got out and moved to the back to begin to pump gas. He put in the nozzle and waited while it clicked away.

Moog got out of the backseat and wrapped his coat around him. "Damn, it's cold." Then, as casually as he could, he slipped away.

CHAPTER THIRTY-SIX

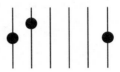

The vibration in his pocket had startled Moog. He'd always carried the phone; it just hadn't gone off before. The phone was only for her. Nobody else called him. Not ever. Nobody knew where he was. Nobody except her.

She always knew where he was. She was his one weakness. His one soft spot. Everyone had one, but he rationalized his away. There was no real danger, because nobody knew about her. Well, almost nobody.

When he felt he'd made as graceful an exit as possible and he was alone, Moog pulled the phone from his pocket and called the number he'd previously declined. He listened as it rang.

Moog Turner was a big, bad monster, but the sound of her voice made him human again. That thrilled and scared him.

She greeted him with a "Goddammit, Vernon, I called you five hours ago."

"This was the first chance I had to call, LaTanya." He was too concerned about the reason she'd be calling to worry about the tone of her voice. "You all right? Is she—"

"No thanks to you," she scolded through sniffles and tears.

Relief felt like a glass of ice water thrown in his face.

She took a long, snotty sniffle, though she would have scolded her daughter for doing something so unladylike under other circumstances. But there were no other circumstances now, and she needed to set herself straight to tell him the news. "It was Arthur."

Men lie to themselves about their vulnerabilities. Sometimes because they need to, and sometimes because they just can't stop themselves. They fool themselves into thinking that they're small lies and easily handled, that they can contain the situation. But all along they know it's not the truth.

Moog had one vulnerability. Just one. But it was a big one. And now he knew it was finally exposed.

"Did he—"

"He didn't hurt us. Not bad. Just scared us. Scared her real good."

Moog had lived a charmed life. This was the first time he'd had to tread the razor-thin line between fear and anger. "Is she—"

"He didn't come for *her,*" LaTanya snapped. "He came for you, Vernon. Wanted to know where you could be found."

The breath Moog couldn't hold slipped through his lips like cigarette smoke. "All right." He tried to think what to do next, but his thoughts drifted off with the frost of his breath.

"It's not all right, Vernon." She tried hard not to start crying all over again. Tried and failed. "I told him, baby. I didn't mean to." Her voice caught in her throat, choked on tears. "I woulda let the motherfucker kill me first, but I couldn't—" There were no words to express a fear she wouldn't let form in her mind. "I just couldn't with her."

"You did right. You hear me? You did right."

"I'm sorry, baby." She stopped crying just long enough to tell him. "I told him about the phone. About our system."

"You did right. Now listen to me. You gonna be all right. Arthur don't want to hurt you two. If he did—" Moog was an infinitely practical man in the ways of life and death and the painful states in between, but he couldn't complete the image. "You gonna be fine."

Even as he reassured her, his mind was trying to figure why Arthur had left them alive. He would've known that she'd warn him. Which meant that he wanted her to make the call to Moog, wanted him to be aware that he was on his trail. And their long-postponed finale was now inevitable.

"I'm not worried about me. He's not coming for me. He's coming for you."

"I know."

"You don't sound surprised."

"I'm not." He thought of something he'd been told once by his teacher. There was resignation in his voice. "Every bullet got a soul mate."

"Did you know he was coming?"

"I shoulda."

"What you should do is get your ass back here and get us out of here. I can't do this shit anymore."

"I will."

"We don't need the money, Vernon. You don't need that life anymore. Let's just go."

"We will," Moog promised, unsure how he could keep his word. "I just can't do it right now."

"Can't do it right now?"

"I've got to finish this out first."

"She's your daughter, Vernon. I thought I was—"

"I know who you are. Know who my daughter is, too. Haven't I proved that to you yet? But you two are safe now. Shit, I'd just bring danger back to you if I came back now. I've got to finish this out."

"Fine."

"And then I promise—"

He knew her silence was her comment on what she'd come to think of his promises.

She sniffed and built herself up again. "Well, at least get rid of this phone. He'll be tracing it."

"That's why I gotta keep it. If I toss it now, he'll just know that you warned me. If he hasn't already found me, that would only send him back to you."

"Then what are you going to do?"

"I'm gonna play this out to the end—"

"And then what?"

He didn't know, but he couldn't tell her that. "I gotta go."

CHAPTER THIRTY-SEVEN

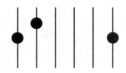

Daniel pulled the hose out of the tank, returned it to the pump, and replaced the gas cap. All the while, however, his attention was focused on the big man who was trying to surreptitiously slip back into the scene. "What's going on?"

"What you mean?"

"I mean what's going on? You've been looking at your cell phone all day." He nodded at the device that was still in his hands.

Moog slid it into his pocket. "That a crime?"

"You and I are well past crimes," Daniel said, half joking. "It's just, who's a fugitive texting?"

"Fugitive?" Moog was more than offended by the classification. "That what I am, a fugitive?"

"That's what we all are," Daniel reminded him. "I just wish you'd tell me whatever it is you're keeping to yourself. Because I can tell it's something. Something big."

"I don't know what you're talking about."

"Like you don't know that Audi's been on our tail on and off all day?"

Moog didn't bother to check the rearview for the black A8 that had been dancing in and out of their shadow all day. "What you want me to tell you for? You been watching it same as me."

"I want you to tell me what I don't know."

"There's some shit you don't know?" Moog served it up with an extra helping of sarcasm.

"That's not what I meant, and you know it."

"No—you wanna know what I know? While you're driving all over the Midwest shooting assholes in the feet and making an even bigger pain in the ass out of yourself than usual, all three of us are chin-deep in some nasty-ass shit. *That's* what I know." He was so agitated that steam began to rise from his uncovered scalp.

"And I know there are half a dozen seriously bad mothers that'd love to shoot us down. Or much, much worse. And I know that while you're taking us on one of your musical field trips, a damn traffic ticket could turn into a life sentence for all three of us. *That's* what I know that you don't seem to know. Or care about."

Daniel couldn't help but be taken aback a bit. "None of that has escaped me. Not a bit."

"Then why are we doing it, man? This is suicide, running around like this. Let's just put your rock-star friend on the long list of dudes whose deaths ain't never gonna get set straight, and get out of here before this bullshit puts us on that same list our own damn selves."

"It's not bullshit." Daniel sounded more sullen than he wanted to. "There's some things you just have to do."

"And there's some shit that you shouldn't mess with. And right now you are running full-bore, straight into a fucking wall of just that kinda shit."

"Maybe."

"*Maybe?*" Moog raised his voice an octave or two. "*Maybe.* Man, you sound like you think you're the only one involved in this situation."

"I know I'm not the only one involved."

Off in the distance, a single shot echoed in the frozen air.

Both men jumped and instinctively looked around them. Neither of them could see where it might have come from. Or where it'd gone.

"What are you two looking at?" Vicki asked, walking up on them.

Moog looked at Daniel and then back to her. "Nothing. Nothing at all."

"It's deer season," Daniel added. "Bad day for the deer."

"Yeah," Moog agreed, "bad day for the deer."

CHAPTER THIRTY-EIGHT

The nose-stinging cold and the frozen ground beneath his belly reminded Pasha of the training he'd received with the Seventy-Fourth Motor Rifle Brigade when he was posted in Yurga. He didn't like it then any better than he did now.

He adjusted the PSO-1 optical sight on his Dragunov sniper rifle and took another look at the target. When he was absolutely certain, he keyed the mic on his tactical headset. "Lavinia. Lavinia. This is Zaichata. Come in."

"This is Lavinia," came the response on the headset. "Go ahead, Zaichata."

"I have the targets. Affirmative on the targets."

"Both targets?"

Pash looked through the scope. There were the two men standing by the gas pumps. The big black man seemed to be arguing with his white friend. "*Da.* Affirmative on both."

"Hold your position, Zaichata."

"Do I take the shot?"

Two miles away, Ivan Nurivov sat behind the wheel of a black Audi, trying to make a decision. His boss had instructed him to bring Daniel Erickson back alive, but there seemed little sense in that. If they took the shot now, they could just be done with it all and go home.

"Do I take the shot?"

What to do? Ivan wasn't sure.

It took Ivan a minute to weigh the pros and cons of their situation. Pasha lay perfectly still against the frozen ground, waiting patiently for his orders, but he never heard the footsteps silently creeping up behind him. He didn't hear the hammer being drawn back. The very last thing he heard was the shot that struck him in the back of his head and made a five-foot splatter pattern on the snow around him.

"Take the shot," Ivan announced over the headset, which had been scattered with the rest of the cranial debris. "Take the shot."

There was no shot. And no response on the radio.

"Take the shot, Zaichata!" Ivan's voice was urgent. And then panicked. "Come in, Zaichata. Come in. Do you read?"

Pasha made no response.

* * *

"Shoot my boy, will ya!" Arthur Beagler holstered his pistol, satisfied with the decision he'd made. "I'm the only big dog on this hunt."

He turned and walked away.

CHAPTER THIRTY-NINE

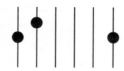

Luck is a way of life for some.

For a time at least, simple good fortune was how Herb Gless got through this world. He didn't have any particular talents and lacked the initiative to make up for that shortcoming with hard work or dedication. Good looks and an engaging personality eluded him. All things considered, he really had nothing but luck. But for most of his life, that was all he needed.

His biggest break had arrived several years earlier on a Metro Transit bus.

After years of nonstop touring, playing every Elks hall, crappy club, and dive bar in the Midwest, the members of Taco Shot had finally landed a recording contract and were headed to LA for their first recording session when their original drummer absentmindedly crossed Hawthorne Street without looking both ways.

Enter the bus.

With deposits down on a studio in North Hollywood and a label waiting for a record, there wasn't time to audition replacements. So as a last-minute stopgap, the vacancy was filled by the only one who had seen enough of those early Taco Shot shows to know the drum parts: the dearly departed's cousin, Herb Gless.

Once he was in place, an odds-defying string of luck kept Herb behind that kit. There were countless times that the band—and that meant Mark—had tried to replace the just-so-slightly-out-of-rhythm drummer, but somehow the hand of fate always interceded.

The drummer from Blue Balls was supposed to take over duties behind the kit, but he ended up contracting meningitis and slipping into a coma before they could announce the replacement. A session player Mark liked a lot would've taken the spot, but after a night of celebrating his new gig the guy wound up beating his wife to death with a table leg. A drummer Mark had met at a festival show ended up winning a patent and left music to go work in aerospace. There was always something.

After a while, the time that passed between Mark's attempts to replace the guy constituted a distinguished and lucrative career in the music business.

Herb Gless was a lucky man. Spooky lucky.

Of course, Daniel Erickson had enjoyed his share of luck, too, and one small bit allowed him to convince the fortunate drummer that he was with a music magazine profiling the best players of the past decade. Gless's ego prompted him to overlook the obvious ridiculousness of such a consideration and open the gates to his Edina McMansion to the "reporter and crew."

Herb Gless greeted them at the front door. "Eric?" he asked tentatively, not expecting a rock journalist to be traveling with a woman and a black man who looked as if his idea of music was the sweet sound of snapping bones.

"That's me," Daniel lied enthusiastically, putting his hand out before him. "Thanks for seeing us."

The drummer's hands were unexpectedly soft and unengaged in the handshake. "And you're with—" The rest of the question slipped into a rising pool of suspicion.

"Such a huge pleasure." Daniel pressed forward, trying to lead him back into his house. "Really. Big fan of your playing."

"Thanks." Herb was too distracted by the scene unfolding in his hallway to recover his hand. "You're with *Rolling Stone*?"

"Guilty as charged." Daniel smiled brightly but couldn't carry off the masquerade.

"Bullshit." Herb withdrew his hand, like a mouse retracting his paw just before the deadly, spring-loaded arm of the Victor trap comes down on him. "There's not a music journalist over thirty." He looked suspiciously at the three of them. "And *Rolling Stone* sure isn't sending the VH1 Classics *Where Are They Now?* version of the Mod Squad knocking on doors."

There was nothing for Daniel to try but the truth. "We're not journalists."

"No shit."

"But we do have a few questions for you."

"We?" Herb looked over his three unwanted houseguests. "And which one of you Alpha-Bits assholes is it this time? MGDOC? DPS? Or are you Feds, is that it? DOJ send you here? DEA? FBI?"

The act was well rehearsed.

"What is it? State's attorneys? You assholes think you're going to walk into my house and what? Twist my arm? If I've told you guys once, I've told you a thousand times. I've got nothing to say."

"I don't think you understand the situation," Daniel offered.

"You're not Drugs and Gangs?" That appeared to be Herb's final, best guess.

"You just wish we were."

"Then it's not about—"

Daniel wanted to make it perfectly clear. "It's about Mark Wannaman."

"Well, you can run along back to whatever cubicles you dragged yourself out from under, get a fucking warrant, and then talk to my lawyer about him, too."

"Yeah," Daniel was less and less amused by the performance. "You're a long way away from lawyers."

The comment seemed to spark a very different thought. "Oh, did the Mystery Tramp send you? Because you can tell him I've got everything covered. I've never talked in all these years, and I never will."

"Who the hell is the Mystery Tramp?" Daniel wondered out loud.

"He didn't send you?" The prospect that he'd said too much seemed to rattle Herb. "Well, I'm especially not answering any questions you may have about him. So why don't you take your bitch and your third-rate Shaq over there and get out of my house before you find out what I can do when you really piss me off."

Daniel hit Herb in the face just for the comment. He hit him a second time to let him know he was serious, and a third time just because Herb Gless happened to have one of those faces that cries out for a fist in it. (What the Germans call *Backpfeifengesicht*.)

The assault knocked Herb to the ground, but Daniel was quick to pick him up by his lapels and shake some sense into him. "I don't give a shit about whatever other game you're running. I don't give a shit about the cops, the Feds, or your lawyers. Someone killed Mark Wannaman. I'm going to find out who."

Herb wiped blood from where the quarters had hit him in the mouth. "Are you crazy? Do you know the kind of shit you just brought down on yourself?"

Another punch suggested he didn't. Or didn't care. "I want to know who killed Mark Wannaman."

There was more blood at his mouth now, but Herb didn't bother to get up from the floor. "Well, I sure as shit didn't."

"But you know who did. I know you do, because they're the ones who told you to steal his body and burn it."

"Who told you that?"

"Mark did. He wrote a song about it. Called you 'Everybody's Bitch.'"

"You're not making any sense, man. How could Mark write a song if he was dead?"

"Because he wasn't," Daniel explained. "And you know that. Or you knew that."

"What are you talking about? Mark died five years ago."

Daniel wondered if the confusion was legitimate or just an act meant to conceal his guilt.

"But you burned his body to conceal the fact he was alive."

"I don't know whether you're stupid or crazy or both, but I wasn't concealing anything."

"So you admit you stole the body and burned it."

"I'm not admitting anything." Gless wiped more blood from his mouth. "If I did anything at all, it was a favor for a friend. That's all."

Daniel couldn't be put off. "What friend? I want answers."

"Well, here's what I'll do," Herb said, getting to his feet. "Why don't you leave your bitch here with me for an hour, and I'll give her some answers. Like a hands-on demonstration of what Taco Shot means."

A second later Daniel had Herb against the hall wall, and Moog and Vicki were trying their best to peel him off.

"Come on, man." Moog was able to separate the two men with all the effort of twisting the twin halves of an Oreo. "We don't need this now," the big man said to Daniel, without letting Herb free from the wall. "Now let's go."

Daniel was powerless to resist the tsunami of Moog's mass, which moved him toward the door.

"That's right," Herb yelled after them. "You better get out of here. Because when my troops arrive, it's going to rain pain on your asses."

Without releasing Daniel, Moog just looked back over his shoulder. "Don't stir the shit, asshole."

"You're not the baddest motherfucker I know," Herb warned him.

Moog turned back again. "I'm bad enough."

Suddenly a buzzer sounded in the house, and everyone turned to Herb. "That's the maid," he explained. "If I don't let her in, she's going to know something's wrong and she's going to go straight to the police. And I can tell the only people who are looking to avoid a talk with five-oh are you."

Herb looked at Daniel, who looked to Moog, who considered the situation and nodded.

"Go ahead. We're leaving anyway."

Herb went to the control panel that governed the gates and screamed into the intercom, "Get up here now!"

Daniel flashed Moog a WTF? look, and the big man returned one back.

They moved quickly to the door, but before they could get out the door came open and five men came busting into the house.

"Now it's a party!" Herb cackled. "Now it's a party!"

CHAPTER FORTY

Outside of their homelands in Asia's most mountainous regions, the Hmong population in the Twin Cities is the greatest in the entire world. For the most part, it is a hardworking community as intent on enjoying the fruits and opportunities of the American Dream as any other ethnic group. But like any other ethnic group, from the Irish immigrants of Five Points to the Cosa Nostra that crossed the Atlantic with Italian immigrants, a small number of Hmong have found their way in the New World through criminal enterprise.

Of the Hmong gangs that have earned a reputation for violence and bloodshed, the Crazy Boyz are arguably the worst. The appearance of five of their top members in Herb's living room changed the mood considerably.

"These folks have questions," Herb announced.

The leader of the group was named Tou, a short, squat man who couldn't have been more than twenty or twenty-five, but whose eyes seemed old beyond measure. "You brought us to cops?"

"They're not cops."

"What are they?"

"As far as I can tell, just concerned citizens," Herb said, setting the stage for retribution.

The five gang members were not alone. They had brought a teenage girl with them, and though she tried to hide herself behind them, she couldn't escape notice completely.

"Who's she?" Moog asked boldly.

"Who?"

"Her." Moog pointed at the young girl.

Tou laughed. "You mean, *what's* she. She the entertainment, fool."

The way the rest of the gang members laughed didn't anger Moog nearly as much as the numbness in the girl's eyes. There was no shame, not in a moral or social propriety sense, but the girl had been stripped of her basic humanity.

"How old?" Moog asked.

"Fourteen. Fifteen," Tou guesstimated with a shrug of indifference. "You like young?"

The other gang members all laughed.

Moog wasn't laughing. "Did I miss a joke?"

"Yeah, asshole. You the joke. Guess you miss that."

Moog ignored the laughter that followed. "She's coming with us."

"What you talk about, crazy man? She not going nowhere. You not going nowhere."

"I'm not going anywhere with you," the girl insisted, nervously looking at Tou and then the other members of the gang.

Moog understood her reluctance, but he didn't care. A spin on the Foster Care Wheel of Fortune seemed a better gamble than the inevitable tragedy of her current situation. "Got a girl of my own not much older."

Tou sneered. "When we done with you, papa, maybe we go see daughter, make her entertainment too."

That was it. Moog reached into his breast pocket, and Tou caught what he tossed to him.

"What this?"

"It's a cell phone."

"I know it cell phone. What I'm supposed to do with cheap-ass flip-top Walgreens phone?"

Moog's answer was simple enough. "I figured you might wanna call someone."

"Call someone?"

"Yeah. I'm going to kill you in a minute, and I thought that even someone like you might have someone they wanted to talk to one last time before they died."

Daniel didn't like the tone the conversation was taking on. Or the odds they were facing. "Hey, Moog. Maybe this isn't the time to—"

Moog turned to him. "You been shooting motherfuckers in the foot and talking all that push-back-man shit since we started. Don't you go all Mormon on me now."

"Yeah, I don't think you mean—"

"I think I mean to leave this room with that little girl. Her days of pulling these boys' train is over. You can help me with that, or you can get out of my way, but I don't need no debate with you right now."

"Fair enough."

"You with me?"

"Till the end."

"All right, then, here's how this is going to play." He turned back to Tou. "You can leave the little girl here, get your raggedy asses on down the road, and live to see the new year, or I'm going to kill every last one of you right here and now and take her."

"That big talk for fat man like you. Tong is bigger, badder than you ever been, old man." He gestured at the biggest of their group, a man who had an inch or two on Moog.

"That right?"

Tou snapped his head and the behemoth started toward Moog.

Tong threw a punch that Moog blocked and held. Moog threw a punch that Tong blocked and held. Both men struggled with each other, until Moog reared back and slammed his forehead into Tong's nose. Moog slipped his right hand away, placed it behind Tong's head and then drove his forehead into Tong's nose again. This time, Tong's arm went limp. Moog reached for a candleholder on a side table, brought it up over his head, and buried it in his opponent's skull.

"Now he's bigger, badder, and deader."

Tou reached for his gun.

Behind them, Lue, Xang, and Ka all reached for guns too. Daniel pushed Vicki to the ground as he pulled out his own pistol. He fired once and Lue fell to the ground.

With Tong's body held in front of him like a shield, Moog rushed toward Tou. The leader got three or four shots out of his pistol, but they buried themselves in the corpse of his oversize henchman. Moog threw the body on him and then grabbed his hand, directing the shots across the room, where Xang was struck down.

Ka aimed at Moog, but Daniel fired first.

In the midst of the shootout, Vicki jumped to her feet, dashed across the room, and knocked the girl to the ground, pulling her to cover behind an overturned couch.

Moog pulled Tou out from under Tong's body. "You big pimpin." Each word was punctuated by a punch to the face. "You wanna tell me what you do to little girls." That was a lot of words, and a lot more punches than Tou could take.

"I tell you what I'm gonna do. I could make good on my word and beat you into the next world right now, but I'm gonna let you live. Not 'cause I got any mercy, but just so you know what it's like to be pimped out." He dropped Tou to the ground. "Enjoy the next ten to twenty years, motherfucker."

The girl Moog had set out to rescue was now in Vicki's arms, crying inconsolably.

Across the room, Herb Gless was whimpering behind the armchair he'd been using for cover. Moog stalked his way over, and only then noticed Herb was struggling to aim a gun he'd picked up.

Without a thought, Moog slapped him across the face, and the gun dropped to the floor. As he watched it fall, Moog noticed a bag of crystal meth there too.

He picked it up and considered it for a moment. "Is this what it was with you and the boys there? You running this shit?"

Herb's answer was unintelligible.

Moog grabbed Herb's head and shoved the bag into his face, covering it with white powder.

Herb screamed, but Moog didn't let go of his handful of hair. "You coulda just answered the man's questions and we woulda been on our way." He rubbed more of the powder into Herb's face. "It coulda been that simple, but you had to fuck things up."

Herb whined.

Moog turned to Daniel. "I think he's ready to answer your questions now."

Daniel came over. "I know it was you that stole the body and burned it. Why?"

Herb was desperate. "Because she asked me to."

"Who?"

"Adeline."

"Adeline Swank? His wife? Why?"

Herb shook his head. "Never asked her."

"Well, I suppose I'll have to." Daniel turned to Moog. "Come on, let's get going before this place heats up."

Moog turned to the girl Vicki was still comforting. "I wish I could stick around to straighten this shit out for you, but I can't. I'm going to call the po-po, come clean up this shit. I'm gonna tell them they need to send someone from Child and Youth Services along with 'em. You can stick around and tell them what happened here. I know that ain't no certainty that it'll all work out, but it'll give you a chance if you're willing to take it."

The girl lifted her head from Vicki's shoulder. "I'm not talking to any—"

"Or you can go back to where you came from," Moog continued. "But we both know that all these boys had brothers and cousins, friends and gangsters, and ain't none of them gonna appreciate the fact that they gonna be takin' up drawers down the morgue. You go back and they're going to take this out on you."

"Fuck you," the girl spat.

"Yeah, I don't blame you," Moog admitted. "But I didn't see any other way."

"You chuckleheads never see any other way," Vicki said angrily. "It's always hitting and shooting. How's that helping anything?"

Neither Daniel nor Moog had a response.

Vicki turned to the girl. "You're going to be all right." She reached into her jeans pocket and pulled out a wad of cash. Then she turned to Daniel and Moog. "Give me the cash you've got."

"What?"

"The cash you have. Give it to me."

Both men looked at one another, but did as they were told.

Vicki took the bills, a few thousand dollars combined, and pressed it into the girl's hand. "Take this. It's enough to make a start."

"A start at what?" the shocked girl wondered aloud.

"Same thing we're all looking for," Vicki replied. "A second chance."

CHAPTER FORTY-ONE

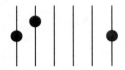

With a holiday snow falling heavier and heavier, the lights of Minneapolis glowed in the winter night like the beckoning torches of Valhalla.

There was no point in getting back on the highway. And Daniel thought a nice night in the city might be just the thing to repair the damage he'd obviously done.

"I'm going to stop for the night." Moog made a grumpy grunt in acknowledgment. Vicki said nothing at all.

"Look, I'm sorry," Daniel said. Although in his heart of hearts he really hadn't done anything to either of them. And, as it turned out, they'd gotten far more from Herb Gless than they ever could've hoped for.

The Graves is one of Minneapolis's finest hotels, and just around the corner from the city's historic music venue, First Avenue. Daniel thought a nice dinner, some great music, and a good night's sleep might be all that they needed to get back on their feet. "You don't think this is just a tad conspicuous?" Vicki asked as he pulled up in front.

"It's the last place anyone will look," Daniel said. "We check into a little hotel in the middle of nowhere, and they'll look us up and down."

"We check into a hotel in fucking Portugal," Moog interrupted. "That's where no one is going to recognize us. We might as well go in there with Prince's assless pants on."

"You forget, Moog," Vicki added. "Nothing we say or think or do matters. Let's just do what Daniel wants to do. That's what's going to go down anyway."

"That's not how it is—" Daniel objected.

"Right, I forgot," the big man answered for Vicki's benefit.

"I'm helping more than you know," Daniel said.

Moog wasn't buying it. "So you keep *not* telling me."

"And so you keep not telling *me*." Daniel looked in the rearview mirror. "You've been texting all day."

"What of it?"

"Who do you know to text? Just tell me that."

Moog took offense at the tone. "Why tell you anything? You never listen to me. Or Vicki."

"Girls, girls," she interrupted before it could get overheated. "Bobby's not asking either one of you to the prom. Can we just get inside before you go all hissy-fit on one another?"

"Can you get the bags?" Daniel asked Moog without sliding out from behind the wheel.

"Sure 'nuff, Miss Daisy." The sarcasm was liberally sprinkled with real bitterness.

"That's not right." Daniel shot back, badly stung by what everyone knew was an unjustified shot. "Just make sure you get that one." He nodded over his shoulder at the cash-filled duffel Moog had been using as a pillow.

"And why can't you get your own goddamn bags?" Moog demanded.

"Because there's something that's got to be taken care of if we're all going to get a decent night's sleep."

The big man instinctively turned and caught sight of the Audi A8 parked at the curb across the street. There was a steady plume of exhaust from its stainless steel Milltek pipes. He turned back. "Let me—"

Daniel wouldn't let him finish. "You have to take care of the really important things."

"I got it." Moog looked hard into his friend's eyes to let him know that he did.

"Of *everything*," Daniel repeated, although he knew he didn't have to. "If anything happens—"

Vicki was growing suspicious. "What are you two talking about?"

"I've got to run a quick errand," Daniel called back.

"Run an errand? We're in Minneapolis in a snowstorm. What errand do you have to run?"

"I'll be right back," Daniel promised.

She tried to lean into the car, but Moog stretched out his arm to stop her. "He'll be right back. Come on, let's us go in and get some rooms."

"What?" She looked at Moog. And then back at Daniel. "What's going on? Now *I'm* the only one being excluded?"

Through the broken bits of ice sliding down the surface of the driver's door mirror, Daniel caught a glimpse of the passenger door of the Audi opening. A large man, his features obscured in the irregular reflection of the frozen mirror, started to climb out. "I gotta go. Now."

Moog reached into the car and pulled out the cash-stuffed duffel. "I got this here. Go!"

"Go? I'm not a set of bags you two assholes leave at the curb," Vicki angrily shouted. There was more, but Daniel didn't wait around to hear it. In the last glimpse he caught of her in his rearview, it looked like she was giving Moog all kinds of hell. Daniel didn't envy his friend at all, but he breathed a sigh of relief when he caught the Audi's HID headlights glowing behind him.

Daniel stepped on the gas, and the truck slid side to side before the antislip regulation kicked in. He took off down the street as a declaration that he'd made his tail and he was slipping it now. Whoever was driving the Audi must've decided that he'd played the pursuit long enough and answered the call by kicking the 4.2L V-8. Both cars raced down the street, ignoring weather conditions and traffic controls with equal disregard.

Daniel hit the brakes and slid to a stop. He left it in gear, pressed down on the clutch, and waited.

Thirty seconds later the Audi slid to a stop behind him, just barely missing a collision on the slippery roadway. A car door opened and slammed shut. Daniel looked into his rearview mirror but was blinded by the glare of the headlights. He glanced at the driver's mirror and saw only the torso of the man who approached and then tapped on the glass with something metal. Daniel didn't have to guess what it was.

Daniel rolled down the window and found himself staring into the barrel of a Tokarev TT-33. He was unimpressed. "It's cold, and I'm really not in a mood for whatever you've got planned for tonight."

"I'm not interested in your mood," the man with the gun informed him. The accent was foreign, but all too familiar.

"You're a friend of Filat's?"

"Preezrakevich is dead," the man replied flatly.

"I heard something about that."

"And just what do you hear?"

Daniel smiled. "Aiiiiiiiiiiiiiiiiiiiiiiiiiiiiii!" he squealed in a falsetto that mocked the cry the Russian had made as he plummeted to his death. "And then a big *splat*. That's what I hear."

The man with the Soviet sidearm put his pistol through the open window so that it was just inches from Daniel's head. "Well, tonight you hear your own screams."

"Take another listen, Boris—it won't be me screaming."

There was a tapping on the passenger-side window. Daniel looked over and saw another man standing there with a KS-23K, the standard-issue shotgun of the Russian Ministry of Internal Affairs.

"My name's not Boris," the man on the driver's side responded, moving his pistol still closer to Daniel's head.

Daniel turned to the man and looked into his eyes, staring straight up the barrel of the pistol. "What's a name to a dead man?"

A second later Daniel reached out and grabbed the hand that held the pistol. As he did, he slipped his foot off the clutch and the car lurched forward five feet.

A second later a blast from the shotgun buried itself harmlessly in the rear passenger door.

Immediately, Daniel grabbed the arm in front of him and pulled it across him, toward the passenger side. As the man's ribs slammed into the driver's door, his hand reflexively tensed and he fired a shot that shattered the passenger window and then buried itself in his partner's chest. Daniel tugged at the arm again and the pistol tumbled out onto the passenger seat.

The man with the shotgun sank to his knees, seemingly more surprised by the turn of events than the amount of his own blood that was already pooling in the snow. He tried to get back to his feet, but couldn't collect himself enough to summon the strength.

By the time the man had decided to take a shot from his knees, Daniel had already taken the TT-33 pistol for himself. Daniel's shot struck the man square in the chest and knocked him back onto the snow-covered sidewalk.

The man who wasn't named Boris tried to pull free, but Daniel had a solid grip on him and pulled him deeper into the car's interior. With his left hand, Daniel shoved the man's head face-first into the cramped area between the dashboard and the windshield. "Now listen up, Boris—"

Before he could finish, there was a violent jolt and the sound of metal on metal. Daniel looked into the rearview and saw a dark SUV buried in the back of his truck.

In that moment, the man not named Boris tried to slip away again. Daniel pinned him again, but a second later the night echoed with another shotgun blast and the rear window exploded in a burst of crystalline shards.

"You brought more friends to the party, Boris?" Daniel tossed a quick look out the now shattered rear window.

"I make you scream," the Russian promised.

"You want screaming, try this." Without releasing the force he was exerting on the back of the man's head to keep him pinned to the windshield, Daniel started the car up and slid it into gear.

With his head crammed against the windshield, the man was twisted in such a way that he could barely stand. When the car began to move, it was a struggle to keep his awkwardly positioned feet moving beneath him.

Daniel picked up speed, and soon the exercise of sidestepping to keep up was an act of futility for the man. His feet fell out from beneath him, but Daniel kept him pressed against the windshield as his feet dragged along the street.

"Stop! Stop! Stop!"

"Yeah. You just scream when you've had enough." Daniel let go of the steering wheel just long enough to pull the gear shifter back to second. He straightened the wheel out again and then repeated the procedure to get the shifter up into third.

Shots rang out from the black SUV that was following close behind them.

As the car's speed increased so did the friction of the man's feet against the pavement. He screamed out as his New & Lingwood calf boot slipped from his right foot and when he lost its mate from his left. He screamed louder as his unprotected feet hit the pavement and dragged along the streets.

"Who sent you here?" Daniel demanded.

"Fuck you!" was the only response he got.

"Fuck me? I got enough gas in the tank to drag your ass across South Dakota, Boris."

"My name not Boris."

"Everyone is going to be calling you Stubby in about half a mile if you don't tell me who sent you."

More shots came from the SUV in pursuit.

"I will piss on your grave!" the man declared as bravely as he could while still wincing at the open wounds that had torn away the flesh of his dragging feet.

"Maybe. But you're not going to be able to stand on it unless you start talking soon."

The man squirmed, but he was too awkwardly positioned and held too tightly to free himself. "Aaaaaaaaaaaah!" he wailed, though it wasn't obvious whether it was a cry of anguish or frustration.

More shots came from the pursuing SUV, and this time they all struck closer to Daniel.

"I've had enough of this shit." Without ever letting go of the man not named Boris, Daniel turned the wheel hard to the left and brought his feet down in unison on the clutch and the brake. The car broke hard, threatening to fishtail for an instant before Daniel slid the gearshift back into second and drove ahead onto the entrance ramp of a parking garage. He started up the ramp. The SUV bumped him from behind, then bumped him again.

"You're running out of places to run."

"Didn't you know?" Daniel asked. "I stopped running a long time ago."

Around and around, they climbed up the ramp until the night lights of the roof were visible. As soon as the car hit the roof, Daniel turned the steering wheel as hard as he could to the left, stomped on the brake and clutch. They spun away to the left.

The maneuver took the pursuers completely by surprise as they headed straight out onto the rooftop deck—and past Daniel. A second later they realized that Daniel was now behind them, but by the time they figured that out, they were going too fast to stop what they saw unfolding.

Daniel was behind them, driving hard, and the deck was too slick to stop. Daniel bumped them and kept on pushing. They hit the concrete wall straight on and broke right through it. There was complete silence for the second or two it took them to plummet the seven stories to the street below. And then there was a huge explosion.

Daniel finally let go of the man not named Boris. He slid out of the car and dropped to the deck as the car rocked to a stop just on the safe side of the now-gaping hole in the wall of the parking garage's roof deck.

Daniel took a minute to catch his breath and let his furiously pounding heart slow to a panicked throbbing. He got out of the wrecked car, struggling to stand on wobbly legs that were shaky from the overdose of adrenaline. He reached down and pulled the Russian up to what had once been his feet. The man cried in pain, but it didn't deter Daniel.

"Who's screaming now, Boris?"

"My name—" Every word was as difficult as the struggle to stand on the ends of his shattered legs. "Not. Boris."

"Well, Not Boris." Daniel dragged the man over to the edge of the deck so they could look down at the fireball that was engulfing his comrades. "Someone sent you here to kill me. To kill my friends. And you're going to tell me—"

"Ivan. Nurivov," the man said with as much pride and defiance as he could muster.

"He's the man who sent you?"

"My. Name." The man grinned, as if somehow he'd won whatever game he'd been playing. "Ivan," he started again, but it was all too much for him. "My. Name."

Daniel understood. "Well, Ivan Nurivov, whoever it was that sent you after me, you save a place for him in hell, because I have a feeling I'll be sending him to join you real soon."

There was no more banter. Daniel merely pointed the man toward the hole in the wall and let go. The man stumbled a step or two and then disappeared into the night.

Daniel looked over the edge and saw the man, now part of the flames.

He didn't feel remorse, or satisfaction. It was something that had to be done, and he'd done it. There were sirens in the near distance, and all he felt was the need to get away.

CHAPTER FORTY-TWO

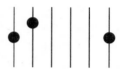

Life is all about rhythm.

This was the thought barely occupying Herb Gless's mind as he listened to the steady beat of electronic beeps on the Welch Allyn Protocol 52000 vital signs monitor. Even his heart kept perfect time.

A slow drip of Naloxone was hung from an IV tree on the hospital bed, and drop by drop, he watched it make the slow descent down the plastic tubing and through the needle embedded in his left hand. The prescription would keep him from slipping into a narcotic-induced coma as his body struggled to clear his system of the ketamine. It was also, however, keeping the K-hole, the narcotic nirvana, maddeningly just beyond his reach, and more than anything else, he wanted to reach the K-hole.

He was convinced that if he could kink the IV tube and suspend the Naloxone for just the right amount of time, he could slip into the state of chemical bliss without risking the coma. He was forcing his hazy mind to make the calculations and estimations necessary to carry out his plan when the door to his hospital room opened.

Herb assumed the two men who entered his room were orderlies because they were dressed in white uniforms, and one of them was pushing a cleaning cart. Also, they were both Mexican.

Whoever they were, he wanted them gone. He tried to say "*Por favor*" to get their attention, but his current status made it difficult to articulate, and the only sound he was able to make was an unintelligible mumble.

"*Que?*" the man with the cart asked his partner.

"*Nada*," replied the one who'd pulled Herb's medical chart from the bottom of the bed and had begun to read it.

He wasn't going to have orderlies reading his chart. He tried to find the words, but it was hard enough to think in English, much less Spanish. *Vamanos.* Was that the word? Or was it *vamoose*? Was there a difference? He made an ill-advised effort to sit up so he could address the intruders, but he couldn't quite manage the maneuver. "*Por favors*," he tried again.

"What's he saying?" the guy with the cart asked.

His partner didn't bother to look up from the hospital chart he was casually flipping through. "I think he wants us to leave."

"Oh. Why doesn't he just say that?"

"I think he's too messed up." The man tossed the chart on the floor like it was something no one would need any longer, and the crash it made as it hit the floor startled Herb in his bed.

"Let's just get this over with," the man behind the cart said.

The other one leaned over Herb and slapped his cheeks sharply. "Hey!"

Herb tried to focus his attention. "What?" The word was barely intelligible and all Herb could get out.

"I got a message for you," the man standing over Herb said as he made a quick survey of the room. "A mutual friend of ours thinks you've screwed this up."

If it hadn't been for the narcotics flooding his system, Herb would have been terrified. "No," he was able to slur.

"'Fraid so, homes," Cart Guy said with a sympathetic nod of his head. "The thin dude wants to know what you told them."

Herb knew he needed to convince them that he hadn't said anything at all, but all he could get out was, "Noth—"

The man standing over Herb only laughed at the pathetic display. "That's the thing, *puta*. Our mutual friend thinks that maybe you've been talking too much." He reached for the drip bag hanging from the IV tree attached to Herb's hospital bed. "That you're a loose end."

Even under the effect of the ketamine, Herb could feel his heart begin to pound more quickly as the sensation of fear settled in on him. "No, no."

"It's not our call," the man explained as he pulled the drip bag away from the IV line running into the top of Herb's left hand.

Self-preservation began to override the drugs in Herb's system, clarifying his thoughts and restoring just enough control to swear, "Didn't talk."

"Maybe," the man conceded as he pulled a knife from the front pocket of his coveralls. Herb's eyes struggled so hard to focus on the blade that he never saw the five-gallon bottle of GD-80 until Cart Guy had handed it to his partner.

"But there's only one way to make sure that you *won't*," the man continued as he took the knife blade and punctured a hole in the cap of the disinfecting industrial cleaning fluid, inserted the IV tube, and secured it.

Even in his muddled state, it didn't take Herb long to figure out what came next. If he could have screamed, he would have shrieked like a banshee, but he couldn't do either. All he could manage was a limp "No. Please."

And that wasn't nearly enough.

The man by the bedside flipped the jug upside down and hung it on the IV tree, spilling its contents down the tube and into Herb's veins.

The two men held Herb down as the poison inched its way down the tube. If he hadn't been medicated, he might have been able to break free. Maybe he would've had a chance. His body wouldn't respond with enough force to break free, though, and his squeaky attempts at a scream were quickly silenced with a pillow over his face.

His body twitched and convulsed as the poison burned its way into his veins. It felt as if they'd set him on fire from the inside out. And as those chemical flames consumed him, the last thought to pass through his head was that he was never going to reach the K-hole. There was never going to be comfort. Never again.

It was a minute or two before someone at the busy nurses' station noticed that the monitor in Room 7371 had slowed to a dead stop. They followed procedure and called Code Blue, but there was nothing that could be done when they got there.

Life is all about rhythm. Herb Gless had lost his for good.

CHAPTER FORTY-THREE

Daniel opened the door and found the room too dark to tell if he was sharing it with Vicki or if she'd left him alone. He let the door close behind him and moved into the room. As his eyes adjusted, he felt his way to the bed and touched Vicki's ankle beneath the covers. An overwhelming wave of relief washed over him.

Daniel took off his clothes and slid between the sheets next to her. Her body reacted to his presence, moving back into his arms, without even waking. He held her tight, grateful for the opportunity.

She murmured, still half-asleep, "Hey."

He whispered back, "Hey."

He leaned out of the bed and retrieved something from the pile of clothes he'd left there on the floor. "Here," he told her. "I got you something."

She took the small box from him and gave him a quizzical look.

"Merry Christmas."

"Is it?" The news took her by surprise, and so did a sudden urge to break down in tears. She bit her lip and struggled to hold it together. "I didn't know." She sniffled. "I didn't get you anything."

He brushed a loose strand of her hair behind her ear. "You give me something special every day."

She smiled. And blushed. But instead of looking into his eyes, she opened the box. "It's…" It took her a moment to realize just what it was. "It's a Zippo lighter. Thank you. So much."

He knew her excitement was feigned, that she was trying to conceal her disappointment as she turned the classic chrome lighter over and over in her fingers. "There wasn't a lot open out there tonight," he confessed.

"I'll bet."

"But I would've gotten it for you anyway."

"Oh, really?"

"Well, I know you're still sneaking cigarettes."

"No, I'm not," she lied.

"Which I don't really understand, because I don't care." They both knew that had nothing to do with it. "And you do whatever you want to do anyway."

"They're sweeter when they're snuck," she confessed.

He nodded. "And I thought it was the perfect thing to remind you of me."

"A Zippo lighter is supposed to remind me of you?"

He took it from her to demonstrate. "It's not anything special to look at, but it's solid and dependable." He flipped it open and thumbed the wheel until it sparked a flame. "And it will always burn for you." He snapped the lighter closed.

She took it back from him, kissed him on the mouth, and pulled him down to her pillow. *Now* the tears came. "I was worried."

He wiped a tear away, but there were too many to catch them all. "It's all right," he whispered.

"Was it bad?" She wasn't exactly sure what she was asking about.

"It's always bad."

She hesitated, not wanting to voice the question that was really on her mind. "And the other—"

He interrupted her with a kiss. "There's no one to hurt you. Not anymore."

She knew what that meant. "But there will always be more, right?"

"No. Not always." He kissed her again. "But I will always do whatever I have to do to make sure that you're safe."

"I'm not sure what I'd do if you didn't come back."

He kissed her gently on the crown of her head and wiped away her tears. "I'm always coming back."

"Promise?"

"Promise."

She rolled over and pressed herself against him, kissing him hard to seal that promise on their lips. They didn't make love; what happened between them was not about affection. It wasn't having sex, a bodily function people perform when they surrender to a basic mammalian urge.

They fucked, like two people whose passions were deeper than emotion and stronger than instinct.

When they were both exhausted, she lay in his arms, exhilarated but feeling guilty about having enjoyed what they'd just done. "You've done something bad, haven't you?" She didn't need an answer.

And he didn't give her one.

"I can tell. You're always like that after you've done something—"

"I did what I had to do."

She knew that was right. What bothered her was that she knew he liked it. And she knew she liked it too.

"I don't know what happens," she confessed. "Sometimes I just feel like I've lost you. And I'm never going to get you back."

"I'm right here," he tried to assure her.

"I know. It's just that sometimes it feels like it's a different *you* that's here."

"I guess I don't know who to be. With anyone. When I'm a nice guy, people take me for granted or dismiss me as a simp. When I'm a bad guy, everyone treats me like a monster." He shook his head, overwhelmed by frustrations he hadn't been aware of before. "I don't know who to be."

It seemed simple enough to her. "Maybe you could just try to be yourself."

There was nothing simple about that to him. "I don't know who that is." Nothing at all.

"In my whole life, I've known three times when I felt like I was who I was supposed to be. The first was when I realized my son had become a man of his own. The second was when I went back to Vegas, stood up to those people, and jacked them all the fuck up." The memory was overwhelming.

"And the third?"

"The third is every time I'm in your arms. Everywhere else," he said with resignation, "I just feel nervous and weird."

"Maybe you should just take a breath and calm down. You're a good man. You'd be a great one if you just let yourself—"

"It's not like that." He stopped her. "When I was about ten, my mother told me I'd gotten sick as a baby. Real sick. I wasn't supposed to survive, but I did. When the doctors brought me to her, she thought they'd made a mistake."

Vicki had never heard the story before. No one had. She could tell that it wasn't easy for him to tell it.

"She told me she loved me, but that she never felt I was her son. Not really her son."

"Oh my God, that's terrible." She brushed his face with her palm, but could tell he wasn't there to feel it.

"No, it's not," he continued. "I never held it against her, because I understood. I always felt the same way too."

Life had required a cast-iron sense of practicality from Vicki Bean, and she never indulged in anything that didn't have real-world applications. "You're saying you died as a baby, and what? Another soul came along and hitched a ride?"

"It's not as crazy as you're making it sound."

"Sweetie, it would be hard to make it sound as crazy as it is."

"It's not crazy. Or even unusual," he insisted.

"It's both, sweetheart."

"Have you ever heard Bob Dylan talk about his motorcycle accident? He went out for a ride as one person, dumped his bike, and when he came out—"

"He was still Bob Dylan."

"Have you ever heard him talk about transfiguration?" He was frustrated by her inability—or unwillingness—to see the broader scope of the picture he was trying to share. "Or Wannaman, after his accident."

"I am with you to the end, angel." He could tell she meant it. "But that we've talked to people who knew the real Mark Wannaman doesn't mean that we ever knew him. Even after everything we've been through, I'm still not convinced the guy we knew back in St. Thomas wasn't just some misguided beach bum." He knew she meant that too.

"Yeah, well, you're wrong." His defensiveness was beginning to just sound angry. "I know who Mark was because the old man told me so."

"The old man?" she asked, struck by how weird that sounded. "What old man?"

It was one of those "Uh-oh" moments, when the magnitude of the unintended reveal becomes obvious from the undue time it takes to conceal. Three or four awkward, gaped-mouth seconds went by before Daniel realized he'd unintentionally thrown open the closet door on the one secret he'd been hoping to hide.

How to explain someone (something?) like Mr. Atibon?

"A year ago," he began. "When I was down in the Delta. I met a man."

It seemed simple enough. "All right."

"At the Robert Johnson crossroads."

"All right." She had a CliffsNotes understanding of the whole "traded his soul to play guitar" legend.

"In the middle of the night."

"Wait a minute. Are you telling me that you think you've met the devil?"

"He's not the devil," Daniel insisted. And then took a moment to think that one over before continuing on. "He's not the devil. But he's something I can't explain."

"Like not being the person you were born as?"

He couldn't help but be hurt by her lack of sincerity, particularly when his answer couldn't have been more earnest. "Yes. Exactly like that. It's something that I'm sure of, but can't explain. Or understand."

"And this all has to do with why we're out here?"

He could, maybe, think of a reasonable answer or two. Or at least a less unreasonable answer—but he decided to go with the truth. "Because he told me to find who was behind Mark's death."

"Wow!" She sat up in bed. "You're telling me we've been risking everything traipsing all over the Midwest looking for someone who may or may not have killed someone who may or may not have been Marco Pharaoh, not because you felt a moral obligation as the friend of a real, actual person but because an old man who may or may not be the devil told you to?"

"He's not the devil." That was the only thing he was sure of. Or at least the thing he was most sure of.

"I don't believe this." She started to rock back and forth as if someone had just let her in on the joke that the winning Powerball ticket she'd thought had changed her life was just a prank. "Oh my God!"

"Vicki." He reached out for her, but she refused his touch.

"I can't believe"—there were a lot of unbelievable things between them at that moment, but the one that disturbed her most was—"that my Chooser was so absolutely dead on the money with you. The one fucking time it got things right, and I totally ignored it." Speaking the words out loud only worsened the panic she was feeling. She rocked harder. And then began to cry.

"Vicki."

"No," she warned him. "I thought we were out here doing something real for someone you felt was a friend. I thought we were trying to find the person responsible so that we can have a new life. I thought there was maybe some little spark of the man I used to know, some ember I could resuscitate. I didn't realize I was freezing my ass off in the nation's meat locker with someone who's so fucking deranged he's following orders from the shadowy blues legends he hears in his head. I just didn't think you were risking our lives for some supernatural bullshit."

"You talk about the supernatural like it's something you can separate from everyday life, but it's not. It's not *super*natural, it's just that part of the natural that we can't understand. Yet."

"I don't believe in the supernatural, Daniel."

"I don't either. I've just come to understand that the natural is far bigger than we think." He searched for an example. "You take writing a song. Keith Richards woke up one morning, and the guitar riff for 'Satisfaction' was just *there* on the cassette recorder he slept with. Jimi Hendrix wrote 'Purple Haze' about a dream of being underwater. Who knows where it all comes from? How can you give a natural explanation to what happens when words and music come together? How can you make music and not *know* that the supernatural exists?"

"I'm not talking about chords and lyrics, Daniel." She ran her hand through her hair. "I just can't do this anymore."

The words were new from her, but it wasn't the first time he'd heard that tone. He knew exactly what her inflections meant. Good-bye is a simple word, but people rarely use it.

He got out of bed and was suddenly reminded of the vulnerability that clothes hide from all but the most intimate. And that there is no colder place in all the world than that void space one is hurled into when leaving a lover's bed.

He slid on his jeans and then a T-shirt, sat down on the bed to put on shoes.

She did not try to stop him. "I'll get you wherever you're going tomorrow. I think I know someone who can take us where you need to go, but then—" She didn't want to say the words.

"I understand."

"I have a friend there," she explained. "The bassist from my band."

"All right."

"She's in California."

"OK."

"I just can't—" She didn't want to say those words.

He didn't make her.

She watched him leave the room, relieved to see him go, distraught when the door shut closed and she realized he was gone.

In her head furious comments about his delusions and betrayal flashed in her head, all of them assuring her she'd made the right choice, the only choice.

In her heart—that treacherous, traitorous, malfunctioning thing she called her Chooser—a quiet, trembling voice broke and quivered as it told her she'd just watched the last happiness she'd ever know walk out into the Minnesota cold.

She slammed her head down on her pillow and pulled the covers up around her. She hated him for having left his pillow smelling like him. She flipped it over and then flung it across the room. She hated him for having deceived her. And most of all for having left.

She lay awake for the rest of the night, too angry to cry.

CHAPTER FORTY-FOUR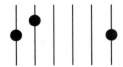

There wasn't a lot of explaining in the morning.

Daniel didn't explain what had happened to the car or why he was now driving a Lexus. He told Moog and Vicki that he'd seen Herb Gless's iPhone and that he'd traced a call he made to an address in Orange County, California. When Daniel thought about it, there was only one person in the 657 area code he was likely calling.

For her part, Vicki didn't explain why she wasn't hungry for breakfast or why she needed to sit in the backseat. She certainly didn't offer any explanation for how she knew Trevor, how it was she still remembered his number, or why—even in the frozen Minnesota morning—he reeked of patchouli. (For his part, he didn't offer any explanation for why he'd taken the rear two seats out of his Piper Cherokee Six.)

Trevor was a gaggle of limbs who probably would've reached six foot or better if he ever stood up straight. He insisted that Vicki sit up front, and his hand touched her knee a lot while he kept laughing about "that one time in Punta Colonet" or "that other time in Puerto Piata."

By the time they landed in the Fullerton Municipal Airport, Daniel had had enough of Trevor's attempts to reminisce his way back into Vicki's life. He was about to say something about it when Moog clapped him on the back with his oversize hand. "I got this."

"Got what?" Daniel asked.

"Our friend Trevor here, let me have a little talk with him."

The big man approached the hippie. "Trevor."

"Dude."

"Dude," Moog repeated with a smile. He shook Trevor's hand and used it as an opportunity to slide the guy a wad of bills.

Trevor took the bills and looked at them. "Thanks, man."

"No problem." Moog humbly shook his head. "But listen, we gotta talk about something."

The high-flying hippie slid the bills into his shirt pocket. "Sure thing, dude. Shoot."

Moog nodded. "That's exactly right."

"What's right?"

"Shoot. That's what I want to do to you, Trevor. There is nothing I like about you. I just listened to you bust my friend's balls for four hours while you tried to climb into his woman's jeans right in front of him."

"Hey, man, I didn't mean nothing."

Moog grabbed him before he could back away. "We all know what you meant. Same as I know a thousand little fucks just like you. You all sell one another out the first time some potbellied cop busts you for possession or some two-bit douchebag thinks he's a gangster slides you a fucking dime bag. I'm telling you now that the best thing you can do is to forget about us. All of us. Because if you talk about us, if you talk to anyone about the little trip we've taken here, I'm gonna come looking for you. And if I come lookin', I'm gonna find you. And when I find you, I'm going to roll you up all nice and tight in paper and I'm gonna light you up. Do you understand?"

"Hey, man—" Trevor protested.

"Do you understand? If you talk about any of this, I am going to find you and burn you to death. I need you to tell me that you understand."

"I understand. I understand."

"Good." Moog set him down and smoothed out some of the wrinkles he'd put in the pilot's shirt. "So we're cool with this?"

"We're cool, man. We're cool."

"Good enough." The big man turned like he might be finished. And then stopped. "Oh, there's just one more thing."

"What is it, man?"

"I think my friend Daniel would want me to pass this along to you." Moog's fist hit Trevor like a cannonball and dropped him to the ground.

Moog stood over him, knowing the hippie pilot couldn't hear him. "All right. *Now* we're cool."

CHAPTER FORTY-FIVE

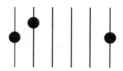

Though there are quite a few homes on Southern California's Map of the Stars' Homes, it didn't take the trio long to find the property they were looking for—an estate so big that it had its own name. *Absinthe Hall* scrolled in twisted iron over the top of the twin gates that appeared to be the only entrance through the fourteen-foot black iron fence that surrounded the property.

Vicki shook her head and tossed a this-is-perfect look up to the perpetually *Simpsons*-blue sky overhead. "How you planning on getting from here to there?" she inquired, making a point of the distance (and fence) that separated them from the massive white mansion that sat at the end of a winding quarter-mile drive.

"I'll just ask," he said, ignoring her snarkiness. "Nice and polite." Daniel pressed the button on the speaker box and waited for a response. Nothing. "Maybe there's no one home."

"Maybe it's the home of a dead rock star and they don't just answer the buzzer whenever someone wanders by the edge of the drive," Vicki offered.

Daniel thought over his options. Turning around at the closed gate and going home—especially in front of Vicki—wasn't on his list. "No problem. I'll just hop the gate here and walk up the drive. Knock on the door. A slightly more direct version of nice and polite."

She wasn't impressed. "A slightly more direct version of breaking and entering."

Daniel didn't bother to respond. He pulled himself over the top, swung his legs over, and then slowly lowered himself until the ground was just a short hop away. "How easy was that?" he asked in satisfaction, his arms raised in triumph.

Vicki was still unimpressed. "You jumped a fence."

"I told you. Nice and polite."

"Well, Mr. Nice and Polite, I hope you can get back over that fence quicker than you made it over," she said smugly.

Daniel cocked his head. "What are you talking about?"

There was a twist of satisfaction in her smile as she subtly pointed toward something unspecified in the distance behind him.

Moog was less restrained. "Holy shit!"

It was the fear in his friend's eyes that spun Daniel around and led him to find that he was the focus of the biggest dog he'd ever seen. A hundred yards away, 250 pounds of canine was moving straight at him, closing the distance at a speed far greater than a creature that large should be able to attain.

Daniel grabbed the iron bars and hoisted himself up. He planted his left foot, but his right slipped, just a bit and just for a half second, and that was enough for the beast to clear the distance.

Daniel braced himself, and on its first attempt the dog only succeeded in banging itself into the gate. The second time was a charm, and its new prize fell to the ground. It shook the ankle it had seized and then dropped it to move on to meatier things.

"Sparkles!" The voice was a girl's, but stern enough that the dog stopped midpounce, waiting for permission to enjoy his treat. "Sparkles, no!" She reconsidered the instruction. "Not yet."

"Come here!" The dog backed away.

"Sit!" He put his ass on the ground, but his shoulders were still tensed as if he was ready to bolt in for the kill.

Daniel pulled himself back as far as he could before the dog rose off his haunches and began to growl again. "Good dog," he said in as soothing a voice as he could muster.

"He's really not," the girl announced proudly. "He's big and bad and he doesn't do this trick very well." The dog growled and licked its chops. "Or for very long. So before he loses patience with me, who are you?"

"My name is Daniel Erickson."

"Should that mean something to me?" She was just in her teens, but the eyes that stared at him, weighing him and judging him, were much, much older.

And they told him exactly who she was. "I was a friend of your father's."

She took a step back, bristling at the reference. "My father had a lot of friends." Her dog responded with a low growl, which she did not ask him to hush.

Daniel could tell he'd gained a handhold in her interest. "Not when I knew him."

"Just you?" she asked skeptically.

"Well, we had—" He paused to consider the proper response. "A mutual friend."

"Who's that?"

"I don't think you'd want to know him."

"You're probably right." She let it pass. "So why are you here, Mr. Daniel Erickson, friend of my father?" She pointed past him. "The fence is there for a reason, you know."

"I need to talk to your mother."

She was quick with her question. "About what?"

"About how he died."

"Why would she know anything about that?"

"Because someone told me she would."

"Lots of people say lots of things." She seemed unmoved by the suggestion. "Like I could tell Sparkles what he's waiting to hear, and tomorrow one of the gardeners would be pooper-scooping you off of the lawn."

"But you haven't told your pooch to eat me yet," he couldn't help but observe.

"I'm still thinking it over." She smiled. "It's called building up the drama."

He hadn't come there with that intention, but there was something in the girl's eyes that made him ask, "What do you know about your father's death?"

"Like I said, lots of people say lots of things. I only know what they've told me."

"And what's that?"

"Merry Fairy!" a woman's voice bellowed from the front door of the main house.

Daniel looked at the girl. Those eyes. They were suddenly filled with fear. And anger.

"Right?" The girl said with a contemptuous shake of the head that she realized expressed everyone's first impression of the raving woman. "Only a complete narcissist names her kid Merry Fairy. 'Look how original my child's name is!'" she mocked.

"Assholes." She shook her head again and then nodded up the drive that the woman was storming down. "All of her friends—her *former* friends—did the same thing. I go to school with a boy named Christmas Tree. Do I have to tell you how fucked up that's made him? I tell everyone that M. F. stands for motherfucker."

Adeline Swank had left the Turtle Rock mansion she'd been born to and done braless tank tops and lace-'em-up Doc Martens punk-rock bands just long enough to piss off Daddy and land herself her own piece of the rock-and-roll dream: Marco Pharaoh, née Mark Wannaman.

She'd parlayed the five minutes of power-couple fame the two had shared into a successful clothing company and a not so successful appearance on a celebrity dance show. And that, together with control of Mark's catalog, was more than enough for a mansion with a big fence around it. And a mammoth fellow with sewer-pipe arms to deal with those persistent types who made their way over it. "What the hell is this?" Adeline panted when she got to the bottom of the drive.

"Relax, Mom." M. F. reached over and attached the loose lead she'd been carrying to Sparkles's collar. The dog didn't seem to like her mother much more than he liked Daniel. "The guy's a friend of Dad's."

The woman looked down at Daniel. "Who the fuck are you?"

Without waiting for an answer, she turned back to the oversize guy who was just reaching the party. "What am I paying you for if a guy can just hop the fence and talk with my fucking daughter?"

"*Language*, Mother," M. F. exclaimed in mock horror, her eyes sparkling.

"I'm sorry, Ms. Swank," the behemoth panted. "We didn't pick up anything—"

"Yeah. You know how I'd already figured that part out?" she interrupted him. "Because the fucker's right here on my lawn."

She gestured toward Daniel, and the oversize guy reached down and pulled him to his feet. He held on to Daniel's arm.

"You two have two minutes to get out of here," she called through the fence to Vicki and Moog. "But your shithead friend here is going to jail. You writers think you can hide behind the Constitution while you go writing all your sick lies—"

Daniel pulled away from the security guy and rubbed his arm. "I'm not a writer."

It was enough to shut her up momentarily. She looked at him as if she was searching for something particular and then reacted with a start when she finally found it. "Who are you?" she asked, although her wide eyes suggested she already knew.

"Your daughter told you. I was a friend of Mark's."

"Mark didn't have any friends." Her words were harsh, her behavior suddenly panicked and nervous.

Daniel shrugged. "He had at least two."

"What is it that you want? You want money? Is that it?" She snapped her now-trembling fingers, and the security ogre quickly produced a cigarette and then lit it for her. "You think you're just going to show up here and throw out Mark's name and I'm going to—what?—give you some money?" She took a hard draw on her cigarette.

"I've got my own money," Daniel told her. "I just want to talk to you about Mark's death."

"What do you care?"

Daniel was eager to tell her. "A friend asked me to find out who—"

"Who?" M. F. wanted to know.

"Our mutual friend," Daniel answered before returning his attention to her mother. "He asked me to find out who killed Mark."

"Mark killed Mark," she screamed, and now her bodyguard was restraining her, but she let him. "He drove into a motherfucking tree, asshole! He killed himself!"

Daniel brushed himself off. No one seemed to notice, not even Sparkles, who was as transfixed as everyone else by the scene.

"How dare you come to my home and talk to my fucking daughter about this! You and your lies!"

"What lies?"

The second that passed then was one of the quietest that Daniel had ever experienced. Maybe ever. It was as if all of the audio had momentarily cut out of the entire world for an instant.

"You get your ass off my lawn," she screamed. "I want you fucking gone!"

"You sure you don't want to call the cops?" Daniel teased her.

The second quietest moment of his life.

Adeline turned to her henchman. "I want them gone."

He grabbed Daniel by the arm and forced him forward. When they got to the gate, the bouncer pushed Daniel face-first into the iron bars as he opened a door in the main gate just big enough for a person to slide through. He pushed Daniel out. "Now don't let me catch you back here again."

"Or what?" Daniel wondered aloud, wiping blood from his nose.

"You think I'm playing with you, asshole?" He opened the gate again and took one step toward Daniel. It was something like opening the bear's cage at the zoo.

In an instant, Moog moved forward, reached past the bouncer, grabbed the opened gate, and pulled it closed—with the bouncer caught in it. Again and again, Moog pulled the gate closed on the bouncer and each time the man slumped farther to the ground.

Moog stood over the man. "You ain't playin' with no one, motherfucker."

The man struggled to his knees, and Moog pulled the gate closed on him one last time. "You all played out."

On the other side of the now-open gate, Adeline was as outraged as she dared to be. "I will have your head bobbing in the Pacific, you ever come back here!"

"Wonder where her head's been bobbing," Vicki said, not quite under her breath, as she went to Daniel's side.

"What did you say?" Adeline angrily approached the fence.

Vicki had been having the kind of week that made her wish there was no fence to separate them. "I said shut your mouth, you has-been pig. You can't sing. You can't play guitar. And you're about as frightening as the fat-assed soccer mom you've become."

The third quietest moment in Daniel's life, and it came just before the screaming started anew from the other side of the gate. But this third moment was by far his favorite. He put his arm around Vicki and led her back to the car.

"That's right, you better run. You better run for your lives! You wait till Haden hears about this!"

Daniel wasn't sure why, but the name struck—not a bell so much as a chord. "Haden?"

"That's right," she confirmed, as if she'd just pressed the big red button to nuke all three of them. "I'm a close personal friend of Haden Koschei, and when he finds out about this he's going to fucking kill you!"

Daniel turned. "Tell him he won't have to wait long. I'm on my way."

More silence.

He gave a smile to the girl. "See you around, M. F."

Adeline was too flustered. "Get in the house, Merry Fairy!" she bellowed. "This is all your fault anyway."

"Hey!" Daniel called after them. All three of them (and the dog) turned expectantly. "The lady prefers to be called M. F."

CHAPTER FORTY-SIX

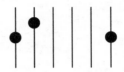

There was a certain energy in the office. Feller couldn't quite pin it down, but he was certain that there was something happening—and that it was big.

The knock on the cubicle opening was merely a formality, a way of arousing attention and announcing an intention to step inside. "Can we talk for a minute?" Feller asked, nervously checking the hall behind him to see if anyone had taken special note of him. "I was wondering if you'd heard anything from the Russians?"

"Really?" Special Agent Schweeter snapped.

Feller knew his onetime subordinate had been doing his damnedest to discourage conversation with the office pariah, but he was every bit as bewildered by the reaction as he'd been earlier in the week when his wife had told him she was through. Simply through. No explanation. No consideration of reconciliation. Just through. "What is it?"

"Can you really be this stupid?" He looked around his small cubicle as if there might be an eavesdropper hiding behind one of the several framed photos of his fiancée. "Ixnay on the Rus-skay."

Feller mistook the admonition as an instruction to simply whisper, as if merely lowering his voice would foil anyone from the FBI from listening to their hushed conversation, "I was wondering how *they* were doing?"

"*They* aren't doing that good today," Schweeter whispered back. "Seems your boy Erickson set them on fire and dropped them off a parking garage. Either that or he dropped them off a parking garage and set them on fire. Forensics team is still trying to work it out. But they're all extra crispy."

"What?" Feller was shocked. Then, although even he knew better than to admit it, he was overcome with an odd feeling of relief, as if the murders of the Russian mobsters he'd helped put on Erickson's trail somehow vindicated his own string of failures in trying to apprehend the man.

"Burned to a crisp," Schweeter repeated. "Yeah, except for the one guy he shot in the head." He shook his head. "The stiff was carrying a Karabin Spetsialniy shotgun. So it's only a matter of time before they make the Moscow connection." He looked around again. "And when they do, some politically ambitious prick is going to be doing his utmost to find out what they were doing here."

That wasn't at all how Schweeter had promised it would all work out. "But you said—"

"Me?" Schweeter had long ago pulled the rip cord on the ejector seat of their arrangement. "You got enough shit smeared all over you right now, with St. Thomas and all. If they find out that you had brought in Russian mafia to hunt down Erickson—"

"*I* had them," Feller gasped. "You were the one—"

"It's not going to do either of our careers any good, true, but you were the senior on the case. You're the one walking around with the hard-on for this guy. I'm going to get a letter in my jacket that I certainly don't want, but you're going to get your walking papers, if you're lucky. If you're not, you're going to see the inside of one of those federal facilities you've been sending guys off to for fifteen years. And frankly, fella, you don't strike me like you're riding on a very long lucky streak right now."

Feller looked down at his shoes.

"The answer is that we both need to keep our mouths shut right now. No one knows about this but us, right? You know enough to just keep your mouth shut, right?"

It occurred to Feller then how quickly the dynamics of their relationship had changed. "Excuse me?"

"Don't get all official on me. You just need to keep your mouth shut."

Feller took a seat in the chair that purposely hadn't been offered to him. It wasn't that there was another fecal front moving in on his personal horizons, or even that his own personal Jean Valjean had slipped from his grasp again, it was what that represented. It had been his last chance. His only chance. His chance to regain his position. Recapture respect in his workplace. Maybe even win his wife back. It had been his last-ditch chance. Now it was gone.

"Maybe if we talked to Bovard?" Feller wondered aloud.

"Didn't I just get done telling you we couldn't talk to anybody?" Schweeter looked back at the file in front of him. "Besides, talking to Bovard would be pretty difficult right now."

Feller clearly didn't grasp what was being implied.

"Do you live in a compound in Pakistan?"

It wasn't Feller's fault. He lived alone now. No one was particularly talkative to him in the office these days, either.

He cocked his head like a big, sad basset hound who can't understand why his owner hasn't gotten up off of the floor in the last couple days. "What do you mean?"

Schweeter didn't see the point in sugarcoating his news. "They found Bovard's body this morning." He held up the manila file folder like the inner-office trophy it was.

"His body?"

"Shot in the head. Execution style." He shook his head at whatever he'd seen inside the file. "Tragic."

Feller wondered if it could be a coincidence. "The Russians?"

"I don't think so," Schweeter said. "But it certainly doesn't create a climate for extracurricular activities like yours."

"Like mine?"

"Listen, just go back to your desk and do whatever it is they have you doing. But keep your head down and your mouth shut. Understand?"

Head down. Mouth shut. If Special Agent on Administrative Probation Gerald Feller had mastered anything, it was that.

CHAPTER FORTY-SEVEN

When he got off the exit, Daniel realized there were only moments left. He didn't see any sense in provoking the inevitable or instigating an argument, so his question was a simple one. "Are you sure?"

"Yes." She was.

But he still wasn't. "Because I could just get a hotel," he offered. "We could talk in the morning, maybe."

"No." Her voice was soft, but definite.

She was too tired to continue the dance.

"Will you be—"

"I'll be fine," she told him, but only because she felt she had to. "The thing about family is that they have to welcome your intrusions. Marcy's my family." She wiped at the thin fog that had formed on the passenger window. "Or at least as much of a family as I've got."

What more was there to say? "OK."

* * *

Marcy Fassure had not proven as resistant to the assault of time as Vicki. Each passing year had added another pound or two, and both smiles and worries had etched their lines on her face. It was difficult to imagine her as the tattooed bassist with the torn hose who'd kept the savage beat for Vicki's band, the Bitch You Miss, but their hug made the bond they shared unmistakable.

"Bitch," Marcy shrieked as she threw her arms around Vicki.

Vicki didn't say anything at all. As he took their bags out of the car, Daniel thought that maybe she was crying.

She pulled herself away from her friend's embrace, quick to wipe away the tear tracing its way down her cheek. "God, it's good to see you." Her smile beamed brighter than Daniel had seen it in months. Maybe ever.

"Introductions," she called out, pretending that no one could see her sniffling. "Marcy Fassure, the best fucking bassist ever."

Marcy made metal horns on her left hand and stuck her tongue out. "Bringing the beat that beats your ass."

Vicki gestured first at Moog. "This is Moog Turner."

He offered his hand and Marcy's disappeared inside his grip. "Nice to meet you."

Marcy checked Moog up and down, flashed a look at her friend, and then returned her obviously impressed gaze to the big man. "*Enchanté.*"

"And this is Daniel." Vicki raised a hand to where he was pulling their bags out of the car.

"Oh, so this is the one that stole you away from the world?" Marcy made no effort to hide the disapproving note in her voice.

It took a moment before Daniel realized he was up. His brain seemed to blank out for a second as he wondered whether he should set the bags down before offering his hand or simply offer her a nod. The result was an awkward gesture while shuffling the bags between hands. "It's nice—"

Marcy wasn't impressed. "Well, it's cold out here tonight. You better come in." She turned and threw an arm over Vicki's shoulder, leading the way inside.

Moog followed, then Daniel at a distance, but still close enough to hear Vicki's friend ask her, "You could have had either of them, and you chose the old white one?"

"Marcy—" Vicki hushed her.

"Would you understand if I told you I was disappointed in you?"

Daniel wasn't sure whether he'd been meant to hear the exchange or not.

Vicki had moved inside and out of earshot before he got her response.

Marcy Fassure's house was small and old. Not unlike Marcy herself, Daniel thought to himself.

"So this is home," she announced, raising her arms as if it were a prize on *The Price Is Right*.

"I love it," Vicki said.

Daniel watched her taking it all in like a hungry child making a tour of the buffet offerings at Golden Corral, more intrigued by the array of things she didn't have than finding anything she necessarily wanted. There were sofas and tables. Pictures and framed photographs. All the things, he realized, Vicki had wanted but had never gotten. There was a life within the walls.

"Come on in," Marcy said to Moog. "Make yourself at home."

The big man took a tentative seat on a couch that looked too frail to hold him, but did.

"Can I get you all something to drink?" She looked at Vicki. "I know you want a vodka and soda."

"No," Vicki said hesitantly.

"I'll make it a double." Marcy turned her attention to Moog. "And you?"

Moog was too tired to care. "I'll have whatever you're pouring."

"Whisky for the gentleman." She turned at last to Daniel. "You?"

"I'm fine." He held his hand up like a civic-minded schoolboy performing his crossing-guard duties. "I can't stay."

"What?" Marcy seemed more surprised than Moog.

And the big man was apoplectic. "What do you mean, you can't stay?"

"I'm moving on, Moog." That was all he could say.

"Just like that?"

"Vicki and I—" He couldn't explain what he didn't wholly understand.

Moog looked at Vicki. "And neither one of you thought to tell me?"

"We just—" Vicki sputtered.

"Well, this is perfect." Moog shook his head in disgust.

"Come on," Daniel said sharply, only to defer Moog's wrath from Vicki. "You've been thinking of moving on since we landed in Florida."

"I been thinking about moving on since you and I took off in Vegas, motherfucker. But here I am." He held up his hands, partly to announce the fact that he was the last man standing and partly as a gesture of frustration and disgust for all of those who had let him down and left him. His father. Arthur Beagler. And now Daniel.

"Well, I can't stay," Daniel told him. "If you want to ride with me—"

"Ride with you?" Moog exploded. "Where? For how long? Till you don't need me again and leave me off at the side of the road like some gimp dog you don't want anymore?"

"I understand." He pushed the cash-stuffed duffel toward Moog. "It's better this way."

"Better?" Moog hadn't wanted to hit someone so hard since he was a kid. "Better for who?"

"For Vicki," Daniel told him. "And for you."

"Don't you go telling me what's best for me." Moog had nothing more to say.

Vicki tried. "Moog—"

He brushed her words away too.

"Listen, I'm not sure what's going on here," Marcy intervened. "Vicki just told me she'd be stopping by with some friends. But really you must all stay. Really."

Daniel's voice was soft. "I can't." He moved to where Vicki sat crying on a couch and stood before her. "I'm sorry."

She shot to her feet and threw her arms around him. "I am, too."

He put his hands on her hips and pushed her away.

"Daniel—"

"It's better this way. You'll be fine." He turned to his ex-best friend. "Moog will take care of—"

"Whoa, whoa, whoa," Moog stopped him. "I'm not taking care of anybody but me. We going our ways, then we going our ways."

"Then we'll—" Daniel looked down at the duffel.

"Forget it," Moog assured him. "I don't want none of it. You give me a ride as far as the next city, and I'll be all right."

"All right," Daniel said, and then looked at Vicki. "All right?"

"All right."

Daniel pointed to the duffel. "You'll be all right."

"I can't take it," she insisted.

"Moog doesn't want it—"

"Not a penny," the big man spat.

"And I won't need it where I'm going."

Vicki looked askance. "What's that supposed to mean?"

"It means, whether you believe me or not, I got a debt to pay."
He walked to the door.

"Kids, kids." Marcy tried to intervene. "Let's all just get a good
night's sleep tonight."

Daniel took a last look behind him and then stepped out into
the night.

He only had one regret. For just an instant he was overcome
with the urge to go back inside just to tell her that he loved her.
The feeling only lasted an instant, however, and he shrugged it off
and returned to the car.

"Wait for me," Moog called out. "I ain't got nothing to say to
you, but I ain't gonna get dropped here, either." He got into the
passenger seat.

Daniel pulled out of the drive and back onto the two-lane
blacktop and headed off toward the highway.

"You're a real asshole," the big man told him without bothering to look in his direction.

"I know."

"She's back there crying her eyes out."

"I thought you said you weren't going to talk." Daniel turned
to purposely engage the big man's eyes.

A horn blared, shocking Daniel's attention back to the road,
where he'd almost drifted across the lane and into an oncoming
Chevy Astro cargo van.

"All the shit we been through," Moog castigated. "Try not to
get us killed with a soccer mom-mobile."

Daniel was too tired to continue the fight with anyone. He drove on in silence.

They'd gone about twenty miles down the twisting road when Daniel's eyes began to droop. He was physically exhausted. Mentally drained. He missed the stop sign at the crossroads. And never saw the dog until it had jumped out of the brush at the berm and straight into the road.

Daniel slammed on the brakes, and the Lexus responded by shrieking to a teeth-shattering stop—just short of the dog.

"Shit!" Moog screamed. His massive hands embedded in the dash.

The dog didn't move. It just stood there in the center of the crossroads, staring straight into the car. Barking.

"What the hell?" Moog was unnerved by the mutt.

Daniel recognized him. "It's Luck."

"What?"

"Luck. Wannaman's dog from back on St. Thomas."

"That ain't—"

"It's Luck."

Moog waved him off. "I suppose the dog hopped a damn cruise ship and then—"

Daniel understood. "It's not a dog."

"You about the craziest white dude I ever met. What do you mean, that ain't a dog? Don't you hear him barking?"

Daniel did hear the bark. It only took him a split second to realize what it was telling him. "Fuck!"

Daniel threw the car into reverse, stepped on the accelerator, and then stepped on the brake as he turned the wheel hard to the right to spin the car around.

"What the hell are you doing?"

Daniel's only response was to pin the accelerator to the fire-wall. The Lexus roared back the way it came.

"Slow down!" Moog screamed. "You're going to kill us."

"I'm going to kill somebody."

CHAPTER FORTY-EIGHT

One of the hardest parts of being a friend is knowing when to ask the question. And knowing when to let it go unasked.

"What is going on?"

"I'm not sure. Not really. I haven't thought about anything," Vicki said as she got to her feet. "But now I'm thinking about using your bathroom."

"Sure." Marcy got to her feet and pointed the way. "Down the hall. Last door on the right."

As Vicki set off, there was a sharp knock at the front door.

"Look who's back," Marcy called down the hall after her friend. "Do you think he forgot something, or just sensed he'd made the biggest mistake of his life?"

Marcy had turned the latch before Vicki could answer in Daniel's defense. A second later, the first of the four men had already forced his way inside. He knocked Marcy to the ground and forced the barrel of his pistol into her mouth to stifle her scream. "Shut your mouth, bitch."

The other three piled into the house, and their leader gave them all things to do. "Chupy. Vibora. Go check in there." He gestured with his head toward the darkened kitchen. "Ogro. Down the hall."

The three men did as they were told, dispersing like army ants with a mission. The man with his knee on Marcy's chest and his gun in her mouth shouted, "Where is he?"

The two men sent to the kitchen found nothing but a dark and empty room. The door to the outside was locked. "*Nada*, Peleon," one called back.

The one called Ogro because he was as big as an ogre lumbered down the hall, checking each room as he passed. The last one he checked was the bathroom, and as he slowly pushed open the door, he was almost certain he heard the faint but familiar sound of someone struggling to silently repress fear. There wasn't any place to hide in the tiny room. Whoever it was, they were standing in the tub, trembling behind the drawn shower curtain.

On the other side of the fish-patterned cloth, Vicki forced her shaking knees not to quit on her. She tried to control her breath, to conceal her panicked need to gasp. She closed her eyes as a desperate measure to calm herself but couldn't help picturing the intruder inching ever closer.

Ogro smiled to himself. He relished moments like this, when he got to see the sudden shock of terror in someone's bulging eyes. He took a step toward the tub, slowly reaching for the curtain, anticipating what he'd find when he pulled it down.

And then something moved in the shadows in the opposite corner. Nothing definite. Not a shape he could discern, just the sensation of unseen movement from the depths of the blackness there.

Ogro screwed his face with confusion. "*Que?*" There wasn't room enough to conceal anyone in the shadows.

Even so, a second later a man stepped from them. He was tall and dark, with eyes that pierced Ogro's withered soul like a stiletto in the back. "*Lef da dawta nuh.*" The raspy warning to leave the woman alone was not so much a collection of words as a single low growl. "*Mi a dogheart.*"

Ogro stood paralyzed, unable to look away from the eyes.

"*Yuh inna big chobble, bubu,*" the man warned him, reaching out with his left hand.

Ogro saw there was something clutched in the man's hand. A gun. No, a stick. A cane. The man put the head of it to the center of Ogro's chest, and a searing pain filled the giant's limbs as a sense of dreadful regret washed over his soul. "*Mami?*" was all he could cry.

"She's as dead as you'll be, you don't leave here," the man growled. Ogro thought he saw an actual flicker of flame in those eyes. "Get out! Now!"

The giant stumbled out of the bathroom and into the hall.

"Ogro!" It took a moment before his senses allowed him to recognize his own name. "Ogro!" He looked down the hall at his leader, who angrily shouted, "D'you find anything?"

The giant looked once more into the darkness and saw only two bright red eyes glowing back at him. "No, Peleon. There is no one here."

"*Merde,*" the man shouted, pulling Marcy to her feet. "We take his fucking *puta* and let her bring him to us, then."

"No," Marcy squealed. "That wasn't our deal," she pleaded. "Mr. Koschei said—"

As suddenly as the men had entered the house, they were gone. With Marcy.

Twenty minutes passed before Vicki could find the courage to look beyond the curtain, not because she was afraid of the men who'd invaded the house, but because she was terrified of the voice she'd heard hissing in the darkness with her.

It was another ten minutes before Daniel came screaming into the driveway in a mushroom cloud of gravel and dust. Vicki burst out of the house and ran across the drive toward him.

He ran straight toward her.

He reached out to take her into his arms.

She slapped him as hard as she could across the face. "What the fuck have you done?" she screamed. "What have you gotten us into? They took Marcy!"

Moog ran over to them and pulled her away. She turned to him and buried her head in his chest, crying hysterically.

Daniel looked on in disbelief. "What's happened?"

"*You* happened," she shrieked.

Daniel looked to his friend, pleading with his eyes for some explanation. He had none.

But she did. "Your Mexican friends were here. They took my friend."

Daniel's head sank, and his heart followed. "Oh, Jesus Christ." He reached out to put a comforting hand on Vicki's arm.

She wouldn't have it. "Don't you touch me." She pulled her arm away and pressed deeper to Moog. "You did this."

"I promise. I'll get her back. I'll make this right."

"Right?" The suggestion offended her. "This is never going to be right. Never."

Moog led her inside. Daniel followed at a distance.

After thirty minutes of Vicki crying and cursing, the telephone rang. All three of them jumped, startled by the sound.

Vicki found the cordless handset and answered. "Hello?" Her eyes closed tightly, as if the voice on the other end were conjuring an image she didn't want to see. She turned to Daniel, her red eyes staring him down accusatorially. "He wants to talk to you." She thrust the receiver out at him.

Daniel dodged her look but took the phone. "Yes." His eyes only narrowed at the sound of the caller's voice. He listened, then gestured for a pen and paper, something to write with. Vicki and Moog dashed to find a scrap and a pen and slid it to him. He scribbled something down. "No, of course I don't know it. But I can find it." He underlined what he'd written. "Thirty minutes."

He put the handset down and picked up the slip of paper without saying a word.

There was something to do now, and Moog was eager to get to it. "What's going down?"

Daniel was already moving toward the door. "They want a meeting."

"All right. Let's go."

Daniel turned. "No. You're going to stay here and watch over Vicki."

She sniffed and wiped at her tears. "I can take care of—"

"You're going to stay here." There was a note of paternal authority to his answer.

Lots of adolescent rebellion in her reply. "Why?"

"Because I can't do what I need to do if I'm worried about you." He was less sure of himself when he looked into her eyes.

"Just what are you going to do?"

"I'm going to get your friend back."

Moog knew it wasn't easy as that. "How you planning on doing that?"

"I'm going to give them what they want."

"And what's that?"

"Me."

CHAPTER FORTY-NINE

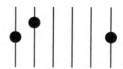

The house had changed since Carrie went back to her parents in Peoria. It was impossible, of course. A house is just brick and mortar, drywall and two-bys. Nothing can *change* it but a fire. Or a hurricane. Maybe a twister. But his wife's leaving was a natural disaster of its own, and Gerald Feller could feel her absence, could sense the lack of her there. He hated being home without her. There was a roof and four walls, but without her beneath it and within them the structure didn't provide shelter from the storm anymore. Impossible, maybe, but undeniable.

He pulled into the garage. It was easier now that there was only one car to wedge into the narrow space.

He let himself into the house, stepping into the kitchen. Somewhere off in the distance Lilith yowled. With all the things Carrie had taken (and she'd taken damn near everything), she'd left her goddamn cat. While Gerald hungered for some last remembrance of her, something he could cling to, the cat did not fit the bill. He'd hated it since the day Carrie had brought it home, and he only resented it more now that she was gone.

Still, he wasn't going to do to Lilith what Carrie had done to him. He wasn't going to abandon the cat just because it no longer suited his life. He wasn't going to discard it just because it'd be convenient to do so. He was going to stick by that damn cat, stick by it to the very end.

He took off his overcoat, draped it over a chair at the breakfast table, and poured some of the dried food into the cat's bowl. The clinking of processed fish by-product and ceramic was the only call to which she responded, and she came trotting into the kitchen on silent paws. They ignored each other, until Gerald noticed that the calico's white muzzle was stained with something bright red, something very much like blood. The cat trotted over to her bowl, happily running her barbed tongue over whatever it was that had stained her mouth.

Feller drifted into the living room, assuring himself that whatever had befallen the cat, he was not going to invest in veterinary care. It was one thing not to toss the cat out, but it was another to take affirmative steps to keep it around. That was far more than the bargain he'd struck with himself.

He absentmindedly wandered into the living room and switched on the lamp Carrie had bought at the antique mall in Hagerstown. (He wished she'd taken that damn thing with her too.) Nothing happened. He tried it again. Still nothing. He stared into the darkness of the room, dumbfounded that the switch had defied him and denied him illumination. That was when he noticed the large form on the couch, darker than the shadows that concealed it.

"Your cat hungry. I give little something to eat," the figure called out in an accent that made it clear that the Russians had found him.

A light came on at the far end of the living room, and the figure on the couch came into view. He was a big man. His head was bald, and a cruel sneer was trimmed in a salt-and-pepper goatee. At his feet was a black plastic bag, the kind that contractors use to clean up a job site. There was something leaking out of it, and it was saturating the carpet.

Feller reached for the firearm strapped to the small of his back, but before he could touch it, another light went on in the living room and revealed a larger man with a pistol already trained on Feller's chest.

"That would be mistake," the man seated on the couch said. "And you already make too many."

"Who are you? What do you want?"

"Don't play the stupid. You know who I am. You know why I am here. No?"

Feller was too far off guard to lie well. "I don't—"

"You think you use me? You think you use me to find this man? This Daniel Erickson? Is that what this was? I was your stalking horse?"

"I don't know what you're talking about." Feller protested, trying to contain the fear that was threatening to overcome him.

"No?"

"No."

The man screwed up his goatee like he was thinking that possibility over, and then offered a nod of concession. "Then how about I have your friend Schweeter explain to you."

With that, the man leaned forward and reached into the black plastic bag, pulling out an object and placing it on the coffee table Carrie had bought at the Furniture Gallery.

It took Feller an instant or two to realize it was a human head. The man turned it so that its lifeless gaze was focused on Feller. "Oh, that right. Your Schweeter cannot explain to you because he is dead. Also, his mouth is filled with his own—how you say—cock."

"Oh, dear God." Feller wanted to vomit, but he managed to catch himself.

"This is what happen to people who try to use me."

Feller said nothing.

"Now I use you. You are going to find this man for me. You are going to find him and tell me where he is."

"What makes you think I can—"

"Nothing," the man admitted. "But something tells me that if anyone can, you can."

"And why would I help you?" Feller asked. "You've just killed a federal agent."

"You will help me because I just kill federal agent. Also because you don't want me to kill two federal agents."

"I don't know—"

"That, as they say, is too bad for you. Because in forty-eight hours you will either tell me where he is or you will be filling your own garbage bag. After that, then I am going to go visit, where is it, Peoria?"

Feller thought of his wife. "No!"

"Then I would get busy finding this man, yes?"

"Yes," he answered in a trembling voice. Unsure how much longer he could continue to stand.

"Also I would not do something stupid like go to your FBI. My bad luck would be your tragedy."

The Russian got to his feet as casually as if they'd been discussing who was going to organize the neighborhood potluck. He walked toward the front door, leaving the bag behind him. "Oh, and you should get rid of that."

The front door closed, and Gerald Feller was alone again. With a cat he didn't want and a corpse's head he had to hide.

CHAPTER FIFTY

The wind whipped along the grasslands and whistled in the windows of their stolen cargo van. It played a high, hollow song that sounded as familiar as the warm Ensenada breeze playing across his mother's Coke-bottle wind chimes, and made Ogro momentarily homesick. "I don't like this," he said, nervously searching the darkness surrounding them from the relative safety of the passenger seat. No matter how much he tried, he couldn't get those eyes out of his mind.

"Don't worry," the man behind the wheel assured him. "He'll come." Then he checked his watch just to see how much time had passed since he'd made the call.

The gringo they needed to nab for their boss wasn't what Ogro was worried about, but he knew better than to share that with the rest of the crew. He wiped at the passenger window with his sleeve, peering out into the black night, terrified something might be peering back. "*La magia negra*," he whispered, louder than he'd intended.

"What are you talking about?" the driver wanted to know.

"It's nothing."

"What's wrong, *esse*? Ever since we left that house, you been like this."

Ogro looked away. "It's nothing."

"It better be nothing. Because when this *puta* comes up in here, I gotta know you're ready to do your thing." He slapped the giant's left forearm and then hung on to make his point. "You ready to do your thing?"

"Yeah."

"Tell me. You're ready to do what?"

They'd been over the same simple plan a dozen times. He sighed. Screw up one little kidnapping in Iztapalapa, and the crew never forgets. He sighed again and began his recitation. "We wait in the van."

That part was simple enough. "Yes?"

"When he pulls up, you turn on the headlights, get out, and call him out of his car."

"And you?"

"I get her out of the back and come beside you."

"With?"

"My gun at her head."

"And then?"

"While I threaten to kill the girl, Vibora sneaks up behind him and zaps him with the *pistol electrica*."

"Next?"

"Chupy gets out of the grass up there." He pointed off to where his comrade was lying in the tall grass with a Sig Sauer 556 to lay down cover fire in case things got cute. "Helps Vibora chain the dude up, and they bring him back here."

"And you?"

"Take the guy's coat and shit."

"And?"

"Drive the girl back to her place." He shuddered at the thought of having to go back into that house. Especially alone.

"Aaand?"

"I kill her. Then drop the guy's stuff there to make it look like he did it."

"And then we pick you up in the van. That's all there is to it." It was simple enough, but the way he said it made clear he was running the plan through in his head yet again. "Then we drive down to LA, drop the fucker with *el jefe* in the morning, and then we are celebrating, *mi* amigo!"

"I got it." He did. But his grasp of the particulars of the plan didn't do anything to address his growing sense of unease. The silence didn't do anything to help it either, so he was quick to break it. "You ever wonder?" he asked tentatively, not sure he should voice his feelings.

"About what?" the man behind the steering wheel answered, without any real interest.

"If there's something more?"

"Something more than what?" The man behind the steering wheel shrugged at the metaphysical ponderings. "I'm here in this fucked-up life because my mother, God rest her soul"—he made a quick sign of the cross—"she couldn't say no to my father, not even after eight kids they couldn't afford." He lit a cigarette and took a puff. "I'm here on this fucking pack road because Koschei told us to get this guy, and if we don't, Carlos will throw us in with his tigers."

It was an answer, but not the one Ogro had been looking for. "No, I mean do you ever wonder if there isn't, I don't know, something else? Something more?"

The man behind the wheel shook his head disapprovingly. "You think too much, you get yourself into trouble. You get yourself into trouble, you get me into trouble, and I don't need trouble. That's how you meet the tigers, *esse*." He took a puff from his cigarette. "Besides, what more is there? I come from a town where there is little work. A boy has little choice but to join the cartel. If you want to put food on your family's table, if you want to protect your sisters and your mother, if you want to have any pride at all, any life at all. Tell me, what choice is there?"

"I just wish there was some."

"And I wish this fucker would show up soon. That's what I wish."

"What do you think will happen to him?"

"Koschei wants him alive, so something worse than death."

There was a noise from the back of the van.

"What's that bitch up to back there?" He leaned back in his seat. "Shut up back there!"

There was another *clang*. And then some scraping of metal on metal.

"Will you go back there and shut her up?"

Ogro did as he was told. When he opened the van's back door, all he could see was darkness inside. For just a second he hesitated, frozen with fear that the man with the eyes that burned red like stoplights might be waiting for him inside.

But there was no man. Only the woman.

She hit Ogro square in the temple with the tire iron. Somehow she'd worked free of the rope with which they'd bound her. He took a step backward, momentarily dazed. A second swing connected, steel smashed into the left side of his head, and he crumpled to the ground.

Peleno heard the commotion and ran to the back of the van, screaming, "Vibaro! Chupy!"

The two men left their positions of hiding and ran out onto the road.

"The bitch is running! Go get her!" The pair ran off as fast as they could.

Then Peleno turned and kicked Ogro in the side. "Get up off your fat ass and go get that bitch."

In the back of the van, Marcy had managed to use the tire iron to pry the ropes off her feet, so she hit the ground running, up the slight incline and then across the dark grasslands.

There were rough swales and deep depressions in the ground. Marcy couldn't run more than a few feet without stumbling or falling to the ground altogether. Each time she fell, she managed to scramble to her feet and kept running.

"Get up! Get up!" Peleon screamed, kicking Ogro again and again "We've got to get that crazy bitch!"

Ogro got to his feet, touched the side of his head, and then studied his own blood. He picked up his pistol and joined the chase, determined now to recapture the woman who'd shed his blood.

The two men set out on the hunt with a predator's inspiration, the charge of the chase energizing them as they rushed forward. Almost immediately they spotted her off in the distance, no more than fifty yards ahead of them.

Looking over her shoulder, Marcy realized immediately she could never outrun the men. Resignation slowed her steps, let her legs suddenly sense how much they burned, how tired they were, how unwilling they were to carry her one more step forward. She fell to the ground, and this time she did not get up.

Fury fueled the men. They watched their prey fall to the ground, disappearing briefly in the darkness of the grass. They both knew she was there. Not ten feet away. Lying in a ditch in the darkness. They could both see the shadow she'd fallen into, and they both slowed to a confident walk as they approached.

Behind them the giant footsteps of Ogro approaching distracted them, and they turned to see his oversize silhouette loping over the grasslands toward them. When they turned back, a figure had emerged from the shadow. Not a woman's. A man's. A man holding a gun.

The first shot hit Chupy in the chest. The second in his gut.

A third shot struck Vibaro in the forehead. Ogro, charging forward, saw the spray of blood against the moonlight and stopped in his tracks. He turned and ran back toward the van.

When he reached the bank above the dirt road, the laws of physics took over and his mass times his velocity sent him tumbling down to the van.

"Where is she?" Peleon pulled Ogro to his feet, but the giant couldn't speak. "Where's Vibaro? Chupy?"

Ogro wanted to explain everything, but all that would come out between the wheezing huffs was, "Shadow. Man."

Peleon struck Ogro with his pistol and knocked him to the ground.

A second later, a thundercloud seemed to rumble in the near distance. The sound grew louder and louder. Lights broke over the horizon, and the scene behind the van was suddenly illuminated by a dozen lights moving closer.

"*Merde*," Peleon said to himself as he took a step back. "Bikers."

They were suddenly surrounded by a half-dozen motorcycles. The glare of the headlamps was eclipsed by the silhouette of a man.

"Well, lookee here," the man at the head of the pack called out above the roar of the engines. "Looks like these two are engaged in a little commerce. Don't you know any better, boys? This is Corpse Corps territory."

Peleon tried not to show the fear he knew would be fatal. "This is none of your business."

"That right?" the leader growled.

With the glare of the bike headlamps in his eyes, Peleon never saw that a weapon had been drawn on him. The shot caught him in his chest and knocked him to the ground next to Ogro.

The giant on the ground looked into his dead friend's eyes, then jumped up.

The leader idled his bike and walked it toward Ogro, "Now suppose you tell me what's going on here."

Ogro just wanted to go home. "Our boss wants a man."

"What is he, some fucking queer beaner?" the leader joked. Every one of his men laughed harder than he did.

"No," Ogro said, not knowing quite how to respond. "It's a business deal."

"So you are here with business."

"No." The giant tried to clear things up. "Just to get the man and go. We had his woman." He pointed off into the darkness.

"Morgan," the leader ordered. "You and Strat go check that out."

Two bikes revved their engines, then climbed the incline and roared off into the night.

The leader turned back to Ogro. "Now you better tell me everything I need to know before my brothers come back here and tell me you're just telling me a story."

"No, no. I swear."

"Biggs," the leader ordered. "Look in the van and let's see what he's got back there."

"There's nothing," Ogro insisted.

"He's got that right," the biker confirmed.

The first shot was just barely perceptible over the loud roar of the bikes.

"What the hell was that?" the leader asked,

The second shot wasn't any clearer, but it convinced the leader that he'd heard *something*. "Cuba, go check it out."

Another bike revved and climbed the incline. He headed off into the grassland, but only got twenty feet before he realized what he *didn't* see.

He turned his bike around and returned to the crest. "Hell," he shouted down. "There's no sign of Morgan or Strat. Can't see shit up here, but I don't see their lights nowhere."

The leader of the bikers—a man called Hell—looked over at Ogro. "You got some 'splaining to do."

CHAPTER FIFTY-ONE

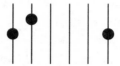

The motorcycle turned into the drive, and Vicki and Moog ran outside to meet it.

Marcy hopped free of the bike before Daniel could shut it down or put out the kickstand. She ran into Vicki's arms and burst into hysterical tears.

"What the hell happened?" Vicki demanded.

"She's all right," Daniel assured her.

"The hell I am," she screamed, pulling herself from Vicki's arms. "I was kidnapped and stuffed in the back of a goddamn van. Then I was attacked and chased through the brush." She turned to Daniel. "And you killed four people, you psycho! I am not all right!"

Daniel looked past her and directly at Vicki. "She'll be fine in the morning."

Marcy had no intention of letting it go. "I'm not going to be fine. I'm calling the police."

"You can't," Daniel told her.

"Watch me!"

"No, really," Vicki interceded. "You can't call the police. Not yet."

"What's going on, Vicki?" she said. "What did you get me into?"

"What did we get you into?" Daniel snapped. "How the hell is it that the Flying Burrito Brothers showed up at your door ten minutes after we did?"

"Are you saying that I had something to do with this?" Marcy asked angrily.

"That's not an answer to my question."

"Daniel," Vicki interrupted. "Stop it."

"If you don't want to listen to me, at least ask the question yourself."

Vicki didn't have anything to say. She looked back at Daniel, but it was sadness in her eyes, not accusation. She was as much a part of this now as he was, and he could tell that she regretted that. Marcy stormed into the house. Vicki gave him a last look, then ran in after her.

Daniel turned to Moog. "Will you look after her for a while?"

"I'll do what I have to," the big man promised.

"Me, too."

CHAPTER FIFTY-TWO

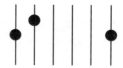

The chains wrapped around Ogro's wrists cut into his flesh as they suspended him above the garage floor, but he still couldn't stop squirming against his bonds in a panicked attempt to free himself. Blood trickled down his forearms in thin rivers that fell off, drip by drip, into a gathering dark crimson pool on the sandblasted concrete floor six inches beneath his feet.

"I tell you everything. I swear it." He was trying to sound convincing without giving in to the tears he felt building on the brink of his emotional overload.

It wasn't working. "Well, I tell you what, boy. I don't believe a goddamn word comin' outta yer mouth."

The leader of the Corpse Corps was David "Hell" Gurger. The word on him was that he was such a beast that while doing a twelve-year stretch at Pelican Bay he had beaten a man to death and the guards had framed another inmate for the crime because they didn't want to have to guard him any longer than they had to.

He was a big man, muscle buried under fat, with all of it covered in the usual assortment of clichéd skin art: demons and dragons, skulls and naked chicks. The only exception was the portrait of a smiling young girl inked across his left breast. No one knew for certain who she was. Some speculated it was the first victim he'd ever taken, and others thought it might be the only one he regretted killing. There were others who thought she was the only thing he'd ever loved, but no one was fool enough to ask him to explain.

"I swear it, señor. We were not there to do business. We were there to get a man."

"So you keep saying. But I don't believe you. And I just lost two of my boys." He turned to the others. "Douse him."

As soon as they opened the canister, the garage was filled with the toxic stench of gasoline.

Ogro knew what was happening. He had done it to others many times. "Please, no," he begged.

Hell didn't give a goddamn. "Make sure you cover him, head to toe."

They did.

Hell turned to the two members who stood waiting with fire extinguishers in their hands. "You make sure you got those extinguishers ready to go. You let him burn too long and he'll go into shock and he won't feel nothin', won't be worth any goddamn thing to us."

"Please," Ogro begged.

Hell was unmoved. He casually struck a match and threw it on Ogro, who immediately erupted like a human tiki torch. The fire roared and the man squealed in pain as the chains suspending him from the ceiling rang and clanged with his spasms.

"Hit him," Hell ordered.

A second later the extinguishers covered him in foam that killed the flames. What was left was only vaguely human, swollen and beet red.

"He's involved in some sorta shit got two of your brothers killed tonight," Hell announced. "Have at him."

The dozen men surrounding Ogro whacked at his charred body with pieces of rusted rebar and two-inch double-loop chains. He screamed out as the metal tore away small pieces of his charred flesh.

"Now," Hell said. "You tell me what you were doing out there, and I'll let you die."

Ogro only had a few words left in him. "Erickson. Daniel Erickson."

"What?"

"Erickson."

"Hell," a heavyset member holding a bloody piece of rebar interrupted. "Erickson. Isn't that the guy—"

Hell knew exactly who Daniel Erickson was.

Ogro had one more word. "Koschei."

The name didn't mean anything to any of the members, but Hell knew the name well.

"Douse him up again, boys."

The members were quick to cover him again.

Ogro's voice was shaky. "I. Tell. Everything!"

"And I believe you." He threw a match. This time there were no extinguishers.

"Saddle up, boys," Hell called out. "Looks like we're riding to LA."

CHAPTER FIFTY-THREE

There is no shortage of barometers of success for those in the entertainment industry. There are sales records and highest-paid honors. There are awards from peers and the public. There are names on buildings and handprints in concrete. But no one has truly achieved success until they've acquired a private table at SHI.

Haden Koschei's was in the back of the club, behind the purple velvet rope where not even the current It kids could make their way without paying their dues.

"Hold it up, Ace." The palm the guard extended was just smaller than the stop sign it was acting as. "This is VIPs only."

Daniel looked more like one of the lost souls who haunt the Strip than the beautiful ones who had earned entrance to the club. "I'm here to see Haden Koschei."

The goon pretended to check his clipboard. "I don't see you on the list, Ace."

"I didn't tell you I was on your little list there. I'm not asking you for permission. I'm only giving you the courtesy of a heads-up on what I'm going to do. And don't call me Ace again. My name is Daniel Erickson."

The man's scowl dropped, and his eyes popped with alarm. "Of course, Mr. Erickson." He slipped the rope from its post and stepped back to clear the way. "Mr. Koschei's expecting you."

Past the rope was a hall with a half-dozen curtains hanging to either side. Daniel assumed that they were private rooms. The one at the very back, with the tied black curtains, was Haden Koschei's.

He was dressed all in black. At his side was a woman dressed in a long, skintight dress as red as newly spilled blood. The thin man rose when Daniel entered. "Mr. Erickson, I presume." He didn't offer his hand.

Neither did Daniel. "You know who I am."

"Please allow me to intro—"

"Spare me that tired tune," Daniel interrupted. "I know who you are."

"I see you're a man who doesn't care for civilities."

"No, I'm a man who's grown tired of bullshit."

"And I'm a man of wealth and taste, who is afraid you're in the wrong place."

"I've got no plans for staying."

"Yes, I wouldn't think making plans would matter much to a man without a future."

"Don't kid yourself. I have the same future as everyone else."

"It's just the timing, then."

"It's just a matter of time for all of us."

"Then let's not waste one another's. Have a seat."

Daniel took the one opposite him.

"May I offer you something to drink? To eat, perhaps?" He gestured toward the woman sprawled across the sofa. "Perhaps another diversion?"

"I thought you said you weren't going to waste my time."

"Oh, I assure you she's no waste of time. She's worth every minute. But if you're intent on getting to the business at hand, then tell me, Mr. Erickson, just what exactly is your business?"

"I'm looking for the man who killed Mark Wannaman."

"You think I can offer you something in that regard?"

"Yeah. I think you're the man I've been looking for."

"If I tell you that I am?"

"Then I guess we'll take care of that."

"What if I tell you that I'm the man who *failed* to kill Mark Wannaman?"

"I'd tell you that you were more successful than you're giving yourself credit for."

"No, no. You misunderstand. I have many…let's call them commercial interests, and one of them is a record label. Five years ago, I had in my roster a band called Taco Shot. Alternative. Post-grunge. Whatever it is that rock and roll is trying to be these days. Not really my personal thing, but they had their following and they made me a lot of money. I mean, relatively speaking, for the digital age."

"Times are hard all over."

"One day I got word that one of my trained monkeys, the man you call Mark Wannaman, had tired of the money and the sex and the drugs and the fame, that he was leaving the band. So a business decision had to be made."

"A business decision?"

"Every band has a shelf life. Some manage to exceed expectations and carry on into their senior years. That's a rarity, though, and a product of the vinyl age when there was some permanence to music, when it was a physical thing. Today music is temporary. It's whatever is being downloaded today. Tomorrow it will be something else. Tomorrow it will be *someone* else. So Taco Shot and Mr. Wannaman had reached their shelf life. That really left only one avenue for continued profitability."

"What would that be?"

"I would think someone who's been in the music business as long as you would know the answer. It's the memorial." He grinned.

"It's always struck me as strange," he continued. "But people go crazy for music from a dead man. Or woman. There may be years, decades even, when an artist does nothing. When they're reduced to playing the shittiest little gigs. Or can't get gigs at all. When their newest album spends a week on the charts before dropping to oblivion. Or doesn't chart at all. Total obscurity. Then they have the good fortune to die, and"—he grinned—"it's like magic. Everyone wants a piece of a dead man."

"So you decided to kill Mark?"

"He wouldn't be the first artist to be worth more dead than alive. Hendrix. Cobain. Joplin. Sam Cooke. Jackson. Tupac. Biggie. Morrison. Buddy Holly. But let's just say I decided to escalate the profitability of the music. Sadly, I suppose, that necessitated someone dying. Of course, I didn't do it myself. Rules are rules, you understand."

Daniel didn't.

"There was a professional. He staged the automobile accident that killed Mark. Or at least we thought it killed Mark. I assure you, if I'd known he'd survived, I would have had him killed all over again. His eventual end, I'm afraid, was not my doing in any way."

"But you know who did."

"I have my suspicions."

"I'm interested in more than your suspicions."

"Well, then, here's a fact for you. There are only four things that kill a man, and Wannaman's death wasn't a result of poor health or accident."

"And the other two?"

He counted them off on his bony fingers. "Money." One. "Pussy." Two. "Follow those trails, and you'll catch your killer."

"The money just leads me back to you."

"I'd already made as much money as I was going to make from Wannaman's death. If he'd come back from the grave, that would've only lit a fire under sales all over again."

"And pointed the finger at you."

"Oh, please. Do you think there's any way to tie all of that back to me?"

"But just the suggestion of murder—"

"Would be great for business," Koschei gloated. "Would make me even more popular than I am. I tell you, Mr. Erickson, if a man with your growing body count could ever settle down enough to come back to the music industry, I think you'd find it a much more hospitable environment now that you're someone to be feared."

Daniel was caught off guard.

"I'm not without my connections, you know. It would take some doing, but I'm certain I could work something out for you. Maybe a year or two of light prison time. That'd be good for business, too. Come out, and I promise you that you'd be a new man. Everything you ever wanted." He grinned as if he knew a secret that only he shared with Daniel. "Everything."

"I already have a job, thanks."

"Well, then, I'd get to work if I were you. Now, I can think of someone who gained significantly from Mark's death."

"And who would that be?"

Koschei reached into the inner pocket of his coat. Daniel made a move for the pistol tucked in the back of his pants.

"Mr. Erickson. I assure you, if it were that easy, I would have done away with you a long time ago." From his coat he pulled out an envelope and slid it across the table. "I think you'll find all the answers you seek in there."

Daniel took the envelope and looked inside. "A concert ticket?"

"Tomorrow night. Backstage pass. Full access." His demeanor changed. "Now, unless there's anything else, I think we've said everything we have to say to one another."

Daniel got to his feet.

"Mr. Erickson."

"What?"

"He didn't explain the rules to you, did he?"

"The what?"

"You really have no idea what you're doing, do you?"

"I'm figuring it out."

"Well, let me know how that works out for you."

Without another word, Daniel left.

* * *

"You look scared," the woman purred into Koschei's ear. He smiled and then grabbed her throat, smashing her to the table.

He looked down on her. "Don't be a fool. Of course I was scared."

He took a cell phone from his pocket and pressed speed dial. "I had a visit just now. Daniel Erickson. I'm very disappointed in you. I'll give you one last chance. Tomorrow at the Staples Center. Don't fuck it up this time. Time is running out and I'm running out of ways to amuse myself with your wife."

Without ending the call, he placed the phone on the table next to her, where she still laid on her back. He flipped up her dress and let down his pants.

CHAPTER FIFTY-FOUR

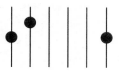

Thirty minutes in Koschei's catacombs with the relentless vibro-acoustic assault of the *oonce-oonce-oonce-oonce* club beat had left Daniel's ears ringing. Despite all that, he could still hear the footsteps as they clipped along the pavement behind him.

Whoever they belonged to followed him down the street, slowing and speeding up when he did, never widening or closing the distance between them. They followed him down Bradley Street and seemed to turn with him as he led them into the parking garage on the corner of Hilton.

As soon as he stepped into the garage, Daniel quickly ducked behind the black Suburban parked in the first handicapped spot and reached for the pistol tucked at the small of his back. He pulled the weapon free, cocked it, and waited for his tail to walk straight into his trap.

No one came.

He waited.

And waited.

Nothing and no one. Five minutes passed, and no one entered the parking garage, or even walked past. He'd been certain that someone was following him, but now he was only certain that he was completely alone.

Even if his paranoia was well founded, he chided himself for having let it get the best of him. He got to his feet, tucked his pistol back into his waistband, and breathed a sigh of relief.

And that was when he heard the long *click* of a pistol's hammer being thumbed back.

"They tell me you're a hard man to kill." When he turned to face the sound, the barrel of the pistol was no more than a foot from Daniel's face. "But then, I haven't tried yet." The man behind the gun had a voice with crazy bass, like a suburban kid blasting Daz Dillinger on the Logic7 in his old man's Beamer. The laugh he laughed would've rattled window glass.

Daniel didn't recognize the man. If he'd ever seen him, he definitely would've remembered.

The man was tall and broad, well dressed in a suit and tie, with a cold, steady look in his eyes. For a moment, in the dim fluorescent garage lighting, it looked as if Moog had just stepped out of a time machine that had aged him a good thirty years. But Daniel had never seen *this* guy before.

Daniel was confused by a new player so late in the game. So he ran over the scorecard he had running. "You're not Russian?"

"No." A little puff of laughter escaped with the gunman's answer. "I ain't no black Russian."

"And you're not with the Mexicans?"

"No." No laughter this time. "I ain't no mariachi either."

There was only one team left, but that seemed less logical than his first two guesses. "You're too well dressed to be with that motorcycle club."

"I'm afraid so."

Daniel was stumped. "So who are you then? Who else wants me dead?"

"It's a dangerous thing," the man said gravely, "to have so many folks wanna kill you that you can't keep 'em all straight in your head."

"You'd think so," Daniel quipped, "but it hasn't been that bad so far."

"Well, that's all about to change for you now."

That's when Daniel heard the long *click* of a pistol's hammer being thumbed back. Again.

"That'd be a mistake."

Daniel had never heard anything sweeter than the boom of Moog's voice echoing off the concrete walls of the parking garage.

It wasn't fear in the gunman's eyes, just the slight squint of concern. "I was wondering when you were going to get here, Moog." Evidently the gunman didn't need to look over his shoulder to know who had gotten the drop on him. Or what he was holding in his hand. "I was letting this fool go on while I waited on ya, but I was just about to cap his ass just to shut him up."

"He does like to talk, Arthur," Moog conceded.

"How'd you get hooked up with this fool?" Beagler tossed the question back to Moog.

"Spent the last year asking myself the same damn thing. I suppose it's 'cause he saved my ass when he didn't have to and—"

"And you owe him now." The story was familiar enough to Beagler that he could finish it for him. "Like I owed you."

"Something like that."

"While you two are enjoying the reunion," Daniel interrupted, "does someone want to clue me in on why we're all so intent on shooting one another here? Because I would really rather go get a burger and shake at the In-N-Out."

Moog offered a question in place of an introduction. "Remember I told you I was trained by the best?"

"Yeah?"

"Well, this is Arthur Beagler. The best."

"Well, Arthur Beagler," Daniel started, with more casualness than the situation warranted. "Any friend o' Moog's—"

"Shut up, fool," Beagler snapped, and leveled his pistol. "I should've just shot your ass."

It wasn't as frightening a prospect to Daniel as Beagler might have thought. But still he wanted to know why the best hit man in the world hadn't just done his job. "Why didn't you?"

"'Cause it ain't about you." Beagler spat the words as if Daniel and his question both disgusted him. "I had to come save my boy."

"How's that?" Moog asked.

"You got some bad motherfuckers want you dead, Moog. Deep-rooted. Folks with reach. Government folks."

"Government?" The prospect of making Uncle Sam's private hit list seemed far-fetched to Moog. "What I ever do to them?"

"They told the world you was dead. And you done a piss-poor job of acting the part. What do you think would happen if it comes out about you?"

"But why you, Arthur?"

"'Cause they knew I was the only one that'd find you. They knew you'd let me get close enough when I did. If I was anyone else right now, you'd have shot 'em already."

"But why'd you take the job, Arthur?""

"Your girl is something special, Moog. She got her mother's eyes. And all of your mean."

"This don't have nothing to do with them."

"I took the job because they threatened *my* girl if I didn't."

"I appreciate that, man. I do." Moog's mind was already focused on the best way to get the three of them out of their predicament. "So how about we all put our pieces down and work on getting all of us out of the shit pool they got us caught up in?"

"It can't end like that." Beagler's voice wasn't threatening, just sad. And resigned. "You know it can't."

"Then how you see this ending, Arthur?"

"The way it has to. With a body." He readjusted his sights on Daniel. "Or two. You just need to decide who."

"What?"

"If I kill you both," Beagler explained, "they'll leave my little girl alone."

Moog tilted his head to the left and then to the right, trying to work out the stiffness that was building. "That ain't gonna happen, Arthur."

"There's only one other way to protect my daughter—"

Moog already knew what it was. "Don't you do this, Arthur."

"It's the only other way, Moog." Beagler's voice was simply businesslike. "If they find my body here, then that's an end to it. My girl is free and clear."

The impact of what was about to happen hit Moog, and he felt he might buckle under its weight. "Arthur, don't you do this." It was closer to begging than Daniel ever would have thought Moog could get.

"Guys," Daniel interjected. "We can work this out."

"Here's how we're gonna work it out," Arthur responded. "I'm going to count to three, and if Moog hasn't shot me by then, I'm going to shoot you in the head." He stole a glance over his shoulder at Moog. "Then I'm going to turn on you, son. Don't you make no mistake on that. If you ain't shot me by then, I'm going to turn and put you down like a dog."

"I'm not going to shoot you, Arthur." Moog pleaded for some reprieve from the chore he'd been charged with.

"I always did my best for you, boy." Moog's voice wasn't the only one touched with emotion. "Even when you thought I fucked you over. I swear I didn't know that fucker Koschei was going to—"

"Koschei?" Daniel interjected. "Haden Koschei?"

"Yeah," Arthur answered, his opinion of Daniel clearly not improved. "Your friend Haden Koschei."

The pieces of the puzzle came together like a sports car slamming into an oak tree. Daniel looked at Moog with disbelief. "You were the one. You rigged the car crash."

Moog didn't know what to say. "I didn't make the connection until we got to Florida. That's the only reason I even came with you."

"Why? So you could spy—"

"So I could cover your ass! Because I warned you there's some shit that you shouldn't oughta fuck with. I begged you to just leave it all alone."

Daniel shook his head with disappointment. "Because you didn't want to be found out."

"Because I was trying to protect you."

"And now what?"

"And now we start at one," Beagler said.

"Arthur, come on."

"Two."

"Don't you make me do this," Moog pleaded. "You're like a father to me." He made no attempt to wipe away the small tears welling in his eyes. "You're the only father I ever had."

"Then be my son and make me proud, Moog."

There was one moment of perfect silence.

"Three."

The shot was loud.

Daniel walked past the lifeless body of Arthur Beagler. He went toward his friend and reached out for the big man's heaving shoulders to lend him comfort.

"Don't." Moog slapped his hand away. "We're even now. All my debts to you are paid, because I don't have another fucking thing to give you. I'm done. I'm out."

Daniel looked back at Moog's mentor, lying facedown on the concrete, a rapidly deepening pool of blood forming around the head. "I'm so sorry."

"Fuck your sorry." Moog's tears were gone now, replaced with an anger that Daniel had never witnessed before. "You think that's some magic fucking word, gonna make everything all right? I told you to leave it alone." He ran his left hand over his head, trying to do something that would allow him to process what had just happened.

"Violence is how I handle my shit." Moog contorted his voice to mock Daniel's. "All that bullshit. I told you all your violence would end like this, because this is all that can happen for men like us. We're all gonna die like this." He looked down at his mentor. "Just not today."

"Moog. I'm sorry." Daniel couldn't help saying it again, though as soon as he had he recognized how hollow it sounded.

Sirens howled in the distance.

"I'm done." Moog shook his head with disgust.

"Moog."

He reached into the pocket of his coat. "Here." He handed an envelope to Daniel. "Vicki wanted me to give you this." Daniel took it from him. "And in case you're wondering, you fucked up her life, too."

"Moog—"

Moog shook his head. "Done with you. With all of this."

Without another look at the only two men he'd ever known as friends, he turned and walked off into the garage, disappearing into the darkness.

Daniel stood and watched him leave. For the first time in a long time, he felt completely alone. He'd forgotten just how much that hurt.

CHAPTER FIFTY-FIVE

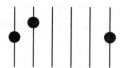

"Will there be anything else?" the guy behind the counter asked.

Gerald Feller couldn't help but be amused by the irony of a young Middle Eastern man with suspicions about the purchase of a pay-as-you-go cell phone by an FBI agent. "Car charger." He put the accessory next to the box on the counter.

The clerk rang them up. "One hundred twelve dollar."

Feller put two Grants and a Jackson on the counter.

The clerk looked down at the bills and then back up at Feller. He took up each of the Grants, looked them over against the light, and then wrote something on their faces before putting them in the cash drawer. "Five. And six, seven, eight," he counted out. "Thank you. Come again."

When he got back to his car, he pulled the phone out of its packaging and plugged its charger into the cigarette lighter receptacle. He drove around for a while, going nowhere, just tracing streets up and down until the phone had stored a sufficient charge to place the call.

He tried to expel his nervousness in a series of quick breaths that left his lips as puffs of frozen smoke. Its only effect was to momentarily fog up the windshield.

The first time he tried, his shaking hand mistakenly dialed a Korean barbeque. He hung up quickly and then carefully redialed the number, deliberately pressing each digit one by one. It rang and then rang again.

A woman's voice answered the phone. "*Allo?*"

"I was calling—" Feller suddenly realized he didn't have a name to ask for or an acceptable way to describe a man like that. He hoped he had the right number and took a gamble. "I'm calling for him?"

The woman made no response to him, but in the background Feller could hear her bellow. "*Mily!* Silly man on phone for you."

A second later the voice that now narrated his nightmares came on line. "*Allo?*"

"Mily?" Feller began, trying to sound more confident than he felt.

"*Mily?*" the man scoffed. "You are idiot, my friend. *Mily* is, how you say, sweetheart or darling. All my women call me that."

There was commotion in the background, and Feller could hear him tell the woman, "Oh, you know it's true."

A second later he was back to business. "But if you call me *mily* again, I will cut your throat." He paused for effect. "Starting at your balls."

"I didn't mean—"

"You find what I ask you to find?"

"I think so."

"Think so? You better be one hundred percent, all-American certain, friend. Because right now I am in room in Mark Twain Hotel. You know place? Downtown Peoria?"

Feller had stayed there the night before his wedding. "Yes."

"I am ten minutes from your wife right now," the voice informed him plainly, obviously not feeling any need to use an inflection in his voice to convey the threat it contained. "So I ask again. You find what I ask you to find?"

"Yes."

"One hundred—"

"Yes." Feller tried to calm his nerves, but he knew what would happen if he misplayed his situation.

"Let me finish," the man scolded. "One hundred percent, all-American certain?"

"Yes. One hundred percent, all-American."

"Good. Where do I find him?"

"He's in Los Angeles."

"How do you know this?"

"Because he's following the members of a band called Taco Shot."

"I know the Taco Shot." The sinister voice was suddenly light with excitement. "'I've got bag full of monster,'" he started to sing. "What does this have to do with man I want?"

"A security camera picked up a photo of him at a parking garage where a murder took place last night in LA. There's only one member of Taco Shot he hasn't run over yet. That's Todd Golding. He's on a solo tour that wraps up with a show in LA tonight. That's how I know—one hundred percent, all-American—that Daniel Erickson's going to be at the show tonight."

There was silence on the other end of the phone. "I don't think you are the hundred percent and the all-American certain like you claim."

The only bluff Feller could muster was silence.

"But it is good for you I like the Taco Shot. I will go to Los Angeles. I will look for the man there. If I find him, it is all good for you. But if you are wrong about this—"

"I'm not wrong."

"Let me finish," he scolded, more angrily this time. "If you are wrong about this, I am coming back to Peoria. I like it here," he said as an aside. "Reminds me of home where I grew up." He took a moment to recollect his murderous thoughts. "If you are wrong about this, I come back here and I kill your wife. Then I go find you and kill you too. Understand?"

"I understand."

"Good. Always good for business, two sides understand."

"I understand you perfectly."

"Good."

"Enjoy the show."

"I hope I do." He paused. "For your wife's sake."

The line went dead.

Feller tossed the disposable phone on the passenger seat of his car and took out his own cell phone. The number he wanted now was one he had on speed dial.

"Good morning. FBI."

"Good morning. This is Special Agent Gerald Feller. I need to speak with Deputy Director Long."

"I'm sorry," the receptionist began as a matter of procedure.

Feller didn't have time for phone protocols. "It's an alpha matter," he told her.

She understood, and her manner changed immediately. "One moment please."

A moment later the deputy director was on the line. "This is Long."

"Good morning, sir. This is Special Agent Gerald Feller." There was no response. "I'm out of—"

"I know who the hell you are. I'm just waiting for you to get to the point. If you've called this in as an alpha call and it's not, that's your badge right there."

"I have some intelligence, sir."

"Then follow procedure and file a report."

"I don't think you want a report on this, sir. I don't think you want to follow proper channels."

"What the devil are you talking about?"

"I'm talking about Daniel Erickson." The name shouldn't have registered with the deputy director, but it was met with silence. "He's meeting tonight with members of the Russian mafia. Members I believe may be responsible for the deaths of Special Agent in Charge Bovard and Special Agent Schweeter."

There was genuine malice in Long's voice. "You're way out of your depth, Feller."

It was true. And he knew it. But he also knew that if he couldn't get the Bureau to the site, his plan would fall through. "They're meeting at a concert, sir. There will be close to twenty thousand other people there when they meet."

"This is it for you, Feller."

That was true too. "Maybe. If you listen to me, you send people to Los Angeles, and nothing happens, then I've given you everything you need to hang me proper."

"I've already got everything I need—"

There was too much at stake to indulge the bureaucratic asshole any longer. "I'm talking here." Whether it was shock or compliance, Feller got the silence he wanted. "If you don't listen to me now, if you ignore me and you don't send people to LA, if

something happens there tonight—to twenty thousand people—
then you'll be hanging from the rope right next to me."

There was more silence and then a contrite, "You're sure
about this?"

He was. "One hundred percent, all-American certain, sir."

"You'd better be. Do you understand me?"

"I understand, sir." And that was true, too. "I understand
everything now."

CHAPTER FIFTY-SIX

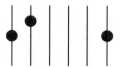

He checked into the Luxe Center City, booking a platinum suite and not bothering to use an alias. He was too tired or despondent to care about any of that anymore. Let them come, he thought.

The room was fine. More than he needed. Or wanted. He stretched out on the couch because he couldn't bear the thought of lying in a bed without her.

He opened the envelope Vicki had given Moog. There was nothing inside but the CD he'd made of Wannaman's album. He turned it over and over in his fingers. A silver disc. A handful of songs that no one would ever hear. No one but him, at least. It seemed anticlimactic to him that this was all that was left of the man's life.

Then who was he to come to such a judgment? Daniel didn't even have that much to leave behind.

He got up from the couch and slipped the disc into the room's stereo. He listened to each of the tracks, one after another. Each song brought back a memory. Some were of Wannaman, some of Daniel's quest to find the individual responsible for his death, but most were of the time he'd spent with Vicki.

The tracks played until they arrived in their natural order at the final selection, the one that Mark had written for his daughter. Daniel listened to it through.

And then it was silent again. And he was alone. Again.

It was silent for a while. Daniel couldn't tell how long—maybe he fell asleep for an instant. But suddenly there was music. One last song tacked to the very end.

It was a staple of the relatively short period in which the compact disc was the primary medium for consuming music. The hidden bonus track. An artist would list out the album's tracks, but at the very end there would be an additional song that didn't appear anywhere on the CD's cover.

Sometimes the track was only hidden in a minute or two of silence, practically a regular track to be included with the others. But there were other bands that favored a more diabolical spacing of ten or fifteen minutes—and those tracks could get lost forever.

The one that Mark had buried for reasons of his own featured a soft acoustic guitar. In his trademark growl, he sang,

I know I swore. I wouldn't hurt you anymore
I promised you. I wouldn't do the things I do
I said I wouldn't be the reason that you cry
I spoke the truth, but I'm afraid I lived the lie

The chorus came in, and suddenly Mark's voice was joined by another. Together the two sang out:

So turn the lights off and put some music on
We'll have a drink, then we'll have another one
We'll sway in time, hold each other while we dance

It'll all be fine, if you'll just give me
Baby, if you'll give me
Give me one more last chance

The sound of Vicki's voice took him by surprise. It had never sounded lovelier. Or lonelier.

He stayed like that for a long while. He couldn't tell how long, drowning in that familiar abyss of nothing.

Then there was the now-familiar sound, like metal scraping slowly across concrete. "Do it!" The raspy voice was unexpected but not unfamiliar. "For once in your life, just fucking *do* something."

Daniel looked across the room at Rabidoso's image, hovering in the shadows of the corner of the room. "You've failed at everything. You lost the girl. The big man hates you. You failed the old man. You've made a mess of everything. As usual."

Daniel had no witty retort.

"You have the answer to it all right there," it hissed, and with its half head the specter nodded toward him, prompting Daniel to look down and realize his gun was in his lap. "It's a one-shot solution to all your problems. You'll put yourself beyond the man's reach. You know he'll come for the girl again. For Moog. For your son. If you want to protect them like you say, then just do it and protect them. Just do it."

Daniel looked down at the weapon and took it in his hand. It felt right and comfortable. Balanced.

"What are you fighting for anymore, *esse*? Just give up."

Daniel weighed the gun in his hand and the ghost's words in his head.

"Just do it. No one will miss you. They'll be glad you did. The only thing you can do that will make them grateful." He put a finger to his own wound. "And I promise, it won't hurt. Much."

Daniel regarded the pistol and knew there was truth in every ice-cold word of it. The sea of hopelessness that threatened to pull him down to its depths with its undertow raged and tossed him about. For the first time he found a calmness in the chaos. "I'm sorry."

"Don't be sorry," the tormenting spirit hissed, sensing he was just six pounds of trigger pressure away from claiming his prize. "Just get dead."

Daniel got to his feet and took three steps toward the corner where whatever remained of Rabidoso lurked in the unseen shadows. "I'm sorry—"

"No one cares."

"I'm sorry for whatever pain twisted you."

"What?"

Daniel took a step closer. "I'm sorry for whatever pain *still* twists you. I'm sorry you never loved anything and nothing ever loved you."

"Fuck—"

"I'm sorry that I killed you. I am." He considered his apology and shook off whatever pride he'd once found in the feat. "But I'm glad I saved my son's life. And my own."

"I don't know what you're playin', *puta*—"

"And I'm sorry, because it seems I'm the only thing you got left—"

"Fuck you—"

"But I'm done with you."

"You don't get to say—"

"I'm exactly who gets to say. I get to say what haunts me. I'm the only one," Daniel said, taking another step toward the darkness. "And I say I'm done with you."

If there was some anguished reaction or if it was simply like flipping a switch, Daniel didn't see. He'd turned his back on the darkness.

He had one last place he had to go.

CHAPTER FIFTY-SEVEN

The concert traffic outside the venue inched forward. If anyone took offense at the biker on the Harley weaving his way through the slow-moving line, no one was foolish enough to call out that he should stay in the queue.

It was a good thing, too. Lincoln "Gandalf" Martin was a bad man with a worse temper. That was when he was stone sober, which was rarely. Or never. But Gandalf had been cranked up for going on three days, and his temperament was already redlining. He was jonesing to hurt someone.

Fortunately for everyone in the crowd, Gandalf knew that would have to wait. There was business to be done. Club business.

He parked his bike and killed the engine. Still astride the Fat Boy, he pulled his phone out of his vest pocket. He pressed the button for speed dial and waited.

"Put Hell on." While he waited for the club president, a guy in his early twenties walked by with his arm around his girlfriend. They were clean-cut college types. Gandalf didn't like the way the guy had looked at him, and he liked the way the girl looked. He watched them walk away, keeping his eye on them in the crowd in case the call wrapped up quickly and he had the opportunity to go after them.

His attention got slapped back to his phone. "No. I'm right here, Hell." He looked back after the couple, but they'd disappeared into the crowd. "Yeah. No, I saw Erickson." His head hurt. Bad. He knew he had to bump again, or he was going to crash. Hard.

"All right." They weren't the orders he'd been hoping for, but they were Hell's orders, and they had to be followed. "Yeah. I'll wait for you and the boys." He looked around for a meeting place. "Union Street side. Entrance under the sign. All right. See you."

He folded his phone and put it back in his vest. He looked around for an out-of-the-way place he could take a bump before Hell and the boys showed up. People everywhere. "Shit!"

Behind him a black guy in baggy sweatpants and a Lakers hoodie was scalping tickets. "Who need 'em? Who need 'em?"

It occurred to Gandalf that he did.

He climbed off his bike and called out to the guy. "Hey!"

The man looked initially hesitant to come over, but must've convinced himself that a dollar is a dollar, no matter whose pocket it comes out of. He trotted over to Gandalf and displayed a spread of tickets for the show. "How many you need, man?"

"All of them," Gandalf growled.

The man never saw the fist coming. His nose exploded like a tomato in a microwave, and he fell straight back and split his head on the curb.

Gandalf reached down and snatched the tickets from the unconscious man's hand. Then he ran through the pockets of the sweats until he came up with a wad of cash.

If anyone saw anything, no one was foolish enough to say.

Gandalf stalked off into the crowd to wait for Hell.

* * *

There were tables piled with food along the far wall of the room. Another table had an assortment of wine bottles and ice chests filled with a variety of different beers. The room itself featured two long rows of picnic tables at which people sat eating and drinking, telling stories and laughing.

There were about a hundred people altogether. Some were obviously members of the band and crew, but most seemed to be corporate types and their spouses who'd overdressed for the occasion. There were a surprising number of children running around, and a disappointing lack of nubile young groupies. A number of local celebrities milled about, but mostly they kept to themselves.

All in all, the event seemed more like a Fourth of July picnic at some municipal park in Smallville, USA, than the backstage of a rock concert.

Daniel stayed to himself. So much so that some of the corporate types were quietly speculating what celebrity he might be.

The cadence of the low, constant hum of cocktail conversation changed as soon as Todd Golding walked into the room. There was initially silence, then a domino-display cascade of "There he is" that followed him as he went around the room, and finally a noisy cacophony of people trying to tell their Todd Golding story before anyone else could tell theirs.

He worked his way around the table, making small talk, shaking hands, and posing for photos. He was pleasant and generous with his time, but all the while he looked as if his mind was busily occupied with other things.

When that ordeal was done, he made his way to the buffet table and picked out a plate of fruit from an extravagant display that had been cut and shaped to look like an overflowing bouquet of flowers. He pulled two bottles of Fiji water from an ice chest, and then he was gone, retreated back to his private dressing room.

Daniel followed.

The woman standing in front of the door that Todd Golding disappeared behind was every bit as big as the largest man Daniel had ever seen. She stood over six feet, and the arms crossed across her ample bosom showed the results of countless hours in a gym—and maybe a little assistance from the good folks at Balco. In no way did her gender make her a less imposing sentinel.

"Hey," Daniel said as nonchalantly as he could. "I just need to have a quick word with Todd."

She barely bothered to look at him. "No one sees Todd."

Daniel understood. The truth of the matter was that he had no real interest in meeting this particular rock star. Or any rock star, not anymore. But one by one he'd crossed off all of the suspects from Mark's list. Todd's was the only name left.

There was a job still to be done and a debt to be paid. More important to Daniel, he knew that the only way he could continue to keep Vicki safe—and Moog, too—was to do what Atibon had asked of him. Right now that necessitated getting through the wall of woman standing in front of him.

He tried the polite way first. "Listen, I totally understand your situation here with the guarding and all. I know that there must be a lot of people constantly trying to get in to Todd just to bother him, and if you let them all in, he'd never have the time or opportunity to get ready for the show. I got all that. But this is really, really important."

"No one sees Todd."

He decided to try the name-drop next. "Listen, could you just tell him that this concerns Mark Wannaman. You know, Mark Wannaman—Marco Pharaoh." He used a singsong tone to convey that he knew they were one and the same. "I think he's going to want to see me when he finds out that Mark sent me."

She obviously didn't agree. "No one sees Todd."

Daniel had tried polite. And the ol' name-drop. He'd hoped he wouldn't have to resort to it, but the only thing he had left was to bring the Big Hurt.

The thing about the muscle-bound—whether they're dudes or dudettes—is that all that sinewy show only goes so far. No matter how big the biceps or triceps or traps, everybody still has a good half-dozen soft spots that make them completely vulnerable to an attacker in the know.

Daniel readied himself, mentally ran through all the steps of his last-ditch plan, and then committed himself to the execution. With lightning speed he moved toward her and stomped as hard as he could on the instep of her right foot.

* * *

When he finally came to, Daniel was staring at a ceiling. White tiles. He didn't think he'd ever seen that particular design before.

"You all right?" The voice was little more than a whisper. Daniel turned toward it and found he was staring at Todd Golding.

Daniel tried to sit up, but couldn't. "I don't know."

Golding shook his head with what seemed like genuine regret about how the situation had played out. "Erda can get a bit severe," he admitted. "But, Jesus, man, you can't go around stamping on her foot."

This time Daniel managed to get upright on the couch he'd been laid out on. He had some difficulty breathing, felt for his nose, and found that both nostrils were stuffed with gauze. He pulled one of the plugs out and was disturbed to find it had turned black with his blood. "Yeah. Well, it got me in to see you."

He looked around the room and found that Erda was now guarding the inside of the door. She didn't look very happy with him.

"So what's this all about?" Todd asked. "Erda said you were saying something about Mark before she had to—" Todd didn't elaborate, but with the way his head hurt he wondered just what the hell the Nordic she-beast had done to him.

"He's dead." That was it in 140 characters or less.

"Oh, wow."

"I'm not talking about the accident," Daniel made clear.

That didn't come as any surprise. "No? I figured."

"You figured?"

"I never thought he died in that accident. It seemed like quite a coincidence," Todd explained. "Mark came out and said he wanted to leave the band, the label, music altogether, and the next thing anyone knew he'd died in a one-car wreck." That wasn't all of it. "That, and his friend disappeared at the exact same time."

The deductive reasoning made sense to Daniel, but what confused him was Todd's openness about the situation. "Well, that makes you the only one that knew he was alive."

Todd disagreed. "No. It makes me the only one who will tell you I knew. Trust me, everyone knew. At least, we all knew that he hadn't died in *that* accident."

"If you knew, then why didn't you go to the police?" Daniel challenged.

"And tell them what?" Todd asked, as if the question was answer enough. "I've got a family, too. I felt sorry for Mark, but I wasn't looking to end up like him." He thought on that a minute. "Or whoever it was in that car."

"And when you learned that he was coming back?"

"Was he? I didn't know," Todd answered. "I didn't know he was coming back. It really wouldn't have mattered to me. I would've been glad to see Mark, glad the dude was all right, but I wouldn't have wanted to be any part of a reformed Taco Shot. That," he said with a well-deserved sense of accomplishment, "would involve a serious cut in pay from the solo gig I got going now."

Daniel sat silently, trying to put everything together.

"And now what?" Todd asked.

"I don't know," Daniel confessed.

"You thought it was me, didn't you?"

Daniel nodded, still lost in his thoughts. "I was kinda hoping it was, because I don't have anyone else."

"Maybe you're just overlooking something. Why don't you stay for the show? Maybe something will come to you."

The comment made Daniel recall Atibon's parting advice, "Follow the music."

Daniel knew he was running out of time, but Koschei had given him the ticket for a reason, and he wasn't going to leave until he discovered what it was.

CHAPTER FIFTY-EIGHT

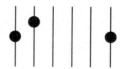

There may be no state-endorsed practice in the United States, but rock and roll is America's religion. Every show, whether it's the smallest dive bar in the baddest part of town or center stage at the Staples Center, is a spiritual revival meeting.

A blue light, barely brighter than the absolute darkness it pierced, appeared onstage, and that faint illumination sparked a deafening uproar, an explosion of anticipation, a unification of twenty thousand souls into one.

The energy ebbed like the tide, and the volume rose and fell with it. Just when it seemed that the crowd might collapse again, might splinter again into the individuals that comprised it, Todd Golding stepped out into that blue light.

His appearance sparked another eruption, an emotional Vesuvius.

He stood confidently at the front and center of the stage, dressed in jeans and a T-shirt, not Mick Jagger's tights and knee pads or Elton John's glittering Donald Duck costume. Around his neck was a black Gibson 335, more of a guitar for the blues, but it seemed to suit him just fine.

With the crowd still roaring, he adjusted the mic stand and sang. His voice was hoarse from overuse, and cracked with obvious imperfections. He wouldn't have won any singing game show on TV, but he sang every word like he felt it and he meant it and if he didn't get it out, it just might kill him.

He opened the song singing a cappella.

There's no way out alive.
This some shit you can't survive.
The game is fixed, the deck is stacked
You take this trip and don't come back

You got foes to your left.
You got fiends to your right.
You can lay down and die.
Or you can stand up and fight.

BOOM! A bass drum exploded

Golding screamed "Get up!" into his mic, and the reaction from the crowd was as if someone had detonated a depth charge of human emotion. People began to scream, not words, but shouted blasts of everything they'd been keeping inside since their last show.

Lights from high above the stage began to prowl the audience like predatory beams looking for a specific victim. The single drumbeat gave birth to a steady stream of successors. It was like a cannon belting out a tribal rhythm. *Boom. Boom. Boom. Boom.*

Over the roar, Todd Golding began to half-sing, half-chant with an inexplicable urgency as he joined the tribal rhythm.

I am the one
The mighty, mighty one
I am the one
I am the one

A quick double beat of the drum. Everyone in the audience began to sing along, screaming out the lyrics as Golding sang them.

I am the one
The mighty, mighty one
I am the one
I am the one

The audience started chanting along, screaming in unison until it was like a single voice making a declaration of its own, with the drum line as its beating heart.

Boom. Boom. Boom.

He repeated the chorus, again and again, until he was satisfied his audience had been whipped into a sufficient frenzy. When it seemed that the collective energy couldn't be driven any higher, he screamed out, "Let's go!" and the loudspeakers erupted with a tsunami of power chords and bass lines.

The show was filled with songs that Golding had written independently, but the people responded strongest of all to their favorite Taco Shot tunes. Daniel thought of Mark Wannaman, bobbing anonymously in his pool three thousand miles away. He had fallen victim to the thing he loved most. It had consumed him, digested him, and would soon forget him—if it hadn't done so already.

It would forget him, but not the music. And maybe that was immortality enough.

CHAPTER FIFTY-NINE

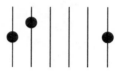

If life were fair, everyone would have the opportunity to experience (even just once) the rush—like an intracardiac adrenaline injection—that comes from hearing one's name announced over a loudspeaker system, echoing off the high rafters, and then greeted with a thunderous roar of applause. Everyone would know the orgiastic ecstasy of being played on by a rocking band and stepping out onto a stage to be bathed in the blinding glow of a hundred lights. Everyone would know the narcotic exaltation of twenty thousand ticket-holding civilians offering shouts of adulation.

Life, however, is far from fair.

And Adeline Swank had absolutely no problem with that.

She stood in the wings trying to tame her nervousness with quick short breaths, two Klonopin, and a short, whispered affirmation. "I can do this...I can do this...I can do this..."

Todd Golding raised his hands to the rafters and called out, "Give a big Angelino welcome to the lovely, the talented, Miss Angeline Swank!"

This is it, she told herself. With a final puff of breath, she took a step out onto the stage and raised her hand in a triumphant wave. At her feet, twenty thousand "cattle" erupted in a shared expression of shock that reflected the cold-spell-in-hell occasion of Marco Pharaoh's widow and Todd Golding embracing at center stage.

She touched her lips to his sweat-covered cheek and then turned them to reveal a toothy, sweet smile even though the experience made her want to puke. The audience loved it.

Give the vermin what they want. She turned back toward Todd and leaned from her waist toward him, embracing him but not slipping him the opportunity to convert it into an onstage doggy hug.

Not that he hadn't had his shot back in the Taco Shot days. She'd bounced on the bassist once or twice, turned getting nailed by Herb into her frequent and favorite way of retaliating against Mark's flagrant infidelities, but Todd had always resisted her advances. She thought it was strange at first, then wondered if he might be gay, and finally concluded that he was just a smug, self-righteous son of a bitch.

And that was before the lawsuits.

In the years following Mark's death—his *first* one—there were a lot of business decisions that needed to be made regarding both the band and his personal estate. Every pop star's death opens a window of economic opportunity, but only for a very brief period, and Adeline had been determined to make the most of it. That included Taco Shot. There was money to be made at every turn of her husband's funeral procession, and she didn't want to miss a thing.

If that meant suing the members of the band into capitulating to her will, she had more than enough law dogs to test the other band members' resolve. There were suits and countersuits. There were joinders and cross-claims. In the end, only Golding stood his ground.

There had been an out-of-court settlement of undisclosed terms between the two last-standing combatants, the kind where neither side is satisfied but both feel they've lost less than the other. The end of litigation had only led to another sort of prolonged conflict, with Adeline saying absolutely anything to anyone else who would listen. And while Todd had been more restrained in his comments, he'd still managed to paint an ugly public portrait of the woman he was now welcoming to his stage.

"Adeline Swank, everybody!"

Outside of their slanderous war of words, they hadn't spoken to one another in years. If left in a room, alone, with a dull knife, it'd be a fair certainty that they'd kill one another in a bloody act of revengicide. But they call it show *business* for a reason.

And the show must go on.

He leaned back into her, and she offered him her cheek. He whispered in her ear instead. "You tell your friend this is the last time I share a stage with a dried-out, washed-up slore like you." The smile never left his face.

Or hers. She leaned right back to him. "The only thing that would make this night better would be if you were with Mark right now." She flashed him a smile that could be seen in the reaches of the back balcony. "And I hope someday very soon you will be."

Golding stepped back and extended his raised hand toward her as if he were offering her to the crowd. They responded with a renewed ovation.

He leaned into the mic. "What we going to sing for the people tonight?"

They'd practiced it for almost an hour during the afternoon sound check, but she responded as if his question were spontaneous and sincere. "I've got a new album coming out in the spring." She was encouraged by the audience reaction. "This is the title track. I wrote this song for my late husband, Marco Pharoah." At the mention of his name, the audience let loose a huge roar, like she'd tossed a gas-soaked Christmas tree on a bonfire. "I hope you like it."

She nodded over at Todd, who'd assumed a spot off to stage left, using his bassist's vocal mic so he wouldn't have to share one with her, and then counted off. "Here we go. One. Two. One-two-three."

The band broke into a rock ballad waltz with a fuzzy electric rhythm line as a bedrock-solid platform for a fingerpicked acoustic lead. Minor chords. Sad and empty.

She sang the first line, "I know I swore I wouldn't hurt you anymore."

Todd did the honors on the second, "I promised you I wouldn't do the things I do."

While she waited for the third line to come around, she looked out into the crowd. Mark had always called them cattle. She always called them vermin.

It wasn't as if she were searching for specific faces, not even as if she were scanning to see what was out there. There was no curiosity involved.

It was more as if she was uncomfortably aware that someone in the crowd was looking—more than straight at her—was looking straight *into* her. There were forty thousand eyes fixed on her, but somehow she could sense that two of them could see something that she'd kept hidden. Something no one else could possibly know.

The third and fourth lines were harmonized with Todd. "I said I wouldn't be the reason you cry. I spoke the truth but I lived the lie."

There he was. Four rows back. Dead in front of her. He was the same man who had come to her house, spoken to her daughter, and scared the shit out of her. The man with all of the questions. And there he was, staring up at her like he knew what she'd done, like he'd gotten the answers he'd been looking for.

The song's chorus called for more harmonies with Todd, and he hit them right on cue. "So turn the lights out and put some music on."

She, however, missed them completely. She was completely caught, transfixed by the man staring up at her with his accusatory eyes.

"We'll have a drink and then we'll have another one," Todd sang out, but Adeline had completely lost her way in the song.

And then for just one second, she thought she saw something different. Not the man that had been hounding her, but Mark. Mark. For just a split second, it seemed—not that the stranger had transformed into Mark, but that the two men had somehow traded places. In that haunted moment, it seemed like her husband was alive and standing there looking up at her. Knowing, but not angry. Just sad and hurt.

The song continued. "We'll sway in time, hold each other while we dance." But it did so without her.

* * *

Daniel knew the next line by heart.

It'll all be fine, if you'll just give me
Baby, if you'll give me
Give me one more last chance

"One More Last Chance" was the last song that Mark Wannaman had ever written, and the last one he'd recorded. He'd included it on *Rock Island Rock*, but only as a bonus track, buried in minutes of silence. There was only one recorded copy of the song, and Daniel had it in the breast pocket of his jacket.

There was only one way that Adeline Swank could have heard the song, and that was if Mark had played it for her live. Perhaps he'd found a muse in the love he wore in a silver braid around his wrist, and called to share with her the newest song that their love had inspired. Maybe he'd used it as a preface to the difficult conversation that required him to explain he'd left her and their daughter for their own good, but he was ready to come back home now. It could've been that he'd reached out to her simply as one songwriter to another.

Whatever the circumstances, the only possible explanation was that Adeline had had contact with Mark just days—or hours—before his death. And that meant that she knew he was alive, that he hadn't died in the accident. As far as Daniel could tell, she was the only one who'd known that for certain.

And that left her as the only one who knew Mark had to be killed. All over again.

There was no shortage of motives either. Mark's supposed death had left Adeline in control of a book of songs that was worth millions and a marketing portfolio that was worth more. His return would have stripped her of all of that.

344

If there was any doubt at all in his mind, he resolved it with a single look. Their gazes locked, and he could immediately see a mournful guilt in her eyes.

Once engaged, she could not pull away from his gaze. He knew she was the one who had put all of the tragic events in motion. But more than that, he could tell that she knew he knew.

She was caught in a trap of her own guilt, and there was no escape for her now.

* * *

She knew it was impossible, of course. It was just an illusion, a hallucination. Just the effects of the soul-crushing stress she was feeling in her high-pressure moment. An unfortunate interaction between the Xanax she'd taken for her stage fright and the Adderall she'd taken to counteract it. The extra Klonopin had probably been a mistake, too. Particularly after all that wine in the greenroom.

"And it'll all be fine." The line from the chorus echoed in the amphitheater, where the crowd was beginning to take note that something was going very wrong up onstage.

No. She knew it was just that terrible man. He raised his hand, some nervous tic of rubbing his chin, and she noticed he was wearing a bracelet. Shiny. It caught the light.

"It'll all be fine."

Even from that distance and under those conditions, she recognized it. Maybe she couldn't actually see it, not clearly, but she knew exactly what it was just the same. It was Mark's bracelet of guitar strings, the one she'd braided for him when they first started out.

She wondered how she could possibly know that. *How could this man have it? How could it have found her here?*

By now the song was staggering without her vocal. And under the weight of her zombielike presence at center stage. "If you'll just give me. Baby, if you'll give me—"

One of the unexplainable wonders of music is that even if a song is being played for the first time, everyone in the audience can instinctively detect a mistake. It was clear that Adeline had missed her lines. Twenty thousand people collectively held their breath, silently noting her flub.

Was it Mark? She looked again, straining to see, using her hand to shield her disbelieving eyes from the banks of lights that now felt like an interrogator's lamp.

"Give me one more last chance." Todd sang the line completely alone. And then flashed a WTF? look from across the stage.

In an instant she became aware of the lapse in time and the gaffe it had caused. Her heart sank and then raced. She wanted to run from the stage, but she knew she had to stand her ground—and hit the first line of the second verse. "I've got good intentions, but I don't have—"

It was gone. The first line of the second verse was just gone from her head. It was as if Mark had come back from the grave to reclaim his song.

Todd got the second line. "Got a predisposition to think of myself."

Adeline knew it was time for the harmonized third and fourth lines of the second verse. She couldn't miss them. She waited. Tapped the beat against her leg to find her place. And then completely missed the cue. She had nothing. Again.

She panicked and froze and looked right back at this guy staring at her. "What the fuck are you looking at?" she asked, as if somehow she could be unaware that her mic was live.

The question boomed out over the crowd, and twenty thousand Angelinos gasped collectively.

Adeline was only distantly aware that the song was still playing, with Todd tenaciously keeping up his part. She could hear the tune, but only the odd, hollow sound music has when it is being played in an indoor environment, but the listener is outside.

The guy with Mark's bracelet was still just staring at her. He was just staring at her like he knew. *What did he know?*

She grabbed the stand to pull the mic closer to her mouth. "What do you think you know? You think you know something?" She was only vaguely aware that the band had ground the song down to a halt. "You don't know anything about me. You don't know anything about Mark. You don't know anything about anything." Her screeching voice echoed against a background of silence.

She felt a hand on her, Todd's hand. She pushed him away. *Fuck him.* She was aware that twenty thousand iPhones were being pulled from pockets and purses to record her performance. Fuck them too.

"You don't know what it was like," she shrieked. "The women, the whores." Tears streaked down her cheeks, black creeks of mascara that lent her an evil harlequin vibe. "He was so weak." Her voice cracked. "He was everything to me. You don't know what it was like to love someone like that. What do you if your soul mate is the one who is dragging you through hell?"

If no one else knew what she was talking about, she knew he did. He was the only one of them who didn't seem surprised, shocked, by what was happening. He stood right there, looking back at her like he'd caught her at something. Caught her? Fuck him. She wasn't guilty of anything but surviving.

"He left us alone," she shouted. "How the hell could I ever let him come back? How could I let him take everything back? How could I let him take everything from me?"

Now the hands on her shoulder were more insistent, trying to urge her from the stage. They tried, but she couldn't be moved.

"I'm not sorry," she screamed at Daniel, and the thousands behind him. "I'm not sorry!" How could she ever make them understand what it was like to love a man like Mark? How could she explain the anguish of loving a soul mate who tore your soul in two? "I'm not sorry." She'd done what she'd done to protect her family, to protect herself, to simply survive. "I'm not sorry! I'm not sorry!"

And now the handlers couldn't be denied, now the hands were not so gentle. They grabbed her and pulled her from the mic. It fell to the ground with a shrill blast of feedback. She struggled against the two sides of beef dressed out in yellow SECURITY polos, but it was no fair fight. They carried her from the stage kicking and screaming.

Over and over she screamed, "I'm not sorry!" but she cried like she was.

CHAPTER SIXTY

Daniel was surrounded by a sea of people all holding up camera phones, hoping to get YouTube-worthy video of Adeline Swank's historic breakdown. It was a great addition to the growing canon of celebrities gone batshit crazy, but Daniel knew he had something more. A confession.

What he was less certain about was what to do with it. Atibon had assured him that once he'd discovered who was responsible for Mark's death, he would know what to do next. For the first time in maybe ever, the old man had been completely wrong. Daniel didn't have the slightest idea what he should do next.

As he watched the security twins escort her from the stage, however, he knew that his window of opportunity was slamming shut fast. As soon as they got her offstage and into the wings, there would undoubtedly be a whole contingent of people "handling" her. There would be rehabs and hospitals and extended vacations to recover from "dehydration" or "exhaustion." And then Adeline Swank would likely disappear for a long, long time.

Without any clue of what he'd do once he confronted her, Daniel knew that he had to get to her before she disappeared for good.

Adeline's outburst had stopped the show dead. And although Todd Golding had retaken center stage and was pleading for his audience to calm down and retake their seats, it was clear that the crowd was more focused on Adeline Swank's meltdown than any face-melting guitar work.

Daniel excused himself, sidestepping his way down the aisle and then slipping through the crowd that was already more involved in talking among themselves and posting things on the Internet than in listening to Todd's next song.

With the backstage pass lanyard around his neck, Daniel had no trouble making his way past the first layer of security. Adeline's onstage commotion, however, had darkened the mood backstage, and the second ring of security was not so easily breached.

"Sorry, chief. Can't let you through." The wall blocking Daniel was young and blond and absolutely adamant. "Can't let you through."

"But I have credentials." Daniel held up the pass.

It didn't help. "Sorry, pal. They got something going on down there. We're not supposed to let anyone by."

"But I got to get back there. It's important."

"It's not important," the blond wall assured him. "It's impossible. That's what it is."

"That's all right. He's with us."

Startled by the *rico suave* voice from behind, Daniel turned and found four young Latin men standing behind him. They were all dressed as if they were auditioning for the role of Tony Montana in a dinner theater version of *Scarface*, including the leader of the group, who smiled wickedly. "Isn't that right?"

Daniel wasn't impressed. He turned back to the security guy as if they hadn't been interrupted. "I've never seen these rodeo clowns before."

That didn't seem to matter to the Wall. "I don't care whether you've never met or you all share a freaking condo in Echo Park. None of you are getting down the hall."

The lead Scarface wannabe smiled and nodded at one of his understudies. The little guy barely came up to the security guy's belly button. But that's exactly where he stabbed him.

Daniel jumped back instinctively at the sudden flash of steel and blood. Before he could process what exactly had happened, the Wall had fallen.

"Now, Mr. Erickson," the phony Tony said to Daniel, "I hope this shows just how serious we are."

It only showed him how stupid they were, but Daniel didn't say anything at all.

"Now, you gonna walk with us down this hall, across the loading dock, and outside to the car we've got waiting in the VIP parking."

"And why would I do that?"

The leader gave a nod of credit to his miniature doppelgänger, who was wiping his blade clean on the dead man's safety-yellow polo shirt. "Because if you don't, Felipe gonna carve you like *al pastor*."

"Is that right?"

"Yeah." The young man smiled. "That's right."

Daniel didn't have any intention of getting in a car with the four of them, but he also didn't have a better plan. "All right."

"All right?"

It struck Daniel as telling that the young man had been caught off guard by getting exactly what he'd asked for. "You don't have a lot of experience with shit like this, do you?"

"Shut up, *puta*." He pulled back the left side of his suit coat to reveal a semiautomatic pistol he had stowed in the waistband of his slacks. "I know enough to be marching your ass down to my car, *puta*."

"But not enough to use a holster," Daniel observed with a casual nod to the weapon the kid thought he'd find intimidating. "You're going to Plaxico Burress yourself there, son."

The kid looked down at his pants and then realized that Daniel had just pulled a *made-you* look on him.

"Let's go," Daniel said with a confident smile. He took a step, and the four rushed to surround him.

"I have to warn you—" Daniel said as they moved down the hall.

"Fool." The leader chuckled. "We the ones with the guns and knives. You don't warn us."

"All right," Daniel conceded, "maybe *warn* isn't the right word. But you guys are so young—" He could tell that all four, especially the leader, were offended. "No disrespect."

"Maybe we kill *him* next," phony Tony said with a smile.

"Come on," Daniel objected. "I'm trying to help you out here, and you go and get all personal."

"Help us out?"

"Yeah, help you out." The leader pushed Daniel to walk faster. "How can you help us?"

"I'm going to tell your futures."

The young man giggled. "You are psychic now?"

"Before you ever get me to your car," Daniel assured them, "something is going to happen. I don't know what or when or where. But it's going to happen. And it's going to be bad for you. Very bad. That much, I'm certain of."

"Certain?"

Daniel nodded grimly. "I'd bet your lives on it."

The hallways ended at double doors. The leader pushed them open and then shoved Daniel through.

On the other side were the facility's loading docks. Five bays, four of which were occupied by the tractor-trailers that hauled equipment for Todd Golding's band.

There were several Cadillacs, and large road cases lined up and waiting to be wheeled in once the show was finished and it was time to break everything down all over again. Just beyond them a group of men—five or six, Daniel wasn't sure at first—hung around smoking cigarettes and talking among themselves.

They were all dressed in jeans and black T-shirts. Jean jackets and vests. Some wore long shaggy beards and others just a 'stache or soul patch, but they all looked like they'd spent the last six months on the road. Roadies, was the logical assumption.

They stopped their nicotine-fueled conversation as soon as they saw Daniel and his four Mexican escorts, tossing their butts to the ground as if they were readying their hands for something else.

Daniel found the attention unusual for roadies who should be working the show or rustling up some crew chew or catching an hour or two of shut-eye in the closest Peterbilt Hilton.

"Now," Daniel said to the phony Tony.

"What?"

"Now," he repeated calmly, almost under his breath. "Now would be the time for you to realize this has all been a huge mistake on your part and just turn and run. Run and don't ever look back."

The leader stopped Daniel long enough to tell him, "We're men. And men don't run."

It was the last thing the kid ever said.

CHAPTER SIXTY-ONE

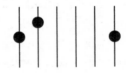

Before Daniel had the chance to tell the kid that smart men run all the time, a .44 slug had ripped through his chest as proof positive of why that's true.

The energy of the shot lifted him off his feet and drove him back a yard or two. He dropped to the ground on the flat of his back—brave, but dead just the same.

There was a reason the kid had been the leader of his crew. The others all subscribed to the same code of macho bullshit, but they were even slower on the pickup than he'd been. None of them stood a chance.

By the time they'd hit the deck, each of them with a large, gaping wound that matched their leader's, Daniel had already dropped for cover. But stretched out on his belly against the cold cement and surrounded by Mexican corpses, he had nowhere to hide. He covered his head, but half expected a wound all his own.

When enough time had passed to convince him that there wasn't a fifth shot for him—at least not yet—he looked up. The first thing he saw was the squared toe of a biker boot. A second later he couldn't see anything at all.

Daniel clutched at his face where the boot had landed. It was wet with blood.

The boot struck again, just behind his left ear. And a third time, square to his temple.

Everything went black.

"Gandalf, get him to his feet."

Daniel heard the words echoing in his head before he could make sense of them or the rough hands that grabbed each of his arms and pulled him from the relative retreat of unconsciousness.

A fist struck Daniel in the abdomen. It would have doubled him over if he hadn't been held so tightly.

His senses slowly returned. He was inside, but the confines were low and tight. He guessed that they had dragged him into one of the idling and empty trailers. At the far end of the open trailer, one of the road-worn roughs stood guard.

Within the trailer, the light was dim, but Daniel could clearly make out the faces of the two men holding his arms back. He could also make out the black eyes of the bearded man who'd punched him awake.

What Daniel couldn't make out with any detail were the features of the man who paced the floor. Every time he walked in front of the trailer's open door, he blocked out the light and cast everything in shades of shadow.

His boots stomped toward Daniel and stopped just in front of him.

"You don't know me." The voice sounded as if it belonged to something that could blot out the light. "But I know you."

"You sure?" Daniel struggled to quip. "I've got one of those faces—"

"Gandalf," the bringer of darkness growled.

The man with the black eyes stepped back up to the plate and punched Daniel again. And again. Then he stepped back and let the bigger one have at Daniel.

"They call me Hell." His breath reeked of methamphetamines and cigarettes. "Most folks think that's a nickname I picked up in the joint or out on the road, but it's what my momma named me the day that I was born." There was a threatening silence. "Because she knew."

A second later something hard and sharp struck Daniel's left cheek. The force of the blow and the pain it left in its wake made it difficult for Daniel to slip off into unconsciousness again.

Hell looked down on him. "You killed club members."

Another blow across Daniel's face, which very nearly snapped his neck from the sheer force of it.

"And you killed my brother."

This blow was harder and crueler than the first two combined. Daniel was pretty certain that he couldn't survive a fourth one.

Hell leaned forward until it seemed to Daniel as if the source of the rancid speed breath was just inches from his face. "I don't have the time or opportunity to kill you the way I want to, because if I had my way I would spend the rest of my life killing you."

"That might not be as long as you think," Daniel said, his voice no more than a hoarse whisper, and slurred with blood that he struggled to spit from his mouth.

"What's that?"

Every word hurt. "Shit just has a way of happening around me."

No sooner had the words fallen from his split lips than there was a commotion at the far end of the trailer, where one of the bikers was standing watch. It wasn't anything definite. No sound that could be identified or sight that could be understood. It was just a general sense of unspecified motion. A presence, maybe.

"Cannon, go check that out," Hell barked. The biker at the end of the trailer looked out of the open end and then stepped out onto the loading dock to have a look around.

Hell turned his attention back to Daniel, "But just 'cause I don't have the time to kill you my way doesn't mean I'm not going to make you suffer. I'm gonna cut you open right here and now, but while you're dying in a pool of your own shit and blood, I want you to know that I'll be visiting your woman. I'll be visiting your son. I'll be visiting everyone you ever gave a fuck about, and every one of them is going to die the death that I'd planned for you." Hell leaned in closer to Daniel until it seemed almost inevitable that their lips would brush. "And I want you to know that the last thing every one of them is going to hear is that you were the reason Hell was released on them. Everyone you love is going to die cursing you."

Daniel raised his head and looked past the shadow that Hell cast. Every word hurt, so he only spoke one. "Shit."

"What's that?"

"The shit that happens around me," Daniel said weakly.

Hell strained to hear him. "What?"

"The shit that happens around me." Daniel took a deep breath. "It's starting now."

A loud *bang* from outside drew everyone's attention.

"What was that?" No one offered any explanation.

"Bronc," Hell barked. "Go see what that was. And see where Cannon's got himself off to."

The man who'd been holding Daniel's left arm let go. Without the support Daniel almost fell to the ground, but he quickly regained his footing. And readied himself for what he knew was happening.

Bronc trotted off toward the end of the trailer, but as soon as he got there, a shadow appeared across the open door. It wasn't quite as big as the one that Hell cast, but it was bigger than Bronc—and it showed the outline of a large pipe in one of its hands.

Before Bronc could stop to retreat or throw up his hands in defense, the big man silhouetted against the light of the open trailer brought his piece of pipe down on the biker's head. Bronc crumpled to the floor, and it was clear from the way he fell that he wasn't ever going to be getting back up.

"Hey." The voice was slow and steady, like the steps he took forward. "You all right?"

Hell turned on the heels of his biker boots. "What the—"

"Hey, Moog." Daniel just smiled. "I ain't never gonna be so pretty anymore, but I'll be all right." He took a deep breath and steadied himself on his feet. "Once we kill these fucks."

Daniel brought the heel of his boot down on the instep of the biker who was still clutching him, then struck him in his Adam's apple. They fell backward against a pile of metal piping and scaffolding, but Daniel was soon the man on top. With one more throat-crushing blow, the battle was over.

Behind Daniel, Gandalf charged toward Moog. The biker hit the big man running and drove him back twenty feet. Moog struggled to get his footing on the trailer's well-worn floorboards as Gandalf pushed him back farther still.

The two men fell backward at the edge of the trailer. Gandalf threw a punch and tried to get on top of Moog, but even with his meth-fueled fury, he was no match for the big man. Moog seized the biker's shaggy head in his oversize hand and brought it down as hard as he could on the trailer's steel frame.

Dazed and confused, Gandalf wasn't able to get to his feet as quickly as Moog, who sprang up and reached up for the gate suspended on tracks above his head. With one motion, Moog pulled the gate down as hard as he could, catching Gandalf's head between the steel frame and the edge of the door. Like a blunt-edged guillotine, it came down on Gandalf's head and put an end once and for all to the biker's drug lust. And life.

In the dim light of the trailer's interior, Hell rushed forward out of the darkness and caught Moog. The two giants tumbled backward to the floor. In an instant Hell had drawn a huge knife, just the same as the Arkansas pigsticker his brother had wielded that night in Vegas. "I'm gonna make you pay for that, nig—"

The *clang* of the metal pipe against the back of Hell's skull rang out as a single note. B, maybe B-flat. It didn't drop him, but it stunned him enough that Moog could push him away.

Both men got to their feet.

Daniel swung his pipe again, but this time Hell was ready. He blocked the blow with the blade of his knife and then slashed out, just nicking Daniel's abdomen.

The *clang* of metal. Hell turned back to Moog and found that the big man had picked up a six-foot piece of tubing, four inches in diameter. Like a knight at the joust, Moog ran forward. He touched the edge of the pipe to Hell's belly and just kept running. The force of the pipe carried Hell backward until his movement was suddenly blocked by a metal rack of lighting rigs. Hell crashed into it with a terrible *clang*, but the pipe Moog was holding kept moving forward—and straight through the center of Hell.

The giant cried out in anguish, but he was pinned to the rack and couldn't even fall to join his comrades on the ground.

Daniel stumbled along the dimly lit trailer to his friend. "I thought you said—"

"Forget the what-I-said shit," the big man said. "I know what I said my damn self, don't need you like a goddamn parrot."

"But—"

"This don't change nothin' 'tween us," the big man assured him. "I just ain't never let a job go unfinished, and I'm not gonna start with you. Now let's get the fuck outta here."

As soon as Daniel and Moog stepped out onto the loading dock, they could hear shouting. It wasn't apparent which one of the corpses had been discovered, but it was clear that the cops and security forces had discovered that some very bad shit had gone down.

The blood-splattered duo on the loading dock seemed to be the obvious suspects.

"Stop!" someone yelled.

"Freeze!"

"It's them!"

"Oh, fuck me," Moog exclaimed. "There ain't no way out."

Daniel looked around and quickly confirmed the observation. Behind them was a swarm of law enforcement and security. In front of them was VIP parking and then a sea of public parking.

"Stuck in the middle with you," Daniel concluded.

"We are properly fucked now."

Honk. Honk. Daniel and Moog were momentarily torn away from their dire straits by a limousine parked among the celebrity rides. It was double-long and white, and the back door was open, with its passenger waving energetically at them.

"Over here! Over here!" the stranger called out to them.

The pair looked at one another.

"What do you think?" Daniel asked, although he'd already made up his mind.

"You gotta be kidding me, right?"

The situation seemed simple to Daniel. "It's the limo or the cops."

Well," Moog said more reluctantly than they necessarily had time for, "when you put it that way…"

CHAPTER SIXTY-TWO

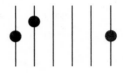

The limousine was the only safe spot, but it was like finding refuge in a fire.

Daniel and Moog climbed inside and looked back out at the gathering groups of security and cops, who appeared to have lost them in the darkness of the parking lot.

They both breathed a sigh of relief. Daniel offered a "Thanks."

The man who'd invited them inside leaned back against the leather upholstered bench and smiled. "No prob-leem!"

And in that one moment Daniel and Moog knew they were absolutely boned.

"How convenient?" the man asked, making no attempt to conceal his thick Russian accent. "I have men inside searching for you. Needle and haystack, *da*? And what do I see coming right to me? It's my lucky day, no?"

The man pulled a phone out of his pocket and dialed. "You excuse." He waited for his call. "*Nyet. Nyet.* I've got them. *Da.* Right here. *Horrosho.*" He put the phone away and explained, "Why have men running around beating woods when the bear is already in the trap?" Daniel looked over at his friend. "You've got a trapped bear, all right."

"That's a good thing," the man assured him. "Trust me, bear always dies."

"And that's what you have planned for us?" Daniel asked.

"Eventually," the man acknowledged. "But first you're going to give me back the money you stole from me."

The degree of offense Daniel took didn't necessarily fit his situation. "First, I didn't steal any money. Second, the money I took was from Filat Pre—"

"You stole from the *russkaya mafiya*," the man corrected angrily. "I am the *russkaya mafiya*."

There seemed little advantage in arguing the point. "And third, I don't have the money anymore."

"You don't have the money?" Moog's shocked reaction shattered the bluff. "Oh. I see what you were doing there."

Daniel flashed him a frustrated look of silent reproach. "Nice."

"How was I to know?" Moog asked innocently.

"It's called bargaining."

Moog disagreed. "It's called I wouldn't put it past the guy to go lose all the goddamn money, is what it's called."

"Really?"

The big man was damn certain. "I said it, fool. I'm not gonna unsay just 'cause you don't like the light it shines on you."

"I don't even know what that means." Daniel phrased his concession as if it was the best evidence of the point he'd been trying to make.

"I *know* you don't know what that means."

"Just because you say something with that *Super Fly* inflection doesn't mean that it actually means anything."

"Super fly? What the hell is that supposed to mean?"

"Gentlemen—" The Russian tried to regain the focus of his captives. "Please. I will kill you both just for the trouble you cause me right now."

"See that, it don't even have anything to do with the money." Moog said it triumphantly, as if he'd won their argument. "Dude, think he woulda killed us anyway."

"I suppose you're right," Daniel conceded. He shook his head, "Stupid."

"Stupid?" the Russian asked. "What stupid?"

"You stupid, man," Moog let him in on their joke. "For thinking you gonna kill us and all. You ain't gonna kill us."

"Oh, yes, I am."

"No," Daniel corrected him. "You may think you lured us in here, but you're the one who's trapped."

Mishka laughed at such a preposterous suggestion. And then realized he was alone. He picked up his phone and dialed again. "Get back here. Now."

"They ain't gonna make it back here in time, baby." Moog looked him dead in the eye. "And you ain't never gonna make it outta here."

It was the Russian's turn to bluff. "You think so?"

"He knows so," Daniel confirmed. "It's all just a matter of time, but you're already dead." He assumed a lethal look on his face to match Moog's. "All of this bullshit we're doing right now is just us waiting around for your lifeless ass to drop to the floor."

There was something in the pair's eyes that left Mishka with the uneasy feeling they were no longer bluffing. "Well, then, I spend last minutes of life killing you two." He tried to sneer as if he wasn't worried and raised his pistol.

Neither Daniel nor Moog flinched.

Mishka might have gone through with his threat and pulled the trigger simply as a result of building tension in that silent moment if something hadn't hit the limo and starting it rocking. It was Hell.

Somehow the Rasputin of Marin County had gotten to his feet and chased them down, without bothering to remove the six-foot piece of piping still run straight through his belly. He collided with the limo window like a bloodied, death-crazed three-hundred-pound sparrow. "I'm gonna fucking kill you!"

Mishka was startled, but quickly recovered. "Is this it? Your great rescue? You think your friend is going to save you?"

More clarification. "First, he's not our friend."

"I'm the guy that busted him all up like that," Moog interjected.

"But...yes," Daniel recovered. "I think he's going to save us. Whether he means to or not."

The wounded Hell pounded on the limo window. "I'm gonna fuckin' kill you."

"You're wrong," the Russian assured Daniel. He casually flipped a button, and the window began to lower. As Hell tried to fit the pig stabber he was clutching in through the open window, Mishka simply shot him.

Hell fell backward to the pavement, although it was anyone's guess whether he was really dead this time.

"There," Mishka announced triumphantly as he held the button to return the window to its upright position.

The act, however, was a distraction the Russian couldn't afford.

In that lost moment, Daniel grabbed a decanter from the bar and threw the amber contents on the Russian. It was such a sign of disrespect that Mishka had to pause for a moment before his brain could even process the fact that someone had thrown liquor in his face.

As he thought that over, Moog leaned forward and snatched the man's smoldering cigar from the ashtray. The big man took two quick puffs from the Cohiba until the tip glowed fluorescent orange. And then he put the glowing end to the Russian's alcohol-soaked clothes.

Mishka went up in flames like an order of bananas Foster in a $2,000 suit. He shrieked as the flames touched his skin and tried to jump forward. Moog stretched out his long leg and kicked the Russian back into his seat. The Russian came back again, this time not to escape his personal inferno but to wrap Daniel and Moog in it.

In seconds the fire had begun to spread to the limo's interior. Daniel and Moog climbed forward in the car to escape the flames and pounded on the frosted glass that separated them from the driver's cabin.

The window came down and Moog stuck the pistol he'd taken from the Russian through the opening. "Drive!"

The chauffeur started the car.

Behind them the fire suddenly roared, and they realized that something had created a fire-feeding draft. They looked behind them and saw that Hell had managed to open the passenger door and was trying to solve the SAT puzzle of how to fit a three-hundred-pound man with a six-foot pipe through him into a limo.

And then from somewhere out in the near distance, a voice called over loudspeakers. "This is the FBI. Step out of the vehicle with your hands up."

Moog shouted at the driver, "What the hell are you waiting for?"

The driver put the limo into gear, but as soon as it began to move forward, a barrage of automatic weapon fire struck the car.

One of the shots shattered the windshield and lodged itself in the driver's heart. He slumped forward, pinning his lifeless foot to the accelerator.

The limo lurched forward, careening off a town car and then off another stretch.

Daniel forced himself through the opening in the privacy glass and grabbed the steering wheel. He managed to steer the car to a clear exit as gunfire continued to strike it.

The limo began to pick up speed, but Daniel couldn't get the driver's foot off the gas pedal. He was helpless to do anything but steer.

Just ahead was a FBI roadblock. There was no way to steer around it and no way to stop. Daniel braced himself and drove right through it. The limo plowed past unmarked sedans as FBI agents scrambled to safety and away from the careening car.

Daniel tried to correct the steering, but there was nothing he could do. And nowhere he could go. The limo plunged into the public parking area, burying itself between a Suburban and a Celica.

In the darkness and confusion, Daniel and Moog managed to slip out of the shattered windshield. On shaky legs they walked off into the parking lot.

Behind them, the flaming limo suddenly exploded with a force that spread fiery debris across the parking lot and began a chain reaction that included at least a dozen cars in an enormous ball of flame.

It was an incredible spectacle. Everyone ran to see what would happen next. They gazed with wide wonder as it burned, but no one noticed the two men limping off into the darkness.

CHAPTER SIXTY-THREE

"It's going to be all right," Moog assured her, but LaTanya Harris knew those were just words.

She tried to read the note, but couldn't make it through. It didn't matter. *They* were just words, too. "My baby's gone." Just words, but they stung worse than any pain she'd ever known before. There was a finality in them that was more than she could bear, and she broke down under the weight of those words.

Moog held her while she cried. He had never held a woman while she wept before, and he fumbled with his uncertain hands, not knowing what to do or how to do it, just like the time he'd held her for the very first time all those years ago. She pressed herself against him, as if there was safety to be found in his arms. As he wrapped them around her, he swore that he would give her that.

He kissed the crown of her head and rocked her. "I'm going to find her. I'm going to find her and bring her back."

"How could she do this?" LaTanya sobbed. "How could she just run away?"

"She's going to be all right," Moog promised, breaking his code about never promising what he wasn't certain he could deliver.

He held her for a long time. At the other end of the room, the mute TV showed footage of the postconcert riot at the Staples Center. Police weren't sure what had initiated the melee, or how many dead there might be.

* * *

A thousand miles away, Vicki Bean was watching the same coverage. Somehow she knew exactly what had been the spark that had ignited it all. Somehow she knew exactly what had caused all the destruction, and in the pit of her stomach she feared she knew what lay at the heart of the rubble.

She curled up in the chair and watched the images. She was aware that she should be crying, that there was reason to, but the thought of it all had put everything on pause. It was like lying on the foreshore and seeing the huge breaker curled up over you, knowing there's a wall of water about to fall on you but still remaining dry, bone dry, just looking up at the wave about to break right over you.

"Sweetie." Her friend's voice was soft and quiet, as if the wrong pitch or volume might shatter her like crystal. "There's a phone call for you."

The thought of it took her completely by surprise. "Who even knows—" She ran to the phone as if she were a condemned prisoner and it was the governor on the line to say he had good news. She picked up the receiver, needing nothing more than to hear his voice, wanting nothing more than the opportunity to tell him what a colossal jackass he'd been. "Hello?"

She'd never heard the voice on the other end of the line before.

CHAPTER SIXTY-FOUR

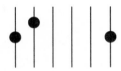

The last morning of the year was clammy and damp, an uncomfortable reminder to all displaced northeasterners that there's supposed to be cold and snow for the holidays. And they've wandered too far from home.

Daniel stood at the gates with his hands wrapped around the iron bars and his gaze fixed on the mansion on the hill at the end of the long and winding drive. There were footsteps behind him, a rhythmic march, but he didn't turn toward them. He knew exactly to whom they belonged.

"What you waiting for, *mi key*?"

"You."

Daniel couldn't see, but he knew the old man would be smiling. "And why you doin' that?"

"Because I've already climbed over this fence once. It was hard, and it hurt. And I figured you'd know a better way in."

"Ain't no better way through a fence"—Atibon laughed—"than the gate." He touched the control panel to the left of the drive, and unseen motors groaned to life and hummed as the large gate creaked open.

Daniel was not shocked or surprised. Not anymore. "Besides," he added, "the girl's got a big goddamn dog. And if I remember right, you're good with dogs."

"Oh, I love dogs." The old man chortled. "Sparkles is one of the best."

"Sparkles? You know their names?"

"Well, ain't all of them got names," Atibon chided, like the suggestion was ridiculous.

They walked up the path a piece in silence.

"How'd you finally figure it out?" Atibon wondered.

It seemed simple now. Hardly worth the odyssey on which he'd gone. And lost so much. "The hidden bonus track."

"The what now?"

"The hidden bonus track," Daniel repeated. "It was a staple of the nineties, early millennial rock. A band would hide a track at the very end of the CD so that you'd think the album was over, but if you let it continue to play, then after a period of silence, at the very end of everything, was a hidden bonus track. Sometime you had to wait thirty seconds, sometime ten minutes. Depended on how diabolical the artist was."

"And how diabolical was ol' Mark?"

Daniel shook off the question. "I can't really say, but the song was about five minutes in from the rest of the album. I didn't hear—until—" His words caught in his throat as his thoughts drifted to Vicki, waking up alone. Or not.

"But then," he continued, although he knew the old man had noticed his pause. And knew the reason for it. "At the concert. Adeline came out and sang that same bonus track, 'One More Last Chance.' She couldn't have known about the song if she hadn't talked to Mark, if she hadn't known he was alive after the car accident. And since she was the only one who knew he was alive—"

The old man was quick to interrupt Daniel's *Thin Man* moment. "She was the only one who coulda killed him."

"Or had him killed," Daniel corrected. "But however that played out, she wouldn't have gone onstage and claimed to have written the song if she didn't know he was dead."

They walked a little farther.

"And you?" Daniel asked finally.

"And me what?"

It was a game Daniel was willing to play. "Why are you here? *How* are you here? If you needed me to find out who killed Mark, and I didn't tell you who or where—"

"Needed you?" Atibon laughed at the idea. "Son, I ain't needed nothin' since the day we met."

"But you said you wanted me to find out who killed Mark."

"You know, you come a long way since those crossroads, but you still tellin' me out loud what I already know for myself." He shook his head like a field trainer who still can't get his dog to hunt. "I know I asked you to find out who killed that boy. I'm the one who asked it."

Daniel threw him a look like a confused hound. "But you already knew?"

"Of course I already knew. Ain't you learnt nothin' about me yet?"

"But if you knew—"

"I asked you to find out. That was what I wanted. I wanted *you* to find out," the old man explained. "Son, sometimes the answer ain't half as important as the steps you gotta take to get there."

When Daniel looked up, they were standing at the mansion's double doors. The old man rapped on them with his bony knuckles, and the sound echoed in the morning like distant percussions of thunder.

M. F. answered the door. Sparkles stood calmly by her side. It struck Daniel that she didn't seem particularly surprised to see him. Or Atibon. She looked from one face to the other as if she'd been expecting the visit and then asked of neither one specifically, "Was it her?"

There are occasions when the hardest thing to do in the whole world is simply to tell a child the truth. Daniel had given some thought to the best way to break the news to the girl, but all he'd been able to come up with was the inescapable conclusion that there was no good way to do it. "I'm sorry."

She saw that he was. And that seemed to matter to her quite a bit.

"Merry Fairy!" the voice bellowed. "Merry Fairy! Close the fucking door! What are you—"

Adeline's attitude changed as soon as she saw Daniel standing there. "What the fuck are you—" Then it changed again when she saw who was there with him. "Oh, Jesus Christ." She drew away in horror, not so much like someone who's seen a ghost as like a ghost who's just been seen.

She looked to her daughter. "What did they tell you, baby?" Her voice was panicked.

"They didn't tell me anything."

The woman took her daughter by the shoulders. "You can't believe them, baby." She tried to mold her voice to approximate maternal concern. "You can't believe anything they say." It didn't really work.

"They didn't tell me anything," the girl insisted.

Adeline's attention switched back to the men standing at her door. She looked at them with the ferocity of a black snake whose hiding rock has just been flipped. "I want you both out of here," she hissed. "I want you gone. Gone and never come back."

"Oh, don't worry." Atibon looked straight at her. "We won't be back."

The old man looked at the girl, right into her eyes and straight through to her soul. "Now you know."

She didn't make any effort to avoid his gaze. "Now I know."

"Know what?" Adeline shrieked. "None of you, none of you know anything."

That was wrong. "We know the truth," Daniel told her.

"The truth!" In her thirty-some years of living on the edge, she'd apparently never heard anything more offensive or ridiculous than that. "Truth? About what?"

Their silent stares were her indictment.

And her silence was her confession.

"Don't you dare judge me," she bluffed, though she knew the verdict had already been reached. She stood up straight and wiped at the tears that ran down her alabaster cheeks as inky black streaks. "Do any of you know what it's like to hate your soul mate? To love the man who's killing you with every fucking word, every fucking kiss? Do any of you know what it's like?" She dropped to her knees, sobbing. "You can't know. You can't know."

No one made any attempt to help her up.

"And her?" Atibon asked M. F. matter-of-factly, his tone suggesting that complimentary trash removal was part of the services offered.

M. F. looked down at the woman now curled at her feet. "I'll take care of her."

"Are you sure?" Daniel asked, wanting to be able to do something more to help her.

She looked down, and it wasn't certain whether her eyes were filled with compassion or a thirst for retribution. "I'm sure."

"All right, then." Atibon nodded. "But that don't have nothin' to do with us," he told the girl. "I done what you asked me to, and you still owe me for it."

Her eyes didn't shy away. "I know." She didn't sound anything but annoyed he'd felt a need to remind her of the terms of their bargain. "I know."

"Hey—" Daniel reached into his breast pocket and pulled out the CD he'd been carrying around. "I think your dad would've wanted you to have this." She reached for it, but he didn't let go. "I think he wrote a song just for you. You take a listen to 'Life Out Loud.' I think that's what your dad would've wanted to tell you."

She smiled, and he let the CD go to her.

Without another word, M. F. pulled away from the door and shut it, leaving the rest of the world on the outside.

Daniel and Atibon turned and looked out over the morning.

"Your debt's paid, son." Atibon took a first step down the drive. "You're free and clear. We're jake."

Daniel followed behind. "Oh. Right."

"You don't sound like folks most normally do when I tell 'em they don't owe me no more."

"What was all that back there?" Daniel pointed to where they'd left the girl.

"What?"

"That 'You owe me' shit?"

"Ain't no shit, son. You make a bargain, you owe a debt."

"She's just a girl," Daniel reminded him sharply.

It didn't have the intended effect. "That's right. Now she's just a girl with a debt." The old man kept walking.

Daniel stopped dead. "I'll take it."

Atibon turned. "You'll take what?"

"Her debt," Daniel answered with determination. "She owes you what? Some service? She's just a little girl, what's she going to do for you? I'll do it instead of her."

"It don't work like that, son. There's a price for wanting things in this life. You make a bargain, *you* gotta pay your debt."

"She's got her whole life in front of her."

"Well, then, she'll have time aplenty to pay off her debt to me, won't she?"

"I'll double it."

"You'll double it?" It took a lot to surprise the old man. "Son, you just 'bout lost everything you had payin' off your own debt. You be best to go off and make the best of what you got left."

Daniel was undeterred. "She owes you a service, right?"

"That she does."

"I'll do you two. I'll double what she owes you."

"I dunno—" The old man paused, clearly intrigued by the possibilities. "It's not supposed to work that way."

"Three. Three for one. That's a hell of a bargain."

The old man thought on it, but only for a second. "Done. You owe me three."

"Done." Daniel shook Atibon's hand and walked on, satisfied himself for a step or two—and then he stopped. "You knew." The realization hit him like an ax handle to the back of the head. "You knew."

"I knew what, now?" The old man had many mysterious skills, but playing innocent wasn't one of them.

"You knew I'd take the girl's debt."

Atibon smiled proudly. "Somewhere down underneath it all, you're a good man, Daniel Erickson."

The full implication began to sink in. "You knew I'd take *her* debt, and you just tacked on another two for good measure."

The old man's smile widened. "You're a good man, but still not very smart when it come to strikin' a bargain." They took a step or two in silence. "But you'll get there."

"And where's that?" Daniel wondered. "Redemption?"

"Redemption." Atibon snorted. "If I knew where to find it, I'd head there myself, *mi key*."

"Then what?"

"You shouldn't be so quick to seek absolution," the old man observed. "Imperfection is the source of beauty. Your sins are what make it clear that every good thing you do has meaning."

"So that's it?" Daniel didn't hide his disappointment.

"It's a dark thing for a man to want to take his own life." Sometimes the truth is the hardest thing to tell. "It's left you wandering a long, hard road, boy. The stone-cold fact of the matter is that I don't know you're ever gonna make it all the way back."

"But that's no reason not to make the trip, right?"

"You keep looking for a happy ending, son. But there ain't none. No one gets a happy ending. That's just the nature of endings." Now it seemed the disappointment was Atibon's. "So you better make up your mind, boy. You wanna do what's right, but you want it to be easy. You wanna be a good man, but you want folks to like you for it. You're too goddamn old to think that's the way life works, son. The right thing's always the hardest to do, and a good man don't never have enough friends. All you can hope for in this life is that your ending—and everything before it—winds up countin' for something. That's all any of us got, *mi key*."

Daniel nodded, not quite understanding but content that he'd figure it all out down the road. "Now what?"

"Now you get busy working off that debt."

"And how do I do that?"

The old man was quick to respond, as if he already had an assignment in mind. "You done a good job as a rock-and-roll detective, findin' out who killed Mark and all. I want you to find another murderer. I want you to find who killed some dear, dear friends of mine."

"You don't already know?"

"I got my suspicions," he confessed. "But I want you to find out for sure."

"All right," Daniel agreed. "Who was he?"

"Told you I don't know," Atibon snapped. "Only got my suspicions. That's why I'm askin'—"

"No, no. I mean, who's the victim?"

"Oh—" Atibon chuckled. "There've been more than a few. Why don't you start with my favorite. He was a fine young man. Loved him like a son." The old man looked off into the cloud cover across the horizon as if he expected to find something there. "Johnny Allen Hendrix."

Daniel stopped in his tracks.

"You know who I mean?" Atibon asked knowingly.

"Jimi Hendrix?"

"Yeah." The old man smiled. "I want you to find out who killed Jimi Hendrix."

"And where will you be?"

"You'll know me when you hear me."

EPILOGUE

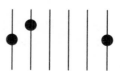

Through the window Vicki could just make out the lights of freighters bobbing on the far horizon of the Pacific as they steamed their way off to Asia. Arranged below her were the million points of light that make up Los Angeles. Buildings and signs, streets and cars. All around her there was nothing but darkness and lights.

For her entire career as a musician she'd dreamed of (and feared) sitting in an office at the very top of LA's tallest skyscraper. For just as long, she'd cursed the establishment that had kept the frosted-glass doors of that office closed to her.

It all seemed like a dream. A wonderful nightmare. She was sitting on a couch so impossibly soft that she wondered what kind of mythical creature it took to provide such leather. She was overwhelmed that after all of these years, she'd finally made it over the wall. At the same time she felt her young, stronger self reproaching her for being there at all.

"Vicki. Vicki. Vicki." He offered her his hand and then smiled as if he'd caught something when she took it. "Now you say my name three times."

She paused in an uncomfortable silence, until she realized he was waiting for her. "Koschei," she started, slowly and awkwardly. "Koschei. Koschei."

He seemed satisfied and smiled broadly. "I've heard about you for soooooo long, it's fabulous to finally meet you."

"Thank you," she said, though she wasn't sure what she was thanking him for.

"Can I get you anything at all?" His carefully sculpted eyebrows arched with anticipation of her request. "Anything at all?"

"I'm good."

"Oh, no, no, no," he cautioned her. "I don't waste my time with *good*. No one even gets my attention until they are fabulous! Can you say that for me?"

"What?" It took her a moment to realize what he was asking, and then another moment or two before she could comply. "I'm fabulous?" It hurt worse than she'd thought it would.

He shook his head sadly, pouty disappointment pulling his Botoxed lips into a faux frown. "That won't do."

She tried again. "I'm fabulous." Even she was unconvinced, so she tried again. "I'm fabulous." He seemed only moderately interested in her, and she hadn't come all this way just to be shown the doors out. "I'm fucking fabulous!"

"Of course you are!" He paused for a moment to savor his victory. "Now there's someone I want you to meet." He pressed a button on his desk. "Send in Malaika."

The door opened, and a girl who looked somewhere between sweet sixteen and second-marriage thirty walked in.

"This is Malaika Harris. She's going to be featured on your new single."

"What?"

"You know. Single by Vicki Bean. Featuring Malaika Harris. Everyone has a 'featuring.' It's the new guitar solo. Remember back in the day they'd have a song and then just stick in a guitar solo? Now we stick in a rapper. And she's your rapper."

Vicki wasn't the only one with objections. "Nothing against rap, but I'm not gonna—"

"Fulfill your contract? Of course you are. Rap makes rock look like an equal opportunity employer. It's a man's game. Unless you get known as a featured…and you're her featured."

"But I do punk."

"No. You *did* punk. Now you're carrying on the long-standing tradition of postpunk pop. Think Avril Lavigne aping Gwen Stefani channeling P!nk."

"But that's not what I do."

"No. It's not what you *did*. What you *do* is entirely up to you. What I need you to do is postpunk pop. With a rap feature squeezed into the middle so that the little girls who buy music will think they're badass bitches when they cruise their mommy's SUV down to the mall. If you two are on board with that, then fabulous. Let's go print some money. If you're not, if your integrity as artists would prevent you from participating in my little enterprise, I totally understand. I maybe even respect you just the tiniest bit. But I also don't have any time for you, and I want you out of my office so I can make room for any one of the millions of young women who would sell their souls for this opportunity. Now is you is or is you ain't my bitches?"

They looked at one another, finding less shame in a collaborative compromise. "Yes."

"Yes, what?"

"We're your bitches," they mumbled together, completely out of sync.

"My what?"

"Your bitches." Tighter this time.

"My *fabulous* bitches?"

"We're your fabulous bitches." Together, with feeling and projection.

He seemed satisfied. "Of course you are. And I've got a guitar player for your band, a kid that can lay down licks that melt faces. Talented kid. Zack something or other."

"Zack?" Vicki wondered aloud.

"Something like that," Koschei said nonchalantly. "If you don't like it, we can change his name. Now, first things first, run along with Cyd. She's going to introduce you to your stylist. I'll be down in a minute to check up on how it's going, but first I have one last meeting to take tonight."

Vicki and Malaika went through the doors and bumped into a pudgy middle-aged man on the way in.

"Come in. Come in. Come in."

The man looked around the office, uncomfortable with the fact that he'd never seen anything like it and didn't know what he was looking at, but still desperately wanting some piece of it. "Gerry Feller." He held out his sweaty hand, but his host was already around his desk and declined to make a return trip just to shake it.

"Sit down, Mr. Feller."

"Boy, this is sure some place you got here."

"Like no place on earth. I assure you."

"Oh, I bet."

"I'm glad that you do, Mr. Feller, because I have a proposition for you."

"How's that?"

"A job offer."

"Well, I'll listen to what you're offering, but I've had a number—" he tried to bluff.

"Don't waste my time, Mr. Feller. I know you've been suspended from your position with the Federal Bureau of Investigations. I know that there are disciplinary actions pending and that when they're brought against you, you'll lose your job, your pension, and with them your wife and your house. I'm offering you something no one else will: a way out. The only way out."

"And just what would I have to do?" he asked, as if he still had a choice to make.

"Exactly what you've been trying to do for almost two years: capture Daniel Erickson."

"But he's on the FBI's Ten Most Wanted—"

"And mine as well. And since you no longer work for them, I would like you to bring him to me."

"Bring him to you for what?"

"Why don't you catch him before you worry about that?"

"And if I refuse?"

"I told you, Mr. Feller. I know about you. I know everything about you. I know your life has fallen apart. You hate Daniel Erickson almost as much as I do. I know you're not going to refuse me—anything."

Gerald Feller tried to regain some note of dignity, but looking into his new employer's icy blue eyes, he realized there was no point in the facade. "All right."

"But don't fail me, Mr. Feller. My disciplinary process is not as soggy with bureaucracy as your previous employer's. I can give you things they never could, though. I can make you a man of respect."

"I understand." For the first time in a long while, Gerald Feller did.

"Good. Then go out there and get me Daniel Erickson."

"Dead or alive?"

Koschei spun around in his seat to look out at the darkening sky and consider the proposition. "For some of us, there's very little difference between the two. But you just bring him back to me alive." In a voice no one else could hear, he added, "I'll take care of his death."

AUTHOR'S NOTE

In this digital age in which we find ourselves (like it or not), there are many who mourn the loss of the warmth and depths that analog recordings provided. Others are nostalgic for the big labels and the stadium acts they produced.

What I miss most are the days when an album was something more than just a collection of songs. I miss the album cover as an independent work of art (even better if it's a gatefold cover). Most of all, I miss lyric sheets. I liked when listening and reading went together and the words were as important as the music.

When I wrote *Blues Highway Blues*, I also wrote about a dozen original songs, a number of which were integral to the novel's plot and themes.

I managed to see a handful of them recorded, but the experience cured me of any interest in future recordings.

Still, when I began work on *Rock Island Rock* I found that I couldn't write the prose without also writing the songs that were its foundations. When I was done with the novel, I was left with a number of songs that comprised Mark Wannaman's album and that Taco Shot greatest hits album as well.

Without a better home to offer them, I've included them here with the thought that they might offer some insight into the book and enhance your reading experience, and because some of you—like me—might be suckers for lyric sheets.

ROCK ISLAND ROCK

Listening to the Clash in my room all alone
Ramones and Dead Boys with Cheetah Chrome
Loved Television, but I didn't watch TV
Just takes three chords to set a soul free

CHORUS
Rock Island Rock
What's in a name?
Rock Island Rock
'Cause it's all the same
Rock and roll, blues, and punk
Grunge and soul and Philly funk
From the stadiums to the bar down the block
Everybody playing Rock Island Rock

Bill had a drum kit and Al had a bass
Todd had some licks that could melt off your face
I had a hook and a rock and roll dream
Make some cash and all the girls scream

CHORUS

BRIDGE
In every city and every town
There's bands of misfits throwing it down

Chase that dream never give in to doubt
Rock Island Rock is the only way out

We rode the charts right to the top
But that's a ride they won't ever let you stop
They own your soul, got the deed to your head
Tried to get free and they left me for dead

CHORUS

NO ONE

This is for No One. You know who you are.
I was strapped into shotgun but you took it too far.
This is for No One, they never knew your name
Flip o' my Zippo and you went up in flames

CHORUS
Stand up. Get up on your feet.
Fight back. Get out in the street.
Shout out. Your voice like a gun.
Stand up and shout out
"I'm not No One!"

This is for No One. A better man than me
I had coins on my eyes and they wouldn't let me see
This is for No One. Wouldn't let you rest in peace
Cover up their sin, they gave the body to the thief

CHORUS

BRIDGE
Never meant to hurt you, cause you any kind of pain
I never meant for my death to take your life in vain
When it's all been revealed, they come to the solution
They'll sing your praise as martyr of a rock 'n' roll revolution

This is for No One. A Hundred Million Strong
You know we can beat them if we sing the same song
This is for No One. You can do just what you please.
You can fight them for your freedom. Or just die on your knees.

CHORUS

BE THAT HARD

Hey now, would it be that hard, one time in your life
Put the motherfucking bottle down, straighten up and get-a one thing right
Hey now, would it be that hard, one time 'fore I leave
Take me by the hand, look me in the eye, say you're proud of me?

CHORUS
I put those things behind me
When I walked out your door
I don't need your shit to remind me
I'm not looking for your love anymore.

Hey now, would it be that hard, catch me once when I fall
Put me back up on my feet and then say nothing at all
Hey now, would it be that hard, not to share all your fear and doubt
Think what you could give, not worry what you're getting out

CHORUS

BRIDGE
All my life I've been trying to impress
And you've been making clear that you couldn't care less
Now you fill my grave with my murderer's gold
And you take your pay from who left me cold

Hey now, would it be that hard, open your eyes so you could see
Every child everywhere got a right to be safe and free
Hey now, would it be that hard, one time before I go
Take all that's left unsaid, look at me and just say, "I know."

EVERYBODY'S BITCH

You call everyone friend when you need them
You don't know them when you don't
Everyone's got their limits
But there's nothing that you won't

CHORUS
You're the prince of thieves
You're the pope of liars
You're the marquis of illicit desires
You're the count of the con
And the king of the snitch
You are what you are
You're everybody's bitch

You got your shoes under all your friends' beds
You're down with OPP when you can get it
You're a snake in the sheets with the ladies
They pay the price and mister you don't regret it

CHORUS

BRIDGE
When there's a chance you advance
When there's a plot you conspire
It not act of bro love
Setting ashes on fire

CHORUS

MIRROR

Fairy tales we tell ourselves 'cause we're afraid to be alone
Compromises that we make, so we won't be left on our own
Little lies twist our tongues, slid in someone else's mouth
Lovers we cling tightly to, just so they won't spit us out

CHORUS
Love, they say, is never real
We only love how it makes us feel
The self-deception couldn't be clearer
Love is a mask
And love is a mirror

So many boys danced at your ball, you found them all
disarming
So many princes you tried out, but none of them were
charming
Now the clock is ticking down, midnight's drawing nearer
Now you only share your bed with loneliness and fear

CHORUS

BRIDGE
The money never was enough
My love didn't make the grade
And everything for nothing
You let them put me in a grave

CHORUS

LIFE OUT LOUD

I don't want you to know that I've known from the start
This mean ol' world is going to try to tear you apart
And I don't wanna be the one, has to explain, the reason why
Someday even…you…are going to die.
No, I ain't gonna tell you all that shit you'll never fix
'Cause you'll do fine if you'll just listen to this (and)

CHORUS
Live your life out loud
Don't be silent in the crowd
You be free and wild and proud
And live your life out loud

Love will come. And it will go. But it'll come again.
Money matters. But not like a true friend.
Don't take your pleasure from another's pain
Don't need to watch the weather if you learn to love the rain (and
you)

CHORUS

Tough it out. But don't suffer their abuse
They'll lie and cheat but that's not your excuse
Don't give your heart to one can't love themselves
The empty ones, they just can't love no one else

CHORUS

BRIDGE
The highway of my life is paved with mistakes
Doing it my way, I lost more than it takes
End of the road with all my bridges burned
Not for nothing if you take what I've learned
'Cause you are loved and I swear that it's all true
Yeah, the only good thing in my whole life…was you

Save your regrets for when you've grown too old
Life's only shame is the fear of being bold
Follow your heart, trust your gut and mind your soul
Then set your sights and just let it roll

CHORUS

ONE MORE LAST CHANCE

I know I swore. I wouldn't hurt you anymore
I promised you. I wouldn't do the things I do
I said I wouldn't be the reason you cry
I spoke the truth, but I lived the lie

CHORUS
So turn the lights off and put some music on
We'll have a drink, then we'll have another one
We'll sway in time, hold each other while we dance
It'll all be fine, if you'll just give me
Baby, if you'll give me
Give me one more last chance

Got good intentions, but I ain't got much else
Got a predisposition to think of myself
It's not lack of love makes me do what I do
I should be good as gold and truer than true

CHORUS

BRIDGE
I swear I never meant to stay away this long
I forgot if you're right or was it I'm wrong?
Pointing fingers can't trade hands, that's what I want to do
Let all the blame be mine to bear, as long as I'm with you

HOT SHOTS THE BEST OF TACO SHOT

BALLAD OF A WALKING DEAD MAN

I was born on the hottest day of July
They couldn't baptize me and they didn't know why
My momma couldn't hold me. Oh, she wailed and cried
"They say you're my son, but my baby boy died!"

CHORUS
You're a dead man
You're a dead man
A walking dead man

My true love didn't love me, put a gun to my head
I did the job for her, thought it left me for dead
I crashed on the table, they called in the code
But I know the old man out walking the road

CHORUS
The walking dead man don't have a soul
Instead of a heart, he just got a hole
But he has a pulse and he draws a breath
And he is the one who they say will kill Death

THAT KINDA GIRL

Crazy things she says and does
Answers "Why?" with "Just because"
She can't be taught and she can't be tamed
And if you fall in love, well, she can't be blamed

CHORUS
'Cause she's that kinda girl
That kinda girl
Love or lust
It's not a matter of trust
She's just that kinda girl

She's got the devil's glint in her eyes
She got Paradise between her thighs
She's got everything that she could need
All she wants is to be free

CHORUS

BRIDGE
Well, someone should've told me she was a danger to my health
Someone could've clued me in I'd never love nobody else

They got CAUTIONS on my smoke and beer and everything in the world
Someone oughta slap a warning label on that kinda girl

CHORUS

NOT FOR YOU

Hey, there mister, what's your name?
What's this little game you're playing
Asking for dances and buying her drinks
You better hold up, son. Stop and think

Boy, you don't know what you're getting into
That's my woman there and she's not for you
That's my woman there and she's not for you

She's a beast in the sheets and I'm not lying
Now you decide if that's worth you dying
'Cause you ain't gonna see her bed
You got a chance to run or you'll end up dead

Ain't no threat, that's what I'm gonna do
That's my woman there and she's not for you
That's my woman there and she's not for you

I'm gonna lay you out in a shallow grave
Curse your soul so it can't be saved
And you won't be the first one there
I'm a bad man in love and you better beware

It ain't no threat, just what I'll do
That's my woman there and she's not for you
That's my woman there and she's not for you
That's my woman there and she's not for you
That's my woman there and she's not for you

SWEET SPOT

The way you dance when you're high on wine
The way your kisses swear you're mine
And I'll be yours till the end of time
You know it's true
I know you do

CHORUS
A thousand angels could dance on by
I swear I wouldn't care
All I want is all I got
I got life in a sweet spot
We live life in a sweet spot
(Yeah, we do)

The way this city makes your heart float
Though you didn't laugh at my beignet joke
There ain't no storm can drown your hope
You pull me through
That's what you do

CHORUS

BRIDGE
And when you go away, and when you leave
Feels like drowning, like I just can't breathe
And holding on, all I can do
Till I got you back and I'm holding you

The way you sleep in my arms at night
The way you love me till morning's light
In a world gone wrong, you make it right
Don't need a thing
You're everything

CHORUS

BAG FULL OF MONSTERS

I got a bag full of monsters
It's heavy and red
I can barely contain them
Like the thoughts in my head
I got a bag full of monsters
Can't believe what they do
Savage and vicious
Like the memory of you

CHORUS
I got a bag full of monsters
It's tearing me apart
I got a bag full of monsters
Instead of a heart

I got a wicked old book
Filled with pages of ghosts
It's the one that you wrote
That haunts me the most
Got hexes and curses
Scratched out in black
But there's no spell
For getting you back

CHORUS

BRIDGE
I got a bag full of monsters
It's all I got left
It's all that remains
Of your vow to the death
I got a bag full of monsters
I got nothing to hide
It's just like my heart
There's nothing inside

SENSE NO MORE

Sun keeps rising in the west and the tide, it won't turn
No spark sets to flame and your old photos they won't burn
Sky's not blue and sea's not green, it's all just shades of gray
The whole world went to hell when you went away

CHORUS
Up and down must've been turned 'round, 'cause I can't get off
the floor
Inside's out and outside's in, since you walked out my door
I keep trying to do the best I can but I don't know what for
'Cause nothing, no nothing, makes sense no more

A thing in motion gonna stay in motion but I lost my get up and
go
A thing at rest tends stays at rest, but I just can't sleep no more
Every action's got a reaction, so what's my reaction to be
I don't know how to live in a world where you don't live with me

CHORUS

BRIDGE
Time moves slower the faster you go, Einstein said that's true
I must be zipping along 'cause every minute's a day without you
Time and space may be relative, but we just don't relate no more
And I got too much time and space since you left me all alone

Friends keep talking about moving on, find someone else instead
I hear every word they say, but I can't understand what they've said
So I don't care if it's day or night, don't care if it rains or shines
'Cause nothing will ever be right if you won't ever be mine

CHORUS

POP CULTURE POP

CHAPTER ONE

"You wouldn't think of it to look at me now," she said self-consciously, as her words drifted to the ceiling with the cigarette smoke she let slip from between her yellowed teeth. "But in my day I was quite lovely. Quite a lovely bit of stuff, indeed." She took another drag on her cigarette. "Not the bleedin' bloater I am now."

An awkward silence passed as she waited for him to contradict her and insist that her loveliness hadn't faded with the years. He would've, but he couldn't.

She took it well in stride. He wasn't the first man to disappoint her. And if God was good, he wouldn't be the last.

"Oh, yes, they all wanted a go," she continued. "And I was ready to give it to them!" She exploded in laugh and spittle. "Oh, those were some days." Her eyes drifted upward and her thoughts seemed to follow.

Daniel Erickson looked at his watch. He appreciated that she'd made time to speak to him—that she'd taken the risk of speaking to him—but he didn't have the time or inclination to spend hours just sitting around Lily Corning's kitchen table. "You were saying."

"About what, dear?" She seemed startled to find herself back in her own home.

"About Jimi Hendrix," he prompted.

"Ooh, right. I was. Well, of all the lads that fancied me back then, the finest of them all was William Gibbons. He was a big man. Big, if you know what I mean?" She winked a droopy eye his way.

He smiled gamely.

"Anyway, William and I were in love. True love. Well, one day he says to me, 'Lil. Darling Lil, if I were to ask you to, would you run away with me?' Run so we could never come back. Can you imagine?" She brushed some biscuit crumbs from her housecoat and didn't notice how uncomfortable her innocent question had made him.

The truth was that Daniel could imagine only too well. "Sure."

"So he says, 'Lil, would you run far away with me?'" She lowered her voice and seemed to please herself with the imitation. "I said, 'Don't be daft, Will. For a year you been telling me that we can't get married 'cause we don't have enough money, and now you're asking me to run off with you.'"

"And this has to do with Jimi Hendrix?" Daniel just wanted to be sure.

"Calm yourself, I'm getting to that part now." She was annoyed at his rudeness, but not so offended that she was willing to lose the first visitor she'd had in six months or more. "Well, my William tells me that a couple days earlier, he'd been walking his beat and he'd just passed the Samarkand Hotel when this young bird, naked as a jay, pops up out of one of the basement stairs there screaming something about some men that've broken into her flat and how they have her boyfriend."

"The Samarkand Hotel?" Daniel clarified, hoping confirmation of that detail might bolster her credibility.

"That's what I just said." The interruption scattered her thoughts like a schoolgirl's composition papers on a rainy day, and it took her a minute to gather them all together again. "Anyway, my William had gone rushing down into that flat, but instead of a baddie, he finds a bunch of blokes in suits. And one of them flashes him a badge. Tells him there's nothing to be seen and he should return the girl and go. Well, beyond the man in the doorway, William said he could see that everything in the flat was all over the shop. And there was a man being held down on a bed—a black man, you know—and that there were men in suits around him yelling at him, doing something to him."

If it was true, it was exactly what Daniel had been looking for. "And that man, the man on the bed—"

"Was Jimi Hendrix." She felt vindicated in being able to interrupt him. "I know that because William told me so. When they came out and said he'd died of the needle and all that, William got it into his head that he was going to get a backhander to keep his gob shut, on account he knew it was a lie."

English provided a formidable language barrier. "What?"

"You know. He knew that the authorities had lied by saying Jimi Hendrix had died because of drugs and that he'd really died accidentally-on-purpose. He thought they'd pay him money if he didn't say anything about it. But I told him, 'William, you're just looking for trouble, you are.'"

"Excuse me?"

"I knew there are some action men that you just don't go mucking about with."

"And did they pay him?"

"Didn't get the chance to," she answered with more than a little resignation. "Two days later he got hit by a lorry, he did."

"And you think that was—"

"'Course it was," she rasped. "On the day of his funeral, right there at the church it was, two men in suits and all come right up to me. They said they were concerned about me on account that they felt bad about poor William. And me being alone, with a baby on the way and all."

"And?"

"And? And I took it." She tamped out her cigarette. "Those blokes give me the screaming abdabs, they did. I knew better than William, and I wasn't looking to meet no lorry in the middle of the street."

"And now?" Daniel wondered.

"It doesn't matter no more," she assured him. "All these years, I can't believe anyone cares about it but you."

Daniel knew that wasn't the truth, but he didn't see any point in sharing that with her. "Is that all?"

"All but the gem," she crowed, like she was playing a trump card. "I know who talked to me at Will's funeral. I know who it was told me keep my mouth shut."

"Who?" Daniel asked eagerly.

"Oh, no," she sneered. "No one else may be interested, but I could tell from the minute you called me up that you'd be very interested. And that means that what I haven't told you is valuable to you." She looked him up and down. "Very valuable."

"How much?"

She looked him up and down again. "A thousand pounds."

"A hundred," he countered.

It was an insult. "A hundred?" But the game was still worth playing. "Eight hundred."

"Three."

She'd been hoping for more, but it was still found money. "Seven."

"Five."

"Seven," she repeated, like it was her final offer.

He got up from his chair to leave.

"All right," she conceded. "Five hundred pounds."

"But it better be worth it."

"Oh, it is," she assured him, and then held out her hand.

"I don't have it on me. I'll have to bring it—"

That was a spanner in the works she hadn't anticipated, but an easily overcome one at that. "Tomorrow then? Same time?"

He didn't want to have to meet with her again, but if she actually had a name for the nameless black hats he'd been chasing all over London, then a return trip to the pub was worth it.

"Fine."

They got up and walked out into the night air. It was cold and dark and dank.

"I'm going this way." She pointed off to her left, although he couldn't tell from her gesture just how far she was going.

A gentleman, he knew, would volunteer to walk with her wherever she was going, and he was just about to make his offer when his cell phone rang.

Daniel had a cell phone solely as a convenience in assisting him in his investigation. There was no one else to call (or be called by), and so it rang so rarely that he didn't recognize the tone for the first three or four rings. "Excuse me," he said, with his finger in the air.

"Daniel?"

The connection on the other end was filled with static and interference, but he recognized the voice immediately. "Vicki?"

He looked back to Lily and made his apologies. "I'm so sorry, but I have to take this."

She wasn't so old that she didn't recognize the look on his face or the urgency in his voice. "Coo, you go along, love. I'm a tough ol' bird that can take care of myself." She started off in the direction she'd indicated.

Daniel watched her take a step or two and then turned back to the phone. "Vicki?"

The connection made her voice sound small and warbled, "Daniel. Is that you?"

He was euphoric to hear her voice again. "It's great to hear—" But he had no answer for how she could possibly have his number. "How did you—"

"It's Moog," she interrupted. Even through the static, her voice made it clear that she was frantic and upset. "He's come to LA, and he needs—"

The line went dead.

He was just about to press Redial when he heard the sounds of a racing motor, a street or two away but coming closer. The Vauxhall Insignia made its appearance with a squeal of tires as it rounded the corner at an ill-advised speed.

Then everything suddenly went silent. And slow. He saw the woman crossing the street, not more than twenty paces away. The Vauxhall accelerating, not braking. It was almost as if Daniel knew what was going to happen before it did. He winced at the collision even before the car had struck the woman and tossed her high into the air. He braced for her impact before she'd even fallen back to the cobbled street.

And then time and sound resumed. The Insignia accelerated to the far corner and then disappeared with the same squeal that had announced its arrival. There was shouting, and more than a few women screaming.

Daniel ran to the woman's side. She'd landed in the most contorted position, with both legs bent back against themselves and an arm twisted back and above her head. A pool of blood had already begun to form at the back of her head.

"Someone call an ambulance!" he called back to the curious crowd that was gathering.

He bent down to comfort her. "An ambulance is on the way," he told her, though they both knew it wouldn't matter.

She looked up at him not in pain or with self-pity, but with fierce determination. "You get those bastards," she told him, although the exertion had taken a toll on her. A trickle of blood began to run from her mouth, and her feet began to twitch.

He took her hand. "Hang in. It's going to be all right." It was a lie, of course, but the right thing to say.

She smiled in appreciation and tried to speak, though she could manage no more than a whisper, "William—"

He put his ear closer to her. "What's that?"

She never answered.

ACKNOWLEDGMENTS

This book would simply not be this book without my editor, Kevin Smith. His insight into my work helped me to pull a novel from a collection of pages. I'm the quarryman, but he's the sculptor.

Jill Marr is my agent, creative partner, and great friend. I can never thank her enough. Thanks, too, to everyone at the Sandra Dijkstra Literary Agency, including Sandra Dijkstra, Andrea Cavallaro, and Elisabeth James.

Thanks to Andy Bartlett, who opened Thomas & Mercer's door and invited me inside, and to Jacque Ben-Zekry and everyone on the T&M team who work so hard to make that house a home.

A number of people have been particularly supportive, and so a note of thanks to Scott and Elizabeth Teel Galante, Anthony J. Franze, Gerard Nolan, and Zachery Petit. Thanks also to Dave Beardsley of the National Blues Museum (www.nationalbluesmuseum.org) and Chefjimi Patricola at Blues411.com. A special note of appreciation goes to Mr. Joe Loveless for his words of personal guidance.

I am indebted to Jaden Terrell and everyone in the Killer Nashville community. Rick Robinson has my heartfelt thanks for his ongoing literary mentorship. Robert Pobi is a constant inspiration and a writer's best friend. (He also taught me a thing or two about Seymore Duncan Pearly Gates and antique bar cabinets.)

My mother, Mary Price, has been my beta reader from the very beginning, and her unyielding support means the world to me. Kaitlin Robertson shows me every day what cool looks like, and Mike Robertson is living proof to me that rock and roll will never die.

My son, Dylan, is my constant highway companion. We've shared more miles, laughs, and songs than I can count any longer and I am grateful to him for every single one of them. My wife, Jaime, has already made all of *my* dreams come true. All of this is just part of my plan to return the favor someday.

Finally, a word of thanks to all of you who started the journey with *Blues Highway Blues* and who are continuing the road trip with *Rock Island Rock*. I sincerely appreciate each and every page you turn. I hope you enjoy the ride and that you'll stay with me on down the road. Please stop by and pay me a visit at www. eyreprice.net.

ABOUT THE AUTHOR

Eyre Price was born in New York and raised in Pennsylvania, and his travels have taken him across the country since then. His debut novel, *Blues Highway Blues*, began the Crossroads Thriller series, an exhilarating cross-country road trip through America's musical history and folklore that continues with *Rock Island Rock*. A former litigator, Price left the practice of law to write and become a stay-at-home dad. He currently resides in Illinois with his wife and son.